A MAN OF LITTLE
FAITH

For Gary
With Warm Wishes
(you asked for
Holy Blossom —
You Got It!)

Rick Salutin

1988

Also by Rick Salutin

1837: A History / A Play   1976

Les Canadiens   1977

The Organizer: A Canadian Union Life   1980

Marginal Notes: Challenges to the Mainstream   1984

A MAN OF LITTLE FAITH

a novel by

RICK SALUTIN

M&S

Canadian Cataloguing in Publication Data

Salutin, Rick, 1942–
   A man of little faith

ISBN 0-7710-7944-3

1. Title.

PS8587.A629M36 1988   C813'.54   C88-094060-3
PR9199.3.S35M36 1988

The Publisher would like to thank the Ontario Arts Council for its
assistance.

Printed and bound in Canada

McClelland and Stewart
The Canadian Publishers
481 University Avenue
Toronto, Ontario
M5G 2E9

And yet – more powerful and more holy than all writing is the presence of a man who is simply and immediately present.

Martin Buber

A MAN OF LITTLE
FAITH

THIS IS THE Book of Oskar. It is not the book of the generations of Oskar, as they say in the Bible; nothing is known of Oskar's ancestors, and he left no descendants. Nor is it the book of the generation of Oskar, singular. He never spoke about his own family, near or distant, all of whom died long before him in catastrophic circumstances. It is just the Book of Oskar.

Nothing is known about his birth either, which was doubtless not that of a hero. According to the Jewish tradition, within which Oskar by his own reckoning wasted his life, birth prodigies are reserved not for mere heroes but for heroes who are also prophets. Moses–yes; King David–no. Oskar would affirm he received no revelations.

He was the ugliest Jew who came out of Nazi Germany. This was the opinion of all the kids, and he concurred. Hairs sprouted from his nostrils and his ears. Little metallic hairs squiggled out of his forehead. His mouth wriggled jaggedly across his face. He drooled. His brows were shaggy and his eyes beady. His nose spread all over; it had been that way since his brief stay at Oranienburg in the aftermath of *Kristallnacht*. Someone else might have had it fixed. Anyone else. Normally, people do not notice facial features in detail unless they are, say, portrait artists.

Everyone who met Oskar recalled each component. He was indelible.

He was a lurker, a haunter. Outside the classrooms, in the sickly-green halls of the religious school. (Or Sunday School, or Saturday School, or Hebrew School. It never found a name everyone was comfortable with, least of all "Jewish" School.)

What did he look for as he lurked? Not truant students. He wasn't scanning the corridors, he was glaring into the rooms. We inside occasionally saw his beak through the clear centre panel of the classroom door. A voyeur, certainly. But he was not observing his teachers, spying on them. Nor on the students. He had a different obsession. He wanted to see what was taking place *between* teachers and students. He yearned to see something *happen*.

It is said that in the practices of psychoanalysts and psychotherapists in Toronto during those years, his image recurs more than any other: in the dreams, fantasies, and projections of those among whom he spent (he would insist: squandered) his adult life. He is a local archetype. He figures in their psychic landscape not just as a convenient icon onto which they project their fears and feelings—as others serve from time to time. He did not simply step into the shared unconscious of that community. It is as though he walked out of it.

Not *walked* precisely. Lurched.

I see him clearest on Bathurst. Bathurst Street rolls up and down: the Pillar of Fire on the hill, the Shaarei Tefillah in the valley. Temple and synagogue, hill and dale, liberal and orthodox; the duplexes and triplexes, the bridge over the ravine. The side streets peeling east into Forest Hill Village and west into more modest Cedarvale, all home to Jews who escaped Christie Pits and Kensington Market, fleeing north from downtown. Jews who got out, as Oskar did, sometimes on the last train. The perfect and smug suburbia of the 1950s, gazing confidently toward coming decades, occasionally to be troubled, never shaken. A community of serenity that knows here, now, is the best time and place in all human history to have fluttered to earth like a driven leaf, and settled. There could be no better time or place. Tell us: where else?

What is he doing there, this refugee from their id? Lurching along Bathurst like a foreign element, a *dybbuk* who has invaded their bubble. Squawking and scratching at them with his voice and his accent while they prefer to incline their ear to the cultivated tones of Abba Eban, Israel's ambassador to the United Nations: *he* talks like an Oxford don. Or the sweet tenor of Rabbi Rosen: *he* used to be a movie star—well, he was in a couple of musicals. Or the measured gravel of Dr Bernstein: *he* quotes the Talmud *and* Freud in his sermons.

Is he a *golem*, under some control they don't know, or none at all—lunging across Clarendon, coming over a rise and tipping down the next incline, out of kilter and context? An alien, reprobate, witch, reproach. A scandal, in the eyes of the *goyim*, but far more to themselves. Haunting their dreams and their analyses. Surely he stands for something. Everything stands for something. But what? And why so much?

A DP, as they called the homeless after the war. Displaced in his case not just from Europe but from farther back, from past ages. Plunked down on Bathurst, where the other members of his people fit so well, just as Bathurst itself—namesake of Britain's colonial secretary in Napoleonic times—fits into the tidy street grid of Toronto: sober colonial city, maybe the last provincial capital in a post-imperial age.

They have struggled to fit this world and this street. It absorbed mighty effort. At length they manage. At last they relax. They belong. Then glance out their windows and *he* lunges by: the *shande*, the reminder, their wandering Jew.

This is his mid-century incarnation, Oskar of the Fifties, like Lawrence of Arabia. Of the many faces he assumed, this one stays with me. I knew many other versions of Oskar, and can imagine more, but this persists, because it troubles me most.

In this incarnation, he shows a special talent for brutality.

He exercises it mainly on the girls. They are named, in those years, Roslyn, Brenda, Joanne, Debra, Cathy, and Judi with an *i*. They are his student teachers. They have exposed their vulnerability to attack by returning to his school *after* confirmation. He has them. They require his permission and his approval because now they are part of his staff. He is merciless. "So, Miss Diamond," he leers, grinning the tormentor's grin. Then he details for her the future that awaits. It is his preferred torture. "You will marry a stupid and successful Jewish boy. You will grow fat in the hips and puffy in the face. You will live in a split-level home on the Bridle Path. A black maid – the *shiksa* or the *shvarze* – will clear the dishes from your table and clean the toilets in your many bathrooms. Your children will be stupid like your husband and will whine constantly. Your sex life will be boring and predictable. After that it will not exist at all. Yes, Miss Diamond, I have a sneaking suspicion" – probably his favourite English phrase – "that you are going to become" – *coup de grâce* – "a baby machine."

Why so vicious? Does he feel they are teasing him? Hinting they want more than the baby machine in the split-level home, that they are willing to embrace the world of his teaching – values, tradition, commitment – while he knows with a vague but rankling certainty, which is as certain as he gets, that even if they stay with him as teachers, department heads, or special consultants, as well as parents of coming generations of students, bar and bat mitzvahs, confirmands, and student teachers, still they are only dabbling in his world. Their real commitment is not here, not him.

What does he do for sex? we wonder. He is not sexless. Sex hangs round him like a haze, thick with something it cannot release. One day in confirmation class, Lois Ellis our teacher announces, "I don't think Oskar goes to prostitutes. I think Oskar is a sensitive person and sensitive people don't do that." No one asked. She raises it so we will think it. Why?

Lois is fiercely competitive. She believes in God and in her ability to make Him real to us. Or us to Him. Oskar hired her and appointed her our teacher. Still she resents his authority and works to supplant him in our eyes. Often she summons us singly to her small apartment, into her tiny bedroom even, since she is plagued by shortness of breath and other respiratory ailments due to incessant smoking. Stranded there, she announces in hoarse, hacking phrases who each of us is and what we are required to make of our lives. We are sixteen and face a mountain of prediction from our elders.

But what *does* he do? A single look provides the answer. He masturbates. He is the embodiment of it. Gnarled, mangled, tense. Wound to a pitch. Every day is an extended jerk-off, an agony of determination. He will get off. He will, he will. It is not an occasional activity for him; it is a state of soul, a one-sided revelation of what he is. A glance at him discloses the emotional reality of the thing, its eidetic essence, its Platonic idea. Oskar is masturbation man.

He believes in belief. He wants us to be committed. He wants us at least to know what commitment is. This desire has nothing to do with his own unconquerable lack of conviction – or is its result.

He brings a scratchy half-hour film into the chapel and gathers us. It is a television interview with Ben-Gurion, Israel's first prime minister. The Old Man sits in a folding chair in front of a bungalow on Sde Boker, his kibbutz. The American reporter asks questions and Ben-Gurion has answers. The program is called "Wisdom."

Wiesel has come to Toronto to speak. *Speak* does not really capture it. Wiesel's eye sockets are burnt out. In their depths you can see pillars of smoke rising like columns from the ovens of Auschwitz, where Wiesel was as a child. He has less than an hour, he must deliver this speech (ridiculously mild term) more than a hundred times each year, yet in that narrow frame he relives the deaths of all six million.

Our temple, the Pillar of Fire, is not spacious enough to accommodate this event. It has the Romanesque height but lacks breadth. So the meeting is here at the even larger Shaarei Tefillah (or Hilton in the Valley, as the kids call it in contrast to our own Church-on-the-Hill, known also as the Pill on the Hill, or just the Pill).

Oskar's friend Hermann reveres Wiesel. He told Oskar recently, "I have met the High Priest of Auschwitz." Oskar asked where. "In Muskoka," said Hermann, "at a retreat for existentialist Jewish theologians."

Forty rows back sit two women. They are here for Wiesel. He pours out his anguish. The smoke of Jewish ashes rises upward past his eye sockets toward the crown of his head. He hurls questions at heaven like a reporter with the final interview. He demands the ancient God of Israel justify His recent behaviour. "What Eli Wiesel needs," says one of the women to her friend, "is a nice Jewish girl."

The rear wall of the sanctuary, separating it from the congregational banquet hall, is actually a partition which is hydraulically lifted once a year to make more room for the High Holidays crush. Anyone passing through one of its doors – though not a soul stirs as Wiesel carries on – would find Oskar pacing back and forth. For weeks he has urged his staff and students to "come to Wiesel." He mutters as he paces. "Bullshit," he is saying. "It's all bullshit. The fool actually thinks he can make some kind of sense of the thing!"

He is a man with only one firm conviction: his own failure. He clings to this article of faith devoutly. He argues it fiercely.

The first time we have the argument, I am sixteen. We are driving to the old airport in his old car, the high-seated Plymouth. He drives the way he speaks English: with continuing unfamiliarity after decades, as though he is from another planet, or species, and his body-type won't adapt to these technologies – the language, the car. He says he comes here often by himself to watch the planes come and go and wonder what, besides a boat and train, ever brought him to this place, Canada.

I am in a shattered state and we are talking about him. It is my crisis, dammit – my father threatening to toss me out, my chaos and despair – and his way of coming to my aid, in his car, is to weigh me down with his own sorrow. "To give you some perspective," he says. Like hell. To make certain we both know which of us is more wretched.

We continue to have the argument till the end of his life, when he is a wraith. His skin by then is diaphanous. You can see through it, especially when he turns on the bed, or is turned, though little remains beneath it to see.

I plead my case: If you were to write a drama, or create a character, you wouldn't take as your model Hermann or Schropp – those men he envies each day as soon as he awakes. (I have a sneaking suspicion of my own: that envy of them is what gets him out of bed most mornings. "I must arise now and begin reviling myself in the light of what *they* have done with their lives.") No, I say. You'd choose you!

"Don't be an idiot," he shoots back – another favoured phrase. Or just a look, with a sneer that says, "So I'd make a character in a book? So what? So failures make good literature. Especially in this country!" I protest, to no effect. He is determined to fail. As a failure, at least, he will succeed.

Yet once after the argument, he brought me "Productivity and Existence" by Buber. It was all of three pages in a volume called *Identity and Anxiety*, which you got for joining a prestigious book club, so allaying some of your anxiety about your identity. I knew he bore Buber some hostility, since Buber believed in God and was a philosopher like Hermann. But he had a soft spot for Buber as well (his ethical writings? his humanism? his aid to the Jewish young of Germany in the darkest days?).

It was an odd fragment. Two men discuss a third who has just strolled away. "Such an insightful and interesting fellow," says one. "It's a shame he doesn't write." "Not really," says the other. "There are things not meant to be written or recorded or passed on, just lived through in a life." That's all. It was unforgettable.

A thought haunts us, as he haunted the halls of the Pillar of Fire. What of him is in us? To what extent is he our fate, which we have by luck and fright avoided so far? He was everything we are not. But how thin is the line separating us from him, how firm our assurance? He was the scapegoat, which the community carefully loads with its sins and anxieties, then sends away into the wilderness; who somehow turned around out there and ambled right back into the camp from which he was just so portentously expelled. Loitering now among us, trying to be useful, grinning sloppily, oblivious to the fact that he carries the burden of all we wish to forget and discard, while we look on his presence in horror and suppress our grimace as he passes.

"Don't be an idiot," he howls one last time from the bottom of the hole, the earth dropping in, the two gravediggers cracking jokes like characters in *Hamlet*, and the voice scratchy with the accent. I know he wants me to, because he keeps saying "Don't."

He is a man of little faith. Very little. He bridles till the end at his incapacity for belief. He resents it, as if Someone in whose existence he doesn't believe has underendowed him. Yet maybe what the world needs is a little faith. Not much, but something.

It seems to me the Book of Oskar is a love story. From Oskar's viewpoint, though, it is a loveless story.

2

LET US BEGIN with the worst moment in the life of Oskar. He would approve. It is May 1960. Schropp is coming.

Oskar sits alone in his office. The private one. The eyrie he keeps high in the old tower of the original ivy-covered Temple building. Downstairs in the educational addition, recently finished under the often ethically dubious pressures of the New Building Committee, Oskar has his other office, the official one. Down there he interviews prospective teachers, living in hope the applicant will be nubile, female, and responsive to the kind of hapless intellectual honesty and moral earnestness Oskar feels is about all he can offer gorgeous young idealists. There too he examines and edits curriculum proposals sent him by the central office for reform Jewish religious education in New York. And heartlessly tears the hearts out of bumbling lesson plans submitted by his department heads. And harasses his irrationally loyal office staff. But when disaster strikes, or the need for his hysterical version of introspection, he flees to the tower.

Where he now sits. He came here to escape the stares of Ida and the secretaries. He entered and locked the door. He turned out the light so no shadow would betray his presence through the opaque door panel. He slumps further in the swivel chair. It groans and tilts to one side because he has never had the bearing fixed.

He clenches his fists, he glares at the hairs sprouting from his knuckles. This is the worst. This is the cursed turn. This makes sense of your survival. Why have you survived? You so often wonder. All survivors wonder, drenched in guilt. This is the answer. You survive to suffer for your guilt for surviving. Schropp is coming.

He grits his teeth, he grinds them. Sometimes he grinds them so hard in sleep that Marshall the dentist has to work on them. "You'll need dentures at this rate," warned Marshall last appointment. "What the hell are you worried about?" Oskar diverted Marshall by asking about his own state. "I'm doing all right for myself," confided the former PFT confirmand, newly risen from the status of mere dentist to oral surgeon.

Oskar starts to froth. He clenches his whole body. He grits and grinds his teeth, and he froths.

It is coming true. This is the fantasy you indulged because you knew it couldn't happen. Now that it is real you tell yourself it cannot be. Schropp is coming. Here, to him. The others will ask, "Did you know him in Germany?" What can he say? He will grin his demented grin and answer with rigid cheer: a good man, a good scholar, good for this place. Good, good, good! Who is he, God looking over His Creation? But what else? Shall he add: Besides which, Willi Schropp of all humans on earth haunts my inner existence and always has because he accepted a scholarship to the seminary in North America even though he was a law student and believed little or nothing at all, while I turned it down because I didn't believe and isn't a rabbi supposed to be a man of faith?

What is driving Oskar? An event that happened in Nazi Germany more than twenty years ago. Sometime between passage of the Nuremberg Laws, which legally stripped Jews of German citizenship, and *Kristallnacht*, when everything just went to hell. The Jewish leadership across the sea in the United States was

18

caught between anxiety over the fate of Germany's Jews and their loyalty to a president who wavered between preparations for the beckoning conflict and an electorate disinclined to send its boys to war for some German Jews. In the paralysis of American Jewry that resulted, minor gestures toward their brothers in Germany ensued. Where was Oskar then?

On foot. He is at the head of a column, loosely defined and loosely ordered, of Jewish youth. They are striding, not marching really but not strolling either, through the soothing countryside near Berlin. This is his group, he is their leader. They sing as they go. It took a while to launch, the boys were reluctant, but now it's taken hold. Some songs are Hebrew, but these aren't well-known, they fade after verse one and chorus. So they sing mostly in German: anthems of the left (*"Wir kämpfen und siegen für dich – Freiheit!"*), folk tunes, wartime songs, even children's rhymes they learned in school. The main thing is to sing. It fuels them.

Were they a more "ideological" group of Jewish youth, firm Zionists for example, they would probably possess a better repertoire. But ideology is not a necessity in this time, Oskar has heard, so much as a clear commitment to seek and guide. Seek and guide what? The sense and strength of one's Jewishness, whatever that turns out to be. Someone said so recently. Perhaps it was Buber. Oskar smells the air. He kicks the dust in the road.

When they set out this morning, the forest's trails were still soft with last night's rain. You could tell by the puddles it had poured. Not the best road for a march, which pleased them all. They didn't want military discipline, or anything military; they preferred to slosh around. Now there is no sign of the early damp. The woods show the first green of spring and echo with the jumble of their songs. At the rear, chatting with kids, then singing too, then chatting some more, walks Willi.

Willi arrived back in Berlin last night, and Oskar invited him along. He left his law course in Freiburg, he said, no surprise. In a country where Jews now lack legal rights, the law is not a promising career. Sad, though, since Willi was made for law. All his life he has been planning it, and everyone planned it for him.

19

Once, around the time they were both bar mitzvah, he and Oskar collaborated on a dramatic sermonette for a youth service. Much later (in Canada), it would have been called a socio-drama. Willi stood in the pulpit and declaimed the rights of man, the glory of emancipation, human equality, the whole Enlightenment concoction, nostrums delivered with proper passion, especially considering his years. Unbidden (so it seemed), Oskar rose amid the congregation and interrupted with sarcastic aplomb: And where has all this moralistic pomposity deposited the Jewish people, the German people, the human race? he begged to know. In the charnel houses of the late great war? The economic calamities of the post-war? The blood-letting of national rivalries? (And all this, Oskar would think later, *before* the Nazi accession.)

They bickered back and forth, Oskar and Willi, to the delight of students and teachers, according to a prepared script with assigned roles: Willi the natural leader, the man at the front; Oskar intervening, querying, needling – until Willi bested him with some thirteen-year-old thunder and a line from Deutero-Isaiah about the universal brotherhood that would come to pass sometime. A brilliant future was a foregone conclusion for that Willi. He belonged out in secular society, like so many Jewish luminaries of the Weimar Republic. He'd always lacked patience with issues that were merely Jewish, that separated us from them. As for Oskar, he was pleased with his part: the one with questions and a troubled soul, whose doubts mirrored the uncertainties of a troubled community.

There is a pause in the singing. The kids are searching, waiting for another melody to well up and carry them farther. In the comfortable silence they hear a faint thin sound. It comes from the direction in which they are heading, just beyond that hill. It is more rhythmic than their sound, they start unconsciously marching to it. Oskar picks up his own step. He knows who this is – Greta and her group of *Habonim*. He anticipated a meeting. The words are still indistinct, but they are Hebrew. Probably, *"Anu holcheem ba-regel, huppa-hey!"* We travel by foot. Since this is Greta's group, the girls' voices are loudest. She inspires them to match and excel the boys, though all share a common dedication to their preparations for *aliyah*, and the new world they'll build in Palestine after they emigrate. He grins at the thought of her, he hopes the kids don't notice. They will tease him anyway, about the uncoincidental routing of their hike.

The song gets louder. Its singers round the edge of the hill. They are still hard to see but a pennant flutters at their head. A pennant – not a flag! Not the blue-and-white *Magen David* but the black-on-red swastika. And behind it a lengthy column of BDM, the German Girls' Organization, female equivalent of Hitler Youth. They are singing, "For us the sun never sets." Oskar turns to ice. They all turn to ice. They have no choice, so they continue straight ahead. They cease all song, banter, sound. They do not march, but they step very deliberately. They look neither at each other nor at the BDM column. They round the hill themselves. It seems a very long time before those voices are inaudible.

Willi catches up to Oskar. He wants to know why they didn't stop, seize the chance to engage the other group. "Where you from?" "How long you been out?" The usual ritual. Perhaps Willi hasn't noticed, says Oskar, but these are not usual times. Willi ignores the sarcasm, it is like a later version of their sermonette. He argues these are not all hardened Nazis, many are young Germans traipsing the countryside as young Germans love to do. They have been snared by the Nazi machine – kidnapped! Why not reach toward them as the human beings they could still be rather than what the hateful state wants to make of them? At least confront them, unsettle them, don't let it just happen. Oskar sighs; Willi is so persuasive in their dialogues, it is as though both know the script will give him a last victorious word. "I decided against it," says Oskar, who made no decision at all. "Why?" presses Willi. Oskar is determined to alter the script. "Because," he says feebly, "they were singing the wrong song."

Next day at the movement office in Berlin Oskar is opening mail. He glances at a circular from the Centre for Adult Jewish Education. A non-traditional Jewish seminary in America is offering scholarships to "young Jewish Germans." Tuition and living expenses plus transportation to . . . Philadelphia. Enter

Willi. "Did you always want to live in Philadelphia?" Oskar cackles. He hands Willi the flyer with a nod to post it. Willi glances, then reads with interest. Oskar laughs. "They want rabbis, not lawyers."

When he tells Greta, she laughs too. Is this what we studied modern Hebrew for, and methods of dry-land agriculture, and citrus fruits of the Mediterranean, and the geography of Palestine? And formed our groups and our brigades? He reminds her he no longer belongs to her branch of the movement.

"Aha!" she cries. "So *that's* what you left us for – America!" He laughs too, but his mind wanders. He knows he could never commit to the life of a kibbutznik. But rabbi? It is possible in a way *aliyah* is not. Thinking, questioning, teaching. Rabbi means teacher, doesn't it? Isn't that basic?

No, he decided eventually, it isn't. Rabbi means teacher, but teacher of what? The faith of Israel. God, prayer, the relationship between Him and His chosen people. Oskar ushered the thought from his mind. Soon Greta was gone, and he was more frightened, more often. He wished there were scholarships to America for youth leaders or educators. He searched the circulars and the bulletin boards. To a diminished sense of surprise – less startled him now – he heard Willi had applied to Philadelphia. To his amazement, Willi was accepted, Willi went. Oskar tries to remember: did he resent that? Willi believed as little as Oskar, maybe less. Oskar can't remember how he felt. He decides not to have resented it. Several years later, between *Kristallnacht* and the war, by sheer accident, he stumbled onto the last train out, the one that became legendary. And twenty years after – more – he sits in a creaky chair in the tower in Toronto and grinds his molars.

On the other hand, what is really driving Oskar?

Is it not bizarre that this event – the announcement of Willi Schropp's imminent arrival – can stand as the worst moment in the life of a man like Oskar? We are speaking about a survivor, a veteran of the Holocaust. One who has become a prototypical human for our time by suffering an ultimate degradation. Can news of a rabbinical posting to a Canadian pulpit during a stunningly placid era in recent Jewish history truly rank as the awfullest moment in this life? Inconceivable! The experience contains, at most, humiliation, resentment, envy, the seeds of a trivial personal despair. No more. To call it The Worst is an affront to reason. It is close to an abomination. This is what *really* is bothering Oskar.

He is not insensitive, he knows his feelings are indefensible. He disgusts himself. What about Franz his brother, whom he survived? Did Oskar survive Franz in order to drown in self-pity in a Canadian suburb? This is not Dachau, it is Forest Hill Village. Dachau is where Franz ended, Dachau was the end of Franz. Why does Oskar feel this moment as his own Dachau? How can he be so despicably self-obsessed? Is it his final punishment: a private Dachau so petty and undignified it deserves to be neither noted nor mourned? Hell isn't other people – only a French intellectual could make a living on such clichés. Hell is Dachau. Yet Oskar's own hell is Willi Schropp, unanimous choice of the board of the trustees and the search committee.

Of course it's embarrassing. Immeasurably. Yet what can Oskar do? Like all of us, he is a spectator at his own emotions. One reason he retreated to the tower was to prevent his staff catching him at it. True, they might not recognize his predicament. They would sense the darkness, the despondency; to these they are accustomed. But it is doubtful they would (a) connect this mood to the coming of Willi Schropp, and, even more improbable, (b) identify it as a more severe source of pain to Oskar than anything he has ever undergone. From them he is relatively safe and his office provides extra protection.

His own perplexity, though, abides, and keeps him in the tower long after the staff have left. Only Mr Oates is left, just below in the Isaac Mayer Wise auditorium, stolidly unfolding chairs for tonight's meeting of the Golden Age Book Review Club. When fury and humiliation are past, perplexity remains.

He wants to see Rosen. This has never happened before.

Rosen is hard to see, and sometimes invisible. This has no relation to the fact that the Pillar of Fire's current chief rabbi–though
not for long–finds it hard to see. Oskar knows the kids say: We
have two rabbis, one blind and one deaf. When Rabbi Rosen
rises to preach, white-headed Associate Rabbi Gellner turns off
his hearing aid with a smirk and a twist. When Rabbi Gellner
starts one of his incredible sermons ("My friends, today I speak
to you on the subject, How . . . Old . . . Are . . . You?" PAUSE.
BEAT. EXACTLY THE SAME INTONATION. "How . . . Old . . . Are
. . . You?"), Rosen's bushy brows arch contemptuously over his
dark glasses. Oskar has never minded their feud. It occupied
them with each other and kept them off his back. Next morning
he goes to the Rabbis' Study.

"Oskar," coos Miss Fitzmorris, when he cranes his neck
around the door. "What sheer delight!" Her bosom heaves to,
as always. Can she be the reason he has avoided this corner of
the P of F for fifteen years? Why is it always *these* women – the
Idas and the Misses Fitzmorris, who respond to him while . . .
but never mind, she is not the reason. Rosen is the reason.

No, the rabbi is not in. She says it as though the rabbi has
never been in and does not intend to destroy a noble record in
the final months of his tenure. He is Out. Perhaps he is having
lunch with the editor of *The Star*, or *The Tely*, or *The Globe &
Mail*. Or all. Or none. Perhaps he is working on a column or
two. He could be reading a book, or reviewing one, or writing
one. But he might call. Oskar raises and lowers his head like a
giraffe finished with the leaves on this branch, and withdraws
from the doorway.

Back in the tower, he wonders why he wants to see Rosen.
The phone rings. "Oskar!" booms a mellifluous voice, the voice
of Robbie Randall, one-time move crooner, who decades ago
forsook a promising Hollywood career for the profounder pleas-
ures of the pulpit, resuming by the same defiant act his real name:
Reuben Rosen. Was Miss Fitzmorris lying when she said he

wasn't there? Perhaps she doesn't notice the rabbi come and go; it mightn't be functional from her point of view. Maybe she didn't even pass on Oskar's message. This could just be eerie timing. "Oskar," says the velvet voice for the first and only time in fifteen years. "Let's have lunch."

So they are perched on a banquette at the House of Chan. Chinese cuisine comes to Eglinton Avenue. Oskar pokes at his plate like an astronaut with the first dehydrated turkey. Rosen starts. "Frankly," he says. Oskar winces. He detests people who "frankly" in conversation, along with those who "indeed" and "of course." As though everything they've just said was less than frank, and they are now going to bless you with the truth.

"Frankly," says Rosen, "I'm just as happy to go. I don't make sense to them any more? Fine. They don't make sense to me either." Oskar knows what Rosen means. "You know what I mean?" says Rosen.

"When I came up here from New England, they wanted my kind of rabbi. A rabbi who didn't look like a rabbi, didn't talk like one, didn't even act much like one. Somebody who could fit in, mix with *goyim*. Who didn't deny he was Jewish, but didn't push it. Anyway, I've got that name, can't miss it, am I right? They didn't want me to talk Jewish things, they wanted me to talk like all the world. Like what? The *world*! The UN, international affairs, human relations, the evils of racism—especially for our Afro-American brothers." Oskar halts a forkful of chow mein. "Once known as Negroes," says Rosen, "but we have to keep up. It was all fine with me. It was jake. That's why I became a rabbi."

"I wish someone had told me that," mutters Oskar, thinking about why people become rabbis.

"Told you what?" says Rosen without interest. "Listen, I never cared much about the *parsha* of the *shavua* or anything else in the Bible and only slightly more about God Almighty Himself. Or Herself. Tell me, Oskar, have you ever really prayed? I don't mean *tried* to pray. God knows, everyone tries that sometime. And I don't mean conduct an experiment in religious feeling. Hell, I believe there's such a thing as religious ecstasy. I just don't know if it's any different than a good fuck. Uh-uh, I mean, prayed to God." He doesn't wait for Oskar to answer.

"So what's happened suddenly? I'm not serious enough for them, not scholarly enough, not – and this one frosts my balls, Oskar–not *spiritual* enough. Feature it. Jack Katz, our chairman of the board, he of the new Chrysler Imperial every year and the wall-to-wall mistresses, thinks I'm not spiritual enough. Frankly, Oskar, it's not that I'm not spiritual *enough*. I'm not spiritual at all. I don't know what spiritual means! I can hardly spell it. I'm a happy *nudnik* and if you want to know, I'll tell you the only thing I'll truly miss when I'm gone." Oskar stares, he wants to know, and he's going to find out. "The music. I'll miss the music. I'll miss the hell out of it. Do you know the highlight of my every blessed year in the rabbinate? Yom Kippur evening. Because I confess my bloody sins? Hell, because I sing "Kol Nidrei" before the open ark. *I* sing that magnificent melody, not our flatulent cantor. Did you ever wonder, Oskar, why that exquisite aria devolves on me and not on the ingratiating set of tonsils they pay to sing everything else? It's in my contract, dammit, I got it in the damn contract!"

They take their cheques and stand in line at the cash register. "Find me a five in there," says Rosen, holding out his wallet. "Listen," he goes on, "I've been working on Friday's sermon. I'll tell you so you won't have to come, not that I could see if you did. It's getting worse, my sight. Sometimes I think at the end of a service I'll take a wrong turn and walk into the ark along with the Torahs instead of up the aisle to shake hands with whoever those people in the pews are. I'm all cataract these days. There must be something spiritual about *that*. Anyway, it's on South Africa, my sermon. They've got a new rotten leader, Verwoerd. I say, they should go *forward* toward equality, instead of *backward* with Verwoerd! I hope Jack the Hack is there to hear it and cringe. I worked all morning for that line and then I figured I deserve a good lunch. Miss Fitzmorris said you came by. Lead me to a bus stop, Oskar. I'll miss these lunches of ours."

"Did you ever wonder," asks Oskar as he guides Rosen along

26

the busy street – the Gaza Strip, the kids call it – "whether you made a mistake giving up your other life?"

"Regrets!" yelps Rosen. "About my career? Hollywood and all that? I was one of dozens. It would have lasted another six, seven films. At most I'd have become a singing cowboy. I'd be the person who was an actor and then drifted into something else. Don't you see what I have this way?" No, Oskar doesn't. "I'm the guy who gave up the movies to be a rabbi! I'll always have that, and I'll always be respected for it. Frankly, I even respect myself for it. Now tell me something."

He pauses. It is the only time Oskar has ever seen him take a breath. "You don't really believe any more of it than I do," says Rosen. It is not a statement and not a question. It is . . . gone with the gusts along Eglinton, thinks Oskar.

A bus comes. Rosen gropes his way on. "Tell Miss Fitzmorris I'm doing an interview at CFRB. It's about age discrimination. Senior liberation, grey power. An idea whose time has come, now that I'm withered myself. Maybe I'll rustle up a congregation of *alte kakkers* so decrepit they make *me* look svelte. Somewhere sunny, by God!" The bus driver revs his engine. Rosen ignores him. "I hope the new man keeps her on – my Miss Fitzmorris. Do you know how often I thought about chasing her around that desk?" Oskar lifts his eyebrows. Rosen seems to see. "Well, I never did," he adds. Oskar realizes Rosen is doing a routine, like a stand-up comic, for him, Oskar. He is being entertained. "What if I had caught her?" concludes his rabbi with impeccable timing. The bus is pulling away. "Tell her I won't be back," yells Rosen. "On the other hand, don't!"

Oskar lurches back down Bathurst toward the temple. He has a friend there now, suddenly, who is about to leave forever. What just happened? For fifteen years he scorned Rosen, avoided and patronized him. Was the man reborn in fifty-five minutes over Chinese food? No, he is as he was: superficial, self-absorbed, unconcerned with education, with tradition, with the students or the school. He prefers, as always, to tend his own garden: the *bon mots*, the interviews, and, as should have been obvious, the music. Yet just this – the shallowness, the narcissism

– was his gift to Oskar. For it meant Oskar had a garden of his own, the Pill itself.

So the kids disliked Rosen and felt distant? So Oskar was there. The teachers *kvetched* because they got no guidance from the rabbi? They turned to Oskar, who knew and cared. What is there to resent in a man who made life bearable for him, because of whom he escaped an ignominious role: educational underling to rabbinical overseer? The temple has been Oskar's empire. He ruled there. Unofficially, sure, but he kept the keys, nobody else. Now he is going to be demoted, exiled to the provinces, tossed out of the garden.

Back at Temple they've already been toing-and-froing with Schropp for hours. He flew in last night on a kind of recon mission and encamped at the Windsor Arms – posh but tasteful. Since the absurd hour of seven this morning he has been summoning them by phone, one after another, like Noah interviewing for the ark. They each comment on his energy, his erudition, his passion for detail. Even Srul is impressed. Srul runs the choir. Schropp discussed liturgical music "knowledgeably" with him. Rosen had that heavenly tenor, it's true, but so what? Rosen never solicited Srul's ponderous musicological opinions, as Oskar points out. Srul bristles to hear Rosen defended, he cannot imagine why Oskar has suddenly and irrelevantly decided to make a case for the poor excuse of a rabbi they have often deplored together.

Srul has been squirming at the prissy repertoire chosen by Cantor Cherniak:

> *Our Father, Our King, keep far from our country*
> *Pestilence, war, and famine,*
> *Aw-aw-men.*

Now he can introduce Israeli motifs on the High Holidays. Schropp liked the idea! And maybe even some of Srul's own compositions, about which Schropp inquired without being told that

Srul is, in addition to being a conductor, a let us say modestly
known composer of Jewish music.

It has the smell of . . . Oskar can't quite get . . . ah yes, yes,
that new brand of politics drifting up from the States, exempli-
fied by the young presidential pretender, Kennedy. An apparent
confident grasp of a massive body of facts and issues, presented
to an adoring press and through them to a credulous public via
a full complement of audio-visual aids, the entire operation
obviously based on a selective briefing beforehand intended precisely for the purpose not of mastering the material but of giving
that impression. Oskar has been watching. He is fascinated. It is
familiar, that fastidious manipulation of the impression.

Sammy comes out chortling. He has run the youth program
for seven years. He never met Rosen. Schropp consulted him on
scheduling, leadership training, and Sammy's own philosophy of
social group work.

They come and they go, they waft to and fro, and Oskar is not
called. He sits in his office and he seethes.

What Oskar doesn't understand about brotherhood is, what
does it have to do with brothers?

This puzzles him, because among the few things that make
sense to him are brotherhood and brothers. Since there are many
things Oskar doesn't understand, and few he does, he clings to
those that seem clear, he chews them over like a rosary. Especially now, in his worst moment.

Take brotherhood. It is one of his favourite English words and
a centrepiece of the curriculum he has created in the school. It is
probably the only element in the whole course of study to which
he can offer enthusiastic, unqualified, unOskarian assent. He has
a sneaking suspicion this is true for his staff as well. They lived
through the war and the first news of the death camps; they still
shudder. Faith either does not interest them or is something they
can at most guess at. From the other end of their experience they
are buffeted by the raucous Rotarian confidence of a suddenly

rich, wildly successful Jewish community with so much to consume, so many homes and cottages to occupy, so many hardtop cars to drive, and no space in their two- and three-car garages for anything as hard to touch as belief in the ancient God of Israel or the mission of His people. Holiness—come again?

Brotherhood, though, they grasp. Had there been brotherhood, it would have prevented the war and the camps, along with the anti-Semitic outbursts that happened right here in sunny, cheery Toronto. Brotherhood would have stopped it dead. Brotherhood is another miracle post-war product, like Gardol, the invisible protective shield in toothpaste.

In grade three, they tell the story of the Churkendoose. One day a strange ugly egg appeared in the farmyard. The hen sat on it with great reluctance. It hatched finally and the Churkendoose emerged: part chicken, part turkey, part duck, and part goose. He—or it—had an awful time with the other animals but, like the ugly duckling, persevered. One night a fox slouched into the yard, the Churkendoose awoke, scared the fox witless by just appearing, and chased the predator till he was long gone. The other animals then realized how valuable differentness can be. They embraced the Churkendoose among them. Oskar and the staff have enlisted in the Churkencause as earlier generations of their people gave themselves to socialism, or emancipation, or the liberation of holy sparks entrapped in earthly shells, or the conquest of *Eretz Yisrael* the first time round, under Joshua. Following the Churkendoose lesson they herd their kids into bright, airy Isaac M. Wise auditorium to sing,

> *I'm proud to be me, but I also see*
> *You're just as proud to be you, it's true*
> *You're just as proud to be you.*

And

> *The world is getting littler every day,*
> *Soon there won't be any places far away,*
> *You can take a plane in China and wake up in Carolina*
> *Or Alaska, Madagascar or Bombay.*

30

Or

> *Close your eyes and point your finger,*
> *On the map, just let it linger,*
> *Any place you point your finger to,*
> *There's someone with the same type blood as you!*

It is a true exercise in the implantation of faith, as their forefathers drilled in the *Sh'ma* ("Hear, O Israel, the Lord is our God . . .") or the Decalogue ("Thou shalt have no other gods before Me . . .") or Maimonides' thirteen principles of faith ("I believe with perfect faith . . .")–and in some ways as abstract. What do these Jewish-Canadian sprouts know about Madagascar, which rhymes often in their songs with Alaska? It is as vague to them as God is to Oskar. But brotherhood *feels* real, and necessary, and Oskar doesn't mind indoctrinating it.

He just can't figure out how it connects to brothers. Brothers is something else he understands. Oskar had a brother, an actual brother; his name was Franz. We do not know a lot about him. He was older than Oskar by many years and died in a camp, like the rest of Oskar's family. Oskar revered him. Franz always seemed absorbed in an intense distant reality–it was called politics–but he surfaced intermittently, after the fashion of fathers more than older brothers. For example, he would often appear to initiate Oskar into significant life experiences. Then he was gone.

Others have felt like brothers. His life sometimes feels overpopulated by brothers and otherwise barren; lacking sisters, parents, cousins, uncles, aunts, grandparents, not to mention friends, mentors, or lovers. Yet there have always been brothers. Like Hermann. Like Willi Schropp.

Take the Bible, which, as a Jewish educator, Oskar cannot really avoid. He finds most of it opaque. God speaking to men and men talking back. Miracles. The Red Sea parts in his mind like the Dancing Waters from Radio City Music Hall in New York that come to the midway of the Canadian National Exhibition every summer. And so much of the Bible is about family:

mysteries between men and women, parents and children. None of this falls in his ken.

Yet he has found you can make your way through almost the entire Bible if you read it as a series of brother-tales with gaps. You have Cain and Abel right at the start, then you have the sons of Noah, then Abraham and poor Lot, Isaac and Ishmael, Jacob and Esau, then Joseph and all the brothers about whom Thomas Mann wrote the novels Oskar tries vainly to impose on post-confirmands, then Moses and Aaron, then some gaps, then the truest of brothers, David and Jonathan, followed by the foulest of brothers, David's offspring, then more gaps. And so on.

But he can't penetrate even slightly what any of them have to do with brotherhood. Those same brothers, for instance, whom the grade two kids sing about:

> O *my quiver and my bow,*
> *They're the only friends I know,*
> *To the hunt I gladly go,*
> *I am Esau, son of Isaac.*

Because when you think about it, Esau, son of Isaac, was blatantly cheated out of his birthright by his brother Jacob. As for Jacob's own sons,

> *Joseph's brothers got so mad,*
> *They were jealous, mean and bad*

So

> *They threw Joseph down a pit,*
> *Tore his clothes up quite a bit.*

Ishmael, Isaac's brother, was driven heartlessly into the desert by his (and Our) father, Abraham, due to sibling rivalry. Cain had long since slaughtered Abel, sure as Bet followed Aleph. Even David and Jonathan were star-crossed brothers. Jonathan had to die so that David could meet his regal destiny, though David sang Jonathan a wondrous dirge. Brothers seem so rarely to behave in brotherly ways, at least not in Oskar's experience. Think about

Hermann again, or Willi. Brothers are vexation, they are distraction. Brothers exist to remind you that inside are feelings that shame you, and so powerful they minimize every other emotion. Think about Franz.

Franz was Oskar's only brother; except for all the others. Brotherdom is not a matter of family for Oskar; it is a condition of existence; he finds brothers every which way he turns, then and now, there and here. He has no faith at all in the reality of an afterlife, but he is certain he will find brothers there, along with the associated pain. He should have known Willi would turn up here.

Brothers are the reason for the tenth commandment – Thou shalt not covet – the sole prohibition of an emotion in the entire Hebrew Bible, a fruitless stricture in an otherwise practical code, since emotions cannot be enjoined. Thou shalt not covet is the only biblical law Oskar understands perfectly, at the same time as he knows he can never obey it. Brothers *are* covetousness. Brothers are jealousy, self-doubt, and perpetual repetition of your sense of failure. Brothers are his fate.

Not parents. However we picture the experience Oskar lived through in Nazi Germany as a young man, it might nevertheless leave a person thinking there is such a thing as a brother in this world. It could even leave him clinging to the thought: *There must be brothers! So many of us have been thrown into this shambles and here we all are, united in our sorrow.* But not a mother and not a father. That person would surely think: *No one can be responsible for all this, nobody would claim to have given it birth.* No father, and no Father. Not a chance.

He wants to see Myrna.

During dinner at the Noshery they talk their way through the outline of the experimental course, the Destruction of European Jewry. Myrna isn't sure. Maybe it's too raw, too frightening for Canadian teenagers, even if they are Jewish. Maybe their parents will object? Oskar says, No, it will be fine, these courses exist all over the States, they will make their way up here the way most things do, five years after the Americans get them. And she is his best teacher, has been for years, since she came in off the street, a teenager from downtown, from the recessive working-class factor in the soaring Toronto Jewish community; she wanted a job; and survived his attempts to humiliate her, and gave it back till he giggled in pleasure. He needs her for the course, end of topic. They pass on to student teacher assignments for next year, he'd like to check them with her, just get her reaction, which flatters her. Then, astounding and delighting her, he asks if she'll compile a sourcebook on modern Jewish history for use in all the reform Jewish religious schools in Canada and the U.S. She demurs, it's too much. Her, the housewife. He twists her arm with a European charm she always forgets he can call on. She is still warm with his confidence in her as they sit in the front seat of his car outside her home. Within is Morry her wonderful husband, the realtor with a heart, happy-go-lucky Jeffrey – drop him on his head and he pops up laughing – and perfect little Lisa, who might even grow up to be the independent rebellious person her mother never became. They sit in the Dodge with the push-button transmission, and years of work and affection between them.

"Do you know I was in love with you?" he says, looking through the windshield. He speaks as though this is not a question, it is information.

What can she say? "Oskar."

"I thought we could have a life together." More data.

"I never thought of you . . . I never thought about you thinking of me . . ."

"Always," he says.

"Oskar, what is it? Is it Schropp?"

He marvels at her instinct. It is perfect. It proves he was right, she was ideal, she was meant to happen to him, she'd have understood him, made him whole, he is insane not to have spoken till now. "Schropp?" he barks. "What about Schropp? Why should it be Schropp?"

"We could never change our feelings about you. No one will ever mean to us what you do." He feels the weight lift a bit, maybe just shift. She continues. She hopes this is what he wants to hear, and it pumps a little distance between them and his declaration. She says it is ludicrous to think he could be displaced by a flashy new rabbi who plays tennis. "Tennis?" says Oskar. Yes, she says, that's all you hear about him. Who needs a rabbi with a forehand? He likes that, she can tell. Good, she thinks, I'm helping. Sure it'll be a little easier, she says, when we have a rabbi the kids get to see once in a while – does he squirm slightly? – but the warmth and the guidance we get from you, Oskar, is not going to be replaced and nobody, NOBODY OSKAR NOBODY, wants a replacement!

She pauses and registers his reactions. She thinks she felt his gloom lighten as she spoke. Now she is certain. She has made him happy. Well, happier. This is what I am for, she thinks, this understanding and compassion for a man who needs and deserves it: for Morry, the kids, and Oskar. Long ago he came from somewhere distant, like a weary traveller, to add something – she cannot say what, she is only dimly aware of it – to her life. To enlarge her. He is nodding slowly in the dark, still testing her words in his mind. He looks like he has come through the valley of the shadow of death carrying an urgent message, which he has delivered, and now he can relax. Something about this irks her.

"Why now?" she says.

"Always. I told you –"

"Why *tell* me now?" she presses. She amazes herself. Confrontation is not part of her mission. She feels as though she is dealing with a bright but belligerent student, the type Oskar always says makes the whole thing worthwhile. She will not let him off the hook. "Are you telling me now because it's too late, there's no chance, it can't mean anything at this point?" He winces; she feels regret. "Sorry. I mean, can't mean anything that's . . ." – she considers the candidates: that's real, that counts – "anything practical," she concludes.

He shrugs. The ends of a smile tug the crooked line of his mouth. She catches it: he *is* relieved. They understand one another, he grants her point. He reaches toward her arm, his fingers brush the sleeve and close around it without gripping. This is an Oskar hug: encircle but do not touch. She leans forward, kisses his cheek, her hands clasp his forearms, she looks at him face to face, as they say in the Bible, and tightens her own hold, which says: Okay, here I am, there you are, we're right here for each other. She flicks a smile at him, he hangs grimly onto his, and she leans toward the car door. A sound rises from his throat, she looks. He shakes his head and lowers his gaze. "If I had had faith . . ." She pauses, but he gestures her out the door.

Right, she thinks, better go. She is on the curb, she is at her door. Faith? She has no idea what he meant.

RING. RING. "Yes?" "Is, ah, Herr Professor Buber there?" "Buber speaking."

Like phoning heaven and God answers. He'd never thought of Buber as an actual person. Buber was a name, the source of many books that Oskar pored over as bad became worse in those years. *Between Man and Man, Tales of the Hassidim*, and especially *I and Thou*, the book that made life make a kind of pure crystal sense to him. Oskar reread that slight volume again and again, sentence by sentence, as if everything might be discovered in it, the way his forebears, by the waters of Babylon, turned the pages of the Torah and turned them again, rock-certain all wisdom would eventually be squeezed out in the process. Of course it was the first two sections of *I and Thou* he read through often, the chapters about relationships between people, between a human I and a human Thou. Then you came to Part III, which dealt with the Eternal Thou, the one you prayed to and answered to, who entered into history and so forth. Oskar stopped when he got to Part III.

He had fantasies about meeting Buber, as he told Gotthold, his former youth leader, when they met at one of the numberless emergency meetings between the Nuremberg Laws and *Kristallnacht*. It's not hard, said Gotthold. Very hesitantly: Could you look into it for me? Sure, said Gotthold, but it would go better if you phoned him yourself. Can you get me his number? Look it up – in the directory of course. Under Buber, M.

He managed to make the appointment and Buber gave him the address. "Oh, one other thing," Gotthold said. "The old man would be just as happy if you told him your problem was choosing between two women. He hears so much philosophy and politics." Oskar's face fell. "I don't have two women I can't choose between," he said. "Uh-oh," said Gotthold. "But you've got Greta. Can you have a problem with her?"

Buber's study was perfect. Buber sat behind a magnificent desk scattered over with books, articles, pamphlets, in German, Hebrew, French, Polish, English, Arabic. Buber looked like God and paid close attention to what Oskar said, so close it was unnerving. Oskar thought: It's because he doesn't want *it* to happen again. In *Between Man and Man*, Buber described how once a troubled student came to see him. He'd listened, yet not really heard the student's distress; that night the boy killed himself. This taught Buber the lesson of living in the moment, the utter primacy of responding fully to each Thou that entered your life. Oskar wanted to tell Buber not to worry. "I won't do myself in just to be included in your next book," he could say. Instead he laboured to describe his "problem," the one that had perplexed him for years.

It was the sunset, any sunset. He had worried it so long, raised it so often, that others called it Oskar's Sunset, like Zeno's Paradox or Ockham's Razor. He'd be on a youth hike, or a day at the lake, or a camping trip, he explained to Buber, and he'd see a glorious sunset, and at that same instant notice himself thinking: Here I am having the profound experience of a sunset! The experience began to sink behind the experience of the experience, sure as the setting of the sun itself. As if a veil, the veil of his own intrusive self-consciousness, endlessly intervened between himself (whoever that was) and the world. He felt such a fool, so insufferably self-obsessed and self-important. Life was out there and he couldn't quite reach it. "Do you know what I mean?" he pleaded, as he fought back tears.

Buber sat immobile. Oh God, thought Oskar, it's even stupider than I thought. What have I done? How can I be so trite? In this hour, in this crisis of our people, how can I place before this great man my pathetic sunsets? What will he say to shame me sufficiently?

Buber leaned forward in his chair. He propped his elbows on the varied wisdom of the human race strewn around his desk. He laced his fingers. After an endless pause he spoke. "Do you have good friends?"

Oskar blinked. "I think so," he said.

Buber exhaled as though an iron bar had been lifted from his chest. "Then it will be all right."

Oskar grinned the forerunner of his demented smile. He wanted to yelp with joy, cry with gratitude, and demand his money back. Buber was being Buber. Buber was . . . Bubering. He was the true scion of Hassidic *rebbe*s, and this was their specialty: the unpredictable aphorism, an elliptical response from some direction not even on the map, an Oriental parable in the middle of a shopping list. Buber grinned back at him. The interview was over.

"I don't understand about faith," said Oskar, instead of rising to go. This was too good to abandon. Not yet. "I have no idea what it is. I read, I listen, I ask questions." Buber asked what Oskar read and Oskar's mind went blank. He wondered whether he'd ever read anything. "I mean that has had personal meaning for you," added Buber helpfully. "Ah," said Oskar, "there's Kierkegaard. He's a philosopher, but I understand some of it. His confusion, his anger, his bitterness."

"And his humour," said Buber.

"Yes," said Oskar, "that too. But not the leap of faith. Or the knight of faith." He started to rub his head as though it hurt from these thoughts. "Especially I don't understand the . . ." Buber helped again: "The willing suspension of disbelief." Oskar jerked his head affirmatively. "That's funnier than anything else he wrote. I start to giggle when I read it."

"Is there a woman?" said Buber.

"Only one," said Oskar. "Will that be all right too?"

Buber laughed. Buber actually laughed. He turned his palms

up, shook his head, and radiated warmth and wisdom. He said nothing. That's really it, thought Oskar, and began to rise. He heard Buber mutter something. It sounded like, "If I had had faith." He turned in shock. "Pardon?" he said. "If I had had faith," said Buber, "I would have stayed with Regina." Oskar was stuck in mid-rise, and stymied. Was Buber now unburdening himself to young Oskar, confronting him with Buber's own problem? Was this part of the life of dialogue about which Buber wrote and Oskar read? Had he now become Buber's Thou as Buber had been his? If so, how could he possibly respond – and how could he not? And who the hell was Regina?

Buber cleared his throat. Oskar had spoken the last question aloud. "Kierkegaard knew Regina," said Buber. "Kierkegaard said that if he had had faith, he would have stayed with her and married her. She was a woman in Copenhagen."

Oskar asked, "Did he love her?"

Buber answered, "He doesn't say. He just says that if he had had faith, he would have stayed with her."

Oskar said, "Can you have faith without love, or can you have love without faith?"

"I thought what you were wondering," said Buber, "is whether you can have faith without God."

Confusion reigns in the mind of Oskar, in his tower. Confusion and embarrassment. How could he pose that juvenalia, that drivel, to Buber in the midst of a historic conflagration? The sorrows of a young Jewish Werther – while their people were being consumed. And why is he reliving it now? There is the past and the present, now, and then. Surely they are meant to be kept separate. Otherwise, how could one ever get a clear view of either?

Oskar likes history, it is his field. Perhaps some day by a miracle he will finish his MA at the University of Toronto and go on to a doctorate. History puts everything in its place and keeps it there, God willing. No wonder Germany has been a nation of historical research. To Germans order is primary. But what place? (Oskar's mind wanders and he follows.) Where is the place that history is in? How can time be in a place? This makes no sense in his own life. History as he lives it will not stay put where it ought to. His past keeps happening as though it is his present. He feels at moments like this as if then is now. Then where has now gone?

Even places confuse him, when you get down to it. There was Germany and there is Canada. The two could hardly be more different, to state it mildly. Then why does he often feel he is in the wrong place? Is he still in Germany, although he is in Canada? Why do times and places frequently seem to overlap, or switch, or even jump ahead and appear from the opposite direction you'd expected them? Something buried in the past looms from the future or takes over the present. Like Willi Schropp! Often Oskar loses track of tense–future, past, present, like the crazy grammar of biblical Hebrew: after an *and*, past becomes future and future becomes past, or became past . . .?

He sighs. He sighed. He will sigh. Hermann would call this mess a paradox. Two things that are opposites occur together. Both seem equally necessary. "Isn't that a contradiction?" asked Oskar. No, said Hermann with authority: in a contradiction only one side can be true, the other must be false. In a paradox both are true. Hermann seemed pleased, as though his words solved the problem. To Oskar they stated it.

And what the hell was he doing, at that awesome hour of Jewish history, human history, cosmic history, talking to Buber about sunsets!

A tap on the door and Schropp oozes in. "Oskar, Oskar, Oskar, it's been *so* long. May I?" He settles into the other chair, the one for terrorized student teachers, or aspiring bar mitzvahs who lack the academic credits that Oskar alone can waive, letting them go the route and collect the cheques, sweaters, season hockey tickets, and other perks of young Canadian Jewish majority. "Naturally I've followed your career," says Willi. He looks gaunt, wasted by the years, his head like a skull–or is this just fit for tennis, lean and lithe according to the taste of the times? "But how could I have been unaware, even had I wanted to! What an honour it will be to collaborate. What a *m'tzee'ah*. I can't wait to hear your ideas." Smooth, silken, superficial, and one hundred per cent *auf Englisch*. Even between Oskar and Hermann, who have spoken English together for years, this is the result of a decision taken long ago, one lonely night on Yonge Street after they both settled in Toronto. The sense of their decision for English still lingers, like a contract that must be renewed. For Willi, though, the thing just flows, as though his German past exists as a subject of conversation but not as anything that ever really was.

"Catherine and I must have you for dinner, our first guest, soon as we move. Allison, Gail and Fiona will absolutely fawn on you!" Aha! His secret revealed: anglicized by marriage. Naturalized and Americanized. May the earth open and swallow this tormentor. Oskar would willingly suspend his disbelief in miracles. "We have so much to discuss. Curriculum, staff. I thought a retreat, so we could all get to know each other as people . . ."

While Schropp burbles, Oskar switches to his other track, the one he rides inside, as he chooses, oblivious to whatever is happening out there. Schropp thinks Oskar is listening, certainly he is nodding and grunting and even speaking the odd sentence. But really he is far away. He wills himself at the airport, the old one, on the observation deck. No, too chilly. The current one then, so he's inside, in the lounge with the floor-to-ceiling windows; the jumbo jets lumber past on their ways to distant runways and lands. Oskar is alone, naturally. He nurses a drink. He doesn't drink but you have to order to stay. If that phantom of the past invaded his solitude even here, what would Oskar do? Launch this drink in his face! Put it to use. Planes come and go, so do the waiters.

"Do you know my *Chronicles of the Delta Jews: A Passionate Portrayal*? Wrote it while I was serving in Jackson. Jackson, Miss. I thought, what about something similar here? It's an approach I've developed – serious scholarly research combined with readability. Has anyone dipped into local Jewish history? Perhaps even yourself? *This* we must pursue. But – ah, I've a tennis date with my new sisterhood president. Remember–soon. Adieu." He slithers through the door.

Tennis. Oskar hisses through clenched teeth. Tennis. The chair moans under his weight. WHOOSH go the jets. SPLAT goes his drink.

But honestly, it still seems bizarre. Can this really be the worst moment in the life of Oskar? Perhaps what is at stake is the term (or term of), a life. When was the life of Oskar? Which life of Oskar are we talking about?

Oskar had a life he was born to; it ended. It began to end when the Nazis came to power. It continued ending with the Nuremberg Laws, which abruptly eliminated Oskar and his kind from public life; then with *Kristallnacht* and the beating in the barracks in the camp after *Kristallnacht*, which stripped him of dignity as Nuremberg had stripped him of citizenship. That life ended finally, with his departure from Germany, or his arrival in a new place, England, or another new place, Canada. There was an interim period, lasting some years, between leaving Germany and being set free from internment in Canada, which might have been yet another life, or some category of between-lives. At length the other other life commenced, the Canadian one.

People talk of beginning a new life, especially in the case of immigrants: immigration as a kind of transmigration of souls without the mediation of death. But perhaps Oskar's real life simply ended when he left Germany. In that case, the many years when we knew him, lurching along Bathurst, was just the long coda to a life; we witnessed only the lengthy afterbreath, an interminable sigh.

Or else, the thing that ended when he left Germany was not his life, it was a prelife, like a prehistory. At least this would make sense of the strange truth that for Oskar, his worst moment came with the relative non-event of Willi Schropp's arrival in Toronto.

His life in Canada was trivial and unmomentous compared to the epochal and traumatic existence that preceded it, but it is the only life of Oskar most of us knew, and it is the life he himself lived out, staggered through to the end, in a private hospital room just south of the stolid provincial parliament buildings. For us, he was Oskar of Canada.

Yet that earlier thing, unspeakable, epochal, full of death – it doesn't sink helpfully into the realm of history; it rises repeatedly into the centre of things. Repeatedly, it rises. In our dealings with him, those of us who knew him, it comes and goes like a bat from another dimension, screeching in, creating chaos and incomprehension, pain and hate, then gone again. For Oskar too. He thinks it is mere envy – at most masochism – that draws him toward self-degradation as Willi arrives. It is not, not only. It is the return of the past, which he longs to have gone, never to reappear. It is the refusal of our past to be history, and of history to pass. If only, he thinks, I could follow through on my intentions and become a historian. Then I could keep what's past in its place.

CHAPTER
3

HOW DID HE GET HERE? What is he doing here? As the Canadians say, Where is here?

Let us try a different image. Instead of the Wandering Jew, the Visitor from Another Planet. This might seem odd, even shocking. The Wandering Jew is a tragic and historic figure. The Visitor from Another Planet is fanciful. What justifies this switch?

Simple. As Oskar walks about Toronto in, say, 1947, four years after he arrived in the city, he feels far more like someone from a distant galaxy than like a wandering Jew.

He is in High Park on a Sunday in summer. Families lounge about the gentle green slopes. Down by Grenadier Pond the band of the 48th Highlanders plays. Behind them, rays of sunshine skip over Lake Ontario. Does this remind Oskar of strolling by the shore of Wannsee, canoeing on Muggelsee, ambling through the piney woods of Grunewald? Not a jot. These musicians wear kilts. On their heads perch high fur hats. Though they are an army band, there is nothing military, in a German sense, to this scene. Kilts? In fact there is virtually nothing Canadian about it. Oskar knows where that get-up comes from: it is Scots. What a strange country.

He has felt this strangeness–theirs, not his–since he arrived in Toronto, after his release from the internment camp. He finds

44

it a comfortable strangeness, it has grown on him. The sense of place here is so lackadaisical, the sense of pride so unpossessive and unassertive. Invisible, almost. It soothes him.

He catches fragments as they chat. They still talk about "the boys." He used to come here while the war was on and watch them listen to the bands and talk about the boys overseas. He wondered how they pictured overseas. Since the boys came home, many have become husbands and fathers. As Oskar lurches through their conversations, he feels protected; no one seems to notice his smashed face, his manic leer. Perhaps they sense his approach at a distance through social radar, and with Canadian politeness, clear a path. He thinks they are innocents, he treasures their absence of passion; it seems to protect him. Maybe it is just this lack which drew him to Toronto. He could have chosen Montreal after his release; but Montreal was a less passionless place.

When their boat sailed up the St. Lawrence, they didn't know what country this was; they didn't know if their destination was on the upper or lower half of the world. Australia was one rumour. Along with Hamburg, where they would be handed back to the Nazis as part of a separate peace that Britain was negotiating with Hitler, according to a plausible report. After a while at sea, they knew it wouldn't be Hamburg, and Oskar relaxed.

Relaxation is relative. When they stopped beating him in the barracks at Oranienburg, he did not relax. They might return. A few months later, when he arrived in England, he relaxed. When the English policeman came to the door right after Dunkirk, with the situation grim for the Allies, and said, "You'll have to come with us, sir, you're under arrest," he did not stop relaxing, for they weren't Nazis. And for the first time in his life someone called him sir. The detention in Scotland, before they were loaded on the ship, was difficult; at sea, conditions were unspeakable. He grew less relaxed.

They landed and settled in a tent camp on a large parkland

called the Plains of Abraham, west of the city of Quebec. He assumed the Abraham in question was Abraham Our Father, who also dwelled in tents. They were safe from death, and together with others. *Hineh mah tov u-mah na-eem*, he thought, in the words of the round they sang in the movement: *Behold how good and pleasant it is for brothers to dwell together.* There were two military monuments nearby, one for an English general, the other for a Frenchman. Before Oskar came to Canada, he never considered the study of history. By the time he was released from internment, he thought of himself as a historian. In waiting, embryonic. It would be simplistic to relate this change merely to his stay on the most fateful battlefield in the history of Canada.

As for the Canadians who received Oskar and his shipmates, they were severely disappointed. It is hard to capture the depth of their disappointment. They had expected Nazis on those ships, because the British promised them Nazis. At the war's outset Churchill's government urgently requested they take seven thousand pro-Nazi Germans living in England. The Canadian government agreed.

They prepared for their Nazis. They expropriated vacant factories and lumber camps in Quebec, New Brunswick, and Northern Ontario. They erected barbed-wire compounds with group huts, and watchtowers with searchlights. They selected and trained special army units for guard duty. Then they went down to the docks in Quebec City to collect their Nazis. They got some. But when they looked up the gangplank, they also saw rabbis, professors, mathematicians, engineers, and *yeshiva bocher*s with earlocks disembarking. Boatloads of Nazis who wanted kosher food!

The Canadians were not easily gulled. They carefully inspected the shipment. Perhaps it was subterfuge: Nazis in clever disguise. They inspected them for the next three years. But the Nazis were Jews, and the Canadians were angry. They wanted Nazis, dammit, and they took out their disappointment by cursing the inmates with racial slurs. They treated them like prisoners of war. They stood them up for roll call three times a day and inspected them for VD with a swagger stick. They black-mailed them and stole from them; threw off their rough blankets in the middle of the night and occasionally gang-raped them.

For Oskar and his fellow German Jews, this situation was at least as perplexing as it was for the Canadians, and as irritating. What went wrong? Who was responsible? Relief turned testy. They did not mind waiting weeks, even months, while the con-fusion dispersed – but not years. They objected to being classed and imprisoned with Nazis. Then they protested, then they resisted.

This climate maintained, in degrees, throughout their intern-ment. Oskar continued to relax less. But he was alive, and not in Nazi Germany. By the time of his release, he was no longer relaxed.

Did he decide to become a historian during this time because he didn't know why this was happening to him and his compan-ions and wanted to find out? There was indeed a reason, which he and the others eventually learned. The British government overestimated when they approached Canada: they had only four or five thousand certifiable hostiles – pro-Nazis and POWs – on hand in the British Isles. They were also holding thousands of other Germans (Jews, Catholics, Protestants, Communists), interned in a burst when the German army rolled through the Lowlands and destroyed the French forces. Only the Channel now stood between Britain and the Wehrmacht, looking less protective than it had. So they arrested all German nationals in the British Isles, just to be safe. The British threw in two thou-sand of these others, to fill their quota with the Canadians and to tidy up a bit on the island while they had the chance; but they didn't tell the Canadians, who learned for themselves by direct experience after landfall in Quebec. So there was a reason, but it made no sense.

On the other hand, this may be one of those cases wherein reason, however senseless, has its reasons. An instance of what Oskar's friend Hermann – a philosopher and not a historian – calls, in a standard philosophical phrase, *die List der Vernunft*, the cunning of reason. Oskar does not believe in the cunning of reason. He doesn't even know what it means. But like most internees, including Hermann the philosopher, he was happy to come to Canada at that time for any reason at all. While they remained in England, they were still within reach of the Nazis they had just escaped. They assumed Germany would soon conquer England, or bring her to heel, and they would be imperilled again, this time round with nowhere to go. The United States would not have them, Australia would not have them; above all Canada would not have them. Canada would have fewer of them than anyone! Canada would have none of those refu-Jews at all, if it had its way. Yet as things turned out, they came to Canada in their thousands, because they came as Nazis! As Nazis, Canada welcomed them, in its fashion.

Yet why a historian? And why now? A ludicrous causal web hardly seems to explain the process whereby Oskar (in his mind only, to be sure) found his calling. The chance arrival on a historic battleground would do as well. Perhaps there is something else.

Oskar had decided long since he would not become a rabbi. But he couldn't go on not being a rabbi forever. He made that choice because he felt inadequate to the religious life: not just that he didn't know God; he took their lack of acquaintance as a failing on his own part. Others, like Buber, like Hermann, like some we have yet to meet, seem to be on close and personal terms with the *mysterium tremendum*, the awesome source of religious experience in every tradition. Not Oskar. But here, in the difficult history of our time where he found himself – the realm around us, not above us – Oskar discovered a mystery, if not quite *tremendum*, to which he could in some manner relate. He would worship where he could.

In those Canadian internment camps, though he was here, he was not really here. His Canada in those first years was a set of negatives. He was not dead, it was not Nazi Germany. At most, Canada was positive negatives: he was alive (not dead), he was here (not there), and in the most potent of positive negatives, he had *survived*. From inside the hut behind the barbed wire, the country was for him only a vacuous surround; he floated in it as a spaceman floats in space, a space significantly drained of European horrors. Then, after nearly three years, his sponsor in Toronto confirmed, the camp authorities concurred, they authorized his release, and he drifted down from the void to begin a true visit to the planet and its inhabitants.

"Go to the home of Jack Katz," said a message Oskar received in fall 1943, just after he arrived in Toronto. It sounded like an instruction in a board game. That Friday night he found the Katz home in a distant part of the city. He didn't know Toronto extended so far beyond its lakefront and the modest downtown. He felt like a pioneer arriving by steamer in the nineteenth century and heading into the bush north of Toronto with nothing but an axe to help him through virgin forest, muskeg, and tundra. His destination was called Lawrence Avenue, but it was mostly mud and unfinished shoulders. He walked over planks as he approached the door to the Katz bungalow.

Katz took a cigar from his mouth and explained he was a builder. This was his subdivision. He'd already named streets after wife Mona and daughters Esther and Rochelle. But first and foremost he was a Jew. They'd been taking poor fellow Jews from the Old Country in for Friday night dinner since before the war, their last one came for two and a half years and just moved on to Winnipeg—

The Old Country! Oskar was aghast. They took him for an Old Country Jew! He knew what the Old Country meant. Russia, Lithuania, Galicia, Rumania, Hungary, and – Poland! Uncouth, uncultured, underdeveloped, the vile pale of Jewish settlement in Eastern Europe. The Old Country was never Germany, nor France nor England. They saw him as one with the wretched mobs, bags of Jewish rags driven by Cossacks and wracked by pogroms: peddlers, cowherds, and mendicant Talmudists. He wanted to fling Goethe and Schiller, Heine and Schubert, Weber and Thomas Mann and Heinrich Mann and Spengler at them—these Katzes of Lawrence Avenue in the Canadian backwoods – like cultural snowballs till they were buried under the mountains of his cultivation. His English did not suffice, so he chose resentful silence instead. The meal passed painfully. By parting-time they gathered he would not be back, they could recruit a genuine Polack, Litvak, or even a Galitzianer to fill their weekly *mitzvah*. He had not fled the furnace to count as a good deed among *arrivistes*.

At the door, before Oskar plunged back into the bog, Jack Katz removed his cigar a last time, shook hands, and offered Oskar a job. Not carrying hods on Mona Road, but teaching and moulding young Canadian Jewish minds. "At the Pillar of Fire Temple," said Jack. "Where we belong. It's modern. We *daven* in English. I mean – " Jack stumbled slightly and recovered, "we pray in English. I'm on the education committee. We need people like you. We don't have anyone . . . worldly." He told Oskar to think about the offer and if he saw fit, "Gimme a shout." Which Oskar did, after an interval long enough to prove he was desperate for no one's charity. The Pill on the Hill has been part of his life ever since.

He began to drop by the temple once a week, to teach Jewish Holidays Then and Now in the religious school. This is how he thought of it, as though he had a detached, optional relationship to the place. Meanwhile his main attention in Canada has been to the rest, the un-Jewish part. What does he find so interesting? That it is so . . . uninteresting. He has grown fascinated with this cool country and its dispassionate people. On afternoons like this in High Park, he wanders among them like an Arctic explorer; they are like penguins. He does not undervalue their negative national trait; *au contraire*, as some of the guards at the concentration – whoops, internment – camp in Quebec would have said. He appreciates their dispassion, treasures it even; without it he might not have remained. For there seems no doubt: he is here to stay.

Only one Canadian he knows lacks their absence of passion: Goldberg. Of course Goldberg is a Jew, perhaps Canadians don't even think of him as one of them. Goldberg however sees himself as Canadian. He doesn't deny his Jewishness. He revels in it along with his Canadianness; he thinks he can be Jew *and* Canadian. To Oskar this is a familiar pattern, he recalls it well. Of all the Canadian Jews he has met, Oskar feels an affinity only with Goldberg. They work together at *World Press Review.*

Goldberg is determined to share his Canadian passions with Oskar. He says he knows Oskar appreciates the true signs of culture because he is German. (Oskar does not wince. He *does* appreciate the finest in European culture.) Later this sunny Sunday afternoon, after he leaves High Park and the 48th Highlanders, Oskar is to meet Goldberg and together they will attend a Canadian play. He has the address on a slip of paper. He wonders what kind of name for a theatre is the ROM.

It stands for Royal Ontario Museum. There are many royal things here in Canada. Royal this and royal that. The Royal Winter Fair and the Royal Mail. Yet there is no royalty in Canada. The royalty Canadians acknowledge is over in England. It strikes Oskar as excellent to be a country with your ruler somewhere else. To separate your politics from your life. To keep the symbols that inflame your passions in someone else's country. Personally, he has had enough of politics for this lifetime anyway; Canada suits his mood.

It definitely is a museum, not a theatre. But here comes Goldberg. He takes Oskar's arm and trundles him down a circular stone staircase that curls around an immense totem pole. (Totem pole? How did Oskar identify that phallic structure? An image from a Berlin grade-school textbook breaks into his memory.) They arrive in a basement auditorium, Goldberg squirms happily, the curtain rises. He whispers to Oskar this is the only professional company in Toronto. They work part-time for no pay. Oskar smiles fixedly. All other theatre here, Goldberg says scornfully, is done by touring companies from Britain and the United States. This is Canadian. They are performing the difficult *Ah Wilderness*, by Eugene O'Neill, an American playwright. The play is scheduled for three performances.

Oskar decides to test Goldberg, or maybe just torment him. It is intermission. "Look here," he says, "Toronto is the metropolis of a country in which national theatre consists of three performances of a foreign play in the basement of a museum. For the whole year!" Goldberg does not collapse like a Canadian culture balloon from which air has been released. Instead he inflates, he puffs up with his cause. "This is a raw country," Goldberg announces loudly enough for others to hear. "It has yet to feel its strength, its cultural distinctiveness. This is frequently the case in the world of art. Think of Ireland, before its renaissance. Think of early America. Think of Elizabethan England . . ."

"Piffle," says Oskar, trying a word he read in a novel. "So this is how they declare themselves, with American plays, English plays, Irish plays?"

"They do Canadian plays," says Goldberg, nearing a pout.

"Their Canadian play, singular," says Oskar, "was garbage. There was nothing Canadian about it. Unquote. I read your review."

"It will take time," says Goldberg. "But I believe it will happen."

Aha, thinks Oskar. So Goldberg is a man of faith. The presence of conviction in someone else stimulates him. It always has. He probes. Goldberg, it seems, was a believer of another sort once: a Communist. But Goldberg's certainty about The Revolution has given way to a deep belief in the transformative power of art, literature, theatre. All the better for his fervour: the man is a convert! He has journeyed hither from the land of politics.

"I think I understand," says Oskar. "Culture. I may not agree, but I follow. However, when you tell me, *Canadian* culture . . ." and Oskar widens his eyes to look as lost as a little boy at the Canadian National Exhibition grounds down by the lake. Goldberg squints, trying to follow. Oskar goes on. "Goldberg, you are a man ready to consecrate your life to the service of art, of culture. You are able take your choice among the great cultures of the earth, not least of all *Jewish* culture. You can if you please reside in the Hanging Gardens of Babylon. Culturally speaking, that is. Don't you find it a little embarrassing to pick around a suburban backyard?"

Goldberg does not look embarrassed. Conversation buzzes around them. No one is discussing the play. "Backyard?" says Goldberg.

"Called Canada!" hisses Oskar.

"It is not a matter of choosing," says Goldberg, with impressive self-possession. "We are what we are."

"I like your answer," says Oskar, echoing Buber whether he realizes it or not. Why does Goldberg's reply appeal to him? Because it is so empty, this devotion to Canadian culture, it lacks content. Oskar, who has had more than enough of politics, has also had his fill of *Kultur*. He is not ready to give up art and literature, but he prefers for now to have his culture, along with his royalty, somewhere else.

Goldberg interprets Oskar's reply as enthusiasm and vows to expose him to the rest of Toronto's teeming artistic life. Two months later they are at the ballet. It is the annual visit of the Sadler's Wells Company from London. London, England, not London, Ontario, a Canadian province which, Oskar thinks, attempts to replicate every street and place name in the British Isles. This time he and Goldberg mount many steps to their seats. They are late. Higher and higher they go, reversing the descent to *Ah Wilderness*, up a stairway with the bare concrete aesthetics of a urinal instead of Indian myth. Why? Because the ballet performs here in Maple Leaf Gardens – the hockey arena!

They emerge in the "greys." A shabby usher glances dully at their tickets. He may be keener on the nights they have the hockey. Far far below whirls the miniature figure of a ballerina. She looks like the decoration on top of a music box. As they settle, breathing heavily, onto their hard seats, Goldberg reproaches himself. "Damn. The binoculars!" He turns to apologize but Oskar is transfixed. Directly before him at eye level, hanging from the roof like a giant overstuffed shopping bag with a clock's face drawn on its sides, is the incredible SporTimer. It hovers above the touching speck of ballerina like a suspended Canadian judgement on someone else's idea of art.

Emboldened further, Goldberg hauls Oskar one day after work to the Casino Burlesque on Queen Street. It's vaudeville, he tells Oskar, and books all the best international acts. This week is special – Gypsy Rose Lee. "An artichoke," she tells the audience as she removes a glove, "is a green tomato that peels." A cymbal clashes. Goldberg glances nervously sidewards. He hopes Oskar takes Gypsy as a sign of Goldberg's cultural eclecticism. Nothing human, and nothing cultural either, is alien to him. He hopes Oskar is not an artistic snob, despite that European breeding. Oskar leers back and bobs his head. Shortly after, he leans in and confides he must leave. Goldberg looks fearful, but Oskar swiftly adds, For a previous dinner engagement. Goldberg nods agreeably.

Oskar is careening up Yonge Street now, on his way to Fran's. "Gypsy needs no introduction," said the host at the Casino. Maybe not, thinks Oskar, but she needed an act! He hears a cymbal clash in his mind. He laughs aloud, a little yelp. A passing couple eye him suspiciously, as though they wonder if he is a German agent sent ashore from a U-boat cruising beneath the surface of Lake Ontario, unaware the war ended two years ago. Ach, he reproaches himself. How would they know I am German? It is merely that on Toronto streets one does not laugh aloud. Canadians and foreigners alike.

He is thinking about the Tiller Girls now, he can't get them out of his mind. It was that sorry imitation of a sex show. Striptease, they call it, an English word he likes. It's touching how the Canadians hem it in with rules and limits. The girls must wear G-strings and pasties (another word he savours). They cannot directly suggest this or that pleasure. Only by negation, by what they are not allowed to do. Ingenious in its way, it can be sensuous. He knows because he watches strippers sometimes at a refurbished theatre on Spadina called the Victory. He wonders if some revue hall in Berlin is now called the Defeat.

He tries to remember where the Tiller Girls performed in Berlin. There were so many clubs. Not the Metropol, nor the cavernous Grosses Schauspielhaus – places the whole family went. Nor the Munzstrasse with a club in almost every house. . Ah, the cabarets, so many cabarets, and each had a specialty: Indian fakirs who invited the audience to stand on their chests as they lolled on a bed of nails; imitators, comics, satirists, yodellers, folkdancers. What range, what choice. All of them had one thing in common, though: naked girls. Even the family shows.

Come to think of it, he's not sure he ever saw the Tiller Girls live. They were just so familiar: their faces gazed from posters on every big tubular street pillar in Berlin. Oskar knew their names – Jessie, Esther, Dorothy, Edith, Winnie, Maisie, Mabel, Molly, Vera, Lillian, Joyce. He still does! Odd, they were English names. Why should beautiful naked women be English? Or were they supposed to be American? The master of ceremonies at the Alt-Bayern started every show with a prayer:

> *Dear God, let me become an American,*
> *That's my greatest wish on earth.*
> *Everything in America is larger, better,*
> * faster than here –*
> *At least I think it is . . .*

American had never meant Canadian. Nor had English. What *did* they think of Canada?

The Tiller Girls seemed to spend every minute together. At least on the posters. They were always putting on makeup in unison, or slipping into scanty bathing suits, adjusting a shoulder strap on or off a white shoulder. There were never men on the pillars. But they were always smiling out at men they surely knew were looking from the sidewalk, eyeing each with a limp suggestion of "Yes, you can have me, if you really want me." That's what they said to Oskar through years of adolescence. So simple and generous: You can have me if you really want me. It eliminated the source of all anxiety: fear of rejection. How wonderful it would be to be loved by a Tiller Girl – it still makes his heart pound. Though he wonders here on Yonge Street whether some of the girls were extending their offer to women passing by, not just men. Why does Canada draw out the perverse in him? There's nothing sexual here to stimulate him, nothing at all. Is that what does it?

The Weisse Maus, he's sure he was there. Franz took him,

not on a special day like a birthday or a graduation, but they both knew what it was: a stage of his manhood. Three women sprawled on the stage, gauze draped their laps and hips, arms raised limply like the stamens of a flower in a botany text, taut strips of white underwear across their crotches, with a little bulge marking the bush (Franz explained and he pictured) and nothing at all above the hips. Then rising from them like the stamen of their stamens, a dark woman with neck arched and head thrust back, gazing to the side as though her lover or master were in the wings, her arms stretched behind as if she were soaring, and a filmy covering that showed everything beneath more clearly than nothing would have done, falling till it was hidden by the rising bodies of her handmaidens, like Pharaoh's daughter bathing just before the basket with little Jewish baby Moses drifted into her life. Tableaus, they were called. You saw them on the stages of every club, café, and theatre of the Berlin night. You looked at them, that was all.

Fran's. They come here often. Oskar passes the Mrs Deck's "That" Salad Dressing across the table to Hermann. They prefer this booth, from which you can see Yonge Street, and vainly imagine life erupting right here in downtown Toronto some night after business hours. Hermann slides the little carousel with the waffle syrup pitchers over. "They call it a Lazy Susan," he says. They pool intelligence like this. Oskar chooses boysenberry.

Hermann has two topics. He starts with Paltz. "Paltz is convinced I'm fixated on my sibling rivalry," he says. "How would he know?" asks Oskar antagonistically. "It's my projections," says Hermann. "It's the way I react to him during treatment. Even though he's my doctor, I treat him like a brother."

It makes instinctive sense to Oskar. He wishes he knew more about this way of thinking, which deals with feelings rather than ideas. It cares little about reasons and logic, in fact it almost revels in what seems silly. Oskar wonders suddenly if the reason he likes Fran's is because it reminds him of Franz. Or does that mean he ought to avoid the place? Or can he avoid its meaning by coming and not realizing that's why he comes? He could ask Hermann, but Hermann wouldn't interrupt his report.

"It doesn't mean I'm sick, you know," says Hermann, who employs "you know" frequently – in English, never in German – as though he wants to check reception of his transmissions via this strange linguistic device, the English language. Oskar sometimes starts counting "you know"s and loses track of what Hermann is saying. "I'm not ashamed to admit I have some neurotic behaviour patterns," concludes Hermann with a healthy glow.

"Look here," Oskar says testily, "do you think I might have some neurotic behaviour patterns too, or is it only your privilege?"

"Like what?" asks Hermann.

"Like sibling rivalry."

"Ah," says Hermann, "you might. You very well might. *Especially* sibling rivalry." Oskar reclines happily. "But you can't take them to Paltz," Hermann adds cruelly, retracting what he just offered. "Paltz is *my* shrink."

Hermann has a way of getting there first. Oskar has a sneaking suspicion he might himself be a better candidate for psychoanalysis, but what can be done? Hermann already occupies the field. He has engaged the only psychiatrist whose name Oskar knows, because Hermann unearthed him here in Toronto, laid siege to him, plies him with hourly fees, and as proof of the spoils, babbles endlessly to Oskar his friend about Paltz's every *aperçu*. Presumably there are other psychiatrists in Toronto. Canadian psychiatrists. Oskar scoffs inwardly at the idea. He wonders about Goldberg. Would Goldberg demand treatment by a Canadian shrink as he went round the bend? Can one practise psychiatry in a Canadian way?

Hermann yammers on about the session he just left. Paltz told him this and Paltz interpreted that. Oskar yearns for someone to show as much interest in the life of Oskar. Naturally, Hermann is paying Paltz for his concern, but that doesn't nullify it. Surely Paltz's attention means Hermann's life is somehow more . . . *worthy* of analysis, thinks Oskar.

Hermann materialized in the life of Oskar, like a puff of smoke, just when the brother-chain seemed about to end. Franz was gone, disappeared into the system of Nazi camps. Willi had vanished too, into Philadelphia, which seemed as impenetrable in its way. Then, on board the transport ship in mid-Atlantic – POOF, POP – and here's Hermann. They didn't agree on anything. They didn't like each other or any of the same people. They became inseparable – except for the many times they weren't speaking – through the rest of the voyage, the years in Canadian internment. Finally they parted. And unerringly rediscovered each other on a Toronto street near the end of the war, vowing a fresh start to what already seemed an ancient and inevitable bond: henceforth they would speak only English. It made no difference, they continue to ride, rile, and needle whenever they meet. They always will. They are made for each other.

Hermann must drive in from Oshawa several times each week to get his head shrunk – another phrase they have discovered together. Perhaps Paltz is Hermann's reward for going to Oshawa. He is rabbi to the little temple there. Well, Oskar thinks of it as little. He has never visited the place. It's just forty miles away, but it's a commitment to Canada that seems beyond Oskar, at least for now, maybe always. Here he is in Toronto, isn't that enough? He has come this far. Like Luther, he can go no farther.

In his mind Oskar admires Hermann – modestly – for daring to go. He knows it is an industrial town, maybe it is like the Ruhr. He once asked Hermann. "How would I know?" said Hermann. "I never went to the Ruhr. Anyway, none of my members is in industry. They're storekeepers, salesmen, insurance agents." Isn't it strange, Oskar thinks, to be in a place and lack a sense of it? Why, he thinks – proceeding along the inner track he often takes while conversation outside goes its own way. Who really has anything to do with anything? What do I know about Toronto? It has a harbour – or does it? Anyway, I never went to the Ruhr either. I wouldn't know a rolling mill from a sockeye salmon. Maybe, he thinks, he should write something about Canada when he begins his MA in history at the university. Maybe he should read something about Canada first. Except Canada seems to have so little history, to linger outside history, in a

pleasant hidden valley bypassed by most of the wars and crusades of the modern era –

They wanted Hermann in Oshawa because he's a rabbi.
That's the difference between Oskar and Hermann; it accounts
for their variant fates. Hermann was ordained just before he got
out, by Leo Baeck no less. Baeck is now a hallowed figure. People
like Hermann called him "my sainted teacher." Baeck didn't get
out, in fact he chose to stay, and he survived the war. They put
him in Theresienstadt, which was the luxury camp, relatively
speaking. There were no death chambers in Theresienstadt.
Oskar knew he wouldn't have been sent there had he missed the
train. After the war the American Jews brought Baeck to the
United States to teach their rabbis. Baeck hadn't much life left,
but he lasted long enough to let a generation of American rabbis
call him their sainted teacher. Baeck never looked like God,
Oskar thinks fondly, even though lots of people tried to give him
the God treatment. Maybe Oskar would have been ordained by
Baeck too, had he not passed on the experience.

Why *did* he pass on it? Maybe it was a failure of nerve, not
a statement of principle. The thought gnaws at him. That missed
opportunity accounts for all the comparative benefits Hermann
receives, like Paltz. Maybe Paltz could help Oskar sort it all out,
if he could ever get to Paltz without assassinating Hermann.
Maybe not going to Oshawa was also a failure of nerve. Not
Oshawa specifically (Hermann is already there – Hermann is
always already there, or somebody just like Hermann), but
another Canadian outport. Windsor, say. Or Timmins. Or Winnipeg. He pictures them all the way he pictures Oshawa: dimly.

He talked with Buber about being a rabbi. On his second visit,
after the scholarship offers from Philadelphia. "Why a rabbi?"
said Buber. "I thought your problem was faith."

"It is," said Oskar, "but maybe with things as they are, there
isn't time to have faith."

That's when Buber said, "I like your answer."

"There's something else, though," said Oskar. "It's embarrassing." Buber leaned forward, hooked. Oskar had learned the sure way to capture this great man's attention: be befuddled and say you feel like an idiot. The more foolishness Oskar expressed, the more Buber responded, as though Buber felt folly alone, among all human reactions, was to be trusted. And valued.

"I'd like to know what a rabbi knows," Oskar continued that time, "but a seminary – it seems so . . . parochial." He hung his head. The word he'd chosen made him sick. Parochial? He sputtered on. "It would be different if the scholarships were to . . . Harvard, or Oxford. My parents, my relatives. They'd feel a rabbi isn't . . . what a man should do. It's not manly." He skidded to a halt, too late, far too late. He had tempted Buber's scorn once, with his juvenile sunsets, and survived. This surely was his Waterloo.

Yet these feelings have deep roots in Oskar's soul. His parents, his uncles and aunts, lived at the end of more than a century's striving among Germany's Jews, striving that predated Napoleon: a brave and persistent campaign to become citizens and equals, to leave the ghettos and pariah status of the Middle Ages and join the life of general society, make a contribution, be a part. Oskar's family were inheritors of victory in this historic effort. They grew up as full members – citizens! – in the confident new empire of Kaiser Wilhelm (namesake of Willi Schropp and others). They shared proudly in its progress as Germany marched to war in 1914. In the liberal republic born in Weimar after the war they felt vindicated, not as Jews but as Germans. They dedicated themselves to the service of their nation. True, that republic was now dead, only a few years after its birth. Never mind, in their hearts the commitments of more than a century lived on. To restrict yourself to Jewishness, especially now, with the anti-Semites ascendant, it wasn't just backward, it was abdication of responsibility, flight from duty, betrayal, cowardice. It was unmanly. (They never used this word. Yet each time Oskar imagines their reactions to the Jewish choices of his life, it leaps into his mind.)

Buber sucked in his lips as though he were fishing for something far inside. He started to look like God again. "My son," he said, nodding as though he'd hooked his fish and was reeling it in, "in the end probably Moses himself was a very . . . *parochial* man."

Oskar backed out of the great man's study like a whipped dog. Buber had done it again. For the rest of his life Oskar lived in awe of one staggering fact: that he had not proceeded directly to a seminary, any seminary—American, German, Bolivian; Jewish, Christian, Buddhist—immediately upon Buber's delivery of that undeniably immortal line. Where had he found the stiff-necked stubbornness to resist that phrase, which instantly pierced his heart? He never spoke with Buber again.

Is *World Press Review* the great unparochial world? The alternative for which Oskar disregarded Buber's searing aphorism? This earnest weekly news digest published on King Street in Toronto, can it be Oskar's portion in the hundred-and-fifty-year secularizing mission of his people? It is not what he pictured.

In one corner sits Goldberg, captain of the national and domestic scene. Goldberg pores through *The Globe & Mail*, then rifles *The Financial Post*. He clips, cuts and pastes, but mostly ponders. Near the door: Jeanette with the falling brown curls, the only French Canadian Oskar has met since he left his Canadian prelife in Quebec. She answers the phone and all practical questions. Oskar sits across from her and tries to keep his mind on his area: the world. Over them presides Andy Keogh, a genuine Gentile sensibility; a *goyishe kop*, in the crass phrase of Old Country Jews. Andy says he is from the Island. For a long time Oskar thought he meant one of the Toronto Islands, a tiny ferry ride away, to which Goldberg has occasionally threatened a trip. Andy, however, means Prince Edward Island, in the Maritime provinces, which sounds to Oskar like a mythical place.

They are dedicated to ransacking the columns of every news source they can buy, beg, or borrow, and delivering a précis to their readers. Oskar suspects sometimes that even Hermann secretly envies this toehold in the secular world, the un-Jewish, adventurous, slightly risqué world of journalism. After all, Hermann is pursuing a doctorate in philosophy, not theology, at the university here. Sure, the courses help Hermann explain his frequent trips to Toronto and cover for his assignations with Paltz. But there may be more. Could Hermann, unconsciously, with secret Freudian intent, be setting the same secular, manly course Oskar has plotted? What about the pitiable salary they pay in Oshawa? Does it rankle . . . ?

"I've been reading your man Goldberg," says Hermann over his waffles. "He's a nationalist." Hermann means (a) Goldberg is a menace, and (b) how can any Jew be a nationalist after what we lived through? "He's only a Canadian nationalist," Oskar replies. Hermann snorts. Hermann knows where nationalism, any nationalism, leads. Oskar, ever the doubter, cannot picture Goldberg leading a march of Canadian Hitler Youth along Yonge Street.

"He grew up in a different part of Canada," says Oskar. "It's called Saskatchewan. Maybe things are different there."

"Ha!" grunts Hermann. "Was he not a Jew in Saskatchewan? Didn't they make fun of him in school there?"

"Not that he remembers," says Oskar. "He says they envied him because he got Jewish *and* Christian holidays."

"Bah!" fumes Hermann. "He was only a child at the time. What does he know? How are things going over there, anyway?"

"Fine," lies Oskar. In truth he is feeling tense. The *Review* is in a financial crisis. He asked Goldberg how bad it would get. Goldberg lectured him that their troubles reflected a post-war economic crisis "long anticipated and now here." Oskar said Goldberg made it sound like a royal tour. Yesterday Andy wondered aloud how anyone felt about deferring the occasional paycheque. Jeanette had the sense not to hear. Oskar and Goldberg both said yes, Goldberg enthusiastically. Later Oskar phoned Jack Katz and accepted the promotion Jack had been waving at him for weeks: intermediate grade department head of the weekend school at the Pillar of Fire.

"How are they treating you in Oshawa?" he says to change the subject.

"I'm going to demand a decent salary," says Hermann. "If they refuse, I'll leave."

"That doesn't sound very committed," grunts Oskar.

"It is," says Hermann. "You just haven't grasped the dialectic."

Oskar fastens his intellectual seat belt. He knows the signs. Hermann is getting ready for takeoff.

"I want them to be serious Jews," says Hermann. "But they're business people. If they get away with paying me beans, they lose respect for me. They don't take me seriously, they don't take Judaism seriously, you know. If they pay better, they'll get more serious about Judaism."

"You have to make them pay you more money because you don't care about money," says Oskar.

"Right," enthuses Hermann. "You hit the dialectic on the head!"

They are now moving obliquely into Hermann's other topic: thought. Sometimes at Fran's, Oskar thinks he sees Hermann's lean body grow even smaller, a diminishing presence tucked into the corner of the booth, while his mind expands the way a parachute unfolds, filling first the booth, then the rest of Fran's, crowding Oskar and the other diners out onto lonely Yonge Street.

Hermann is talking now about his doctoral thesis. He has chosen a subject: the confrontation – one of his favourite words, along with dialectic – between faith and reason in the Middle Ages. He'll examine the works of the Rombom, a Hebrew acronym for the famed physician and philosopher, Rabbi Moses Ben Maimon. In Germany they always called him Maimonides, a Latinized name by which he was respectfully known through centuries of Catholic and Arabic scholarship. Rombom makes Oskar giggle, it has such a funny sound in English, with its connotations of rumbum. Hermann scowls. He doesn't approve rough-housing the Hebrew language as they do English. "We have to make proud use of our own tradition," he says, "rather than non-Jewish equivalents. You know?"

"I think I see," says Oskar, moved by Hermann's show of conviction.

"Anyway," says Hermann, "I've decided his problem is not our problem." Now who is Hermann talking about, thinks Oskar. Paltz? Goldberg? Or the Rombom? Oskar is awed by Hermann's ability to treat the great names in the history of thought as intimate acquaintances, as if he and they are puzzling out the same matters together and a few of them just stepped out of the room for a pee. "I would say," Hermann goes on, "we have to take his problems seriously. That's the only way we can be sure he is irrelevant."

What a wondrous ocean it is to Oskar: theology, philosophy. He has plunged in now and again and always emerged bone-dry. Not a drop clings as he clambers ashore, nothing to suggest he's been immersed in Meaning. God, prayer, revelation, the covenant between God and Israel – their unreality is so strong Oskar can sometimes taste it. He thinks Hermann might call this a dialectical thought. He thinks of dialectical as meaning silly but clever.

"They've asked me to teach a section of the Introduction to Philosophy next term," says Hermann casually. *Gasp*. Oskar feels the abyss open beneath his feet under the booth in Fran's. Was Hermann sent into this world to torment him? To emphasize every failed ambition Oskar ever dreamed? And at this very moment, as he congratulates himself for adhering to the secular alternative in the face of Buber's pious challenge. Surely he, Oskar, who stayed in Toronto close to the university, carefully planning a course of study that will lead to an academic appointment – once he gets it underway – ought to be making this off-hand announcement to Hermann, who exiled himself to the Jewish community of a Canadian backwater! "I'll use the standard humanist textbook," Hermann continues, unheeding the volcanic emotion across the waffles. "It could be a valuable encounter. You know?"

This serpent Hermann, flinging one of Buber's choice terms

in the midst of a sneak attack on his closest and probably only friend and confidant. Who else has sat through countless hours of tedious reportage on Hermann's psychiatric excavations? Hermann has Paltz and now he has a teaching position – a university position, not grade six or confirmation class at the Pillar of Fire. What an asinine name for a temple. It sounds like a gospel church or a tent revival. At least if the louts could use the proper Hebrew – *Ahmood Aysh* – the place might sound remotely Jewish! No wonder Hermann is ready to tell the burghers of Oshawa's only reform congregation to go hang. This alternative, the tree-lined road to Academe, is the source of his sudden *joie de combat* in salary negotiations. Hermann has an opening. He is on the way. He is going to Get Out again.

"So, have you been dating anybody?" asks Hermann. It is the first personal question he has posed during their meal. Oskar breathes deep. He wants to calm down, he has made himself miserable enough. It is time to get back to ordinary conversation. *Dating* strikes him as a very odd English word. Is it just because it's in Hermann's mouth? If the Rombom walked into Fran's right now, would Hermann ask if he'd been dating anybody? Without a doubt.

"Not at the moment," says Oskar. He pauses for Hermann to talk about his own love life. It usually has some content, though nothing enviable, Oskar assures himself. Isolation is surely better than combination with some of the cows Hermann has presented to Oskar. He thinks about the latest. Is Hermann still dating her? She was so ugly she was magnetic. To step into the street looking like that, it shows character, it might manifest itself sexually, in some astounding originality.

Hermann ventures nothing. This is untypical, thinks Oskar. Now is when he tells me about what has happened in his relations with women, his worries and ambitions, and I in turn sympathize and encourage and hate him for it. Why is he holding back?

Oskar has not failed to date since he arrived in Toronto. He has, he does. Nor does he experience a diminished sex drive, in some predictable psychic reaction to the historical trauma he has lived. Just the opposite, actually. He dates and he lusts. He just doesn't, well, connect.

When he went to the P of F, in response to Jack Katz's offer, he met Ida. Other women too, including some he found attractive, unlike Ida. But Oskar knew she wanted him, so he asked her out. To tell the truth, he might even have liked her at first—he has a vague memory of desire—but any attraction vanished once he knew she liked him. She was larged-limbed, yet graceful, with an African cast to her features. Maybe it was this exotic quality that initially appealed to him, before she became repellent by wanting him. She had an artistic bent. She offered to sketch him almost the instant they met. She ran the drama program.

Their first date was brutal. When not scoffing at her artistic interests he ignored her. When he did not ignore her he patronized her. He dropped crumbs – travel, European architecture, literature; she snatched them like one of the beggar children of Naples. Then he looked away, around the restaurant, as though nearly anything would outrank her company. She kept scratching for his attention. Finally, when she was about to cease trying, he turned back, tossed another nugget–Mann's novels, when in doubt – hooked her again, played her briefly, and scanned the room once more. This strained encounter laid the groundwork for forty years of . . . friendship? unrequited love? permanently postponed sex?

As for Ida, she was smitten. The man was cultured. He knew art, music, literature, food, wine. Especially food and wine. There were those in her Toronto who spoke of Goethe and Beethoven but not cuisine. He was Jewish and he had lived (which meant suffered). Yet it was not only what he knew, who he was, and all that pain. It was also–how he looked! "He was so handsome," she could say years later, and if someone snickered: "Oh, he was. He really was." The portraitist in her tarried over his features. The dark wavy hair, the deep-set eyes, and especially the long thin fingers, the delicate hands. A man's hands are his secret weapon.

Does this mean Oskar was *not* the ugliest Jew who came out

of Nazi Germany? In honesty, I must acknowledge Ida is not the only woman who would deny Oskar was ugly. They disagree, they found him attractive. This means either that he was not ugly, or perhaps that being ugly is no hindrance to being attractive. Hermann might call this a paradox.

CLICK-CLACK, CLICK-CLACK, the little mystery of Hermann's reticence is solved. Along the parquet floor of Fran's comes the signature of high heels, directly toward them. Wily, vindictive Hermann has prepared a surprise for this dinner. *She* is here. Hermann's latest horror. She needs no verbal proxies, she bears down on their table in the gruesome flesh. She looms above them. She passes a smile across Oskar's decomposed visage and settles on Hermann's side of the booth. He wiggles over to make room. His face wrinkles happily at Oskar in mock protest as she plants a peck on his cheek.

"So," says Oskar, "I see you're still dating old Carp-face."

Oskar, we know, chose history about the time he reached Canada. Ever since he has considered "historian" his true calling. He has decided intellectual humanity can be divided between those (like himself) who toil in history and those (like Hermann) who labour in abstract thought – philosophy or theology. He plans an academic career as a historical scholar. *Plans* is weak; he counts on it desperately; it gives shape to his wanderings and solace in moments of pain, such as daily conversations with achievers like Hermann. Running the intermediate grades at the Pillar of Fire is just a stopover.

It is also true that Oskar thinks about his own past. Are these two tendencies – autobiographical and historical – connected? It seems likely. One scrutinizes *the* past, as one examines *my own* past: out of curiosity and for the sake of insight. In each case, we seek to learn from the past. Yet in the mind of Oskar a sneaking suspicion is starting to form: everything can be a way of avoiding what it seems to be doing.

He likes history because it is out there, in books, and back there, in time. He thinks of it as a big old family chest. You crawl into the attic when you're free and you rummage around. You find interesting items and aged family photographs. You dust them off and contemplate them. You keep them out awhile, then return them. Sometimes he thinks of history as the cars on a long train. You climb down from the engineer's cab and wander back along the track to a car that interests you. You mount the steps and poke through it, like a conductor collecting tickets, or the inspector in a baggage car checking freight, or the crewman in the caboose having tea. When you want, you climb down again and amble back to the front. The trip continues. It is all very . . . interesting.

This is not how he feels about his own past. He does not inspect it at leisure. It closes in on him. He finds it suffocating. He can run in various directions, no matter, it stays with him, step for step. He has no choices about his own past. It is there at random or its own behest, disregarding what he might prefer to think about. Now this moment, now that event: arriving and departing wilfully and erratically. Unlike history, his own past is out of his control. It does not pass before him like flashbacks in the cinema: it ambushes him. He does not recall it: he lives it still. Above all, his own past is not interesting because it is not facts. The facts of his past are secondary, and often irrelevant. His own past is really feelings.

Aunt Hilda, for example, is ranting in his head. She pats the *Journal of Political Psychology and Sex Economy,* which she removes from her bag. It is the wellspring of her authority. She is saying, "He must masturbate. It's your responsibility. You cannot take no for an answer." She is speaking to Oskar's mother, who shakes her head gently. She appreciates her sister's good intentions, but she "doesn't know." These events are biographical facts. What Oskar feels is: tense.

"Have you made a point of bathing nude before him?" Hilda presses. "Sometimes," says Oskar's mother. "But are you sure he has witnessed it?" says Hilda. "Look here," says his mother, "what makes you so certain he doesn't do it? Masturbate." In her voice the word is less flamboyant, it doesn't stream from her mouth like a banner.

"Regard him," shrieks Hilda, wheeling on little Oskar. "Grumpy, dissatisfied, bored. Doesn't he bore awfully easily? You told me that!"

"Yes, but . . ."

"Obviously he does not possess a genital structure!"

Why doesn't Oskar participate in this conversation? Well, he is nine years old. But there is more.

"You must talk to him about it. He clearly suffers intense genital anxiety."

"Why suffers?" says his mother. "Maybe a little genital anxiety is a good thing." Her tone is unconfident.

"All children require a positive sexual outlet or they will be damaged and experience severe sexual distress."

When Aunt Hilda and her bag are gone and no one else is downstairs, Oskar pads across to the oversize dictionary on a stand in the sitting room. He opens it and after several attempts finds the word. The dictionary tells him its meaning is sexual self-gratification. He glumly flips the book shut, unenlightened.

His glance darts here at her, then across the room, at her. Riveted on her back, her hair where it falls between her shoulders. His intensity astounds him, as usual in these moments, as though this gaze at this girl is all that matters in the world. At the same time he manages to hear the discussion.

The subject is *aliyah*, going up. To Palestine, of course. Anywhere else in the world you migrate. In the case of Palestine, if you're Jewish, you ascend, like Moses on Mount Sinai, or the High Priest in the Holy of Holies. In their Blue-White group these days, Palestine has become the only topic. This wasn't so when he joined. Then they talked about youth in the society of the future, or classical versus surrealist models of culture, or the sinuous attractions of Buddhism in Hesse's novels. They also planned the old clothes collection for the poor Jews of Poland and menus for next week's hike.

He clears his throat and the others swivel to listen. He says he finds the information brought by their guest, the *shaliach* from the Jewish Agency in Palestine, useful. But he keeps thinking that maybe the reason they talk *so* much about *aliyah* lately is because they want to avoid thinking about the situation right here in Germany. He doesn't mean to offend their guest, he just wanted to raise the suggestion and see what others think. On the contrary, says Gotthold, their group leader, as the room shifts back to eyes front. But in the instant before their attention is gone, Oskar catches the narrowing glances of appraisal, jealousy from the boys, admiration from the girls. This kind of contrary reaction, Gotthold is saying, which forces us to look at some unpleasant possibility – it's what we all value in Oskar.

But already his gaze has returned to her back. Her hair. The hint of her neck. The memory of her open mouth and freckles when she turned in her seat to look at him. What would they think with their respect for him – Gotthold and the others – if they knew all he really cares about at these meetings is the girls. Heads, bodies, backs, and necks. Dotted about like centres of gravity competing for his concentration. How craven. The world is turning to ashes around them! Urgent decisions must be made. By them, the youth, hope of the future, whose own hopes crumble in their trembling hands. Much as he tries to evade and deny it, while he continues to make his regular, idiosyncratic, highly valued contributions, what genuinely matters is only them, the girls. Despite all he firmly, idealistically intends, the energy of his being turns to them alone. There has not been a meeting or an event since he turned twelve and became active in the movement at which his real focus was not their hair, their necks, thinking about meeting them, speaking together, nearing them physically, seeing their smiles at his searing intellectual honesty. They occupy his field of attention like a mountain range. From behind and between peek glimpses of the worrisome history of the age: the threat to his people, the catastrophe of German politics. What sham, what shame. He is serving the cause, but he serves, like the sons of Aaron the priest who were destroyed for it, with the flame of the impure fire.

70

This group is different. "Why do youth join groups?" says the leader. He is thin, unlike cheery, chubby Gotthold, and he looks straight at them in turn. He seems to hold on Oskar. Then he answers his own question. "For sex."

Oskar has found his way to a counselling centre at one of the sex-hygiene clinics run by the Institute for Sexual Advice and Research. There is such a muddle of groups and organizations, solutions and quick fixes, as German society twists and dangles. What is he doing here? "They're Communists," his father said once, or was it his Uncle Charles, or a teacher?

"What is the real purpose of the child-rearing you have been processed through?" says this leader, a more directive presence than Oskar has seen elsewhere in the youth movement. "And what about the education you're force-fed? To create sexual weaklings and slaves!" he booms. "What else?" Some kids seem cowed, others nod slowly, as if against their will. "And religion?" he barks. "It exists to terrorize the young about masturbation and sexuality." Oskar is flicking his gaze around the room, searching for the girl to concentrate on during this meeting. On her hair. . .

"You!" he hears the leader say. "Do I detect a sneer on your face?" He is addressing Oskar.

"No," says Oskar, who has learned to parry these sudden thrusts, delivered as his mind wanders. He deflects panic as he reconstructs the discussion. "I just don't think it's so obvious."

"Well, then," says the leader, "why do religions make such a point about God seeing everything you do?"

Touché, thinks Oskar. He has been masturbating furiously since they moved and he and Franz got separate rooms. Once his godlike older brother was out of sight, he really got on with it. One day, in an exhausted afterstate, he realized the meaning of sexual self-gratification.

"Masturbation won't eliminate anyone's sexual distress," says the leader to a question someone must have put while Oskar drifted away again. "It's good and it's healthy, to a point. Beyond that it's just a rotten substitute for intercourse." One of the boys asks whether prostitutes are a solution. The leader sighs as though he is used to better questions. "And what are the girls supposed to do?" asks the head of hair Oskar has been fixed on; it has a voice. Some people laugh at her question, others shift nervously. "Prostitution does not provide a satisfactory outlet," says the leader wearily. "It is like masturbating to excess. It just creates more need and more frustration."

Something odd starts. Oskar finds his attention divided, tugged between his usual obsession with her – whatever her of the moment – and the talk around him. They are speaking about friendships between boys and girls, so-called Platonic relationships. His mind wanders to Greta. Now he is split three ways. "They seem oh so meaningful, don't they?" says the mocking voice of the leader from some far place. "And they are. Because they never get down to basics. They are daydreams and you wallow in them at no cost!" Oskar has been mooning about Greta. This snaps him out of it. Or was it the girl? "All that intense conversation between true friends of the opposite sex . . ." Oskar floats easily into the feeling of the long talks he and Greta often share, expressing everything, never really finishing so they never really have to start again, like a long soothing ride through a peaceful countryside. "A form of intellectual masturbation instead of the thing both really have on their minds . . ." Oskar winces at this, he hopes no one noticed, but the leader did, he fears, though the man rolls relentlessly on, condemning in persuasively reasonable tones the "endless self-absorbed fantasies that drain the vigour of youth in our society . . ." Oskar wills his thoughts back to her, and her hair. He doesn't want to share languid musings with her, thank you. He wants nothing between them, not even words, as he presses against her –

Rubbing against her in a line entering a cinema, or getting on a bus, or sitting in one, or standing on one, looming over her seat, her knee meeting his calf as the bus takes a corner, or in the darkness around a campfire, their fingers touching "accidentally" and then . . . or on one of the stairwells at school or in the movement office with nobody else there, feeling her through winter's heavy clothes –

"And none of it works! That's the trouble! The masturbation,

72

the wallowing in daydreams, the rubbing against each other furtively, even intercourse itself if it's only rushed and shabby. It won't do, because it's not what's really wanted, because it's not what's really needed: healthy, full, satisfying, orgasmic, sexual . . ."

All right, all right, it's true, he has tried it all ways. Jerking off tirelessly in the hope he can get his mind off sex and onto schoolwork or his tasks in the movement. Resisting masturbation so as to store up energy to pour into assignments and responsibilities. All leading to masturbation again and more masturbation, and fantasies and a piddling amount of work done, and more daydreams and furious energy and exhaustion!

"God knows, pardon the expression," says the leader, and all the young men and women laugh with relief, "there is work to do for everyone, especially youth, in times like these. But how can the young concentrate on work, on politics, on resisting, when their minds are irresistibly drawn to sex, exactly because they are interminably pressured in every way NOT to think about it. I defy you not to think about sex, as I say to you: DO NOT THINK ABOUT SEX! Stop it, stop it, you're all doing it, I told you not to." They all laugh, some uncontrollably, hysterically even. "And the worst is when youth are ordered not only not to *think* of it, but NEVER EVER to *do* anything about it."

"Are you Communists?" says Oskar, as the room settles down.

"Some of us are," says a boy turning toward him near the front, right beside her with the hair. "How about you?"

"No, I'm not," says Oskar, "but I'm Jewish." And they all laugh again.

On the way out, the leader asks if he has found this meeting valuable. "I don't know," says Oskar. "How would I know?"

"If you come back again," says the leader. Oskar smiles a precursor of his demented grin. Never, he thinks. Not ever.

Keogh says, "Stay on, boy. Stick with us. We knew this crisis was coming. Goldberg said so." Goldberg carries on typing, with muffled pride, in his corner. "He quoted the prime minister,"

Keogh continues. " 'The nation that does not control its own currency will not long remain a nation.' Hell, we're part of a national crisis. I'm almost glad. Goldberg has predicted catastrophe so often we're losing credibility. How can you publish a magazine about urgent political and economic issues when nothing urgent or political or economic ever seems to happen?"

Oskar says nothing, because he is paralyzed. He knows others often mistake this mode for icy determination. Keogh keeps talking, desperate to keep Oskar aboard his sinking ship. He can't pay, the magazine can't pay at the moment, but if Oskar sticks with it, and things improve, as Goldberg wrote somewhere . . .

Oskar's mind is meanwhile at play on the other track he moves to so often these days. He nods; Keogh assumes he is listening. He is thinking hard about the last job Jack Katz tempted him with. Full-time director of education at the Pillar of Fire. "You make it sound like admiral of the fleet," said Oskar brusquely, and with no thought of accepting, "but I have a sneaking suspicion you mean principal of the religious school." Jack lowered his head and breathed through his nostrils. He didn't like backchat.

Oskar relished the reaction and left Jack hanging. He wondered, on his other track, how it would be to deal with Jack regularly, as a tormenting colleague. Now as Keogh begs on, the thought returns, it comforts him. Someone else wants Oskar, someone who will not just plead, but pay.

He freezes. The parochial world beckons again, the one he inhabited centuries ago, and which he escaped when he came to this strange non-country, Canada. The little Jewish world with a regular salary. How persistent it is. He never meant to enter it, it was against the family tradition, but in the crisis he found himself immersed. It tried to snare him, first by capturing him for the movement and sending him on *aliyah*, then by the more insidious route of a seminary scholarship. He evaded both. Now it is back again. Heedless of his stiff neck and reluctance.

Do his own choices play no role in his life? His weighty decisions, deplorable though they may be, fly up and disperse like the smoke of a campfire. Or else they count in the worst possible way. He will finally be in a temple, despite his choice, but because of that choice he will not be the rabbi, he will be educational director. A mere teacher, camouflaged by terminology. All the parochial unmanliness his elders scorned, plus minor bureaucratic status.

What of Andy and the magazine? What of Goldberg's passion for Canada? Does Oskar feel like an opportunist for deserting them and their mission? Yes, and . . . not at all. The job here at *Goyish Press Review*, it was the real opportunism. He escaped the fate no one else – with pathetic exceptions like Hermann and himself – eluded. By what right? Out here in the secular world, the worldly world, the un-Jewish world of journalism, of NATO and SEATO and the Marshall Plan, of quotations by Prime Minister Mackenzie King, with opportunities for adventure, a career, maybe even wealth and fame – he has lived and frolicked. As though a Jew could live such a life and get away with it! As though the Nuremberg Laws never happened, never stripped Jews of normal, natural, national rights.

That was the true betrayal. The assumption one could ever be other than a Jew among Gentiles, a permanent other. Perhaps Oskar has been searching, or awaiting with messianic patience, another opportunity, the chance to scrap the opportunity and turn back. Buber's sanctimonious phrase still sounds. "My son, in the end probably Moses was a very parochial man." Even now, after all the global and private history that has come between, it whispers on the streets and in the restaurants of this provincial city in which he washed ashore.

And on the other hand.

This too may not be forever. If Katz's little job tides Oskar over, helps him through Goldberg's crisis, till the dollar improves, whatever that means (maybe he'll read Goldberg's article), and if his plans for a degree and an academic career pan out, and he uses the interlude at the Pill on the Hill to cushion the transition . . .

The dilemma renders him helpless. He knows he is moving

from *World Press Review* to the Pillar of Fire Temple, from the universal to the parochial, from the profane to the sacred. He has no idea why. Is it a cowardly retreat from adventure? Affirmation of his destiny? Self-denial out of guilt? Is it for Franz? For Buber? For Greta?

He never tells Keogh. He tells Goldberg, Jew to Jew. Next day he feels Keogh's gruff Gentile presence at his shoulder as he snips and assembles. Keogh says he understands. If only *I* did, thinks Oskar.

He is a sad young man standing outside the Institute for Sexual Advice and Research. He has returned. It is boarded up. The windows are broken, the walls defaced. The official sign reads:

CLOSED.

PERMANENTLY.

BY ORDER OF THE FÜHRER AND THE PARTY.

He wonders, years later, Did I become a teacher and remain one all this time in order to learn the secrets and knowledge that were boarded up in that building? Does one teach because of what he does not know, rather than what he has to offer? How ignoble. He hopes it is not so. Adam never got back in the garden, but at least he learned what he wanted to know before he left. One thing is clear: if Oskar is searching for knowledge, he will not find it here in Canada. In Canada they know not, and know not that they know not. They don't know from history, or from politics, or from sex. They are innocent in the biblical sense. Ignorant.

Canada. What is it about Canada?

Canada is the term that was applied at Auschwitz to inmates who were not slated for death but instead unloaded the extermination trains – including the tiny corpses left behind in the boxcars – after all those who survived the trip were herded into trucks that carted them to the chambers where they were gassed to death.

"There's a train arriving, Canada."

"Canada, get out to the unloading ramp."

Canada were those who reaped the food, clothing, and valuables that remained in the boxcars or at the side of the ramp or in the trucks that took people to the "showers" or in the "changing rooms." With the proceeds, Canada made themselves comfortable in the camp. Canada was a state of privilege, relative to those who were murdered straight away.

Oskar did not just come to Canada. He stayed. Is it because he is a true Canadian?

THIS IS WHERE I come in. It is the 1950s, the Golden Age of Education in North America. Why was education golden then? Because the world we lived in was perfect, no further changes were required. Therefore no politics were necessary, beyond managing the current state of perfection. What remained to be done? Admire the perfection, study and appreciate it. What a time to be an educator.

I am about eight years old at the start of that era. I am cowering in the hallway of the PFRS, the Pillar of Fire Religious School. I am apprehensive about walking through the classroom door before me. I know none of these classmates; I am a stranger to their middle-class, suburban part of town. Suddenly a ramshackle presence bears down on me, hooting like a train whistle. "Ding, ding, ding," it screeches, "I am zee bell!"

This works. It scares me out of the corridor and into the classroom where I swiftly make a connection. My new friend wears a little blue suit like mine and shares my scorn for the inefficiency of opening-day procedures. We cement relations with a giggle about the man who is zee bell.

The highlight of this, my first season at PFT, is the unit Miss Greenstein teaches us on the Holocaust. "Imagine," she says (we squeeze our eyes shut), "that all the Jews in the world were like three apples and Hitler took away one apple!" She asks us to pretend we are little Jews in Germany at the time, and send letters to friends our own age in Canada. I write, "Dear Harry" – my idea of a period name – "things here in Germany are pretty bad. There is an awful man named Hitler. He should be called Shitler instead of Hitler." I recline and contemplate this with nascent literary pride. Miss Greenstein calls for volunteers to read. With pleasure, Miss G. She retains her composure till I finish. Then she assigns some seatwork and bolts from the room. I see her head bobbing in the centre panel of the door and then the leering, drooling visage of the ding-ding man, gazing, I think, at me. Does a smile inform the twisty line of his mouth?

Next time I am maybe eleven, maybe twelve. I am in the hallway again, this time ejected from my Hebrew class, which I attend two afternoons a week, after real school. Our teacher, *Mar* Sachs, is a former Mr Ontario bodybuilder, according to rumour, and we have taken as our mission to rile him and survive. Our previous instructor, *Mar* Zachary Helkam, fresh off the boat from Israel, as we delicately say, was no challenge. He fled raving in weeks. (Why are we so hostile here, in the educational half-world of the Pill? Perhaps it is a safer place to explode than real school, where the stakes seem higher. At real school – junior high over on Spadina Road – we feel misbehaviour carries heavy and official consequences: the power of the state, maybe even the police. Not so at Temple.)

As a result of our latest eruption I am in the hall, though as God is my witness, I am not the real culprit. Guilt lies with Yitzhak (Jimmy) Marcus, who incited Yosef (Joey) Banks, who laid his palms on the table round which we sat, and moaned, "Let the table rise," sending it flying with his knees. "What's your problem?" I whined, when the mighty Sachs seized me and heaved me out the door. "The problem," he choked, "with you," he wheezed, "it's your face!"

Suddenly I am alone together in that hall. There are two of us sneaking looks into the room, as though we were both thrown out. "So, Mr ——." He doesn't exactly speak, he emits a low scream, like something coming through an ancient filter. And how does he know my name? And what else does he know about me? "Follow me," he emits, and leads the way.

Along the dank corridor, up the broad stairs that lead to the auditorium where we go for music ("Some day you may be in danger / Then along will come a stranger / With a bit of blood to pull you through / A stranger's blood may save your life for you"), up a few steps I thought led only to the girls' washroom, but past it is an unobtrusive opening, and through it a narrow winding stairway to a dimly lit landing. He fumbles in his pocket for a key, fumbles in the door for the lock, motions me in, and we sit face to face, knees nearly bumping. This isn't an office, it's a lair.

"And so, Mr ——," he repeats, as though we've just been interrupted by a commercial, "What is the problem?"

"It's my face," I blurt, near tears despite my toughness. "That's what he said. What's that supposed to mean?"

"Aha," he says with great seriousness, as if he has long been preparing to deal with this question. "I have a sneaking suspicion that you sit in the classroom, slouched back in your chair, with a supercilious, Olympian sneer on your face, glaring down your nose at the teacher. Or else you turn and gaze out the window as if anything, anything in the world, must be more interesting than what is happening in his class."

I am torn between hurt and curiosity. "How do you know?" I say. He grins in an eerie way. Does he want me to think he is omniscient, like God who sees everything? "You hang around in the halls," I say. "You peek through the windows." His grin loosens and little gobs of saliva appear at its corners. "It's my job here," he says, almost sheepishly.

He skips from topic to topic. I have the feeling he is prying at things to see how close to my surface they are. He takes a topic, pries a little, and if it gives, pries till it loosens. Then he looks under it and moves on. I feel like a roof being reshingled.

I tell him I'm pretty nervous about my bar mitzvah. He pries some more. I say it's the service I fear, and the moment when I'm finished reading my section of the Torah portion for that

week, which happens to be the grisly tale of Abraham ready to
sacrifice little Isaac at God's command. I tell him, I picture that
I've got through reading it in Hebrew and translating for the
many not fluent in the Holy Tongue. "So everything is fine!" he
says, actually clapping his hairy hands. "Wrong," I say. "But
you've got through it, the worst is over," he maintains. "And
that's the tricky time," I say. He stops, like he's frozen in mid-
motion. Then he leans back in the swivel chair and it creaks.
"Yes," he says, "you're right, that's when it happens."

I have no idea how I got this far in our conversation. I am
quite lost. "When what happens?" I say. "That's what you have
to tell me now," he says, "what happens then?" He adds helpfully, "At your bar mitzvah."

I describe in sorrow, but with relief at finally being able to
tell it, what has been revealed to me in many a daytime nightmare
during these months leading up to the gladsome day. As I hoist
the twin scrolls of the Law for the congregation to see, open at
the passage I have just read flawlessly – I drop it! The Torah
itself. It does a half-gainer to the centre of the chancel and starts
to unroll down the steps into the midst of the faithful. It unrolls
and unrolls, everything comes undone, no one has ever seen a
catastrophe like this in the middle of a service before, and I am
its detestable cause. Today I am a mess!

He is grinning and nodding and leaking spit and looks absolutely delighted. I haven't felt so appreciated since the Seder one
Passover night at Aunt Sadie's when I entertained my aunts and
uncles with jokes and riddles I'd memorized from my Big Joke
Book. By the time the bell rings – the real bell, there is one – and
he ushers me downstairs to pick up my coat and galoshes and
waves weirdly at me as I leave the classroom while he stays
behind for a chat with *Mar* Sachs, I have the odd feeling I have
been doing *him* a favour.

Where did we think he came from: the Berserker who roamed
the halls and streets of our little paradise. We, the young, inher-

itors of the earth, living in a community that had escaped history, it seemed to us. Escaped so thoroughly we did not really believe history existed, or that we were its outcome.

Yet to us he seemed to come right out of history, that place which didn't exist for us, the realm from which we were disconnected, thank God. He hauled it on his back like a hump. To us he *was* history.

How can that be? Perhaps it's because we said history when we thought of Oskar, but we really meant myth. History is something you are connected to in an uninterrupted flow; it has shaped you so you are unimaginable apart from it, as you are inconceivable apart from the air and your parents. Myth is different. It deals with great events and figures, which it locates in a past completely separate from us. Myth may or may not have power over us, but it is a power that comes from outside. The realm of myth does not issue in ourselves like an underground spring, the way history does. Myth stands apart from us, making demands or just exposing itself vainly. The Oskar we saw in the corridors was sheer myth: a grotesque character from an otherly realm: the Wandering Jew, the mark of Cain, Sufferance is the Badge, Survivor of the Camps. He scared us, and we felt the urge to flee his arrivals.

Who is he in this incarnation, at this time in his life? He is a character none of us have ever seen and whom we don't recognize: a denizen on every little stage of all the *Kabarett*s in the Berlin of his youth. He is the funny little man who appears repeatedly through the evening. He wears garish makeup – lascivious lips and wide eyes – and natty clothes, he sometimes carries a cane as he rushes around the stage, often he has a funny walk. He gets things going ("Good evening, ladies and germs.") and provokes the audience ("The couple on their way out – will you take the garbage?"). Sometimes he provokes the powers that be as well ("Heil!" he says, shooting his arm out stiffly, then glancing up at his palm: "That's how high we are in shit."). He does the odd turn himself but mostly he keeps things going ("This performer needs no introduction. What he needs is an act."). He is always there to bring on the next number, and the next. He makes sure we enjoy ourselves and guarantees our satisfaction ("*Mesdames et messieurs*, ladies and gentlemen, *meine Herren und Damen*, I give you now – "). He is the *conférencier*.

The year after bar mitzvah he gives us a different kind of club leader. Instead of Marv "Juno" Katzman, remarkable for the number of potato *latkes* he can down at a sitting, we get Norm "The Legend" Reese, a law student already making his mark in civil liberties. When Norm leaves suddenly to launch a survey of housing discrimination against Negroes, we aren't handed to the obvious choice: Harry "The Horse" Soberman, best (and only) Jewish starting player on the U of T Blues. Instead Oskar imports Stuart Lipowitz, so principled a figure, by the standards of the time, that his friends are betting he'll attend his own imminent wedding in blue jeans. Stuart shows us filmstrips about the kibbutz movement in Israel and how a baby is born; he makes us think about our future service to humanity. These bright young Jewish professionals-in-training parachute in to help us out, for we are a special audience with unique needs. Oskar starts to think of us as his Great Class. As a skilful *conférencier*, he tailors the show to his audience's taste.

A year later we move up to intermediate clubs. Suddenly there is a new group for us. It meets Tuesday evenings instead of Sunday afternoons like other clubs. Oskar gives us as our leader Harold Oelbaum. He wears a tie and in later life will join the New Democrats, the Liberals, and the Tories in turn, depending on what public post he is applying for, and in which part of the country. Harold sits us down and explains the world. He even uses the blackboard – in clubs! There is the world, then there are communism and capitalism, and if the world is a pie, the two forces are out for the biggest bite. We nod sagely. We are fourteen. What are we really learning? That we are special, people think so, and they're taking pains to please us. Two years before we were the Temple Terrors. Now we are the Jewish community's hope for the future. The responsibility rests lightly on our slim shoulders.

When we are sixteen and enter confirmation year, he gives us Arnie Torno. We file into class for the first session of this, the big one. Our individual bar and bat mitzvahs, eons ago when we were thirteen, were just preparation, private liturgical boot camps, for the coming collective event. Our teacher, the swarthy, handsome Mr Torno, steps around his desk, dramatically removing the barrier between him and us, creating a common playing space, as though he is standing on a thrust stage instead of beneath a proscenium arch. He is indeed an actor, and life to him is theatre.

Outside in the halls, Oskar is cruising. He is not ding-dinging today. He saves that for Saturday mornings, when the primary grades meet. Sundays he is on silent patrol. As he lurches past the window of our room, he is arrested by the same sight that mesmerizes us inside. Arnie – Mr Torno – stands before us, a Bible in one hand and a lighter in the other. He flourishes the Ronson, he flicks it with his thumb, he ignites the holy text! We are transfixed. We are rooted to the linoleum, wedged between chairs and desks.

Out in the hall, perhaps because he is shielded by the door from the full numbing power of this moment, Oskar retains some freedom of action. He bursts through the door like a fireman responding to a call. If he were carrying a hose he would douse the whole display. "Mr Torno, what do you think you are doing?" he screeches like the siren atop a fire truck. Arnie turns coolly, as though this sputtering figure has arrived on cue. "I am demonstrating," he announces in a modulated manner I will come to recognize as projection, "that it is not this book which is sacred, but the thoughts which it contains."

We react to Arnie in our varied ways. That week, for homework, he orders us to attend a recent Cecil B. De Mille film, *The Ten Commandments*, with Charlton Heston as Moses. "Moses?" I blurt. "The guy who was Buffalo Bill in *The Pony Express*?" Our mentor responds with a slight dismissive movement of his head, as if I am a gnat. "You will review the film," he continues, "as your assignment." We think he is finished, but he has just warmed up. He talks about the significance of "the review," the difficult necessity of being reviewed – we do not realize he is describing the harsh lot of the actor – and the exacting critique he expects.

I take an afternoon off school and attend the film at the grandiose University theatre on Bloor Street. Back in our apartment on Briar Hill, I chase my little brother from the room we share and consider my judgements. I begin to write. I refer to the villainous character Dathan as "good old reliable Dathan," played by Edward G. Robinson, "with a built-in sneer." I snicker. I lean back in amazement. It is possible to be funny when you write! When Mr Torno returns the assignment, across the top is scrawled, "Talk about built-in sneers!" We have entered a conspiracy.

Oskar, for his part, hands Arnie an extra assignment of his own. He asks Arnie to produce the confirmation service toward which our year is geared. It is a massive project worthy of a De Mille. The confirmation class has exploded in recent years: there are now over one hundred of us, and the service has acquired the logistical problems of the invasion of Europe. The congregation expects it to be beautiful, meaningful, tasteful, and a unique experience for each kid. It is *more* intricate than the Normandy landing. Arnie accepts Oskar's offer on condition: no interference. He plunges in, less like De Mille than Moses. He posts an onerous rehearsal schedule – "That's what it is and that's what we'll call it," he snarls when Oskar agitates an eyebrow. Oskar is reduced to silence, but he can still eavesdrop.

From the balcony that runs round the sanctuary's edge, he sometimes observes us during these preludes to glory. Occasionally we glance up and spot him. Then he takes off like a bat in the belfry. He careers around the upper level as though going from one point to another by the shortest route, which is absurd. He moves swiftly on these tours, his beak in the lead. He looks to us like a bird of prey, or pray. When he has exited from the other side, he often slips into the old choir loft, which is screened from view by a grillwork like a lattice of dinosaur bones. From here he spies on us unseen, doubly secure in our conviction that we have rousted him.

(What does he see from up there? Certainly not *The Ten Commandments*. Perhaps *Triumph of the Will*, a brilliant Nazi documentary unknown to us. Row on row of dedicated youth, pennants fluttering, marches, campfires, numerous low-angle shots of the Führer. What does he make of these images when they come to mind? Does he suppress them? Does he jerk off to them?)

Here below, Arnie storms up and down the centre aisle of the sanctuary, where so many brides have marched in and caskets rolled out, waving his arms like the mad genius he will one day be proclaimed (he knows), while we on the stage – pardon, *bimah*, that is, chancel–cower. He agonizes resonantly over our inadequacy, he threatens us: he will quit, he will expel us – one at a time or *en masse* – our shame on the day of our execrably executed confirmation service will be insupportable. He has recently read *Act One*, Moss Hart's autobiography of a life in theatre, and he is determined to experience nothing less soul-destroying than the religious equivalent of a Broadway opening. He harasses us for not projecting and he bullies us for being insincere. Just when we are on the verge of rebellion for treatment as a chorus line, he reverses field and attacks us for *our* obsession with appearances and surface effect on this, a sacred occasion. He is brilliant and uncontrollable. Oskar resigns himself to spectating. So do we. In the end Arnie puts on a great show, and the confirmation service isn't bad either.

Afterward Oskar congratulates him, and Arnie accepts. Oskar starts to talk about next year, but Arnie thrusts his hands into his pockets, hangs his head, and swings it slowly from side to side. This reminds Oskar of a young actor named Brando he saw recently in a movie called *On the Waterfront*. "Then how will we make it happen again?" asks Oskar. "Ah," says Arnie, "the eternal dilemma of the theatre: how to make the magic happen tomorrow? Oskar"–he blurts with a sudden insight into his own favourite subect – "perhaps I'm not made for theatre at all, but for film, where you get it right once, and for all time!"

The year after confirmation he gives us Hermann.

We file in for Jewish Theology, sensing the spectacle is over; now comes the hard part. At the front of the room sits an elf smoking a cigar. His eyes twinkle. He blows a ring of smoke heavenward. "Vell, you know –" he begins, and we are his. He is physically self-effacing, vocally ingratiating, and intellectually intimidating.

What is it he says that enthralls us? He argues the case for immortality of the soul! Why does this win us? Not because we need to believe we will live forever. We are sixteen or seventeen. Immortality is assumed. Nothing worries us less. I am far more concerned about the fragile state of the Maple Leafs in the National Hockey League and the paralytic timidity that seizes me each time I speak – or rather, hopelessly struggle against my tongue in a vain effort to speak – with the exquisite Vicki Freed.

It is that he argues for something so unlikely. So unpopular. It is as scandalous as life gets in our placid community, the gilded ghetto as we say with a sense of daring. The *immortality* . . . of the *soul*! Brilliant. They are so hard to shake around here, impossible to shatter. Yet this could halt them in their tracks. Old-time religion. Everything they worked to escape, abandoning the faith of their fathers, leaving it downtown in the musty houses and tenements, where Yiddish accents cling to the wallpaper in the halls like mildew. But there is more.

Hermann *argues* his astounding claim, as if he is making the case for a balanced diet. "Vell, you know," he says, "what is the mind? Nobody can see it. It's not the same as the brain, you know. You can't see it on an x-ray." Two-ton Herbie Firestone, king of the black marks in our Hebrew School days, foolishly begs to differ. Hermann responds – with respect! He leans forward, he raises his glasses from his eyes to his forehead, as if to see now with the penetrating eyes of the mind. He questions Herbie, he listens carefully, he leads him along, till suddenly

Herbie is making a further point for Hermann! What's going on? The rest of us assail Hermann with questions. Can he do this trick to us too? Our puzzlement pours forth, the mental maunderings of adolescence: How do I know I exist? How do I know you exist? Was there ever nothing? Can nothing exist? What's good about being good? And, is there a God? He replies in his modest, methodical, magnetic way. I suddenly feel the world is not opaque. There is a reward for asking questions: answers! Hermann peppers his discourse with references that fly by us and ring the occasional bell: Hegel, Kant, Schiller, Schopenhauer, Kierkegaard, and someone named Buber. They all sound German. We decide every serious insight in human history was acquired in the German language. We applaud his performance and look forward to the next show, next week.

We become devout Hermannites, after a manner in which we were never Oskarians. We imitate his choice of words, like "encounter." We mimic his irresistible accent. We have Hermann contests; Joey Banks is the easy winner. He has a God-given (theological phraseology too slips in) knack. Joey is so good at Hermann that we persuade him to phone Oskar one day and be Hermann. Oskar tells, because next class, before Hermann starts on Revelation – a delicious term because of the way Hermann rrrrrolls his *r*'s – he turns to Joey. "I like your deadpan," he says.

Does our conversion bother Oskar? We are his Great Class. Unknown to us, Hermann is one of the "brothers" who people his biography; and here his own children – the closest he has – have transferred their loyalty to a man and a way of thinking that all his life Oskar has found abstract, dubious, delusory, and perverse, even if he afflicts himself for being unable to do it himself. But talk about perverse, he made it happen. He gave us Hermann and Jewish Theology! And he seems proud that we, his unrecognized offspring, can enjoy – silly as it is – what he cannot.

Anyway, he has other matters to resent in Hermann these days. Hermann is happy. He is a professor: he has passed the stations of the academic cross from visiting lecturer through to the frontier of tenure; the rabbi of Oshawa is no more. Hermann is a husband too; Carp-face is a memory, but the lovely Merle has come and stayed. Merle's only drawback, aside from her personality (thinks Oskar), is her religion: Jesus is her saviour. "It's predictable," explained Hermann one night in Fran's before the wedding. "It's a hundred per cent dialectical: to be serious as a Jew in this materialistic community is like being in exile in Exile. Only with a non-Jew can a serious Jew affirm his Jewishness." Oskar nodded: the dialectic strikes again.

But mainly, Hermann has a son. This means more to Hermann than Oskar ever guessed it could. Hermann's eyes fill when he says, "We are pregnant." And by phone on a winter night, "We are in labour." Finally, "A boy."

When Hermann meets Oskar in the days following the birth of his heir, he displays a photo and says, "Unto us a child is born," deftly mingling epochs and religious traditions. He is making a joke, puncturing a joy he cannot express or contain. Oskar smiles his twisty way. He will never have a child, and would not say such a thing if he did. But he thinks: Would one blessing less to Hermann be missed, for the sake of a single goodness to me?

We are all affected by Hermann, but I – perhaps this is where I start to separate myself from our adolescent community of the elect. I carry my new consciousness like a banner. I march into a student council meeting at high school and demand the senior prom be rescheduled. Friday night is *shabbat*, I say, it is holy, it is not meant for jive and chiffon in a school ninety per cent Jewish. They are as shocked as I'd hoped. "You're not orthodox," they say, "you're not even conservative – you're reform!" My parents wince as I leave for services each Friday night and Saturday morning. They feel my pity for the shallow lives they lead. Saturday afternoons, the waning last act of the Sabbath, I saunter through the streets of the Village, one hand tucked in the big paw of my Father above, the other clutching a thin tome called *I and Thou* by the writer named Martin Buber whom, come to think of it, even Oskar might have mentioned.

I am obsessed with the march Nathan Wineberg has stolen on me. Nate's family is orthodox, he has been onto this mine of meaning longer than I. He has been Jewish, really Jewish, all his life. He is also a year ahead in school and already taking Philosophy of Religion at the university *with Hermann*. The more I think, the more I read, the more I believe in – all the more do I agonize over the leap of faith Nate took long before I got the chance. I will never catch up, because he is so far ahead. But I have a plan. He has snaffled Hermann, I will snatch his mentor – Morton Mandelbaum, the orthodox rabbi. I mount my CCM bicycle and pedal to the Haarei El synagogue. "Someone wants to see you," they tell Rabbi Mandelbaum. In I come. "Teach me Jewish," I implore. He squints, he's not sure, then he barks into the intercom: "Bring *t'fillin*" – the phylacteries traditional Jews bind on their arm and forehead each morning at prayer. I leave with my own set, and I know how to use them. I have entered a mystery of my past. I have passed from the banality of modernity into the depth of meaningless ritual. Here is a secret weapon with which to attack their smug community. Watch your rear, Nate Wineberg, I'm moving up.

One morning weeks later I stand wrapped in my *t'fillin*, sun streaming in, rushing to finish my prayers and get to school, when my bedroom door opens. My father! Still in pyjamas, sleep in his eyes, smelling of bedclothes. He and I are not getting on. He dislikes my piety, my jousts with school authorities, the mania I have developed for leaving Toronto after high school to study Judaism somewhere in the United States. The University of Toronto, he assures me with the complacency of the world I am out to destroy, is one of the finest universities on the continent. Yet God in His heaven knows my father never expected the hoary apparition he now sees. I look back in dumb terror, like a child caught masturbating. He groans deeply and with a staggering dismissive wave of his hand turns and lumbers out, leaving me alone with my accoutrements and my God.

Late that spring Oskar and I talk. We sit in the old secret office, knees nearly banging, as usual. He knows I need money if I am to escape the unspeakable U of T. He has spoken with

Ben Fink, chairman of the temple brotherhood and owner of Sanitary Sal Healthcare Products. Ben has a booth at the Canadian National Exhibition in August. He has offered me a job there; I know Oskar is behind it. Three straight weeks – no days off – for a full summer's pay. Manna is falling just outside my tent.

I am telling Oskar I have said no. I will not work on *shabbat*. He sighs. It is a religious commitment, I say. He rolls his eyes. Why do I feel guilty telling my principal that I put Jewish obligations above lucre? Hermann would understand, he would approve, why the hell don't you? The twisty smile starts. He says: It's your life. No approval, no judgement. What kind of attitude is that for a religious educator?

Whenever Hermann's act is interrupted by, say, a prestigious academic convention, Oskar fills in and does a turn himself. Where Hermann gave us wisdom, warmth, and erudition, Oskar gives us sex. Sex in the Bible.

He starts with the truth about Rachel and Leah. "You remember that lovely story we taught you in grade two, how Jacob loved Rachel so much he worked seven years to win her? Then her father gave him her older sister, Leah, instead; so Jacob worked another seven years for Rachel, too? Well I hate to inform you" – a patent lie, just look at his pleasure, his relish, as he speaks – "this was false. The truth is, Jacob got so drunk on his wedding night he couldn't tell who they sent into bed with him, and next day he threatened so much violence they immediately gave him Rachel as well. The very next night – picture the stamina of the man! Then he worked seven years for her! You see the real story is a lot seamier than we taught."

By now he is drooling. His mouth writhes, his eyes are wild. It's hard to know what is arousing him. The lurid details of a drunken wedding night in a desert camp? A look at him gets the rest of us thinking such thoughts. Or is he thrilled by watching our innocence fade and crumble as we encounter contemptible reality – because of him? Is this his idea of education?

91

He moves to the rape of Dinah. As he tells it my mind wanders to Dina Libman, who is cute and dusty and wears makeup. Biblical Dinah was Jacob's daughter. One day she went to town and got raped by Shechem, son of a prominent citizen named Hamor the Hivite. We picture Shechem as a *shaygetz*, but not the kind who attends Forest Hill Collegiate with us, those lower-income Gentiles who rent on the fringe of Forest Hill proper. Shechem's parents could have afforded to send him to private school – Upper Canada College or Ridley – away from the little sons and daughters of Abraham. Dinah's twelve brothers were furious. They said all would be well if Shechem married the girl, but he and his whole village must be circumcised first. The *goyim* stupidly agreed, and while they lay about moaning and feverish, Jacob's boys snuck into town, killed the men, and stole the cattle, women, and children. Their father, Jacob, was disgruntled when he heard but, as they told him, "Shall he treat our sister as a harlot?"

Then Oskar does Judah and Tamar, another Bible story that was skipped in primary grades. Tamar's husband died by God's hand, so his brother Onan had to "go into her." "The unsavoury biblical practice of levirate marriage," Oskar notes for us. But Onan "spilled his seed on the ground." Oskar gets one of the girls to read this verse aloud. "It does not mean he urinated, Miss Donnerstein. It means he pulled out before he shot his wad." He leers as he speaks, like a radar beam sweeping for reactions. God killed the brother, too. So Tamar disguised herself as a prostitute, and seduced her own father-in-law, Judah!

From there by nominal association to another Tamar, King David's daughter, and her half-brother, Amnon. Amnon had such a yen for his sister it made him ill, he took to bed, called her to nurse him, then raped her. "Afterward Amnon hated her with very great hatred. Greater than the love with which he had loved her." Oskar lingers over this part, as if it speaks to him. "Men are disgusted when they finish the sexual act," he says. "It is well known."

Sometimes he skips to sex in the Talmud. We've been told that Judaism has "a healthy attitude toward sex." We've been told it so often we start to wonder who denies it. The proof is always that the Talmud says it's a *mitzvah* – a comandment – for pious Jews to have intercourse on the Sabbath. "Is that so?" says Oskar, tilting off-centre like he's getting a left hook ready. "If sex is so healthy, why do men have to be *commanded* to do it?" We shrink into our chairs uncomfortably. "Listen," he says, "these fine scholars, they sit in the House of Study all week, then they go home and they're so busy praying and celebrating the Sabbath, if they weren't told to do it, they never would! What about the wife? Is once a week fine and dandy with her? Women have multiple orgasms! They are voracious. You think *they* think once a week is healthy?"

One day he mentions the Kabbalah. The what? we say. Jewish mysticism, he answers. Did you know there were Jewish mystics? It sounds like he just read about it in *Reader's Digest*. The left side of the Godhead is masculine, he says, the right side is feminine, and the two have intercourse in the universe.

"Why do you say these things?" I complain. "You want us not to believe anything?"

"I'm telling you," he shoots back, "because I want you to think."

This is preposterous. He tells us because he gets a charge, he looks like he's goosing himself as he talks. He is a parody of one of Julius Streicher's anti-Semitic caricatures – "The Jew as Seducer," for instance, rich and swarthy and ravishing Aryan virgins, obsessive Nazi fantasies of Jewish power. Anyway, it's obvious Oskar couldn't stop if he wanted to. He says these things because he can't not.

Also to voice his doubts. Why, he must ask himself, does he run an institution he finds questionable when it is not ludicrous? He has spent ten years feeding us fables like Jacob's fourteen-year service for Rachel and Judaism's healthy attitude to sex. He is warning us, in a dirty-minded way: let the believer beware.

Oskar steps close to the edge of his role as *conférencier* at these times. The *conférencier* is blasé and continental – a modern. He undermines and debunks but with detachment. He is above it all. There is too much passion in Oskar when he does

Sex in the Bible for us; he is engaged, there is something positive to his negativity. He has become someone else: a *misnagged*, an opposer. What a different figure!

Misnaggdim were sheer Eastern Europe, obscure and unmodern. They appeared at the same time as Hassidism, a vibrant movement among Polish and Russian Jews in the seventeenth century. The *hassidim* danced and sang their guts out. They brought some life, for God's sake, into the desiccated Rabbinic Judaism of their time. Who said no to the life-affirming *hassidim*? Who denounced their joy in the name of orthodoxy? The dreary, dried-up, chaste, miserable *misnaggdim*.

Who withheld approval when I became a teenage *hassid*? He didn't say no, but he never said yes. I took off on my mission and my relationship to the Eternal Thou, but he held back. Long after, when I had no bonds left to my mentors and fellow enthusiasts from the days of my *hassidut*, he remained accessible to me because he had stayed aloof, a well-wishing *misnagged*.

It is curious to watch Oskar shift from *conférencier* to *misnagged* as he does Sex in the Bible. Sometimes both images drop out of focus and another starts to emerge, then vanishes. The *conférencier* is detached. The *misnagged* is cantankerous but remains a disbelieving believer. Both undermine and attack, but neither aims to destroy. A different role impends then, like a storm cloud.

These are lonely times in the life of Oskar, lonelier than ever. He hasn't been dating anyone, aside possibly from Glückel of Hameln, who died in 1724. She was a lusty woman of her age who went through two husbands and, Oskar is convinced, numerous lovers among the Court Jews of Frankfurt, Bayreuth, and Vienna, with whom she also conducted her husbands' business dealings after they were buried. Oskar pictures her like a woman tycoon in the *shmatah* business: severe suit showing a firm, resistant body, hands on her hips, brazen. She left a book of memoirs, which Oskar is condensing and sanitizing for the grade six course, Jewish Life in Olden Times. He thinks about her often, especially when he beats his meat, except when he is concentrating on the bottoms of some of the girls on the pre-confirmation council. He disgusts himself for what he is becoming, and he has a nasty hunch who that is; he is turning into Professor Unrath.

It was during Oskar's puberty, before the Nazis. A smarmy little gang of them played hookey and went to Sternberg's film at a cinema on the Friedrichstrasse. They giggled like maniacs – it was Herr Professor Shaffer, their teacher, on the screen. Panting for the unachievable chanteuse, Lola-Lola, being such a fool, running off with her, losing his job, then returning and cock-a-doodle-doing at her command on the stage of the local *Kabarett*, the Blue Angel, while his former students hooted from the audience, and finally staggering down to his one-time kingdom, the little classroom, and dying there! It amazed them as they sat in the cinema watching Professor Unrath's pupils sneak into the Blue Angel to watch their mentor humiliate himself at the end of Dietrich's cool gaze – just as *they* had snuck down to the cinema to watch . . . Where did reality end and image begin? Who was onscreen, who in the audience? Tomorrow morning they would go back to Herr Shaffer's class and the fantasy would reverse, it would be like seeing Professor Unrath transported to their school, a film made real, and the others who weren't there wouldn't be in on the secret.

Oskar alone did not giggle with a whole heart. Was he the only boy there who identified with the bathetic *teacher*? At thirteen or fourteen?

A lifetime later he feels he has joined Professor Unrath in humiliation. *Ich bin von Kopf bis Fuss auf Liebe eingestellt*, she sang as her ludicrous lover pined. I too am made for love from head to foot, he thinks. I am made for it and nothing else – *und sonst garnichts* – but it eludes me. I would follow any of them, Dina Libman, busty little Miss Donnerstein, Myrna my most lovable student teacher – any – if only they would lure me to my doom. Instead I prate about sex in the Bible and torment children. Even as Unrath I fail. I am un-Unrath. I am not worthy of his fate.

Such images proliferate in the life of Oskar. A wandering Jew, a visitor from another planet, a *misnagged*, a doleful *Gymnasium* instructor who is not even an image, but the image of an image: a play of light and shadow projected onto a screen. Or the image of an image*maker*–the *conférencier*–a trafficker in images, for your pleasure, *meine Herren und Damen*. This abundance is not surprising, since Oskar comes to us direct from one of the original image factories of modern times: the propaganda machine of National Socialism. It's true, Oskar also comes from a people who long before, in the shadow of Mount Sinai, were commanded not to make unto themselves any graven images. But think of it this way. If the children of Israel weren't already busy turning out images at the time, why would it have been necessary to forbid the activity?

A while later, when I am finishing high school, he gives me Maribeth Fine. He found her at JYGGL camp.

Oskar at JYGGL. Oskar in shorts. His knees bony and white, like clenched fists. His chicken's neck inside the collar of a short-sleeved white shirt, and a sparse clump of hair to suggest that down there somewhere is a chest. He looks more like a survivor than ever. Well, this *is* a camp–the summer leadership institute run by JYGGL–Jewish Youth Groups of the Great Lakes.

He adores these camps. He loves to hear Rabbi Rocky's voice singing "Wakey, wakey, wakey in the morning" as he pulls himself out of sleep and squints through the window; he sees Rabbi Rocky and his banjo burst into one of the cabins. He wishes Rabbi Rocky would barge in on him. What a way to start the day! He likes the capers kids play on each other. Yesterday they carried their outgoing JYGGL president down to breakfast roped to his mattress and smeared with shaving cream. Oskar wishes they would do that to him. He'd shift drowsily, dimly aware he was encircled by stealthy teenagers. They'd whisper, "Now!" then pounce, swathe him in ropes, and bear him to the dining hall, where he would be the source of so much *fun*.

They won't, though, because he is Oskar – might as well be one of the rabbis. Maybe more intimidating because he is foreign and intense and so unpredictable that even in shorts he won't ever seem to Canadian kids like an ordinary guy.

The shorts hang from him like they're on a rack. The rabbis all wear shorts too. The first night of camp, after cabin prayers, they met in the staff lounge and discussed how the rabbis could prove to the kids that they're human. Hermann disagreed. He said they should worry about proving to the kids that they're rabbis. Oskar found it witty, he was glad he'd invited Hermann to join the camp faculty, even though Hermann's a professor now, no longer a rabbi. Rabbi Denny from Syracuse and Rabbi Bob from Buffalo weren't amused. "I don't think they got my deadpan," said Hermann.

Oskar likes the Americans. They created these camps. The first one he heard of was in a place called Zionsville, Indiana. Imagine putting a Jewish camp in *Zions*ville. Did they find it on a map and say, "We'll show them we're not ashamed to be Jewish!" In Germany, a nation of youth camps, Jews were never so bold. (Except Buber, who changed the name of his journal from *Der Israelite* to *Der Jude*. "Why gild the lily," he said, "even if it worked?")

Oskar likes Americans' enthusiasm and confidence, their sense of attack. "Oskar, I live three things," said a boy from Akron, Ohio to him. "I live youth group, and I live football, and I live my girl!" Sometimes at campfires Oskar looks around: he's virtually alone, the kids have vanished two by two, some into the woods, others into huddled balls just out of the fire's range.

The American kids pray with the same energy they play football and pet, and they make it up as they go. Oskar likes that too. Hermann doesn't. Hermann prefers the old liturgy, from the ancient *siddur* or the modern prayer book, but Hermann thinks God listens when people pray. If Oskar felt Someone was listening, he too might get queasy about the sludge these kids generate for their "original services."

"Why are Americans obsessed with originality?" asked Hermann when they were alone. "Everything has to be new, it all has to be better than ever! They even insist on doing original *mitzvahs*."

"That's the only way a youth group can get its *mitzvah* certificate," said Oskar. "You need to do some original *mitzvahs*."

"What's wrong with the old hackneyed *mitzvahs*?" said Hermann. "Like loving your neighbour, and honouring your parents, and keeping the Sabbath. The Rombom listed six hundred and thirteen *mitzvahs* in the Torah. Not even including the rest of the Bible and the Talmud. Why can't you get a *mitzvah* certificate for them?"

"They've been done," said Oskar.

"Not by me," said Hermann. "Or you. Or them."

Yet this morning a girl astounded them both at the chapel-in-the-woods. "O God," she read from her notepad, "when I awoke today all I saw was the bedpost. It was rusty. Outside rain was falling. The girls in my cabin lay asleep and snoring. O God, help me see the gleam in the bedpost, the sun through the drizzle, the compassion of a sleeping friend." The boughs of the fir trees heaved Amen. She made Oskar so happy he hurt.

This afternoon he lurched by the sailing area, where Hermann holds a daily class in Modern Jewish Thought. The kids stretched and sunned, their fingertips lightly touching in the sun on the yellow painted dock. She was there, in a blue two-piece, chin cupped in her hands, listening. Lucky Hermann, again.

Now, after dinner, the dining hall sings the *birkat*, the grace after meals. Oskar loves it too. In Germany the *birkat* was a dreary drone. Here in the New World it's a rousing singsong: antiphonal, lilting, changes in tempo, melody, mood. Oskar settles into its musical folds, he could swoon. "Rock o' my soul in the bosom of Abraham," as they sing after breakfast and around the campfire. He sways with the promise of emotional release he connects with true religious feeling, whatever it is and wherever you get it—religion minus the intellectual problems you have when you need to believe something in return for that feeling. A dicey deal, and one he can't ever negotiate. He sways on. He knows the *birkat* is a prayer, but it's an old sock of a prayer. No one sweats the meaning of the *birkat*. You sing and you feel. As it winds down dreamily –

> *I have been young*
> *And also old*
> *And never saw the righteous abandoned*
> *Nor their children seeking*
> *Bread*

– Oskar rises from the bench at his table and starts to dance!

He thinks dance; they see a spastic lurch around the dining hall. He shuts his eyes and moans. He wonders, Is this *hitlahavut*, the indescribable ecstasy that Buber described in his books on Hassidism? Oskar wants them to see how happy human fellowship can make you, that self isn't everything, nor family, nor the college of your first, second, or third choice, nor career, nor money. Nor loving the Lord with all thy might. Other people matter – they can suffice, for some of us they have to. He is educating them with his dance, leading them out from folly and illusion. That's it – this is a teaching technique! He presses his eyelids very tight as they sing and he dances; he weaves and sways, and stumbles suddenly against something, he opens his eyes, it is Rabbi Bob from Buffalo. Rabbi Bob glowers like a Shriner at a convention who's just had a wet kiss planted on him by a stripper – with his wife right there!

Is Oskar drooling and frothing? So? Isn't this how bands of prophets behaved in the days of King Saul, as they went about the country prophesying? Is Oskar too, as they used to say of Saul, among the prophets? Perish the thought, he thinks, the wonderful thought, as he sinks onto the bench and the little hand of Hermann pats his shoulder.

That night it is his turn to give Cabin Prayers in the oldest girls' cabin. He doesn't know there was debate among the rabbis about this. They've been edgy since last summer when Rabbi Chuck from Cincinnati went through the boys' cabins at night groping under their covers. They made Rabbi Marty bunk in with Rabbi Chuck till the end of camp. With Oskar, they worry but no one speaks. Who the hell knows what the guy might do?

He ticks like a time bomb. He's not American, not even Canadian. There is absolutely no way to figure him out.

The girls have fallen off to sleep. For a long time in this darkness he thought they were listening quietly to his musings on the importance of people, with a few notes from Jewish tradition and a wagonload of personal anecdotes. But the silence has thickened. Silence can be awfully unresponsive. He sighs and packs away his memories. He plants his palms on the mattress and starts to push up.

"Oskar," says a voice from the other end of the cot, "that was very nice. Thank you." It's her.

They talk about *everything*. Around them is sleep; outside, only darkness. He wishes he could see her face. It is there, at the far end of the cot, backlit by a wispy blonde halo. He tries to remember her, from the creative service and the sailing dock.

How they talk! The darkness is like a foreign land in which two travellers from the same country have been unable to speak their own language; when they meet they fall into each other's company, conversing feverishly, though in the bright light of home, who knows, they might have nothing to say, they might look right past one another and go their ways.

She is from Shaker Heights, Ohio. The perfect American suburb, a *Doppelgänger* to Forest Hill. Her family belongs to Temple Hillel. Their rabbi is "a legend in the Ohio Valley," she says, a phrase she has heard since she was tiny. "I thought he was God. He was so far off, miles away, over the heads of everyone, high on the chancel, with a huge white head." (Her own blonde aura flickers as she tips her head to remember.) "How else would God look?"

Oskar describes Buber to her: the white hair, the beard. He starts to cackle, he can't help it, he says that all the religious leaders he's ever seen look like God: Heschel, Mordecai Kaplan, Tillich. God is never bald, he says. "Hm," she says, tilting her halo. He wonders if Hermann will start to look like God. A giggle breaks from her – she knows it was a joke – she claps a hand to her mouth. He shivers and tingles.

"The rabbi," she says, "has nothing do with the kids. He is

100

there for the parents, with his sonorous sermons, his weekly columns in the paper, his public presence. They call him the Father of Unemployment Insurance in the Ohio Valley." A New Deal rabbi, thinks Oskar, a Jewish FDR.

The kids have their own rabbi at Temple Hillel, she says, Rabbi Randy. Oskar feels the resentment rush in. Another brother, one who didn't exist a moment ago. Are they always there first? "Rabbi Randy's so honest," she says, "he tells us about his doubts. He's not sure he believes in God. We respect him for that." Oskar clenches his jaw. Rabbi Randy employs Oskar's own best *shtick*—searing honesty. What else can he offer her but uncertainty? She continues, "Sometimes I don't think he understands much, though. He's not wise, like you."

He doesn't know what she means and doesn't care, he glows in the dark. In the light, he would blush. Thank God he stifled the acid remarks about Rabbi Randy. He waited and she gave him her admiration! Words stumble on their way from his throat. "If I know anything at all," he manages, "it's because a few people along the way were interested in what I thought."

Then a wonderful moment. "Who?" she asks. She wants to know, she is one of them. She cares too.

He tells her. She is simple, decent, and deserving. What does age matter, or sex, or anything that ever happened? A human being is a human being: naked they come into the world. He wants to connect.

As they talk, the sky outside brightens slightly, imperceptibly. Then it flickers. Then it shines.

"Oh, Oskar," she says, "the northern lights! I've heard about them."

Hours later he walks across the big field toward his room in a staff cabin. The lights died a sweet death while they spoke, and her need to communicate, unlike his, gave in to sleep. Now hints of tomorrow rise over the basketball court. He stops, looks around. He feels strangely open, pleasantly . . . vulnerable. Is this the beginning of a religious experience? Is it what they mean by God? He laughs, but it doesn't sound like Oskar's voice. He jerks his head up and around like a bird. Has it gone, that feeling?

No, it's still there. He relaxes and plods back to his bed in the Faculty Village section of JYGGL camp.

This was quite a night in the life of Oskar, one to recall alongside the many baneful times. It was a night of love and intimacy, relatively. Love was not mentioned – nor thought – and the intimacy was verbal. Next fall, he keeps things moving by presenting Maribeth to me. He mentioned me to her during their night at JYGGL. She and I meet at the JYGGL autumn conclave in Erie, Pennsylvania – dreary Erie, the mistake on the lake – and our own teen story begins. I suppose it is an appropriate role for him: matchmaker. It suits his age and status. But was there cowardice too? Did he pull back from a connection between the two of them? What if Oskar had ventured something? For she was one more woman who failed to find him ugly.

Another connection also nearly happened that night, as Oskar passed the basketball court. He didn't think of it as God, just "something." For once something, rather than the blank he always draws when others meet God. Was there a connection between these two near-connections: with her and with God? He felt a feeling like it once before.

It is after Nuremberg. How can you stop being what you are? German Jews are no longer German. What are they, then? They feel the same. They speak the language impeccably, Buber remains its supreme stylist, they are cultured, they take pride in German thought, art, and industry – they produce them, in fact – as though they are their own! Sense is slipping away.

Panic is widespread, but it doesn't affect Oskar. Maybe it's his natural gloom. When things go well, he is tense; when they misfire, he relaxes. This is the way of the world, this darkness feels right to him. Because he seems to handle the catastrophe, others turn to him. Their confidence gives him confidence. Leadership falls his way. People come with accounts of those they know. Will he speak with them, take a walk, transfer some of his own solidity? It is the hour of Oskar. One after another he counsels them. He never felt so necessary.

On a late afternoon, the sky darkening, he is alone in the movement office. He just dealt with the crisis of a group leader. He spoke to her calmly, without superficiality. She responded. Greta took her away, an arm around the girl's trembling shoulder, a glance of admiration back toward him as they left the room. He feels so useful. You are put here to *do* something. This is a terrible time, everyone is victimized, but at least he's not standing by, not pissing his life away, passive. He turns to the study program they are designing for teens. It is their main function now, Jewish education and study, instead of the customary activities – hiking, camping. It is as though young Jews, stripped of one identity, are urgently grafting on a new one. It cannot wait, the way the woods and trails can. What matters is pride. If one is forbidden to be a proud young German, one will be a prouder young Jew.

They rely on Buber for these courses. His advice, his occasional presence, especially his books. Oskar flips idly through *Tales of the Hassidim*. They are making a selection of Buber's selection. He skips from page to page, he decides to slow down and enjoy the task. Who knows, he might find something useful for the next crisis. He worked well with the girl, Greta was impressed, he's earned a moment for himself. He will lower himself into one of the tales.

Rabbi Jacob Isaac the Younger, Oskar reads, was a disciple of Rabbi Elimelech of Lizensk. On the way to his teacher's hometown, Rabbi Jacob Isaac stopped for the Sabbath in a small village and heard the local rabbi pray with great *hitlahavut*. Rabbi Jacob Isaac asked the man who taught him the secrets of such ardour. He was astounded when the man said no one had instructed him, he reached this state alone. Rabbi Jacob Isaac persuaded this remarkable man to join him and visit Rabbi Elimelech of Lizensk. But when the two arrived and crossed Rabbi Elimelech's threshhold, they were nonplussed. Instead of extend-

ing the traditional greeting, the Great Man turned and looked
out the window. Oskar smiles. There is a leisure to these tales.
The punch line will come.

Rabbi Jacob Isaac the Younger deposited his companion at
the local inn and returned to Rabbi Elimelech, who now greeted
him and asked, "Why did you bring me this person, in whom
the image of God is defiled?" Rabbi Jacob Isaac was stunned.
Rabbi Elimelech went on. "You know," he said, "there is a place
where one brilliant star provides all the light, and in that place
are mixed good and evil. Sometimes a man begins to serve the
Lord, but pride and secret motives are mixed in and he does
nothing to dispel them. He may not even know it. He might
seem to act with great *hitlahavut*, for nearby is the flame of the
impure fire, which he uses to ignite his own worship, and he
doesn't even know where he got it!" When Rabbi Jacob Isaac
repeated these words to his travelling companion at the inn, the
man saw their truth. Weeping, he ran to the house of Rabbi
Elimelech and sought his help.

Oskar collapses. His head hits hard against the desktop. He
sobs. He slips weakly from chair to floor. Buber's book falls
beside him. The flame of the impure fire. He is serving with the
flame of the impure fire, and didn't know. What is it but his
pride and secret motives? Using the desperation all around not
to truly serve but to aggrandize himself in the name of selfless-
ness? What are he and his service worth? Is forgiveness possible?
He prays. He does not know if there is a God, but he needs
forgiveness. He knows it with perfect faith. Is this what others
mean by God – the *need* for God to forgive you? At this rare
moment in his life, similar to the dawning moment on the big
field at JYGGL, it makes some sense to him. Not the God of his
Fathers; still – something. Oskar reaches for the book and finds
the end of the tale. It says the man ran weeping to the house of
Rabbi Elimelech, sought his aid, and with the rabbi's aid, found
his way.

When Greta returns – Oskar doesn't know how much later –
he is still on the floor, as though he's been waiting. He lets her

see him, then rises, and paces as he tells her. She listens and nods.
He starts to feel quite . . . connected. But he asks himself, on
his other track: Why am I telling her, what am I trying to gain?

Decades later, she walks the paths among the orange trees.
Ahead of her scampers little Uri on his way to bed. With her is
Chana, her eldest daughter, on leave from the army. She has his
letter that says, Willi Schropp is coming to me in Canada, why
am I here instead of there with you? She speaks aloud to the
trees. *Attah loh ratzeeta l'hitkashair*, she says. *You didn't want
to connect.*

The slumber of the decade falls gently around Oskar, like the
curtain of a modest *Kabarett*. He has settled finally, far from the
storms of Europe, and even the minor turbulence of downtown
Toronto. He is a Jew among Jews, in a community seized with
a comfort deserved after centuries. They repose in their dens and
rec rooms, their two-car garages; he selects well-upholstered
furniture for his apartment and installs capacious bookshelves.
The *Kabarett* he conducts among his students and staff is aggres-
sive, in the nature of a *Kabarett*, but only mildly so. Neither
politics nor the Eternal Thou interrupt his daily comings and
goings. Life at its riskiest is a shopping trip.

He feels light qualms about being so protected, like hearing
distant calls from beyond a thick wall. The call of the harsh
angular world of secular learning, for which he once rejected
Buber's unforgettable challenge. Or the exploration of history,
and the lure of an academic life. Dim echoes, too, of debates
with Goldberg at *World Press Review*, along with the goading
of Andy the editor and the sensuousness of . . . what was her
name, the French Canadian?

He hates it. He would not exchange it, but he reviles himself
for making this peace. He is certain he has betrayed himself; he
teaches a life of harmony and integration within the Jewish com-

munity – all right, but he was not meant for it himself. Tocchet strides into this plush world like an intruder in the temple. Oskar runs to greet him.

Oskar adores Tocchet; perhaps he loves him. When Ida or one of the secretaries calls from downstairs and says Tocchet is on the line, it is the best moment of any day. When they buzz and say Tocchet is here, his tiny body present in the flesh, Oskar is humble and proud; he wants them to know who is calling on their Oskar, to see that the hard reality beyond their bubble recognizes him, even here in hiding. Sometimes when Tocchet comes Oskar feels like King Saul, journeyed far from his palace into the hills, fallen asleep in a cave, and little David, whom the king drove from his court, has found Saul, stands over him and looks down on his monarch with love despite the king's vicious rejection.

At those times Oskar meets Tocchet on the stairs (Tocchet wouldn't pompously wait for Oskar to hurtle all the way down; he has been here before and knows the way); together they mount to the little sanctum, where Tocchet curls up in the chair opposite like a genie popped from a pop bottle. His mind seeps gently from the crown of his head, like the smoke from his ever-present cigarette; his thoughts expand through the small, friendly room. In this way he is like Hermann, but Tocchet's mind is comforting, it is like a pillow. Tocchet's generous insights calm Oskar, even as they nudge and stimulate his thick mental process. Tocchet goes about relieving guilt and self-doubt, as Jesus went about doing good. He is a sociologist.

He enters the life of Oskar like a miniature angel, sent scurrying hither with a puff of divine breath in his sails. He comes to Oskar on a rescue mission, and not a moment too soon. Tocchet is here to lay intellectual siege to the stifling smugness of this community.

He came straight from the completion of his previous study: an urban slum. "I wanted to know if the rich are as miserable in their way as the poor," he says, sounding suspiciously unscientific. "Are they?" asks Oskar. "They talk like they are," says Tocchet. "They whine more."

Tocchet doesn't feel like a brother, unless he is Oskar's ideal brother, the one who exists in the perfect world of his fantasies. Tocchet is too much other to be a brother. Tocchet is not Jewish, nor is he Christian. He is a Quaker. He tried the Unitarians, he says with the warmth he extends to all life forms, but they struck him as intellectual. Think of Tocchet, superbrilliant Tocchet, saying they were too intellectual. Tocchet is so smart, he knows being smart isn't everything.

What Oskar needs, to feel at home, is another outsider, a brother alien. What else is a sociologist except a legitimate outsider, an outsider with a licence? Back in Germany, sociologists were weighty and theoretical, cousins to philosophers. Here in the New World, the hell with theory. Sociologists aren't philosophers, they're voyeurs. This suits Oskar. He teams up with Tocchet, they form an anti-community; he starts to scrutinize and categorize those who stigmatize *him*; he mediates the community for Tocchet; he is after all, the *conférencier*: I give you, my dear sociologist, this bizarre society, so chaste, so painfully normal . . .

And he gives them to Tocchet. He can't resist. They're in such a panic these days – "aggravated" as they say. It's those fraternities and sororities their children are joining. Like everyone who meets Tocchet, the parents of the Pillar of Fire will sense immediately his understanding; he will alleviate their fear and anxiety. He just needs to be brought before them. *Meine Herren und Damen* . . . At this very moment, beneath the tower office, Mr Oates is readying the auditorium for a meeting of Parents' Council.

They do whine. What the hell is with their kids? Who ever heard of frats for *Jews*! With Greek names? It makes them nervous, like "restricted" hotels and resorts, like the Granite Club. It grates on their liberalism. It's snobbery, isn't it? What goes on at those meetings? They haven't a clue, because *there are no adults allowed*. Lily Cohen says they blackballed her Lewis! She phoned their mothers, she even phoned the *pishers* themselves. "Look,

Mrs Cohen," they said, "you've got drive, why don't *you* join our frat?" They have conventions? What for? What do they do at their conventions? And why do they hold them in Buffalo?

Oskar drifts, he is on his other track, the twisty smile slides across his mouth as the lament swirls around him. He is thinking about beer gardens, whoring, duels – he could tell them about fraternities. Out in the Parents' Council there is a hush. Someone says they go to Buffalo for the whorehouses. Oskar slips out of his thoughts and back into their world. So that's what frats are for – first fucks. Some of the fathers in the room seem easier. Were they wondering how their sons would learn what came naturally on the downtown streets where they themselves grew up, so unlike the sidewalkless roads and crescents of Forest Hill? What a jumble. This wasn't part of the package for which they travelled west from the Old Country and north from downtown. Who will make sense of it for them and tell them what to do? They look at Tocchet. He rises, compassion pulsing from him in compact waves.

Tocchet clasps his hands in front of his chin like little paws, as though he is going to pray for them. Sometimes he looks to Oskar like the teddy bear on signs outside Travelodge motels who promises you a good night's rest if you stop here. Tocchet crinkles his face. He is concerned, he almost hurts with their doubt and trauma, then the lines around his eyes relax and the resolution of their dilemma seems to arrive in his mind like a telegram. "These organizations," he says, with his trace of a lisp, "these little adolescent enclaves – they are the only refuge in this entire community offering some independence and dignity to young people. Where they do things for themselves without parental supervision and control. You must thank heaven they exist and do nothing to endanger them." He smiles. He looks pleased that he has been able to help.

The storm bursts silently. It consists of glares and glowers. Speech will come later. They are in trouble because this man is an expert. He speaks treason, but he is an expert. Experts tell you what to do. They are a feature of the new age, like frost-free refrigerators; they engender security and save labour. They occasionally surprise you with advice you didn't know you wanted, but they *never* tell you what you *don't* want to hear. The parents will have to regroup, reassure each other outside his presence, and declare him a false prophet. He doesn't understand "our" kind; yes, a *goyishe kop*; doesn't know what it means to get kicked in the balls in Christie Pits before the war by an anti-Semitic mob of toughs who probably all belonged to a fraternity – or would have if they could. One way or another decertify him. The chairman of Parents' Council observes there are no questions and thanks Tocchet without profusion. The meeting disperses.

Oskar is quiet as he walks Tocchet to the temple parking lot. "They're funny people," says Tocchet. This statement explodes like a starburst over Oskar, like the liberation of Europe or the storming of the Bastille. It is like a steel band snapping from around his head. He is so happy to hear Tocchet's words – *They're funny people* – he could weep. For so long he has been the aberrant among the normal, the fugitive from a madhouse, the DP, the scapegoat come from the wilderness into the settlement, into the place of complacency. Now, to hear Tocchet say *they* are funny, say it to *Oskar*, as though Oskar is the regular one, looking on bemused along with Tocchet, at these deviates.

"The signs of mental distress are enormous," Tocchet confides, unlocking his car and feeling as much compassion for the bloated rich as he does for juvenile delinquents. "I'd say one in four needs a shrink fast." Tocchet knows because he is a shrink himself, he teaches shrinkage at the university, he's probably been shrunk himself – pre-shrunk, from the size of him – but not in Hermann's competitive way, fascinated by his own mental landscape and hotly possessive of it. In Tocchet, therapy has bred generosity. Oskar imagines being in shrinkage with Tocchet, though he continues to long for Paltz, since Paltz belongs to Hermann.

Tocchet, a man who can turn into an emotional antenna, loses interest in the meeting they just left. "What about you?" he asks.

"I am engaged in a contradictory enterprise," says Oskar with rare certainty. "That is why I hate what I love doing." He stops.

Tocchet seems so interested; as though he wants to crawl into Oskar's head and play among his tangled thoughts. "Religious education," says Tocchet, as though they are both reading from a neon sign flashing messages into the darkness of the parking lot.

"We tell the children," Oskar continues slowly, "that Judaism respects them for being what they are. And then we tell them that they have to be good Jews, no matter what. It doesn't make sense."

"Maybe," says Tocchet, "someday it will."

"Really?" says Oskar with hope.

"And maybe never," says Tocchet.

"I'm the teacher," says Oskar, "but I don't have anything straight." Tocchet starts to launch a soothing response, but Oskar isn't finished. "It's worse," he says. "I'm not just the teacher. I'm the teacher of the teachers."

"In my experience," says Tocchet, "all real learning is equivalent to pain." Oskar is disappointed. He doesn't know if it shows, but he expected more than this nostrum. Tocchet, though, isn't done. "I never realized till this moment," says the sociologist, "that all real teaching is also equivalent to pain."

It is the best conversation Oskar ever has about his life's work.

On Christmas Day, Oskar goes to Tocchet's. They asked him to drop by; he supposes this is what Jews do on Christmas. Tocchet lives near Casa Loma, Toronto's stupid castle. As Oskar parks, he thinks of the way medieval peasants gathered near the lord of the manor, ready at hand if he chose to declare a blood libel and send them out to harass Jews. Tocchet has a Christmas tree and four boys, who are scattered around the foot of the tree like

110

presents. They offer their affection to Oskar; like father like sons. Harriet Tocchet rocks in a chair by the tree; she could be the mother of all of them, including Tocchet himself. She is as plain and unexpressive as the grey December afternoon outside. Tocchet and Oskar talk about Christmas and Judaism, the boys join in, she rocks. How do people choose each other? How do they cross the distance? How do they connect? Perhaps this is the mystery of Christmas – or is it Easter that's a mystery? He shudders, on his inner track, thinking about how they teach Christianity to the grade eights in the wildly popular Comparative Religion course. No matter how Oskar cuts that curriculum, it comes out as Three Cheers for Us. JUDAISM AFFIRMS LIFE WHILE CHRISTIANITY IS OTHERWORLDLY . . . CHRISTIANITY CONCENTRATES ON THE INDIVIDUAL BUT JUDAISM STRESSES COMMUNITY . . . JUDAISM HAS A POSITIVE ATTITUDE TO SEX . . .

At the door, Tocchet says he and the family are leaving for a while. "Did I do something wrong?" says Oskar. Tocchet laughs. He says sociologists always leave town when their studies appear. His book will be out in the spring. Oskar can't believe it. "Are you sure it's not me?" he persists. "Hell hath no fury like a suburb studied," says Tocchet. Oskar is delighted at the thought. He says he'll miss Tocchet. "One thing you might do," says his friend, grasping Oskar with both hands, "is get together with Wetherford. He teaches math at the high school."

Wetherford is curt. Oskar is embarrassed; he is on the phone with a stranger – another Gentile – asking for what amounts to a date. Oskar doesn't phone strange women, not even Jewish, for dates. What's got into him? Loneliness. He misses Tocchet, the outsider he feels at home with. But Wetherford sounds very unTocchet-like. He doesn't extend human solidarity across the wire; his voice is clipped, his sentences state their case, then end. Silence hangs and it doesn't seem to bother Wetherford. Oskar stammers. "Tocchet," says the voice. "Well then" – and Oskar hears the background clamour of a staff room – "I think you should come to my lecture on the fourth dimension. It's the first

time in many years. Next Tuesday at three in the school cafeteria.
I'll meet you in the lobby just before."

The lobby is lacquered wood. Oskar stands across from the
glass-walled office. The secretaries are inside. They must be
discussing him. He's sure they think he's a bum who stumbled
in off Eglinton. Though you never see bums on Eglinton. What
if the janitor asks him to leave? Toward him strides–Wetherford,
it has to be. He steps briskly, like a sergeant-major. He is lean
and starched like a riding crop; his moustaches bristle. But his
eyes are wild. They seem to start far back under the crown of
his head and hurtle forward like projectiles, firing out from his
eye sockets into the world, seeking objects to penetrate, palpable
targets like Oskar. Wetherford wears–well, the main thing is the
tie.

As Wetherford approaches, the tie seems to enlarge more
swiftly than the man. It enlarges exponentially, blotting out
everything else. Oskar is saying hello to a tie. "I'm very excited,"
says Wetherford. "I wear it only when I give my lecture, every
four or five years." The tie is Dali, a clock bends and flows as it
passes over a waterfall. Time curving, or something like that.
From behind the tie, near a trophy case, comes a voice. "Hello,
Oskar, nice to see *you* here!" It is Dennis Pierce, music teacher,
who brings his high-school choir to the Pillar of Fire each year
for Brotherhood Week. They sing "No Man Is an Island" and
"Millions of People Lift Up Their Hearts to ONE GOD." What a
sane thing to do, what a sane person to be, compared to this
garrulous tie. Dennis is already gone, he is vanishing down the
hall. Along the walls are plaques naming year after year of school
prefects, whatever they are. Oskar feels he has stepped off the
boat in a foreign land. He is checking his pockets for his vacci-
nation certificates. "You know Pierce, do you?" says Wetherford,
as though opening a new file: The Oskar Dossier.

The students are packed in the cafeteria like tuna fish sandwiches in wax paper bags. They crowd around tables and press against vending machines. They lean against the railing beside the counter where they normally order their hot and cold meals. Some of the kids are familiar, they must have attended the religious school, but none of his best are here: the student teachers, the club leaders. Oskar is the only adult. Behind the counter is a window in the wall, probably opening into the staff lunchroom; it is covered by a plywood panel. Oskar wonders if any teachers slink there, curious. Wetherford bursts through the door like a trim thunderclap.

His face is illuminated; it shines the way Oskar pictures Moses when he descended the mountain with the tablets. Maybe it's high blood pressure. Oskar has sometimes wondered if it's the same thing: revelation and exasperation. Wetherford is electric movement, he seems to float, to jump spaces like a spark; his eyes dart around, his tie seems to exhale and inhale. He launches his presentation in the middle, as though it has no start or finish, as though it is part of the existence of the universe, a rounded whole, a snake swallowing its tail, a world without end, *l'olam va-ed*, as Jews say when they pray. Oskar is drawn in like all the kids in the room; this is initiation, they have become a secret brotherhood, witness to the rites.

When Oskar relives this "lecture" at various times for the rest of his life, it is all images. He has sat through Hermann's discourse: "Historical Faith and Faithful History" for example; he felt like a blind man groping for a shape, knowing a structure was there, but missing it; as he felt in music appreciation at *Gymnasium* when his teacher explained the *Architechtonik* of the Eroica symphony, and Oskar sat listening to it on the phonograph, unable to find any of the articulations just laid out for him. Wetherford, though, does not lecture; he launches dazzling pictures.

"Here is a point in space." He holds up a fist. "We roll it in one direction." He runs his fist across air between himself and his audience. "This line has one dimension." They see the straight line he has made in the air. "We unroll the line in another direction." He seems to bring the line he has made in empty space

113

down toward them, as though he is unrolling a carpet; a surface lies before them, an invisible surface, which they see. "This surface has two dimensions." They nod. "We extend the surface in another direction again." He lifts the tangible unseen surface toward the cafeteria ceiling; a cube fills the empty space. "This cube occupies three dimensions. Now we extend the cube in yet another direction, as we have been doing." They await, transfixed, the unfurling of this cube into yet another shape, to form the characteristic four-dimensional structure, just as the line, the surface, and the cube are the typical shapes for the first three dimensions.

Of course it does not appear. But Wetherford has led them to the brink. He has made the fourth dimension a logical expectation that just happens not to emerge, like a reliable bus that one morning fails to come. The fourth dimension at this moment is as real for them as length, width, and depth. What is it, then? thinks everyone in the room. Time, thinks Oskar, looking at the clock curving over the waterfall, billowing on Wetherford's chest. It is the best teaching he has ever seen.

Now Wetherford flourishes scissors, a blunt pair of little scissors that kids can't hurt themselves with, like they give to the toddlers in arts and crafts at the Pill on the Hill. Oskar feels he is light-years from there. Wetherford takes a cardboard, the sort the dry cleaner puts in with your shirts, and cuts a flat little cardboard man from its centre. Then he cuts a small door that swings out flat to allow the flatman in or out of the cardboard enclosure. "His house," says Wetherford, and they all see it. He holds the little man and his house up vertically, facing the audience, and conducts them through a day in the life of the flatman. "He gets up in the morning," says Wetherford, "he has breakfast, he goes out the door to work. He comes in at night, shuts his door, and falls asleep exhausted." Then Wetherford simply, dramatically, pivots the flat world he holds in silhouette against his taut body upward – and it becomes a line. They gasp, Oskar among them, yet they don't know what they saw that just took their breath away. Wetherford pivots the cardboard back; there is flatman again, home in his bachelor pad. "We," says Wetherford sententiously, "see him, all his comings and goings, from our three-dimensional world. It never occurs to him that he is failing to see all there is. He does see all there is – in his two dimensions. It doesn't enter his mind that there might be a dimension to reality – his very own reality – that extends it into another realm. Now what would happen if we entered his world, or let's just say his room?" And Wetherford thrusts a bony forefinger right through the living room of the flatman. A dizzying, kaleidoscopic piece of incomprehensibility passes before the bewildered gaze of flatman. They all see it. "My God," screams Oskar soundlessly, "it's a miracle!" He believes he just understood what the children of Israel felt when the Red Sea parted before them. Not what they *saw* but what they felt. He thinks about all the efforts among Jewish educators he knows to explain, or explain away, and figure out how to teach the biblical miracles. Wetherford meanwhile is looking at him, aiming eyeball projectiles directly at Oskar.

The last image is the worm in the Persian carpet. Wetherford doesn't gesture, move, or illustrate. They see the worm as he speaks in his clipped voice, passing from a brown to a mauve to a green patch of carpet. From the viewpoint of the worm, life is open and free; the future is undetermined. From the worm's point of view, the many patches he has not yet traversed are the future, they are ahead in time, they don't exist yet at all. But from our vantage point above, a dimension beyond the flat world of the worm, every possible future already exists. What for the worm is future time, is for us above merely more space. "Everything is foreseen," thinks Oskar in the words of Rabbi Akiba, flayed to death in the second century for joining rebellion against the Roman Empire, "yet freedom of choice is given."

They stand on the steps of the collegiate, the main entrance with big glass doors, which students are forbidden to use. Oskar balances the two large books Wetherford has loaned him; they are by a Russian mathematician who collected the teachings of the mystic whom Wetherford mentioned quietly a moment ago.

"You may have heard of him–" And then the name, like a grunt. "Here, look!" says Wetherford, snatching one volume and leafing through it with the enthusiasm of the Tocchet boys opening Christmas presents. Wetherford folds the book back to a chart where lines join circles, and labels sit in the circles. "See," says Wetherford, "the highest energy is transformed into sex! Isn't that gorgeous?" Oskar shivers. Is this a sexual advance? "I have one question," he says.

"Why do I do it, why pursue the Truth?" says Wetherford with sweet resignation, full of a happy sense he has no answer to this question, but he can do no other, it is his fate. "No," says Oskar, looking back into the foyer with the athletic trophies and the prefect plaques. "Why are you here?"

"Aha," says Wetherford, satisfied with a question to which he has an answer. "Some of us are sent out into the world to check what we know from the Teaching against the world itself. I am here, you might say, on a secret mission"–he looks around –"but no one must find out." He moves his head up and down; he is glad to provide useful information. "Let me know what you discover," he adds, glancing at the books. Oskar opens them occasionally during the months to come, but never reads them. He is not really interested in the Teaching. But he is fascinated by its teaching.

There is a last image for this period in the life of Oskar.

One summer he sends my friend Jimmy (Yitzhak) Marcus to a Jewish creative arts camp on the rocky coast of Maine. It's called "Genesis," and they don't just write their own worship services: they sing, dance, paint, and act them. Jimmy is creative to his toes. He returns inspired and begins to build an ark of the covenant – the enclosure that houses the scrolls of the Torah – for our children's chapel. He tells Oskar, who is pleased, and starts to fret. Jimmy locks himself in the family garage and toils in rapt seclusion every day after school. He shows no one his unfolding vision. The annual P of F Brotherhood banquet nears. The Brotherhood sponsored those two weeks in Maine; they hold the purse strings for future Jimmys to attend future creative arts camps. Oskar starts to hector Jimmy for the completed ark. Jimmy hurries, Oskar harasses, Jimmy starts to stumble, Oskar presses harder, he demands a look at the ark in whatever state it is. Jimmy succumbs. Oskar comes to the garage beside the Marcus home on Rosemary Road, he regards this splendid effort, the abstract shape, off-centre doors, the enormous piece of driftwood that seems to hover before it, the plexiglass impressionistic Hebrew lettering – he explodes. Oskar simply erupts. He heaps up a curse of biblical proportions. He refuses to let this monstrous *crap* be seen by anyone in Brotherhood, he trusts it will not ever be completed, it will certainly never pass through the doors of Temple, toss it in some junkyard where the derelicts and perverts whom it mirrors can appreciate it, they maybe could put it to use for firewood – just the way the original ark of the covenant, as recounted in the Book of Judges or somewhere, sat and rotted in a field for *twenty years* because it was such misfortune for all who touched it! The field of Abinadab the Beth Shechemite, you biblical illiterate. They died, they got boils, I don't know what – but that wouldn't interest you, would it, Mr Art-for-Art's-Sake! Are we running a religious school, or a training camp for pansies and degenerates who belong in the prisons and the workhouses? Mr . . . Mr . . . Futurism/Dadaism/Surrealism – go and join them – it's where you belong – with your bizarre and ugly notions of art, and leave us alone forever – at least!

This is a typical outburst for the Oskar of those years. Young James is shattered. Futurism? Abinadab the Beth Shechemite? Jimmy has never heard about the Exhibition of Degenerate Art, which the National Socialist government of Germany mounted in Munich in 1937 to publicly expose the gulf between healthy Aryan artworks and the disgusting afterbirths of Jewish and Jew-inspired artists. What can Jimmy know of the link between the fit Oskar throws inside his garage and the thicket of assumptions against which Oskar flailed during adolescence, according to which Jews were responsible for everything evil including Marxism, pacifism, internationalism, psychoanalysis, the Treaty of

Versailles, atonal music, organic architecture, and abstract expressionism? Is even Oskar himself aware of a link?

Consider that for Oskar, education is not the creation of expertise or transmission of information. It is a matter of values. "The goal of our education is the formation of character." He would concur, but he did not speak these words. The minister of education for the Third Reich in 1936 said them. Oskar wants to create a positive response to Jewishness in his students. To accomplish this he utilizes emotional experience as well as teaching techniques. So in our school we have music, arts and crafts, and drama – routes to young hearts and minds. He creates a youth program. He sends us to inspiring camps. It is the whole person he wants. For him education is, in a word of religious origin, propaganda. In this respect he is more or less continuous with the pedagogic traditions of the state that stripped him of citizenship and murdered his family. Religious education can hardly be anything but propaganda.

This is starting to sound like the modern literary sport of thinking the unthinkable, and in this case, the improbable too. Toronto is not Berlin. Comparison seems idiotic. Yet Toronto is white, western, European, northern, and Gentile. It is the Berlin of Oskar's childhood held in his mind's eye, a mild and tolerant Diaspora. It is exile without a vengeance, Berlin on the other side of the sun, a Berlin to which no Nazism ever happened. It feels like home to Oskar, in a way that home never did. Why else has he not only come here but stayed?

It's true, he had enough politics back then to last a lifetime, thank you, and that's why he's here. Leave politics to others if it must be done; he has chosen the life of the mind, he has chosen to teach, not do – and the perfect place not to do it. But if he, the teacher, has learned one trite lesson, it is that everything may be a way of avoiding what it seems to be doing. Each time he forgets this lesson, he rediscovers it. We are free to doubt that Oskar is actually aware of hidden parallels between what he does now and what was done to him then, and yet –

There is a quandary that has never left Oskar. It concerns how much the Nazis called on, that was basically good and positive: their sense of belonging to a collectivity that is more than oneself, for example, and of pride in one's heritage, and sacrifice for what is greater than oneself. These are values praised in the Jewish tradition and every other noble human discourse. In the Comparative Religion course for grade eights, the jewel of Oskar's curriculum, these values rise like dandelions. It is confusing: how could cretins and degenerates take all that good and twist it so?

According to the concise Havdalah service, which ends every Sabbath sweetly, it is God who creates the distinction between the holy and the profane. But who makes them indistinguishable from time to time, and how? What was the move in those dark days that blurred the separation between good and bad? Was it a unique event or does it frequently recur?

One afternoon during this period in the life of Oskar, I call at the apartment of my classmate, Joey (Yosef) Banks. Joey is a splendid eccentric at age sixteen. My knuckles are poised to rap on his door when I hear, from within, a double sound: the static bark of a harsh, foreign harangue, and the live, unmistakable voice of my buddy Joe following and mimicking the voice of Adolf Hitler on the same record Arnie Torno played for us in confirmation class. As we laughed, Arnie noted that this same voice, now funny for its excess, once conducted millions of our people to the gas. Joey, I have said, is the mimic among us. He does Hermann perfectly. He also does Oskar. And to me the strange part of this event, as I retreat from the doorway and wander through the shady streets of Forest Hill, is that I am not really surprised. I couldn't explain it. I am puzzled, but I know it makes some kind of sense.

I feel the same years later when I hear about another ex-member of the Temple Terrors, Teddy Stein. I am in Europe and receive a news clipping in the mail from good old Jimmy (of the obscene ark). It reads, RESPECTED LAWYER ARRESTED AT AIRPORT, CHARGED WITH ARSON. Teddy, who was the soul of reason and compromise, Most Likely to Succeed among us. I don't know why he did it, but again I am not surprised. It too makes strange sense.

Survivors vary, like everyone else. Nazi Germany was not on another planet, nor does severe pain and suffering–even a Holocaust – entail a general exemption from the rules of human behaviour. There are those who emerge in a kind of stupor, utterly uncomprehending; others go through and come out not understanding, but not surprised either. Such is life, think those, and among them was Oskar.

He sometimes even wonders: Would I be much different had none of that happened to me? The answer is yes. And also no. He would not have become virtually all the things he became, including a Canadian, a Jewish educator, and a would-be historian. Along with, probably, barren, alone, misanthropic, vicious, and depressed. On the other hand, it is the same person who would not have become those things.

At any rate, to get on with saying the unsayable, among his many faces, Oskar was also the Führer of PFRS, the Pillar of Fire Religious School, a refracted other world he created and pervaded with his obsessiveness, his paranoia, and his sadism.

But let's not cut off discussion at this point with a specially grisly face of Oskar. Let's go back to one we passed quickly; among all these images it is the one Oskar would detest most, even more than the scurrilous Führer of PFRS. I am thinking about the *misnagged*, the smug and pious East European rabbinical foe of Hassidism. A small-minded, unappealing epitome of all that Oskar wished never ever to be taken for.

A *hassidic rebbe* once opined that God made *misnaggdim* too. Why? Because the *hassidim* in their purity rise from the mundane weighed-down world of sin most of us inhabit and ascend far into the upper realms of holiness, where they disport themselves. Who then will remain below, among the lost and exiled sparks of holiness still trapped in these lower worlds, and try to redeem them? Who will continue to stagger about in the muck down here along with ordinary humanity, once he has entertained visions of pure joyful holiness such as *hassidim* know? Who would be so foolish and inelegant to remain in this mean and foul place – yech! – after he has beheld the radiance that the life of the spirit can yield? No one in his right mind! And so the Holy One in his wisdom made *misnaggdim*.

CHAPTER
5

WILLI SCHROPP HAS come and stayed. He is ensconced, he is the new regime, like John F. Kennedy in the United States. Oskar adores the young American president. Why? Maybe it's the audio-visual techniques Kennedy employs, the same methods Oskar has laboured to bring to the religious school. When Kennedy announced he was sending American military advisers to Southeast Asia, he stood before an array of multicoloured maps, wielding a pointer. He even used flip charts! Oskar couldn't have been prouder if the president were teaching confirmation. But that's not all. Kennedy is a man of action–such a man, such action.

To Oskar it is a source of wonder that change ever occurs. One day things are this way, next day everything is different. Like the coming of Willi. It was unthinkable; now it is a state of nature. They pass each other in hall, they meet to discuss school business. They almost never mention the past–their own past – as though there is no past, only the magisterial present. Others know the secrets of change, they turn that into this. Willi knows. Even Hermann knows. Hermann has transformed his life. He has gone from Oshawa to Toronto, rabbi to professor, alone to coupled, barren to parent. Not Oskar.

He never seems to do anything. His life is a swamp of pas-sivity, a Jewish passion play. He is rich in feeling: anger, despair, regret, elation. But what does he *do*? Others change lives–their own if they are ambitious and egocentric like Willi, the lives of others if they are idealistic and–

He sighs. He knows what Myrna would say, and Hermann too if they ever get to have another long wonderful talk in Fran's. You, Oskar, you touch the lives of others profoundly. You are an educator, a teacher. You act on the *future*. What could be more effective . . .

He knows, he knows. So why does he *feel* ineffective? Because anything can be a way of not doing what it seems to be doing. By acting on the future, he evades the present, his own life.

He concedes, his staff worships him. Those who don't worship him need him. How would they manage all that costly audio-visual equipment without him? He's built a fine library, he has implemented methods of pedagogy that surpass the public school system, if he must say so himself. Under his leadership they have moved into the new addition, at a cost of hundreds of thousands of dollars–talk about action! He hires and fires. He brings experts and inspirers, like Buzz Friedkin from the Center for Vital Jewish Values in New York, to provide a conviction he cannot dispense himself. Among his American colleagues he is becoming a legend. Well, he's starting to be known. One day he may be their first Canadian president.

So? *So?*

Anyway, who wants to be a man of action? He had enough action once in his life. He's seen politics, what it does to people, how they try to make things happen and things get happened to them instead. If some still want to engage, good, let them, but not Oskar. He found a way out, he got out cleanly, he's an educator, a noble calling, especially a teacher in Israel. ("Even the idle chatter of the students of the sages deserves close study.") So why does he still feel he ought to *do* something?

A man may be typified by what he is not, as well as by what he is. Oskar is the Man of Inaction.

A Saturday morning. *Shaharit b'Shabbat.* The legions of pre-confirmation–grades seven, eight, and nine–are herded into the Children's Chapel. Bonnie Bell, whose squat, muscular body has always appealed to Oskar, plays the organ as they enter; her thick fingers glide surprisingly over the keys. Off in a corner sits Jimmy's ark. During the first years here in the new addition it served, over Oskar's dead body, until the last touches of the architect's design for the Children's Chapel were in place. Now a proper traditional ark of the covenant faces the young congregation. It houses several Torah scrolls, slightly downsized from the adult version for this congregation. Irma Dean faces them too. She is their department head. She is a wife and mother and part-time cub scout leader, in addition to her duties here. She has an English accent. She must have been an air-raid warden during the Blitz. She starts to intone everyone's favourite prayer, "Grant us peace, Thy most precious gift, O Thou eternal source of peace." They adore this prayer because it asks for something they all understand, and desire deeply. For those who find prayer a little strange, and God a little distant – or a lot – it associates Him with so plausible a need that they can pray for the result without worrying too much about the source.

Oskar is at the back, as usual; pacing, as usual. All seems fine on this opening day of a new school year. He knows this is the sure sign something is wrong. He scans the room. His eyes pass across the front, along the sides, over rows of students and teachers. *Alles in Ordnung.* He relaxes slightly. He starts to join in the Prayer for Peace. Then it hits him, right between his beady eyes, which swing back to Irma, behind her, above–

He bursts from the chapel, along the hall, past the neat bulletin boards with multicoloured construction paper displays about tree-planting in Israel and the youth group hayride in two weeks. With a desperate lurch he negotiates the fire door between the new addition and the old building. He is alone on the landing. He hurtles into the office, his ancient one. He seizes the microphone for the up-to-date public address system, which was installed during the last phase of construction. Few know that, in an emergency, he can control it from here, without having to battle through the secretaries in the main office. He squawks into it, to the one man who can rescue him from this travesty. "Mr Oates, Mr Oates," he implores. "Report immediately to the Children's Chapel. The Eternal Light has gone out!"

At this moment he knows he must act. He makes a decision. He is going to leave this place, like Abraham Our Father, who at God's command left his homeland, his birthplace, his father's house, so that his real life could begin. He plans his escape with great care and German thoroughness.

Plan One. Tocchet is the key. The soulful sociologist has travelled widely since their times working together (Oskar indulges in the fantasy of) on his study of the beleaguered rich in Forest Hill. The furor following publication was even fiercer than Tocchet predicted: news reports, denunciations, sermons – Rabbi Rosen delivered a scorcher. Now Tocchet is back. He landed on his little feet at Beaverbrook University. It barely exists – it is mainly a construction site on an estate overlooking one of Toronto's ravines – but its future is glorious. The post-war babies are blooming into young adulthood; they want higher education, and no politician dares deny them. The provincial government has guaranteed Toronto another university; it will be the Harvard of the north, or Oxford on the Humber. It has few students and faculty so far; it will be daring and innovative; it will chart new ways in contemporary scholarship. Why not, thinks Oskar, why not *me*? A professor at last. It would be *better* than the University of Toronto, because Hermann already has the U of T. Oskar would be a late comer there. But he could become the Hermann of Beaverbrook, with Tocchet's aid. After a life perfectly ill-timed, he has a sneaking suspicion: his hour has struck.

Tocchet, he read in the paper, was the first faculty member appointed to Beaverbrook. His job is to sit in an office and think about the ideal university. Only Tocchet would have the chutzpah. "I'm off to work, dear," he says each morning to the unprepossessing wife Oskar met on Christmas Day, then puts on his thinking cap and drives to the office. For months Oskar broods on this leap into action, then, surprising himself, he unearths a small stash of entirely personal stationery; nowhere does it say Pillar of Fire. It merely records his name and MA. He feeds a sheet into the typewriter – why does he feel he is photographing secret files, why does he expect the security police to break through his office door? – and composes a simple, heartfelt note of congratulation to Tocchet. On the twenty-fourth attempt, he declares victory. He carefully folds, seals, and stamps the envelope.

Then he uncrates his MA thesis. He has not inspected it since the day he gave it into the unsympathetic care of a proconsular American professor in the history department who eventually agreed to accept it in fulfilment of degree requirements. "I have work of my own to get on with," the man said when he finally returned Oskar's call and gave him the good news. My God, thinks Oskar, did I write all this? It is a monster; he is impressed. He starts to read. He finds it tedious. He ploughs on, expecting to be drawn in by a combination of sweep and insight. It never happens, and he returns his opus to its resting place. He is a pedagogue, not a scholar. He will play from his strengths.

He tears open the sealed envelope and starts over. This time he inserts an artful aside about his teaching expertise and alludes to a willingness to try something new at this late point in his career. On the seventieth try he surrenders. He retypes the result of his original drafts and sends it off, convinced he has destroyed this opportunity while creating it.

The phone rings, it seems, instantly. Tocchet! What a delight, thanks for the good wishes, could Oskar possibly find time to drop over and see their little operation. And by the way, Harry Hall would enjoy meeting him over lunch. All right? Thanks.

Tocchet, not for the first time, has read his tortured thoughts. Harry Hall, it was recently announced, is the new president of Beaverbrook University.

Tocchet is actually doing it. He comes in view as Oskar peers around the office door. Tocchet sits behind a desk that dwarfs him: tilted back in his chair, chin on his hands, eyes scanning the ceiling and doubtless cosmic tracts beyond as he thinks about the ideal university! Oskar could watch the spectacle of Tocchet in thought for hours. He hauls the rest of his body into the office, along with a slide projector and carousel – the very latest in audio-visual–and a sampling of slides coincidentally illustrating Oskar's insights into the history of Canadian Jews as a proto-typical ethnic community. He happens to have these with him. "You can leave them on the desk," says Tocchet, rising with no notable effect on his height and leading the way to the Promised Lunch.

They cruise through the corridors of the only usable building at Beaverbrook, students scattered about. Oskar feels like a bumper car; Tocchet is the wild mouse–he skitters from side to side, group to group, approaching them like a fairy godmother, drawing their attention down and whispering puckishly, "Why don't you lean against the wall and see if there's anything holding it up?" This could be mine, thinks Oskar. They are my students, I am their professor. No more meetings with department heads; no shepherding the primary grades into music; no ludicrous announcements over the PA; no frantic efforts to rekindle the Eternal Light. He has been granted a vision of heaven. Tocchet ushers him into the president's office.

Harry Hall is hearty, though more red-faced than Oskar considers healthy. Cultural differentia, he supposes. He meets so few real Canadians, the kind that whip off to ski slopes or the hockey rink; Hall probably tobogganed into work moments ago. The president pours red wine, like his complexion, and quickly raises his glass. Everything depends, Oskar now feels, on the subject of conversation. He has prepared a number of topics, and prepped himself, but with a deep futility. What can he and Harry Hall have in common? They were flung into this situation from opposite corners of the universe. If only, Oskar thinks, *I* could choose the subject, like a contestant on a television show. I would select Bible tales for children, or Jewish history at grade six level, or sex in the Talmud. But it is too late, it is hopeless, Harry Hall has opened the discussion, the trap is sprung, Oskar is dropping to his doom, the noose tightens, for the subject is–Jewish Youth!

Jewish Youth! The president of Beaverbrook wants to discuss Jewish Youth. Instead of relief, instead of salvation, Oskar feels patronized! Why not bagels? Why not Yiddish humour? But this is foolish, it is excess sensitivity. Harry Hall has his reasons. This boozy source of Oskar's highest hopes made the sole serious foray of his academic career, it turns out, with a thesis on the Jewish youth movement, for which he received a doctorate in psychology, subsequent to which he never darkened a classroom doorway, but leapfrogged from one administrative plum to the next.

Fate breaks down and grins a crabby grin. Oskar sits across from a man with power to reshape his life into the stuff of dreams, and the man chooses a subject about which Oskar knows merely everything! He rummages furiously, he drags it all out, he smiles at his most manic; he is happy. It is a boring conversation; he doesn't care. The president of Beaverbrook seems at ease only with the trite and shopworn: the time of the youth movement, he says over salad, is past; a utopian institution on its way to extinction under the pressures of *Realpolitik* and a new generation lacking the idealism of its parents, blah blah blah blah. Oskar loves every trivial syllable. He applauds Harry Hall's dreary observations and contributes his own. He barely notices Tocchet.

But Harry Hall does. He glances frequently toward Tocchet, whose attention is diverted outside the room, toward the swirls of dust created by steam shovels, dump trucks, earth movers, and Italian day labourers Oskar can see through the window. Tocchet's distraction seems to distract Hall, then disturb and then distress him. A tension is growing between the two men that has nothing to do with Oskar. Naturally, he feels responsible for it. "What are they building out there?" he asks fatefully.

"A haven for excellence," says Harry Hall, in the same breath as Tocchet spits, "A degree factory." Pleasant conversation is concluded. "We have an obligation to deal with the university-age population of this society," barks Hall. Oskar looks at him; he hears the voice of a liar. He thinks Hall hears the same voice. "I am here, and so are the rest of us," says Tocchet, "on your promise that we were joining the pursuit of excellence."

"You are," says Hall – to Oskar, since Tocchet has whirled and faced the dust clouds again. Tocchet has been through this before, they both have; it feels like an eternal spat, something that began one day over a tiny thing and has expanded since till it is a maze neither of them can or wants to exit from. Oskar knows the signs. He knows it is folly to speak, it is folly to merely be present, caught between them. Perhaps Tocchet even brought him in a vain attempt to bridge what divides them. So he speaks again: "Faced with a difficult choice between two alternatives, I have always felt it is best whenever possible to choose both." They regard him with equal contempt – he has brought them momentarily together – then they turn from him and each other like two men pacing off a duel. Oskar's heart sinks like a stone. He feels like he just woke up in a married couple's bedroom. Have these people no sense of privacy?

Tocchet gazes at the construction crews and breathes heavily. Harry Hall speaks. Not *speaks*, precisely. He goes a brighter red, then explodes. "I may be a liar and I may be a bastard. I may be everything you people say I am." Oskar's heart sickens at his inclusion with Tocchet, just as it would have leapt to it moments ago. "But I'm here like those buildings are here," Hall goes on, wheezing like a calliope and spinning his arms like a windmill, "and anyone who doesn't like it can get out!"

They step across the planks that cover the mud and around the poured foundations toward Oskar's Dodge. "He used to be a teetotaller," says Tocchet. "He was once director of the Boy Scouts of Canada. He was an international eagle scout. Now he's drunk halfway through lunch, he's boffing the wife of the chairman of his board of trustees, he's climbing out the back window while the sonofabitch himself comes in the door."

"How did he change from an eagle scout to a fornicator?" says Oskar. This might be worth knowing. It is the kind of information his own curriculum doesn't cover.

Tocchet shrugs his little shoulders, his arms rise and fall like stunted wings. "It had to be a transformative event," he says, "a hideous parody of the Maslovian Peak Experience." And suddenly Tocchet is full of inquisitive compassion for horrible Harry Hall; he is the Tocchet Oskar has always adored, unaware the spirit of an angry Hebrew prophet also stirred in that little frame. "He told me once," Tocchet continues, looking like the chase has started, as if he is sniffing the wind, "that they took him on a hunting trip to a lodge up north owned by one of their companies."

"They?" says Oskar.

"The trustees," says Tocchet. "That's where the real university is. The classrooms, the students, and faculty are a sideshow." Oskar shudders; there are lessons a teacher doesn't want to learn. Tocchet persists, hot on the trail of something. He will track it and analyse the hell out of it. "They drank a lot, they went hunting and bagged a moose. Then they made jokes about fucking it." Oskar blinks. "The moose?" he says. Tocchet nods. "I don't know if they actually did. I suppose not. What do you think?" Oskar shrugs too. Tocchet carries on. He is wrapped up. He is waving his arms much the way Harry Hall did moments before. "It really seemed to shake Harry. He went on and on about it. He kept bringing it up when we were supposed to be doing course studies or enrolment projections. It sounded like an initiation. They made him part of it. Part of them." Tocchet winds down. His arms slow gradually, then stop. He looks bereft, he has lost a friend; humanity has lost a potential benefactor. RIP the real Harry Hall. Oskar almost lays a hand on the little decelerating forearm. "I won't be here much longer," Tocchet finishes. "I don't know if I should try to bring him down first or just go. Thanks for coming over, Oskar. You're lucky, you know." Oskar stares. "To be where you are," says Tocchet, "in an institution that makes sense. Instead of one of these grandiose, deformed paeans to conformity and power." He starts to walk away; he is passing into the distance like a squirrel crossing the lawn. He is gone.

Oskar looks at the mess of foundations, half-walls, and excavations. He pictures a Harry Hall Hall here one day. On its handsome façade is sculpted a quotation from the wise words of Beaverbrook's first president. It says, "I may be a liar and a bastard; I may be everything you people say I am – but I'm here like these buildings are here, and anyone who doesn't like it can Get Out."

His eye catches a line of contruction workers filing toward the parking lot. A canteen truck toots its horn. They are silhouetted against the sky. They squint in Oskar's direction, into the sun behind him. He wonders what they make of him and this place. He wonders if they were watching the dialogue between him and Tocchet, and what they thought about the gesticulating mental rotor Tocchet looked like. They seem to be scratching their heads under their hard hats.

What are they thinking? Oskar wonders. And where did they come from? He never notices people like this; not even when they were right under his smashed nose for four and a half years building the new addition to the P of F religious school. All that time, he never saw them watching, or wondered what they were thinking. Maybe because they were always *doing* something. They were always *making* something.

He has a frightening thought: Maybe they are there all the time, these doers and makers, watching and thinking, and Oskar simply fails to register them! They could be anywhere, not just on the street: in his office, in his bathroom! From now on and for months, when he lurches up and down Bathurst, or goes to a movie, or the Power Supermarket on Eglinton, or climbs on a bus, he checks to see if "they" are there. And often they are! Heavy women with kerchiefs and bundles; men with plaid shirts and scuffed work shoes. But the amazing thing is, unless he remembers to look, they stay invisible. If he does not engage a special effort, like an extra gear on a car, he will finish the bus ride unaware he has seen and been seen by them. Or do they not register him just as he doesn't see them? Is this what God is like,

He who sees but is not seen? Is this what Hermann, on his latest kick of Godtalk, calls the Ineffable? Why does Oskar always get so far and never farther in his search for the Absolute? Why does it always happen at moments like his post-Hall depression, when he is completely unprepared to continue the quest, and then vanish at times like Yom Kippur when he is? Right now he does not want to pursue the Godhead. He has something else on his plate. He still has not *done* anything. He still has to Get Out.

But how? Ecape to Beaverbrook is a nonstarter; his decisive act misfired. Plan Two. A rest is as good as a change. He will take a sabbatical.

A man who never observed the Sabbath goes on sabbatical. In his youth, the two eligible Sabbaths, Saturday and Sunday, meant a tram ride to the amusement parks outside town, a row on the Muggelsee or Wannsee, or a wander through the woods. As he aged, like a wine, he advanced cautiously toward beer gardens and dance halls. Just as he was ready to celebrate the transition from celibate Nature Sabbaths to riotous ones, the Reichstag went up in smoke, along with his plans for a lusty adolescence.

In later life, at the Pillar of Fire, *shabbat* means severe anxiety: classrooms must be ready, blackboards clean, student lists up-to-date, teachers are calling in sick, bell schedules are complex, there could be a surprise visit from the rabbi, or the unforeseen ("Mr Oates, Mr Oates – "). Surely this is not what the Creator had in mind.

Oskar on the other hand was not made for rest. The thought of a holiday in the sun fills him with dread. You go to a steamy island, you undress, you lie down – then what? Go hard as a board, probably. He prefers a basic Teutonic vacation: tight schedule, arduous sightseeing, constant movement, in Switzerland, if possible, a country like a clock. So where does he go for his sabbatical?

He rides the bus in from Kennedy. At Port Authority he changes for the subway. The trek from bus to subway is long and sub-terranean. "You don't have to be Jewish," crow the ads along the passage, "to love Levy's Rye Bread." Do Jews run this country? Do they think they run it? Would the Jews of Toronto be so brazen, or those of Berlin? He has a vestigial reaction: he cringes. Yet none of the glassy-eyed pedestrians seem offended. This is the New World in a way Canada dares not be.

On the filth-caked platform, waiting for the train, he sees a man wearing a sandwich board, gazing intensely at a man wearing a different sandwich board, who is looking closely at Oskar. The train comes.

Opposite him sits a man with two hats on his head, one inside the other. No one asks why. No one but Oskar seems to notice. At 72nd and Broadway he ascends. He looks down Broadway, then up it. A convertible comes toward him; it is driven by a gorilla. No one looks except Oskar. The gorilla turns left onto 72nd. Oskar goes in the same direction. He carries a valise. The rest of his luggage has, with typical foresight, been shipped in advance to his new temporary residence.

How do they not look? he wonders as he totters down the street, thrown out of his usual disequilibrium by the weight in his hand. There must be a secret. Clearly those sights pass through their field of vision – the hats, the gorilla in the convertible – yet they don't gawk. Do they just not think about it, or do they think . . . *very quickly*? Aha! "Some guy delivering a couple of hats – easier than holding one in each hand – this way he can read the paper!" And, "Probably shooting a commercial, must be a camera somewhere." So there is a rule to their behaviour: Only one look. And a principle: There is an explanation for every oddity. And a purpose to the code: Never look foolish, always be "in on it." Oskar even knows the name of this code: street smarts! He breathes comfortably. He is acclimatizing.

A thought comes to him like a pardon from the governor. In this place a man could be free. He could do anything. Why? Because he knows almost no one and no one knows him. The city is so vast, it is like a licence. Whatever you do, you will not be seen and reported. This is not the only source of freedom here. It is also because no one looks. They pass over the bizarre. They take in everything but they don't stare. It is the badge of their sophistication and a shield for every deviation and outburst. Here he is, the Master of the Deviant Outburst. Could he be . . . home?

He lurches past a pizzeria. Standing at the counter is an extraordinary black woman. She could be an African princess. Her hair is streaked and tawny, her lips full and red. A leopard-skin top trusses her breasts and thrusts them out. Her behind is jacked high by soaring pointed heels. She balances a slice of pizza in her long curving fingernails and directs its flapping tip toward her mouth. Oskar freezes in mid-lunge. Her eyes flicker toward the window, past Oskar's stare, into the traffic beyond. Then they stop, her eyes stop, they slide back along their route, they halt slowly, calmly. What are they looking at? Him! Her face nearly shatters with delight. It is a moment arrested in time. She raises a finger, indicating "Just a minute." ("Just a minute, *honey*," he hears in his imagination.) She wolfs her slice, wipes her mouth with a paper napkin, steps in a businesslike way to the door, and takes his arm.

"Where to?" she says.

"I don't know," he says. "Where are you going?"

"Home," she shrugs pleasantly, and steers him down the street. He goes along like a hovercraft, ungainly but afloat. They stroll a block or two – but who's counting? – up the steps of a run-down brownstone, into her apartment, she deposits him on the couch and excuses herself.

Now, he keeps thinking, now I'll tell her. Tell her what? That he doesn't intend to go through with it. With what? What it? He isn't even sure what she thinks he signed up for. That's the only problem. No one here is looking. They wouldn't condemn him if they were. He watches, fascinated, to see what he will do. This feels like the beginning of a new life. Why rush it?

It's a matter of pride. He doesn't want to fumble, to look ill-informed, not just in her eyes but in his own. He apologizes for taking her time, with deep respect, because he knows she is working to make a living, an honest living, he adds, but he just got to town and is preoccupied with finding his hotel and con-firming the arrival of his luggage, which he sent ahead with precise instructions, aside from the small suitcase she has prob-ably noticed, but he is confident they will meet again, when he definitely will not waste her time, but will swiftly conclude any business they have together, because he certainly won't be so distracted (as if the fifty-five-minute trip from Toronto to New York has blasted him with jet-lag) and they do seem to live in the same neighbourhood.

She shrugs again. He finds it less charming, but still a thrill. He trundles downstairs, manoeuvring the leather valise with the stylish straps that the staff gave him for the sabbatical. It is true, he mutters to himself, they can do "it" again, because running into each other seems likely, probably inevitable, here in their part of town. All he has to do is lunge by the pizzeria from time to time. (Of course months will pass, the year will pass, he won't see her again.)

He is back on the street now, exactly as experienced as he was twenty minutes ago. He came here to do something. This was a hell of a beginning.

The Parkside is an apartment hotel almost but not quite over-looking Central Park. The husband of the chairman of the library committee of Parents' Council has a cousin who knows the man-ager who said, Sure, just for you there's a special rate. They have assigned him a corner suite with a sitting room and a view onto 72nd. His other window looks into the "court," a square chute in the centre of the building into which he must extend his neck, then swivel his face upward to find out whether it is sunny or raining. Squinting out the side of his front window, he thinks he spies a sliver of the big park itself. Why not? he thinks. He has come for spontaneity and adventure. He doesn't even unpack.

He descends to the street, finds the park, and plunges in. He feels like Livingstone. He winds stealthily through, but it is an uneventful crossing. No muggers, many relaxed blacks, girls in school uniforms, businessmen holding briefcases, nuns with ice skates. At length he hears the rush of traffic again, like the source of the Nile. He quickens his pace, breaks through and lo, on the other side, visible beyond the taxis and busses, goal of his journey, the Center for Vital Jewish Values. He gazes at it: this may be the least imposing building he has ever seen. Somewhere inside is Buzz, the true reason he travelled here on his sabbatical. Buzz, as in Buzz Sawyer, the comic-strip hero.

Is Buzz another brother? Probably. Not an evil brother like those who vex Oskar's career. Nor an ideal brother, like Tocchet. Buzz has too much gusto for the ideal. He is Oskar's American brother.

The first time Oskar met Buzz he was smitten. Such manly confidence, thought Oskar. This man would settle coolly into any setting. Like a lone cowboy he rides into town and steps through the saloon doors. The cardsharps and barmaids register him casually; they are impressed. Like the people on the subway, they take one look, then make room for him at the bar. Or in the sleaziest pool hall on the waterfront. He offhandedly selects a cue through the beery haze. Or in an elegant men's club, where sophistication means not doubting for an instant you possess the style required. This is a man of the world, thought Oskar. He could go anywhere and receive respect. And a rabbi too?

But such an *American* rabbi. A Jewish Joe Palooka. Oskar first saw him lecturing excitedly to kids and leaders at a youth conclave in Kunkletown, Pennsylvania. Buzz wound them round his finger: outgoing, lollygagging, making them laugh in fits at him and themselves; lanky and athletic though he never actually played any games Oskar knew of, just a Gary Cooper reticence that said, I could if I would; along with a fine intellect in the patented American vein. Nothing roundabout in his thinking, no twists and dips of the dialectic—though Hermann too likes this young theologian cum stand-up comic. Buzz serves his ideas straight, convictions from the shoulder, plain as the Jewish nose on his American face. He is articulate too—outspoken, the Americans would say—everything said clear and loud, just the way he means it.

And spirit! Religious conviction that comes at you like a tank. It is all in the way Buzz says "God." GAWD, he pronounces it, like a Yankee, drawled long and loud as though he is tasting it in his mouth and enjoying the result. There is no hush or whisper when Buzz speaks that name, Gawd, none of the paraphernalia of reverence. Gawd is a divinity who lives free and proud on the wide-open spaces of the American frontier, where a man has to shout to be heard and wouldn't voice his mind any other way. The God of Buzz is like everything else Oskar admires about Americans, lacking centuries of European, and before that Asian or Middle Eastern, subtlety and complexity. Just state your business, say the Americans. All right, then, GAWD. God, you say? God it is.

So different from Canadians. An American you've never met tells you his whole life story in ten minutes while you're waiting for a bus. Canadians aren't as relaxed and upfront as Americans, though they aren't as defensive and uptight as Europeans. What *are* Canadians? It is much easier to say what they are not.

Oskar brings Buzz to Toronto often, the way Canadians in those years go to the States and return with portable radios, alligator shoes, and rock cornish hens from Victor Borge's farm in Connecticut – things not readily available in Canada. Buzz comes and says GAWD. The staff, or the kids, or the congregation –whomever he is addressing–recoil. The word lies in their midst like a stink bomb Buzz has smuggled through Customs. ("What is the purpose of your visit?" "I have come to bring to the complacent members of the Pillar of Fire Religious School the awesome presence of GAWD." "And what will be the length of your visit?" "Forty-eight hours.") Long after he has left, and left *it* behind among them, they circle it, fascinated; a few touch it, imagine what it would be like to have this . . . thing a part of your life. Oskar feels indifferent to GAWD himself, but the process, the disturbance, delights him. He feels: This is education!

Buzz likes Oskar back. How does Oskar know? There's an

old American trick – Buzz says so. "Oskar, I like you." It pleases
Oskar. Buzz reminds him of those all-around kids from his childhood in Berlin. Good at carpentry, built his own crystal radio
set and knows how it works, outstanding in sports, attractive
girlfriend with whom he has a solid, mature relationship, parents
admired by other kids, knows what he is going to do with his
life when he grows up. Oskar always marvelled when one of
"them" liked him. He felt blessed, but stayed insecure. They
might withdraw their affection as capriciously as they bestowed
it. It never occurred to him that they got something back from
him. Like your older brother, whom you always needed, but
who never seemed to need you. Like Franz.

So when Buzz said, "Oskar, my friend, come spend your
sabbatical in New York," Oskar thought, Where else?

And after the incident of the Eternal Light, he thought, like
Hillel the Elder, "If not now, when?"

Time speeds up. This is the nature of Getting Away. Events
compact, they tumble into one another and pile up with no
spaces between. When it is over and you go home, you are
amazed. So little has changed in the place you left; how did all
that happen?

"Take some courses," says Buzz when Oskar wonders what
he'll do besides meet Buzz frequently to discuss their Customs
and Folkways syllabus. It's fine to be on a jailbreak from his
horrible life in Toronto, but what about the many days and
months that must pass before he can return happily to it? "On
my sabbatical?" moans Oskar. Those that can, do; those that
can't, teach. When they can't teach – they take courses?

He registers for Sociology of Religion in the graduate faculty
at Columbia. I follow in the steps of Tocchet, thinks Oskar, and
relishes the exchange of views they will have next time they meet.
It's true, this is still religion, but it's religion as an object of study,
not commitment. He'll stand back from it, he feels better already.
This must be why the kids love Comparative Religion at the Pill
on the Hill, the only course on his curriculum for which they are

not expected to believe anything; instead they look at what others believe – Buddhists, Jains, Hindus, Sikhs. It's interesting – that's all, full stop! Don't serve – observe! Oskar doesn't really approve; he still thinks a proper human life is committed. But this distance from commitment is such a . . . *relief*, like when you stop banging your head on a wall. He should have tried it long ago. They don't study religion this way in Toronto. The university there has faculties of theology attached, like adult religious schools for *goyim*, like the *yeshiva*s of the Pale. Ah, Canada: a little of these, a little of those, never anything its own. But this is different – New York is his kind of town.

Columbia, he thinks, the great world of secular learning. He has reached its shores. The landfall from which Buber's brilliant epithet deflected him, the forbidden realm entered by Hermann the viper even as he piously proclaimed his loyalty to Buberian principles. Buber himself didn't spend his life in the religious school of his local *shul*; he was a *Herr Professor* too! Of religion! Oskar recalls Buber's sweet phrase – In the end, my son, Moses was probably a very parochial man – he feels guilt still, it flooded his heart, it was so good to feel that deeply. He forgives Buber, he carries on, he registers at Columbia.

He sits in a seminar and studies the students. These are serious folk, much his junior but scholars. None know the truth about Oskar, that in his real, ugh, life, he is principal of a suburban Saturday school. They accept him as a colleague in the scientific study of religious belief. He thrives on their fraternity. Enter the professor. He is dry and brittle, as though he has not been properly watered and might flake away. The seminar is called the Religious Sociology of Everyday Life. It sounds down-to-earth. It reminds Oskar of the Back to Reality session they do for the kids at the end of JYGGL camp, to help them make the harsh transition from services in the woods to daily life in dreary Erie or T.O.

In class he meets Sweet Eustache. He rivets on her, as he used to fix on the girls in youth meetings when he was young. She is gaunt; he's never seen such emaciation. She could be a fashion model, she could be on the cover of *Vogue*. Other men must covet her, he can tell. She is ideal for Oskar, because she attracts him but does not, as the Americans say, turn him on. In her way, she is as ghastly a sight as he. They could be fellow prisoners in a death camp, about to expire on the day U.S. troops arrive to liberate them. He feels they are soul mates, but there is nothing earthly about her, no facet that corresponds to his own crude, corporeal self – the smashed nose or beady eyes. She is like a being from one of Wetherford's other dimensions. They chat, they become friends. She is so polite, sensitive, refined, demure, un-Jewish. Every morning and night he whacks off to the thought of her frail body. One day she invites him to dinner.

She lives in a cluttered residence on a tiny street in the Village. It is a home for women run by the Southern Baptist Mission Society. He does not associate New York with places like this; it belongs on a dusty path strewn with magnolias, whatever they are, in the Deep South. The home exists, he supposes, to maintain the virtue of southern women; the missionaries are probably all expired; their widows retire here and guard the gate against men who would assault the chastity of Sweet and women like her – if there are any. She welcomes him to her tiny apartment. He is fascinated. He has pictured her in many ways, but never eating.

She serves a Bay Salad. He has seen these at Murray's restaurant in Toronto, eaten by small grey ladies who recall Toronto in the days before people with foreign accents lived there. The ladies pick at little mounds of egg, tuna, and cottage cheese, such as Sweet has prepared for him. She says she is a minister's daughter. She grew up in Connecticut, not far from here. "Why are you studying religion?" he asks. She shrugs, like a skeleton dancing on a string in the closet. "The same as everybody else," she says. He doesn't understand, he is not like everybody else. "We grew up religious," she explains, "most of us are the children of clergy. We don't believe like our parents, but we miss the singing and the prayers, the church dinners and picnics. I guess it's our way of staying connected even when we've lost our faith. It may sound weak," she ends feebly. Oskar is bitter. They are not hard-nosed scholars, they are fearful people in flight from their pasts, but too scared to make the break. Tepid refugees, just like Oskar. He excuses himself and goes to the bathroom of the tiny apartment; he wants to ravish her, now that his other fantasies have dissolved. He leans against the medicine cabinet above the toilet and banks his stream off the sides of the bowl so as not to embarrass them. A familiar voice trumpets from beyond the bathroom door. "Shoes!"

He hears her rise. "I knew it!" exults the voice. "I knew I'd find him here one day, whoever he is. Look – his shoes on your doorstep. And him still in your bed. Come out, you – " Oskar steps from the bathroom nearly into the arms of one balding, brittle professor of sociology of religion, who is glaring into the bedroom, which must be just off the bathroom. His instructor whirls. "You're not naked!" he shrieks. "You're not in bed! You're in my class!"

Not much later, Oskar exits the subway at Broadway and 79th. He missed his stop on the way home. Maybe he doesn't want to go back to the Parkside. The restaurant at the corner looks drab and hostile. Good. He has a terrible cup of tea at the counter. "Hey," hails a voice behind him. It is Gerald from the seminar, a massive man. Gerald kindly orders Oskar into his booth, like a priest asking the next penitent to enter the confessional. Gerald is finishing a meal, one of several, to judge by the stacks of plates, cutlery, and saucers pushed to the side of the tabletop.

"Your trouble," says Gerald during the long pleasant night that follows, "is you think a university is where people pursue knowledge." "Don't they?" peeps Oskar. Gerald shakes his shaggy head. "All suffering is caused by ignorance," he says. "All right," says Oskar, "what *do* they pursue?"

"Each other," says Gerald. "They pursue each other. The drippy, sex-starved men with tenure who teach; the gorgeous, brain-starved women taking notes. They come together, Oskar, in profound mutual need. You and me are just spectators."

"Even in the department of religion?" says Oskar.

"Especially in religion," says Gerald. "Religion drives people wild."

This makes sense to Oskar. It is almost . . . sociology! He revives. He switches to his other track as Gerald proceeds outside. She has a body, scraggy perhaps, but all her life that body is what others have responded to. Sociologically speaking, she *is* a body. *Herr* Columbia *Professor* has probably always been a brain, as the kids at home say. No pretty girl, no cheerleader or prom queen, ever liked him. She gets the brain she always wanted, and he gets her beautiful body. What an excellent arrangement. It's like a proof for the existence of God – the one where you find a watch on a desert island and assume a watchmaker must have been there.

Oskar looks gratefully on Gerald and the pile of plates still rising. He feels he has just attended his first real class on the sociology of religion. "It was such a disappointment," he muses, "when she said they're all in religion because they miss the church choir. It's nice to talk to a real intellectual. How did *you* get here?" Gerald shifts his torso modestly and waves to the counterman; he wants another meal. "I was a Jesuit for seventeen years," says Gerald, "then I quit. I wrote for TV and worked in advertising. But I knew I'd have to get back to it somehow, someday."

Oskar is restless. His sabbatical is passing. He has a mission. He is here to do something, so he moves. He leaves Columbia and goes to Union.

Union Seminary is just up the street from Columbia, but worlds away. He likes it. They are so earnest, these young Protestants. They sit in the oak library, aisles of milk-fed blond kids, like rows of Iowa corn. They hunch over their RSVs, the authorized Wasp version of the Old Testament, as they call our *Tanach*, coloured pencils in hand, underlining the "sources" of Genesis, decoded long before even Oskar was young by bloodless German exegetes: the E, J, and P codes, and the tireless Deuteronomist (D) with his tell-tale cadences. Oskar is touched by these children of mid-America, switching colours from word to word, not just verse to verse, as though they are dealing with an original text instead of a distant English translation. It is like going on an archeological dig for remnants of the Exodus in the Hollywood lot where De Mille filmed *The Ten Commandments.*

"I never knew what Jesus meant," says Ellie Burns to Oskar, "till I lived in the slums of Amsterdam after I graduated from Vassar." Her ringlets jostle like little bells. She could be Lorrie in *Oklahoma!* "Don't throw bouquets at me, la la." In the library others like her, kids from a Broadway chorus, shush them politely. They will be part of their difficult times. "The Church has got to get where the action is," they say. They publish a weekly newsletter called *What's Happening, Man?* It tells you all the protests and political meetings in Manhattan. They remind Oskar of us, his Great Class, throwing ourselves into the clothing blitz in confirmation year, wedding our Jewishness to our exploding adolescent solidarity with humankind.

Funny, Oskar never thinks of Bible as *Tanach* – such a traditional Hebrew term – except at Union. Here he is the Union Jew, a modern *Hofjude.* He always liked those Court Jews, he thinks he'd have made a good one because he'd have killed for the access, the chance to eavesdrop on lives of real power, even share a little himself. Sometimes in the packed lectures on New Testament theology, the lecturer suddenly stops and queries Oskar, "What is the Jewish point of view?" Oskar rarely knows, but he answers anyway; it would be churlish to refuse. He stuffs an Israeli newspaper in his jacket pocket when he lurches through the stony corridors of Union. He buys the papers at a kiosk on Broadway at 96th. He can't read them very well, and it would take the rest of the week to slave through the *shabbat* edition of *Ha'aretz*, but he lets a Hebrew headline peek from his pocket like a periscope so they will whisper as he passes: Can you believe it? He reads the news in *Hebrew!* He feels like the Connecticut Yankee who startled the locals in King Arthur's court by making a bicycle and a firecracker for them.

He is starting to change from passive to active, he can feel it happening, like Gregor Samsa the morning he awoke and knew he was becoming an insect. Perhaps it's because he is here like an explorer, a Jew among Others, discovering things. Compared to old Oskar, he is a dervish of decision. He registers for the

Jeremiah seminar at Union. He can picture it without seeing it. When he gets there, it is like walking into the picture: around him are the buds of Protestant biblical scholarship, inheritors of biblical criticism as practised to insipid perfection by Wellhausen, Albright, Noth – humourless, *goyish* footnoters. Oskar fits into the seminar like a pickle in a meringue. They have prepared their chapter, checked their concordances, pored through Gesenius's Biblical Grammar – a single example and a hundred exceptions for every rule. They read aloud their lifeless translations. Their haggard professor, the fabled Munch, peers over his glasses. He looks like John Calvin. No – he looks like Yahweh, the God of the Old Testament, as they call Him in their unfamiliar way. Munch is a God of Justice but not Mercy, approving and disapproving their dreary renderings of Yirmiahu's feverish words. This professor is just like Him on Rosh Hashanah, the Day of Judgement, deciding who to inscribe in the Book of Life for another year and who to consign to the pit, and *how*. Who by fire and who by water, who by sword and who by beast, who by hunger and who by thirst, who by earthquake and who by plague, who by strangling and who by stoning, who shall rest and who shall wander, who shall have peace and who shall be troubled, who debased and who exalted . . .

At which point Munch calls on Oskar, as these majestic figures in his life usually do. Oskar stumbles through a spontaneous English rendering of the chapter, in his scratchy accent. The God of Justice is outraged. "You have not prepared!" he thunders. "I have," whines Oskar, feeling maybe ten years old. "I have too, just because I don't write it out like the rest of you as if it's Latin!" Munch concentrates his formidable brow. "You mean," he intones, wonder in his voice, looking fit to receive a revelation, which may not be beyond him, "you mean *you* read Hebrew the way *I* read German?" The seminar draws a stunned breath: this one reads *Hebrew* the way we read German! Daniel has escaped the lions, he did it again.

Oskar is not singled out alone at Union. The professors also pause in mid-lecture to solicit Arthur the black, Jan the feminist, and former Father Gerald the Jesuit – who has also been drawn to this place – to speak for their respective minorities. Union exists inside those brotherhood songs the grade threes sing: "We'll soon be one world / One world / Nations great and small / We'll treat each one like a brother by protecting one another / We'll be all for one and one for all."

He makes Union his new home. Afternoons he sits in the basement coffee shop – it's how he pictures a prayer cell in a monastery – surrounded by the coffee and soft-drink machines. He nurses a chicken noodle soup in a plastic cup, like a drunk on the Bowery. He enjoys it here because the girls pass by. They've taken to him, you can tell. They treat him as a likeable old Jewish man. Till the day, the one that always comes.

"Oskar, Oskar," chirps Karen McCarthy from South Dakota, entering his cell. She comes direct from the office of the newly arrived visiting professor of interfaith theology. "He's a Jew, Oskar, like you. From Canada. You're from Canada, aren't you? Do you know him? You won't believe what he told me. It was wonderful!" She pauses to get the right voice for telling this, she is like an actress waiting for her stage light to come on before she delivers her speech.

Oskar's stomach makes the customary drop into the bottomless pit. He has been preparing for this since Hermann's postcard. "So. They invite me to be visiting professor at Union Seminary this winter. You could visit me there. It is on upper Broadway. Would you ever have believed it when we lived in tents on the Plains of Abraham? It's a long way from Tipperary, my friend. See you soon. Regards from my lovely wife Merle. Yours, Hermann."

How did Hermann know his old confederate had gone to ground at Union? Oskar had no plans to study here when he left Toronto. Maybe Buzz talked. But how did Hermann arrange to be invited precisely when Oskar has established *himself* as the Union Jew? At the moment he relaxed! Hermann's diabolical inventiveness knows no limits, not in the torture of his dearest friend. On the other hand, it is mere coincidence. Sure it is. Sure. Coincidence *that* strong beggars the leap of faith, it requires willing suspension of disbelief, or whatever Kierkegaard said.

Oskar never wrote Hermann back. Nor has he replied to any of the phone messages at the Parkside in recent weeks, since Hermann arrived in New York *en famille* and began his Union lectures – "Jews and Christians: Lost Together in the Twentieth Century. A Paradox." Oskar has been patient, knowing the full weight of humiliation would come in its time. Soon, he told himself – and now it is here.

"My dear," says Karen to Oskar in the basement, "it was right after I told him I sometimes feel guilty about just being me! A Christian, comfortable, safe, loved. My dear, he said – the visiting professor has such a *spiritual* manner, you can tell he has suffered – my dear, you have a beautiful soul!" She melts again, as she did minutes ago, when Hermann spoke the fraudulent phrase up in his office. Oskar smiles a strychnine smile. Karen smiles back, her grin is as high as an elephant's eye. She exits. Next. Nancy Vrchoda from Sioux City, Iowa. "Oskar, Oskar, you won't believe what the visiting professor of interfaith theology said to me in his office just now. He told me I have a beautiful soul." Suzanne Durocher from Vermont – her soul too. Oskar swills his soup, he crumples the plastic cup like Zeus weary of a thunderbolt and flings it in the waste. He will not return Hermann's calls. Never again. But if he did, he would say to his alter ego, "*Liebchen*, have you got shit in your mouth? Is that why you talk that way?" It is a line he heard in an off-Broadway show; he has been waiting to use it.

But cancel that, this is a new Oskar, Oskar as Action Man. He doesn't retreat, he swings onto the attack. He appears suddenly one day, like Jesus on the road to Emmaus, in Hermann's class. It is a bold *geste*. Immersed among the Gentiles, nearly concealed by their blandness and decency, he is here to blow Hermann's cover. Hermann, like the travellers to whom Jesus showed himself, seems at first blind to this luminous presence. Then he offers Oskar a cold embrace, hands to elbows, for show, for the *goyim*, a façade of solidarity. Oskar fiendishly agrees to play Hermann's game.

He scrunches in his seat and hopes to survive a climate he is not made for, as though they are basking in a Florida sun while

145

he shivers through a blizzard. They are reading Teilhard, a "natural" theologian. Teilhard is a philosopher, a scientist, and a priest. He talks about Being. There is a prayerful mood. A student speaks softly. "A kind of . . . crackling," he says. The others lean forward, Hermann steepest of all. "Then," says the student, "then" – his voice lowers to a whisper – "Powwww."

Hermann puckers his face. He leans in even farther. They are witches in a coven. Hermann slowly opens his mouth, wets his lips. "POW," he repeats with care. Then, "Powwww . . . *er?*"

They sneak sideward glances. What a conspiracy this is. They are delighted. Being is loose among them, flitting about like a bat, they take care not to disturb it, lest it flee. The student who spoke takes in Hermann's daring suggestion. He shuts his eyes as though he is chewing the idea with his eyelids. Then he opens them carefully. "No," he says. He holds, cautious not to disturb the Higher Reality still hovering. He responds serenely. "Just . . . plain . . . POW . . ." His reiteration slips gently into the void, they watch it go, they bid it adieu. Being still flutters in the room.

Oskar saw Hermann pull this once. They went together – that is, he dragged Oskar along–to a question-and-answer, Faith After Auschwitz, at Hillel House in Hamilton. A student said, "Tonight the *Shechinah* is flying around in the room, I can feel it," and everyone nodded reverentially. Oskar didn't feel the wing-beat of the divine presence, all he felt was their smug agreement. He didn't speak on the drive back, and Hermann didn't notice.

Oskar leans back. He has been leaning back since he wriggled out of Hermann's half-embrace, tilting his chair in reverse flow as they hunched forward. Now he looses his balance altogether, he'd be ass-over-forehead but his chairback strikes the wall with a loud clunk. ZAP. It's gone. Being no longer in attendance. Dispersed with not even a goodbye. They turn on Oskar in silent fury, ready for an ontological pogrom. They glare at him. Hermann grunts. Oskar knows he must take a stand.

"I don't follow," he scratches, struggling to rebalance, four chairlegs in search of a floor. "Being was in the room, and some of us felt it, and the rest of us" – he looks around hopefully, perhaps one or two nod – "didn't. I want to know how you can tell you are feeling Being" – he searches, he has to get it right, it will be his final word in an institution he could have loved – "and not the tickle of an erection just before it starts?"

In New York the snow doesn't fall white, as in Toronto, and after becomes brown slush on the ground. In New York slush seeps up through cracks in the pavement, just as the anemic trees on the curbside grow from subway grates. Occasionally the works department spreads a layer of earth and grass over the natural covering of Manhattan, which is pavement, and declares a park. But everyone knows it's a façade, pavement is just below and extends to the planetary core. Oskar knows he'll see no white snowfalls here.

One brown day in February he sits in the lobby of the Parkside with the house copy of *The New York Times*. Near the back of the paper, where they put stories that don't seem to belong anywhere, a headline says, "Math Teacher Wins International TV Award, Vows Never to Lecture Again." Behind him the switchboard buzzes and hums. Oskar lowers himself into the article like a man in a bathysphere. He knows who it's about. "Oskar," calls Ernestine the operator, "it's for you."

Wetherford, of course. He doesn't seem surprised, either, that Oskar was reading about him at this instant. Someone persuaded him to make the television program of his fourth dimension lecture. Then he got this award and a detestably superficial notoriety. They act as if the prize is what matters and not the Teaching. As if it is all about him, Wetherford, and not the nature of existence. Thank heaven it's over. But he's calling about something else.

Oskar tenses: did he return those books Wetherford gave him? Yes, he did. But he never read them; so he didn't speak with Wetherford again, after the wondrous lecture in the cafeteria. Now Wetherford will face him with his cowardice and inability to explore Truth and Meaning – to even show interest. Which isn't the case at all. Wetherford is in New York, would Oskar like to see him, and meet Mme de Koning? Definitely, says Oskar. These days his social life is nil, he will go anywhere he is invited. He has avoided Union since his commando raid on Hermann's class. He hasn't spoken to Buzz, who must have heard a horrid Hermannian account of the event. He doesn't return calls from either of them, his dearest friends in New York. As a result, he still hasn't discovered the purpose of his sabbatical; perhaps it is Mme de Koning, whoever she is.

She lives in a townhouse on the most fashionable street of the East Side. They drink Russian tea. The furniture is old enough to have been stolen from under the noses of Bolshevik commissars after the Revolution – as Madame herself and her entourage were. Wetherford sits stiffly, almost prim, as she tells her tale to Oskar. She and Monsieur were students of Gurdjieff, who originated the Teaching. When the revolution came to St. Petersburg, now Leningrad, the seekers fled south with their master. They lived in India, absorbing the wisdom of the East. Then they settled in Paris. The Old Man died, and the Russian writer whose books Oskar didn't read took the leader's mantle. When he died Monsieur de Koning took over. Now he too is dead and, well, here I sit. She is the inheritor of the Teaching and Wetherford's guru.

As she speaks, Oskar sips and glances at watercolours pinned with thumbtacks to the parlour wall. They are familiar. He reads the name signed on them: Kandinsky. Yes, she sighs, we were very close. In Paris. He was one of us. Wetherford fires several eyeball projectiles at Oskar, then turns toward Madame. His look says, It is confirmed: this person with the smashed face, he is one of us.

After, Oskar and Wetherford walk through the slush along 53rd. They stop in front of the Museum of Modern Art. "We could go in, but it's merely images," says Wetherford, moving on. Oskar is enjoying the afternoon, but he feels it is time to admit he could not feel less like one of whoever it is Madame and Wetherford are members of. Before he can, Wetherford says, "I understand perfectly. Come tonight." He scribbles an address.

It is a dance. Sort of. Or a gymnastics class. The music comes from ancient 78 rpm recordings played on a portable phono-graph. A dozen people are there. Do they represent tribes? Apos-tles? Wetherford introduces him, first names only; they are friendly, he is there with the knowledge of Madame. They are about Wetherford's age, that is, Oskar's own age. They are middle-class and professional. In coming years Oskar will see some of them in newspaper and magazine photos. One is the publisher of a prestigious newspaper. She is his partner for the physical routines they do to the music. The music, she says, is by Monsieur de Koning. Has Oskar met Madame, who never attends these sessions herself? There is a Canadian. He intro-duces himself. He dabbles in public life, he says, he is a member of the Supreme Court of Canada.

It is odd – with these people Oskar does not feel graceless. In the movement, they danced Israeli circle dances, but he held back. At the Pillar of Fire he schedules folk-dance clubs, and the kids have parties. He likes to watch them grope each other, especially from the projection booth far above the auditorium floor. But he never steps out there himself. Even if he attends the bar mitzvah dinner of some teacher's child – a rare and unlikely event – they seem to know: don't create a situation by asking Oskar to dance. (There was the time at JYGGL camp during the *birkat* when he rose in the dining hall. He does not consider he danced then. More like he was danced. A force compelled him.)

Here with Wetherford, it's not really a dance either. It's an intellectual exercise, a physicalized quest for truth. Dance embarrasses Oskar; so does mystical talk. But put them together in the city where deviance is normal, elide truth and dance, mind and body, in a combination as awkward as Oskar himself, and he is easy. Wetherford must have known. No more talk, let's do something.

It is the social highlight of his sabbatical, maybe his life. He is disappointed they do not go afterward to a bar, or a coffee-house with folksingers, or a flamenco club, as the parents of his kids go out when they've spent an evening learning the mambo or cha-cha-cha at Latin American Dance Studio on Eglinton. After an evening together, these are his people.

They part, he and Wetherford, sensing they will not talk

again. They have spoken enough to know they have nothing more to say. But they shared a dance and dark tea. They did something, they were united in action. Wetherford gives Oskar a little salute and struts away in the slush and night thinking maybe about wheeling suddenly in an unexpected direction and breaking finally into his beloved fourth dimension. Oskar has a strange thought: He is my astral brother.

Revived, he recalls he may try anything in this place, since no one who knows him will see him. He registers for a singles weekend at Grossinger's. It is in the Catskills, the Jewish mountains as they say here where people are never embarrassed about being Jews.

Time speeds on a singles weekend. It's like a sabbatical from his sabbatical. Life cycles pass in an evening – such as tonight, Friday. They start with a monster cocktail party. Back at the Pillar of Fire, Mr Oates is spiffing the sanctuary for the modest congregation who have finished their chicken dinners and are about to leave for the service. Everyone but Oskar in this vast room knows what to do. They have the script and he doesn't. They scurry around, coupling and recoupling. The men have pens and pads. They spend a brief time with each woman, then separate on an internal timer, like an efficient production line.

"Why are you still standing here?" says the woman with the tossed raven hair. She is Oskar's type. Kind of slutty. There are crow's feet beneath the makeup around her eyes. Heavy red on her cheeks. Too much lipstick. The line of the dress shows an abundant body. Her hair must be dyed. It excites him. If she works so hard to look sexy, she wants to be. "You've got my number," she says. He had to ask her for a pen. "Have I seen you before?" he says, thinking of some openers he read in an article on singles bars. "Oskar," she says, using his name as though it's not something she just heard for the first time, "are you kidding? I was at your session in north Jersey on teaching the Holocaust and the audio-visual revolution."

He could have stood here lusting for hours without connecting her to Jewish education. That weekend Buzz drove him across the George Washington Bridge to meet some teachers at a retreat. He fixed on her immediately, hungrily. They sat around the fireplace singing songs after his talk. It was dark enough, in the firelight, to look her up and down and turn her like a pig on a spit in his imagination. That night in his little room he whacked off as if he had found the meaning of life–to the thought of her. This is the same her. They have something to talk about. He asks where she teaches, why she's here, isn't she married? "So," she says, "we're on to phase two."

Phase two, she explains as they move into the cavernous dining room together, is committing themselves to each other for the weekend. She knows, she's been here before. They pass serenely through dinner. He is entranced. She chose *him*. They talk Jewish education and European culture. "What now?" he says when dinner is over. "Table tennis, walk in the woods," she says. "Going out on the lake is nice."

They take a rowboat, though there are canoes. The night is a little cool, but what the hell, he feels reborn. He is not klutzy Oskar on a JYGGL weekend with skeptical kids from Toronto and their livelier American cousins; he is dynamic Oskar, leader of German Jewish youth on a country hike. Tomorrow, by God, they will canoe. They dock. They walk arm in arm, they reach the main building. She tilts her face up. Her mouth melts straight into his. It is his first kiss, again. He recalls another first kiss: with Greta on the second-floor landing of the movement office in Berlin. He stammers. He bobbles the words. "I feel – " She nods. "Phase three," she says.

Three is infatuation and it's full of ardour. It lasts all Saturday. They explore the grounds of Grossinger's in intense conversation, crawling over each other verbally. This is love, he knows, though he doesn't say the words. He's not sure why, he figures there's time. They brush each other, they explore with a light touch. That night they kiss, and he starts to go. She says, "That's it?" He points out they are each sharing a room. She tells him there are ways around that and explains some. He feels criticized, he pulls back. He kisses her again and cranks up another goodnight. She says, "Phase four started early."

Phase four, she knows, is the time-waster. It comes out of

the weekend at Grossinger's and carries on and on until the next Grossinger's weekend probably. In this phase he reveals the monstrous truth to her: he is a man unable to love. To love anyone, not just her, it isn't personal. On the contrary, he says (in this phase), if I could love anyone it would be you; I just don't think I can, it isn't in me. She rolls up her sleeves, she'll work like hell to convince him he too can love, he really can, he can too. It's a long hard miserable job, she thinks as she heads into it once more.

In the weeks to come he sees her often. They are in love, they attend plays and concerts. For long periods he feels trapped in Lincoln Center, circulating like forced air between the ballet, the symphony, and the theatre. They still haven't bedded each other. There is time, he thinks, this is special, I will know. He likes the phone calls best. When he comes in at night and shuts the door of his room, he does not have to stare at the phone; it is his right to call. After a month, he notices she never tells him anything; he is always explaining things to her. She talks to him, but always about himself. At first he adored it, his thirst for her interest in him seemed bottomless. But he has decided, I am boring. He grows irrational, he starts imagining the old awful sessions with Hermann, hours spent stifling yawns and disinterest in Rrrrevelation or ultimate integration. Should he abandon principle and call Hermann in his visiting office at Union? Oskar shudders. Hermann drove him from there, he won't return like a cur. This is what being in love – or as she says, the hard work of trying to love – is doing to him. He misses Hermann the snake.

On Good Friday Oskar returns ruefully to Union. It is midnight. No one knows he has come. To all appearances he abandoned this terrain, his one-time New York home, to Hermann. He doesn't know if he is back because he misses Union or Hermann. He needs, he feels, to say a final goodbye; without it his misery over this episode in his sabbatical year will be incomplete. He huddles in the farthest corner of the Union chapel and watches his Jeremiah professor, the austere Munch, mount the lectern.

Munch is typically ageless and haggard this night, but more so. His face shines with glory and torment. He is no longer the vindictive Old Testament God; that was only, it appears, for the seminar. On this sacral midnight, Munch is someone else. Oskar, from his darkened corner, tries to discern the new character. "Time, time," Munch speaks, and his thoughts float, searching for an anchor. "History," he says, and seems to falter. *This* is the quest for truth, thinks Oskar; it really is, and it's happening before me. "We see it always . . ." Munch is still searching, his face rotating like a searchlight in a fog. "Ah!" he cries. "We see history from ahead!" His eyes gleam, as though they have caught sight of a barque in difficulty. "From afterward. From the future. We view history from the future, looking back." Oskar leans forward, caught by the mention of what he still fantasizes as "his" field: history, a life he never had, more truly his than the one in which he's mired. "From afterward," says Munch, "as though history stretches behind us and we glimpse it over our shoulder. We look back on the most momentous event in that Long March: the Crucifixion of Our Lord; we spy it from afar, from the future, where we reside, from the perspective of Easter Sunday, and we joyously cry, He Is Risen!" Munch's voice rises triumphant on "risen," then tumbles to the depths. "But I say to you–" Oh God, thinks Oskar, he is disappearing before my eyes, he is vanishing into that event of which he speaks, he is going to pass right through it, and emerge *before* it happened! And Munch does!

"My friends," he moans, "let us join those Christians, our analogues, who had to view the Crucifixion not from Easter Sunday, but from Good Friday, from before the Resurrection." He is there, thinks Oskar in terror, he made the move! Munch's frame gaunter than ever, his eyes hollow–like Wiesel's who lives the Holocaust from inside–and his voice sounding with despair and hopeless, truly hopeless. A man of constant sorrow, after Oskar's own heart. Of course! thinks Oskar, with the reproach he always heaps on himself when he reaches an insight, that's who he has become–Jeremiah! "Woe unto you my mother, that bore me, a man of strife and contention to all the earth."

153

Oskar careens up Broadway. This doleful Gentile has led him to the light. A Bible scholar who reads German as well as he reads English – but can't read Hebrew the same way! A natural object of pity and scorn, just like Jeremiah, yet this strange man understands history with a depth that makes Oskar feel he has never properly used the word. As if Oskar has been saying history but thinking taxidermy. A historian! Oskar curses the day he was born. Woe to you my mother – a man of scorn and nonsense from Berlin to Toronto to New York.

At 113th, former Father Gerald steps from a bar. It is Good Friday; Oskar is embarrassed to see him here. But Gerald is not abashed. He is concerned as always, defrocked but involved. Gerald claps Oskar on the shoulder, he enfolds Oskar, he is so vast, now going to flab but once a handball champ. They pass some 24-hour groceries, Gerald steers Oskar into an all-night restaurant. He orders dinner. He orders dinner for Oskar, who is ravenous. Then another for himself. In the coming hours Gerald orders three more. Each consists of an appetizer, a main course, a salad, a dessert, and coffee. Dishes are stacked before former Father Gerald like towers of Babel. He rarely stops talking. He is possessed, he has an answer. Oskar does not know the question, but he has learned this is not essential. The answer is: Search for meaning without cease. So, though Gerald has left the Church, he maintains the quest, like a knight of faith with one small element missing: faith. The platters mount. "Meaning," former Father Gerald is saying. "Emotional meaning. Intellectual meaning. Spiritual meaning. Oskar, a man needs meaning, even if he's lost his faith, especially then. If one type of meaning is stripped from a man's life, he will find a substitute, sure as if he is hungry or thirsty. Oskar, if you had been alive in the sixteenth century when the Reformation abolished the confessional, you could have predicted the rise of the novel!"

"Why?" says Oskar.

"Because people need to put their inner life someplace. If they can't pour it out in a confessional, they'll live it through in the pages of a book."

"Not that why," says Oskar.

"Then what why?" says Gerald, with a mouthful of mashed potatoes.

"Why did you leave the Church?"

"I was forty-two years old," says Gerald, spearing a pea, "and I had never kissed a woman. It's the same story for every goddamn one of us. I never lost my fucking faith. But after a while, what did I need it for?"

Passover comes. Buzz breaks the communications blackout and invites Oskar to the seder at his home on Long Island the first night of the holiday. "Er . . ." says Oskar. "Ahhh . . ."

"Oskar my man!" says Buzz. "Is there a woman?" Oskar chokes. Buzz says she must come. Buzz has class: he doesn't even ask if she is Jewish. Hermann will be there, with wife and infant son. Oskar hasn't seen him since the seminar. On impulse he says yes. He is armoured; he will have revenge. *His* woman is sexier – and Jewish! Oskar thinks he could have a peak experience, as Tocchet calls them, and in a way he does. It rivals the day he heard Willi was coming, and the afternoon they took him from the barracks in Oranienburg.

Buzz is perfectly avuncular, as though he has proudly given birth to everyone at the table, not just his own kids. He's invited Murray, a publisher he knows–perhaps Buzz thinks Murray will be a buffer between his other two friends. Murray is alone. This makes Oskar tense; he is used to being the alone one. Murray has some impressive credits – an encyclopedia of espionage, a huge seller called *The Cookie Bookie*; but like everyone in New York, he'd rather talk about himself. He is learning to fly. It gives him a reason to go on living, he explains. He needs it because his analyst, with whom he is entering year fourteen, is no help any more, though Murray can't quit, because the shrink needs *him*! Talk lingers on Murray just the way people usually focus on Oskar, but tonight Oskar doesn't rate, because he isn't there by himself. He has a woman. They are treating him normally; they've found another charity case – just like that! Their conversation moves around the table like an echo to the Seder ritual they are also conducting. Buzz's youngest squeaks, "Why is this night different from all other nights?" – as it says in the Passover Haggadah. In the spaces between prayers and rituals they ask amiable questions about each other's lives.

They ask in the way *hassidim* pour drinks: never for yourself, always for someone else, and then he'll pour for you. Oskar twitches and waits his turn. Murray has spoken, he was questioned by Buzz. Now it's Murray's turn to question Oskar. But Murray skips Oskar; he proceeds directly to Hermann! Hermann is in form. He is cultured and European and Murray is a mere New World Jew. Hermann quotes Goethe and Heine the way that always impresses Americans who want to seem intellectual. They roll over like dogs having their tummies tickled.

Oskar looks around the table. It could be a séance. Hermann is the darling of their gaze, like a spirit they have called from the Other Side. Hermann wins again. If their gaze shifts from him a moment it is to the adorable children by his side – there are two now–whom Oskar could crush like *charoses*, the condiment mixed to resemble mortar with which the Israelites built the pyramids. Or flatten them like a slab of *matzah*. He sees his own date gaze on Hermann. He has lost her. He has lost Buzz, and Buzz's kids who used to claim to like him, and even pathetic high-flying Murray. After a brief orgy of ego, Hermann sits back, spent. Murray is flushed, he looks as if he is going to rise in a standing ovation. "There can't be many like you up there in Canada," says Murray. Hermann blushes. Modesty yet.

It gets worse. Now Murray is soliciting a book. A memoir maybe, or something heavy and philosophical. Or what about a book for young Jews? asks Murray. Hermann mentions, in an artful aside, the classes he once taught at the Pillar of Fire Religious School. He has been dining out for years on that quaint experience, which Oskar terrorized him into. Who is scripting this? Everything Oskar tries to dismiss as mere morbid fantasy happens in his life like the arrivals and departures of Swissair: absolutely dependable. Now – Oskar conjures it in his fevered brain–Hermann will become Mr Jewish Education to everyone

Oskar has struggled all these years to impress, not to mention –
he wishes he hadn't thought of this – the royalties!

Murray turns casually to Oskar. "And what do you do?" All
hope drains from him. A lifetime of sucking it in, finding the
will to keep going. "I am a religious school principal," he says,
forlorn. He never calls himself a principal; he is an educator.
Principal is self-hate. It says to others: nothing about me would
interest you; it doesn't even interest me. He sinks in his seat.
There is a pillow beneath him, part of the Seder ritual: once we
were slaves but no more, we recline in comfort to show we are
free and easy today. The pillow slants him downward, he slumps
lower in the chair, he wishes he could slide right under the table,
and farther, down to the lowest worlds, the realm of the *klipot*
– the shells and husks, the crudest level of existence where nothing sparkles, nothing shines. If only Oskar could get that far
down where nothing is lower. Oh for an end to hope. Oh for
the blessed relief of losing hope.

They are singing *Eliyahu ha-nahvee*, Elijah the Prophet, for
whom a spare place is set at the Seder table. *Speedily, and in our
lifetime / May he come to us.* Elijah the tease, who went to
heaven whole, vanished in a flying chariot over the hilltops of
Judea, and since he didn't die on earth, he still is out there,
beyond the blue horizon, ready to pop back and announce the
arrival of the Messiah, should that one ever choose to make time
on his busy schedule to bring peace to the Jewish people and the
human race. Oskar hates Elijah, he's the prophet who makes
everyone keep hoping. Christians have the right idea: their Messiah came and went, their hopes are retrospective, they're fas-
tened on the past, which is no real hope at all, it is mere history.
Our damned Jewish Messiah who is yet to come, right after
Elijah announces him, he makes you wait for the future. The
future has no history, you can't examine, study, analyse, and
bury it. It leaves you clutching at hope. Oskar hates Elijah.

He excuses himself. Maybe he just gets up and stalks from
the table, or droops to the floor and slithers out. Oskar's chair
is empty as Elijah's. No one notices, none of them care. They

are absorbed in each other's perfections. He mounts the stairs to Buzz's bedroom. He picks up the phone, he calls California. Tocchet is in California. His next stop after the dreadful last act at Beaverbrook U. Oskar gets through. He hears Tocchet's gentle voice. He pours it out. Tocchet says, "I know what you mean."

"Will I ever lose these feelings of hate and jealousy?" Oskar implores, long distance. There is a pause. "I never have," says the wisest and best person Oskar knows, and he feels less alone. "Will you be all right?" says Tocchet. There is an edge in his voice, he is worried. Oskar is tempted–he could retain Tocchet's attention with a threat. "I don't know," he stammers. This isn't fair. He shouldn't do it to Tocchet. His voice firms. "I'll be all right. But I wish I had . . . a *sign* . . ." He feels as stupid as he felt with the other wise man in his life, the Jewish one, Buber. A sign? "Ah," says Tocchet, with the note of relief he strikes when the answer starts coming through, "isn't that what every prophet wants, a sign?" Oskar lays the phone down like it is a sacrament. Me a prophet? How absurd, how comforting.

When they say goodnight, after they're back in magical Manhattan, she says, "I don't think I'll see you again." He nods. He isn't surprised. He didn't speak on the train, just quietly inflicted his pain on her. "It's not personal," she says. "It's just, I don't need this." She steps into the elevator, the door closes in front of her, he is left in the lobby of her apartment building. Alone, bereft.

There is a mirror beside the elevator door. He raises his gaze from his shoetops till it meets his reflection. He looks at the shaken visage of the man in the mirror. It is smiling, grinning back at him like an idiot! They almost got him this time, but not quite. A snare was set but he escaped. He got out. Nothing remains except the last few months of this torture holiday. Then he can go home.

His sabbatical is now spent. He has little to show, and it is raining. He has not seen Buzz since the night of the Seder. He hasn't seen Hermann, nor Hermann's wife and son, nor former

Father Gerald, Munch, nor any of the Midwestern beauties who pass through the Union coffee shop. He has cut them off. He's spent the balance of his sabbatical with the people of the Parkside. Archie the desk clerk, Ben the black doorman, Ernestine the operator, to whom his mind wanders when he masturbates these days, and the manager herself, possessor of an ill-defined relationship to the wife of the chairman of the library board.

He lingers now in front of Chock Full O' Nuts, after his third cup of coffee today. He detests coffee. Across Broadway, the grimy gates to the Columbia campus are withstanding a spring shower. He could go back into Chock Full O' Nuts. Or browse in the Paperback Forum. Or amble up the street a block and a half to Salter's Books. There's a grey-jacketed salesclerk with long straight brown hair, he figures she irons it, he hears that's done. She has a severe look, older than the usual student employees in the area and, he suspects, a trace of a Southern accent. She has escaped, probably, a decadent Southern family in an incestuous community. He misses Sweet Eustache. He pretends to have trouble recalling her name.

An abbreviated double column of New York City police march-steps across Broadway right beside Oskar and wheels through the iron gratings onto the campus. It is raining harder. Umbrella stands bloom like morning glories outside every storefront. It would be prudent to buy one. It would be Oskar-like. Instead he pursues the police toward the campus interior.

He strides briskly, he can accelerate that lurch, he has nearly caught them. They break into a sprint, heading on a diagonal up the broad, long steps mounting to Low Library—not a library at all but the administrative centre of the university. It has pillars and a dome like the Campidoglio. He knows a phone booth was once incongruously stuck in front of Low Library so Frank Sinatra could call Lee Remick in a movie called *The Detective*, which was shot here. He saw it in a theatre down Broadway. Frank was taking a night course, probably criminology, and he hurried down these steps when Lee didn't answer, just as Oskar now scurries up them.

The action is at the top, between the pillars and a revolving

159

glass door that leads into the lobby. Dozens of students are there. They are being, well, they are being beaten by the police. What he immediately notices is the fun of it! The fun the police are having, not the students. How can he tell what they feel, these armed, uniformed, shielded enforcers? Easy. Look at their bodies: tense and excited. Look in their eyes, which glisten. Look at their clubs, raised in taut anticipation of the satisfaction they are about to receive. They toss the women back and forth with the thrill of an activity normally prohibited, but now, owing to special circumstances, permitted. Like religious festivals such as Mardi Gras, where the forbidden is temporarily allowed. (Dressing up at Purim is the feeble Jewish version, though there is also *ha-mitzvah haba'ah ba-averah*, a commandment fulfilled by sinning, a mystical concept not taught at the Pillar of Fire Religious School.) The women are flung about, their long hair falling with them, to the hard concrete, then seized by the fistful to pull them back and heave them again. Oskar gapes.

He is aware of his reactions to this moment, as he used to be aware of the sunsets. This is a sunset in his latter life, these drizzly beatings on the steps of Columbia. Oskar knows—and knows he knows—that he is not instantly reminded of *Kristallnacht*, or the afternoon in the barracks. It is violent, yet he does not assimilate it to violence he has known. Nor does he experience the event as if he is one of those attacked, clubbed, and brutalized by the agents of the state. Maybe his past and that of his people—a past he is dedicated to perpetuating—should lead him to identify with these victims of organized terror, but he does not. Hm, he thinks, the rising generation of middle-class America are expressing their resentment toward Mummy and Daddy. It is all happening here, to them, now; not there, then, and to Oskar as well. History is history, and now is now. *Blessed art Thou, O Lord, Ruler of the Universe, Who makes a disinction . . .*

This may be a matter of denial, a well-known psychological mechanism. However, there is more at work, for Oskar does feel the experience—but from the other side, the club-wielders'. He is virtually in their skins. The tension, emotion, anticipation, release, almost immediately the remount of tension; he leans forward into the melee and gawks, mesmerized, absorbed in their feelings, wondering what will be revealed to him next – as he is flung down the rainswept steps!

He clambers back. The show has continued in his absence. That tumble was not meant for him, no way. They don't realize he has nothing to do with the whole skein of causes: the demonstration, whoever organized it; the protest, whatever it is against; the clandestine expression of Oedipal resentment – it's easy enough for a bystander to be mistakenly included.

Standing outside the glass door now is a porcine man in his fifties. "I regret this," he says, "but you people are interrupting a university exercise."

"ROTSEE must go!" shout several students unimpressively.

"You should see the exercise we have been having out here," squawks Oskar. He blinks. That was his own voice!

Heads turn. Is it his accent? The scratching sound? "Are you a member of the university community, sir?" says the fat man to Oskar. Oskar realizes – probably he knew before he spoke, that is, before the voice burst from his throat – that he is talking to the president of Columbia, and numerous banks and corporations as well. "This is the seat of reason," the man continues.

"Stay out here and find out how reasonable these storm troopers are," Oskar says. "Right on," yell the kids. Is there a *dybbuk* inside him? He feels himself pushed to the front of the crowd. "That's an interesting approach the old guy's got," somebody mutters. "Confront the motherfuckers." Someone says, "Who is he, an old Bolshevik?" "Maybe a Wobbly," says another. Oskar is face to face now with the president. He knows Eisenhower was once president of Columbia. If this were Eisenhower, he could salute and say, "Have a good exercise, sir," and Eisenhower would say, "Thank you, son, carry on."

A fresh-faced man, also in a business suit, places himself between Oskar and the president. "I'll take care of this, sir," he says, filching a servile tone Oskar admires. "Sir," says the young flunky to Oskar, "if you are registered here or on faculty, may I see your Columbia ID?" Oskar stares dumbly. He hopes he is doing the idiot grin, it may be his only chance. The president

161

turns away from Oskar and says, "You people will have to find out what it means to deal with the state," and disappears beyond the revolving door like a villainous character in a left-wing play staged by Piscator at the Volksbühne in the 1920s. "Is hooliganism your idea of dealing with the state?" he hears the voice of the *dybbuk* hurl at the vanishing figure, as the tumult revives around and on him. He falls down the steps again and lands on one knee. The same unflattering position as the fresh young man in the suit three steps below. Oskar pushes himself up, he starts to mount the slippery slope again. No one asks why and he does not even ask himself.

But what is the reason? Why did the *dybbuk* announce itself at the entrance to Low Library? Was it the porker who purports to head this noble place of learning? The *dybbuk* appeared simultaneously with him – they are a matched pair. Oskar is a man committed, with grave misgivings, to education. Was something in him offended by the blunt instrument who spoke to these students in its name? Or was the *dybbuk* buried elsewhere, not in Oskar's identity but in his history? Is it a response he failed to make on *Kristallnacht*, or earlier, at the time of Nuremberg, or later, when they came for him in the camp? Is it belated politics? The problem with these central moments in one's life is not that they lack a cause but that they often have too many causes.

He slips once more and lands against the steps, this time on his hip. On the way to his feet he feels a hand on his shoulder. "I think you've had enough for now," says a voice neither his own nor that of the *dybbuk*. He looks up and sees a face framed against an umbrella. It is not the face of someone he knows, nor is it unfamiliar. She stoops slightly and helps him rise.

They sit in her office in Butler Hall, which *is* the library. The office is narrow and high, like a canyon. Her face is framed now against the window, which is darkened by dusk outside; the window rises almost the height of the room. From every direction books hang and balance ominously. Oskar cowers, in case the books leap from their shelves and pelt him like hail. Kroitermann is discoursing as though they have conducted a lifelong colloquy. Why does he find her so familiar, aside from the many articles and interviews with her he has seen, though rarely read, over the years, and all those works of hers he knows he ought to buy as soon as the book clubs and literary reviews announce their publication?

It seems only yesterday – it *was* yesterday – he saw her on the public television station in the lobby of the Parkside, debating with a mushy liberal academic about foreign policy. The academic yapped about the war in Vietnam, but Kroitermann refused to descend to the level of the daily news. She was there to discourse on democracy and the Greek ideal. Oskar liked her strength.

"They are enamoured of violence," she proclaims now, as though more than she and Oskar are in this canyon, as if history too is listening. He wonders if she is talking about the police. "Why enamoured? Because from violence they derive a misplaced sense of power. Power of all things!" She is oblivious to the metallic German quality of her English. Her accent does not scratch like Oskar's, it rasps with confidence and authority, like a heavy file working over a flawed piece of equipment. "They are unaware, of course, that violence is the opposite of power, that it is the sign of impotence. Those with power have no need for violence." Oskar realizes she means the students, not the police. The talk of power and impotence thrills him to his crotch. "Do you think I was violent?" he asks.

"I was mystified by your behaviour," she rasps. "That is why I intervened. What did you think you were doing?"

She is gloriously confident, and very ugly too. He marvels at people like her who can speak so directly, their thoughts seem to run along a straight highway from their minds to your ears. He has noticed they are usually women, like the Advice to the Lovelorn columnists. "Listen, toots," they snap, "wake up and smell the coffee." Forthright wisdom, like the Book of Proverbs. What else is Proverbs except . . . aha! Greta! That's who she reminds him of. So German, so imposing, so ghastly.

163

"Did that scene make you recall the rise of the Nazis?" She speaks as though she locks everyone she meets in a confrontational embrace, like Jacob grabbing the angel of death at the ford of the river Jabbok and refusing to release him without a blessing. "Not a whit!" she explodes in answer to her question. "A ludicrous analogy! Sheer intellectual alarmism. America is no more Germany than I am the Queen of the May!" Every word a percussion grenade, every speech an artillery barrage. He can tell she is always this way; you can count on her to be contrary and unpredictable, like those free spirits he is often attracted to because they are so totally different from other people, until you get used to them.

They have been talking for hours. He knows he must fire back, a burst if not a salvo. He has tried to hold his own with references to history, his field. "You have not asked me about my relationship to Heidegger," she bellows, shifting course again. He knows he must comment on Heidegger, who has not crossed his mind in ages, if ever. Who is Heidegger? He associates the name with Hermann. Is that why he feels so used to this woman? Is she a female, godless Hermann, whose passion is politics, not theology? Was she married to Heidegger? Is she married at all? He has been trying not to think that thought.

"The great question is," she says, exhaling with compressed energy a puff of unfiltered cigarette smoke, "was Heidegger's Nazism a result of his existentialism – or its betrayal?" Oskar doesn't know and he couldn't care, but he thinks he is falling in love again. He has to say something to declare his competence, his intellectuality, his existence.

"I'm afraid I don't believe in it," he says. What else, he thinks, do I ever offer?

"Don't believe in what?" she shoots back.

He ventures a bit farther. "Politics," he says. "I don't believe in politics."

"Ha!" Hers is a joyous yelp. He gives thanks, he caught her interest. "Politics isn't like religion," she says. "You can't not believe in it. Though that is an illusion of our consumer society. It's like not believing in the law of gravity. Sure you can not believe in it, but what the hell does that have to do with the price of eggs?"

He is rolling now. He prepares to defend his unbelief. He opens his mouth – and the lights go out.

"Gadzooks," she huffs. "I don't have any spare light bulbs in here. I wouldn't know where to screw them if I did."

He looks around. "It wouldn't help much," he says. "All the lights outside in the hall are gone too."

She rises and peers through the vast window. She looks like Alice, from the rear, staring into the looking-glass. "Every light on campus has been extinguished," she declares definitively. "And so are the lights on Broadway. I wonder if those twerps from the demonstration pulled this off?"

"A power failure would suit their style, according to your analysis," he says. She squares around toward him and thrusts her chin in his direction, a silhouette against black. That last crack did it, for the first time she is impressed. He beams. He knows she can't see it.

"I must rush off and make sure my husband is all right," she says, and he has the Reaction.

The Reaction consists of one part devastation to one part elation. In the less intense form it is one part sadness to one of relief. It is always equal infusions of opposite emotions. In this case, his anticipations of love with this woman, along with a share of her vitality, and children, companionship, plus glorious orgasms and unthinkable sexual experiments, are dashed. Meanwhile the fear of failure, rejection, exposure, and responsibility also lift from his heart. In a short time he is back to normal. The blessing of the Reaction is, it always returns him to equilibrium.

"He's a cripple, he's stuck in a wheelchair," she says bluntly as she crashes around her office in the dark, searching for the door. She grabs her nondescript coat and her umbrella. "You're welcome to stay here till the lights come on."

Hours later she arrives back with a huge flashlight in her hand and pockets full of candles. "How did I know you would still be here?" she asks in the dark, opening the door. "How *do* you know I'm here?" he answers from her chair in front of the window, which he cautiously occupied after she left. "You're making some kind of noise," she says. "What is it?" He has to think for a moment. "*Niggunim*," he says. "I was humming *niggunim*, but I thought I was humming inside my head, not out loud. I guess it doesn't matter since I am the only one here. I was, I mean."

"What are *niggunim*?" she asks with no nonsense.

"Melodies," he says, "mostly religious. Although some of them just . . . are. Usually they come from the Jewish communities of Eastern Europe, which are no more."

"Ah," she says, as if she rarely comes across new information.

"I love to go over them," he says, knowing the dark makes it possible to confide like this. As though he is still alone. As if she is inside his head with him, looking out the portholes of his eyes at his view of the world. He starts to hum the theme for the High Holy Days. To him it begins in the depths of the ocean, then climbs its way to the stars – like the glittering staircase in a 1930s Hollywood musical – holding the heights and the depths together in what he imagines as holy tension. He closes his eyes and swings his head as he moans. He has no sense of pitch.

"I will return now to my husband," she announces, as she lights a candle on the table in front of Oskar.

"A woman of valour who can find?" he recites solemnly in his head, as though it is Friday night and she has just lit and blessed the Sabbath candles on their groaning dinner table, their children and grandchildren all around. "You may remain," she says, "but when you leave, as you eventually will, please be certain to pull the door locked behind you."

Up and down Broadway, the coffee shops and restaurants and bars have become *shtiebelach*, dense enclosures in which people huddle and worship, huddle and study, huddle and conspire. Even the interior of Chock Full O' Nuts dances with candle flames and a limp spirituality. They are grottoes where small groups gather, each to a candle, as though poring together over a *daf gemara* from the Talmud, or more perilous, a Kabbalistic text, their faces dark and rosy above the flickering lights. There is no background music, only the static stutter of the odd portable radio, independent of the electric flow, detailing the awesome extent of the blackout, up and down the East Coast and spreading cancerously all the way to the Canadian frontier, as they call it, at Niagara Falls. Oskar feels a sudden connection to Toronto: darkness enfolds them all, him and Willi Schropp, and Myrna whom he should have married, and Hermann, who has already returned there with the Holy Family and has no more time for Franburgers and cranky conversations. Oskar walks. People everywhere glow as they talk, talk as they glow. He wanders from place to place, knowing nobody, thrilled by the low hum of words and thoughts and the anonymity that makes community possible for him. He doesn't know them, they don't know him, they are all the same to each other, therefore they can join and feel together. He thinks again, Is this all I can ever grasp? Is there more, as Hermann and Kroitermann and all the brilliant voices of heaven and earth (Buber, especially) proclaim? Or are they wrong, and am I right – is this all, this alone?

Former Father Gerald looms from the comforting darkness. His huge arms overflow with books, newspapers, writing pads, pens and pencils – he even juggles a cigarette. Gerald asks what Oskar thinks of this sacred moment, then listens to his answer. "You must have been a wonderful priest," says Oskar. "I was," says Gerald. "It was the training. Never forget a name, and I never do." Oskar does not believe it is just technique. Gerald really *is* interested.

"Oskar – in the dark as usual!" It is Lorna Honeywell from the Union basement coffee shop. Oskar introduces Gerald. "Hi," she says. They are suddenly a little family within the big community of the blackout. Oskar is less alone than he has been in years, maybe ever.

Gerald perks up. His shambling bulk seems to smooth out slightly. "A sister," he says, and a grin lopes across his face.

Oskar assumes Gerald feels that family feeling too. "Nope," continues Gerald, correcting himself, "an *ex*-sister!" She smiles back, not a blush, a forthright smile. "Order of St. Winnifred," Gerald says confidently. She nods, amused. They are off on a conversation, not like old friends but like members of one far-flung clan who never met before. Oskar has become a bystander; they are leaving him behind like a hitchhiker. "How did you know?" Oskar asks Gerald. They turn affectionately. They forgot he was there, and are terribly sorry. He brought them together. "Hard to miss," says Gerald. "Should we have a coffee?" The restaurants and bars are full of life, though none of the coffee is hot, after hours with no power. "I'm going this way," says Lorna. "I'll come," says Gerald. Oskar is not going any way, he stands like a lamppost. As they leave, Gerald glances back. "I'm gonna marry that ex-nun," he says quietly.

From the street where Oskar is rooted, the Gayway Tavern looks like a pirates' den, the ne'er-do-wells inside cluster about dripping candles plunked in the necks of spent rum bottles: they plot the seizure of a prize from His Majesty's fleet. They don't look like *yeshiva bocher*s in there. As he dawdles she catches his eye. Or he catches hers. It is the same event of mutual connection that happened through the pizzeria window on 72nd the first day of this, his fading sabbatical. He is certain it is her. Almost.

"How are you tonight?" she says smokily.

"I'm fine. What's your name?" he answers with a resolve he lacked in their past encounter. Is it the panic of imminent return to Toronto and the school, the urgency a prisoner on a weekend pass must feel? Is it a yearning for action kindled by the battle of Low Library–those kids thought he was a Bolshevik! Is it his unrequited lust for Kroitermann? Or a residue of the current that flowed between Gerald and Lorna?

"Bella," she says breezily, as though any name will do. She does not recall him. They walk together. He had forgone all hope and fantasy. Now he has a last chance to see if he can be another person. "What could we do together?" he says. The students at Low Library felt they were doing something. If you're not part of the solution you're part of the problem, they chanted. Why didn't he feel they were doing anything, or that he could do it with them?

"You name it," she says, terrifying him.

"I don't know," he says. "Maybe we should forget it." Does a shadow of memory cross her face as he dithers? Is it even really her, forty blocks north of their meeting at her apartment? Was it her apartment? Has she moved? Does a being like this have apartments and move with her furniture like ordinary humans? How can this creature and Kroitermann exist on the same planet, much less the same night and inside Oskar's experience? He blinks. He wonders if other people talk this much inside their heads while pretending to converse on the outside.

"There's lots of things in life," she says languidly, "you might never have experienced." They are strolling now, like an old couple walking by the lake after dinner at the lodge. "You think so?" he asks, the scratchiness intensified by anticipation. "I've gone with other professors," she says. "I've shown them things they didn't know there were."

Something like the fingers of a masseuse run up and down inside him. She thinks he is a professor. A Columbia professor! "Where do we go?" he asks. "This way, my friend," she says, steering him off Broadway onto 107th and into the first doorway. She guides him down a hall and through a door. Nothing is seen, only felt and heard. "Ten dollars," she says. He has no idea what kind of room they are in, whether they are even alone. "I don't know," he says. Damn. Does he ever know? Does he never do? "Tell you what," she says, "two for the price of one. First we suck, then we fuck."

"Yes," he says, in close imitation of a decision. He fingers the bills in his wallet; she helps herself to one, as though she can tell the denomination by feel. Now she is moving lower on him, she is pulling his pants down, she is starting when, of course, the lights go on.

He is looking down – not at her, she is under his line of sight – at the toilet bowl in the hall bathroom of this dingy hotel.

Against its stained, discoloured sides are the turds and piss of whoever lives here. How long has it all been roiling there? Do they never flush, is it hopelessly broken, don't they bother with repairs?

She pulls off, looks over her shoulder at the bowl, and rises. "Okay," she says, "let's go." She takes his hand, the other one is hauling up his pants, and leads him down the hall. She knocks on a door, sticks her head in, says "Half a minute," disappears for thirty seconds exactly, and pulls him inside. There is a bed, he sits on it and lowers his pants. "In here first," she says from the bathroom. "We'll go by the rules this time, professor." In the sink she is washing my dink, he muses. This is better: clean, orderly, an act preceded by preparation, like a lesson plan before class.

Much later, it feels like very much later, she looks up from his crotch. "Sorry, professor, I haven't got all night to suck your cock. I got to go make a living. You understand." He does, and he's grateful to be asked for something he can do. "Thank you," he says, and gets up.

During lunch next day at the Parkside, he opens his wallet and wonders, Is this what's left? Where did it go? Was someone else in the room, hiding in the closet behind the chair over which she draped his pants, while he shut his eyes and moaned, mostly to encourage her to keep going? During the half-minute before he entered, did someone slip out of the bed and hide? Or when she dipped into his wallet in the dark . . .?

Back home in Toronto. Oskar steps into the airport. No one is here to meet him. His life consists of not being met at airports. At least his sabbatical is over.

He passes Immigration, then Customs. He has nothing to declare, a moment of shattering self-exposure. Hermann has so much to declare. So does Buzz, and Kroitermann. Even Bella has a philosophy of life. He steps through the opaque door into the airport lounge. There are no businessmen swinging attaché cases in figure eights as they pass wrist watches before their faces.

They have been driven from the place, for it is Friday night, immigrant night at Pearson International. Charters arrive and leave, families are bawling. It looks like a bazaar. Is this home?

Orange juice, he thinks. He walks toward the fresh citrus booth. Life resumes a little meaning after the searing passage through Customs. There is no one here he knows, or who knows him. It could be the Seventh Avenue subway.

But it's not. On the edge of a black leatherette couch – on the edge of more than that, and on more than the edge too – is someone he knows. Not just a student, but one from the Great Class. Why does Oskar pause? Is it the strangeness of the familiar, after he grew so familiar in New York with the strange? Or is it a message from this person – he has passed through some process, he has been somewhere, in and out of one of Wetherford's dimensions? It has changed him as mere time or experiences like hate, failure, and pain never change you. (At least so Oskar thinks later that night.) It is Teddy Stein. Teddy the moderate, Teddy the measured, Teddy the Most Likely To Succeed.

Oskar veers from his OJ vector. He crosses in front of Teddy. He doesn't register as even a blip on Teddy's screen. He continues a few awkward steps. He would like to talk to Teddy. It would feel slightly like being met. But he is reluctant to intrude, though he's not sure why. Anyway, Teddy should notice him first. He was the teacher, Teddy the student.

Oskar retraces his route. He slows as he is about to sweep past again. He swerves and stops. He is making an ass of himself. He stands directly above Teddy and says "Mr Stein," as though he's caught Teddy in the boys' room when he's supposed to be in the Children's Chapel. Teddy hears, he seems to have known all along, he tilts his head up without surprise. His face lights slowly, no one in normal life reacts to anything at this rate. "Would you like to sit down?" says Teddy, and waits with infinite patience. Oskar sits, and starts to converse normally.

As he does, Teddy's life flashes before Oskar's eyes. This is not so strange, since of all the young Canadian Jewish lives that have slipped through Oskar's fingers, Teddy is one of the few whose parents came from Germany. "They're very white," said

171

Jack Katz once, "compared to the rest of us." They participate proudly, they give to the building fund, they buy Israel bonds, they wouldn't think of denying their Jewishness. But they stand apart from the hordes of members from Russian and Polish stock. They don't speak Yiddish, not even the occasional phrase, and they never ever raise their voices. Oskar thinks he understands Teddy: the rigidity, the control, the striving after high – impossibly high – ideals.

Teddy organized the clothing blitz in confirmation year. It made their endless classroom chatter about social justice real. Teddy sent his teenage troops through the streets of Forest Hill like Panzers overrunning Poland. They returned victorious, arms and station wagons full of used cashmere and polyester. Teddy believed what they taught at Temple about changing the world. He had difficult relations with faith, but he was at home with practice. He won the sermonette contest that year, on the theme *Na'aseh v'nish'mah*, "We shall *do* and [then] we shall *hear*." A biblical phrase spoken by the children of Israel at Mount Sinai, which suggests, according to a tortuous Talmudic interpretation, that one learns through doing, not theorizing. Teddy liked doing – though at the moment he seems to hear something Oskar cannot. Around the leatherette couch a space is widening, like the ripple from a pebble dropped into Teddy's mind. Oskar feels alone with Teddy. He chatters about his sabbatical as though Teddy is an intelligence officer debriefing him after a mission. Teddy seems interested, and also absent. Oskar does not ask Teddy what he is doing. He doesn't say: Why are you here?

Teddy adored John F. Kennedy, as Oskar did. When Teddy won the Farber Oratorical Cup for his sermonette on doing and (then) hearing, he chopped at the front edge of the pulpit, just like JFK in a news conference or debating Nixon. When Kennedy was shot, Teddy flew to Washington and filed by the coffin along with the stricken Americans.

Teddy pleased his parents when he went to law school. It was good preparation for taking over the business: high-quality stationery. Oskar ordered his letterhead from them. Then Teddy started going to Yorkville, where the hippies are. Then he began helping them in court on their drug charges. He said he wasn't going into the business after all; he would practise law and aid the underclass. He dropped his long-time girlfriend, Ruthie, and moved in with the *shiksa*, a legal secretary who worked for him. He hasn't married her yet, but if he does, Oskar suspects, a tightly controlled Jewish-German hell will break loose.

"Why aren't you in Temple?" says Teddy. Oskar halts. Has Teddy heard nothing Oskar said about his sabbatical? He probably heard, but it didn't matter. This Teddy is not concerned with the paltry details of day-to-day. He is no more the practical Teddy of the clothing blitz. He is fixed on eternal recurrences. He has cut past the things one happens to have done recently; he wants to know what persists through time, uncontingent. It is Friday night, he points out – one prays.

Oskar can play this game. He says, "And you? Why aren't you at Temple, or your parents' home for Friday night dinner?"

"I was," says Teddy. "I was at Friday night dinner. Then I went to Temple."

Oskar senses a risk in proceeding, but Teddy has baited a hook. "Then why are you here now?" he asks.

"That's a very good question," says Teddy with a big smile, like teacher rewarding a student.

"How was the service?" says Oskar, trying too late to pull back. "How was the sermon?"

"It was a mess," says Teddy.

As they speak, a circle of men is tightening around their conversation. Oskar doesn't notice. The conversation is constricting enough, it draws in like a noose. "You see, Oskar," says Teddy, "it's really a question of interdating, to put it the way we did in Youth Group." Oskar nods, he is committed to Teddy's world now, he'll participate if he can.

"They don't talk reasonably," Teddy says, "the way we always did on youth weekends. They won't listen to the other side. Why does an intelligent Jewish boy like me do it with a girl who's not Jewish? I might have a very good argument for them. They should listen, instead of repeating everything. That's when I left. I drove straight to the temple."

173

A man with a chubby face stands before them. He wears a shiny suit. Beside and behind are other men, some in suits, some in uniform–police, airport security. The man speaks. "You move away," he says to Oskar.

Oskar moves. When they came to the barracks that afternoon, they told others to move away. Oskar wished he had been among them. He starts walking toward the exit and the downtown bus. Another man in a suit takes his arm. "Stay here, sir." The first man is talking to Teddy, Teddy is answering as though *he* is now being debriefed. Maybe he is asking why the man isn't in Temple. When they put handcuffs on Teddy, Oskar is surprised. If they had beaten or killed Teddy, he would have been less surprised. The man snaps them on delicately. "It's an arson," says the man beside Oskar. "He tried to torch that Jewish church on Bathurst."

"The Pillar of Fire?" says Oskar, hearing how silly it sounds.

"Yeh," the man chuckles. This must be the kind of humour that enters the life of a policeman.

"Did it burn down?" says Oskar. All he thinks of is his MA thesis in history, and he wonders whether the eternal light is still on.

"No," says the man. "Somebody caught it in time."

"But everyone was at Friday night dinner with their family," says Oskar.

"It was an old guy who works there," says the man. Oskar sees Mr Oates. "Is he all right?" asks Oskar.

"He put it out before it spread outside the choir loft," the man answers. "Then he called the fire department. Then he opened the front door for the service. Then he collapsed from smoke inhalation. He's at the hospital now."

As Teddy is led away, he passes Oskar. "It was a symbolic act," he says, "but I don't know what it means." It seems important to him that it was not irrational, it had significance. Teddy is not someone who acts from sheer emotion. Oskar says, "Ah," and Teddy is gone. The other man asks Oskar who he is and why he is here. "I just finished my sabbatical," says Oskar. He gives his name, which is hard for the man, who settles for Oskar's

174

position at the Pillar of Fire. Oskar can't remember the phone number there; this has never happened, but he never took a year off before. The man has enough information, or he has decided Oskar is not worth attention. When the man is gone, and the others, Oskar looks over to the orange juice booth. He sits down on the slippery couch. He touches the spot where Teddy sat. "Another first," he says softly, "for the class of '58."

His sabbatical is as though it never was. The staff wave their lesson plans, the students giggle at the eccentric man in the halls, Willi Schropp golfs and tennises through his board and the Toronto establishment. Years pass.

Oskar and Hermann have not made up over whatever Hermann did during Oskar's sabbatical; eventually it matters less. When Oskar can't remember why he hates Hermann (this time) he decides they can talk again. They are like family; their feelings about each other are irrelevant, they will always be connected. Oskar realizes: it doesn't matter what I do, what he does, how I feel, how he feels. "Our problem," says Hermann when they are talking again, after not talking, because of something neither recalls, "is we can't just get a divorce."

Sometimes they still walk, though the streets of Toronto have changed. People say the city is cosmopolitan. It has lost its provincial character. It has "come of age"; it is "world class." There are French restaurants that serve quiche. Toronto is sophisticated, they say constantly. Oskar wishes Toronto would stop coming of age. He misses the old days—ballet at the hockey rink, the 48th Highlanders in High Park.

Hermann is a *paterfamilias*. Three children now, his lovely wife Merle, the family home (two-storey brick, lawns front and back, double garage, imitation lantern with a street number on it). Oskar has not become Uncle Oskar. He is an infrequent guest, because they only invite him on Friday night. Merle still thinks Jesus is her saviour, but she has become adamant about Judaism, she's even a militant Zionist. There are times Oskar wants to pull out his circumcised dick and say to her: Look,

Merle, I *am* Jewish, you know. He wishes they would ask him another night, without candles and wine and Hermann blessing everybody. They never do, so he doesn't go, and they see each other less. Today Hermann has an announcement.

"You know, for twenty years I have been doing something and thinking I was doing something else," Hermann says. They are trudging through Yorkdale, the largest indoor shopping mall in the world, or North America, or Canada anyway. Hermann's family adore Yorkdale, like thousands of Canadian families. Merle and the oldest vanish into a cave of a shoe store. Hermann pushes little Jonah past the indoor palms.

"Why have I been writing all this time?" asks Hermann. "I have been striving to prove faith is not *ir*rational. I have tried to clear a space in which one can believe in God and not feel like an ancient relic." Oskar dodges a trio of thirteen-year-old girls, arms linked; he is listening with mild interest. Hermann does not usually associate his thoughts with his life. "I have shown that God is not impossible, you know?" Oskar nods. He is not on his other track. "I have argued for faith every which way, always on abstract grounds, like a medieval philosopher establishing universal truths. And I suddenly ask myself, Why? What did I need it for?"

Oskar laughs. "That is like feeding a sick horse with a pill through a blowpipe. Everything depends on who blows first!"

"I know," says Hermann, wincing. "That's what *I* always say every time anybody questions *my* motives for faith. I say it is like feeding a sick horse with a pill through a blowpipe. It's my dead pan."

"I know you always say it," says Oskar. "That's why I said it. I was quoting you against yourself. It's a joke." He pauses at a trash bin that has a name: Ricky Receptacle. Everything in Yorkdale looks like it is for sale, even the garbage cans. Oskar is sorry he interrupted Hermann. He enjoys seeing Hermann on his intellectual bicycle. "So?" he says. "What *did* you need it for?"

Hermann hesitates. This is historic. In the past, Hermann's pauses were like someone walking over to a filing cabinet, pulling out the necessary file, then carrying on. This time he doesn't have an answer, he can't find the file, maybe not even the cabinet. He temporizes, he is avoiding the question. "I wrote 'Self-Fulfilment and the Search for Faith,' " says Hermann. "I wrote 'Modern Man and the Arguments for the Existence of God'; I wrote 'Revelation and Reason, Reason and Revelation: Horns of a Dilemma'; then I wrote . . . well, I counted them. I wrote a hundred and fifty-five articles about the possibility of having faith, or the impossibility of not having it." Hermann is floundering; it is not a pretty sight. Oskar wishes he could help, he has never seen Hermann intellectually adrift, it makes him seasick. He has often thought he would like to see Hermann fail, or sad; but not *uncertain*. It is too cruel, it is unnatural.

"I never made it through any of your articles," says Oskar. "I tried, but I always quit." Maybe if he mentions how far above him Hermann's thoughts are, Hermann will cheer up.

"The point is," says Hermann, "nothing I wrote was connected to anything real!"

"What do you mean connected?" says Oskar. "Never mind that. What do you mean, *real*?" As though he, Oskar, is now the metaphysician, St. Thomas Aquinas prodding a dull seminarian.

"Why don't you ask me what I mean, *seemed*?" says Hermann.

"What do you mean, why don't I ask you?" says Oskar. "I'm asking you!"

"I mean," says Hermann, "nothing I wrote seemed connected to anything that was happening in my life and in the world. I mean history."

"You write about History all the time," says Oskar.

"No, not History," says Hermann. " Just . . . history." Each of them can hear, as they walk, the difference between History and history. Of all the people manoeuvring through Yorkdale mall while winter blusters outside, only Oskar and Hermann speak a language in which some words are capitalized and others are not. It is English, of course, which they have spoken together since Fran's, but they continue to capitalize the nouns, as in

German. "Plain ordinary history," says Hermann. "Not Metahistory, not Superhistory, not Election, Revelation, Redemption – " *Heilsgeschichte*, they think together. Both men glance quickly at the shopping throngs, wondering if anyone overheard this word they each thought in German. "Not Redemptive History," says Hermann *auf Englisch*. "Just the real stuff that happens in our times and our lives," he concludes with a kind of stammer Oskar has heard often when they are together, but always in his own mouth.

"Which?" says Oskar, with the fervour of the Grand Inquisitor. "What events are you talking about in our lives that explain everything you've been doing for twenty years? This all sounds pretty complicated and intellectual to me."

"We got out," Hermann says. He does not elaborate.

"Yes," says Oskar.

"Others didn't and we did," says Hermann. Around them swirl the strains of Canadian shopping.

> *Just hear those sleighbells jingling*
> *Ring-ting-tingling too*
> *Come on, its lovely weather*

"You have to do something because you got out. So for twenty years I have tried to deny Hitler one final victory, you know? That's what it's been for. That's why I did it."

"So what about God?" says Oskar. "What about faith?" Hermann shrugs. Oskar presses: "Was that wrong? Was it just so Hitler wouldn't win?"

"I don't think so," says Hermann. "But it wasn't the point."

"What wasn't the point?" says Oskar.

"Faith," says Hermann. "And God."

Oskar feels like Moses in the divine presence. Not the time when Moses got it all from God straight, face-to-face as they say, on the top of the mountain. But another time, when Moses huddled against the cleft in the side of the mountain, and God passed by, with a great noisy wind, and all Moses got to see was His back. That's how Oskar feels now. Something has happened, something just went past, he's not sure what, but he knows it was important.

"I always felt like your idiot brother," Oskar says to Hermann, "because I was interested in history, not theology." Hermann nods as if he is running these words of Oskar's through his brain and verifying them. Can it be: has Oskar been ahead of Hermann all this time because of his interest in history? Then Hermann wags his head side to side; he will snatch away, as always, what he just granted. "It's not your kind of history either," he says heavily, "that I'm talking about," and Oskar knows he will get no points even in Hermann's rare moment of self-doubt. Nor does he deserve credit. Because history has been for Oskar what theology was for Hermann. Avoidance. Detachment. Thinking about, instead of living through. Disconnection. "So what kind of history is it you mean?" says Oskar sadly.

"It's history as it makes us," says Hermann in the middle of Yorkdale. "And history that we make. It's . . . politics really. It's . . . what's *done*."

Let us blow through the blowpipe from the other end one more time and ask, Why did Hermann raise this issue and reach this conclusion about himself, at this point in his own history and that of our time? The moment is January 1968, the winter sequel to the glorious summer after the Six Day War.

It is difficult to reconsruct the effect of that momentous clash on the Jews of Toronto and the world. Let us begin in the middle, while the war of June 1967 rages.

Israel's ambassador to the United Nations stands before that body; he is imperturbable yet impassioned. He documents the right of Israel to strike in self-defence. He assails the "obscenity" of Soviet comparisons between Israel and Nazi Germany. His voice carries eloquently. Here is balm for the anguish Jews have felt in past weeks and millennia. It is balm because this moment is *not* a reprise of others, evoked by names like Nebuchadnezzar, Antiochus, Torquemada, Hitler. This moment leapfrogs those

179

names in reverse; it arches back and connects with an ancient situation, because once again there is a Jewish state, a Jewish army, and a Jewish voice among nations.

"When you get to Damascus, phone home and ask for yourself," says Mrs Moshe Dayan as her husband, defence minister in Israel's new unity government, leaves for the Syrian front. This joke voices the feeling of the After, when the war was decisively won. It is the voice of Jewish relief after two thousand years of passivity, of a people who now *do*, and don't only suffer. The relief is like an explosion.

Now consider the Before. This is harder to reconstruct than the After ("When you get to Damascus . . .") or the During (the United Nations ambassador). Still, one learns from trying. (Remember Oskar's experience in Union seminary on Good Friday. "We see the Crucifixion through the portal of Easter Sunday," said Munch. "But view it through the eyes of those at the foot of the cross two days before."

The Before of North American Jews in early June 1967 is as gaunt and despairing as Munch on Good Friday. They hear Arab millions howl, "THROW THE JEWS INTO THE SEA." The enemy seems overwhelming. The catastrophes of Jewish history are about to receive another. Perhaps the Befores of all those disasters contained a little hope, less as the chain lengthened—until we came to expect calamity as routine. It amounted at some point to inevitability. What we never learned was the alternative: victory.

Now put the event together, from its Before, through the event, to its After. What did Hermann experience? Why did he ask his question: What did I do it for? and reach his answer: To deny Hitler another victory–just then?

For many Jews, the lightning victory of 1967 came as a great surprise. The fate of Israel, state and people, seemed to have been sealed before the war began. The experience of Exile meshed with the accounts of the press, the experts, the sorrowful mood in the air they breathed. Yet the catastrophe failed to happen. There appeared to be no explanations available, all options had been canvassed and a unanimous prediction voiced.

Even the heroic behaviour of the Israeli people seemed necessary but hardly sufficient, to the result. Something else must have intervened. Or Someone. Him. El Shaddai, the ancient God of Israel who went before His people and they smote their enemies. It was difficult to find another explanation. The hand of God in contemporary history was, well, a logical conclusion. Nothing fancy, just–God has spoken. The victory of the armed forces of the state of Israel was, sorry to put it this way, a miracle.

In those days, Hermann, along with many Jews, and many non-Jews as well, felt he saw and heard the voice of God in headlines and bulletins. For two decades he had tried to clear a modest intellectual space for the ancient Lord of Hosts. Suddenly, in a few days, God existed not as a theoretical possibility but an active force. What about his own faint-heartedness those many years, when for the most part he sought a mere theoretical permit to entertain the hypothesis of a living, acting God? He felt scandalized by his own lack of faith–all in the name of faith. God was acting while he *kvetched*. It was the moment of a new beginning.

> *The lion has roared, who will not fear?*
> *The Lord God has spoken, who can but prophesy?*

From now on he would speak less of theology and more of history, of what was actually being done, of politics.

What about Oskar at this volatile moment in modern Jewish history? How did he pass through the phases of the Six Day War? Like other Jews. When it was over, he was ecstatic; he swooned to the news of the victories. In the street, on the subway, at a committee meeting, he cackled wildly at the joke about Mrs Dayan and the collect call. Inside, though, nothing changed. The event did not restructure him. Unlike Hermann, he believed no more nor differently than he had.

If Oskar chooses to think of himself in his ideal life as a historian, perhaps it is because he wishes to be, in his daily life, historical. He does not seem to require life to have great significance. Modest significance will do. He does not mean to be selfish or petty: he'd like to educate well and help others as they cross his path. But he does not need to be a character in a cosmic drama of salvation, a *Heilsgeschichte*. Others say history and mean myth. For Oskar, history is the opposite of myth.

Maybe this is why Oskar developed his futile fantasy about being a historian—as a sort of personal stand against myth. What makes you suspicious is he never came close to actually doing the thing: no doctorate after the MA, no scholarly publications. You start to think something else was involved, something less practical than a normal career goal. A statement of belief, or unbelief, a symbolic act of his own. It's true he dealt in myth and faith: the courses and syllabi he designed were full of them. He even looked like a myth and often acted like one: alone, disproportionate, imperious. Perhaps, although Oskar personified myth and inculcated it, he tried to struggle against the mythifications that his age, his people, and he himself practised.

He is always a fascinated onlooker at mythic dramas and celebrations of faith, especially when others he knows, like Hermann or Buzz, participate. Sometimes he mimics them, wondering whether he could take part if he wanted. But in the end he always learns it is not his game, and he doesn't play it.

6

ON THE DAY Oskar arrives in Israel, some years after the Six Day War, he has a problem, naturally. It is: How does one set foot in the land of Israel? Why is this a problem? Because for a Jew, arrival in the land of our fathers has always been an event that must be specially marked. Yet for Oskar, it should not be a puzzle; he has been here before, has already planted his foot on this terrain. It was nearly forty years ago, when he was still young, still German even, in the time before the war. Then, however, although this was *Eretz Yisrael* – the land of Israel, his people – it was not yet the land, Israel.

He felt like a biblical figure in those days. Not a judge, a prophet, or a king, however. He was an anonymous player, one among thousands. He was the "wayfarer turned aside for the night" whom someone – Oskar thinks it was Jeremiah – mentioned in passing. A character role.

He turned aside, from Berlin, politics, fear, responsibility. Oh, he travelled there for a serious reason, on assignment from the movement, and he completed his mission after he returned. Yet while he actually journeyed, it was as though he turned aside from that responsibility and entered something airier, like stepping into a fable or legend he once read.

He came on a Turkish ship, from the port of Naples, through

the heart of the seas. He felt he was a charmed traveller, nothing would stand in his way nor prevent his arrival. The hustlers of Naples assailed him when he descended from the train on his way to the port. They ringed him round with imprecations. They lunged for his valises. He broke past them and cut his way among the crowds along the ramp, then burst through the doors into the great marble interior of the station Mussolini had built there. The beggars of the city spotted him as he entered. From every corner of the compass they streamed toward him with their demands for alms and hire. He held his ground, stood frighteningly still, and howled a mighty NEIN! into their faces. It echoed from the vaulted ceiling, it rattled against the windows and wooden benches. They retreated in the face of his Nein. *Retreat* is insufficient – they melted from his presence. He prevailed utterly. This was the power he felt, by the grace of which he undertook that voyage.

He barely slept during the passage. This was due not only to the rapturous state of his anticipation but also to his travelling companions on board, especially the bald man with the bulging tumour on the left side of his head who slept directly below Oskar, and the seven snoring, phlegm-producing voyagers with whom they shared a narrow metallic stateroom. Creatures whose company in another circumstance, any other circumstance, at any other moment, on any other mission in his life, would have filled Oskar with bile. No matter, he went happily up on deck each night. He scanned the skies, he hummed to himself. No inconvenience was potent enough to dent the sense of well-being that accompanied him – not just accompanied but transported him like a magic carpet, on which he lolled as it whisked him toward his goal.

When they berthed in Haifa, he wafted down the gangplank. What did he do as he transferred his presence from sea to land, not just land, but *the* land – *ha'aretz* – as distinct from all other mere "lands"? He did not do as, for instance, an elderly couple, the Metzenbaums, who shared the voyage but never appeared at the mess table, owing to the absence of kosher food. He did not, like them, lower himself to his knees and drop his face to kiss the concrete dock. He smiled as he watched them. Nor did he skip briskly from ship to shore like sailors and merchants, lifting his eyes to scan the surroundings in search of a welcoming face, or merely for orientation. Instead, though he had given no thought to this moment, he did a wholly appropriate thing. He firmly, consciously, shifted the weight of his corporeal presence from one foot to the other, one reality to the other. He stepped more intently and deliberately from *that* place (Outside The Land) to *this* (The Land) than he had ever planted a foot before or would again. It was a completely private act, it contained no outward manifestations. Yet he felt certain that he had stepped a decisive step, he had truly *done* something. It was, he thought afterward, an example of what the *hassidim* call *kavanah*, or perfectly concentrated human attention. It was as unequivocal an act as he could perform in his life, though no one knew but him. It marked his arrival. Now it was time for *aliyah*, going up.

Travelling directly to Jerusalem was unsensible. It lacked *yekke* logic, the hardheaded calculus of efficiency German Jews are known for. The movement office was in Haifa where he landed, the educational centre was in Tel Aviv; nor was the kibbutz to which Greta had been posted along the way. Yet here he was, like Bing Crosby and Bob Hope, on the road to the Holy City and nowhere else. When ushered into the King's presence, does one tarry to chat with courtiers who line the approach?

Up and up they mounted, the little bus grunting and creaking, the day fading and hiding behind one hilltop and another. One truly did "go up" to Jerusalem. No wonder every trip by a Jew to the land of Israel was a going up and not just a going to. Slowly and painlessly, but always mounting. A gradual ascent, human and measurable; not a sudden elevation, an Ascension, as Christians would have organized but a worldly and manageable one, Jewish, real. Through stands of scruffy little trees – one might almost have thought one was in the climbing country of Thuringia (or the lakes and woods of northern Ontario if one had ever been there)–the road slanting gently, then twisting back on itself to continue its painless rise, shepherds and their flocks, truly, and by the roadside the scrubbed white exteriors of homes belonging to Arab peasants and their families, like little mosques. The hillsides were terraced, row on row of terracing, what patience to farm them, what evidence they gave of generations – no, centuries; no, millennia – of human care. What a humanized landscape. It made the well-worked fields and valleys of Europe appear to have only just met the effects of human tendance. (Not to mention the virgin forests and newly cleared fields of North America, which, of course, one had not seen and did not expect to.)

Gradually one became aware of the tops of these Judean hills, fading gently and amiably into the sky, a friendly relationship at the horizon, just the way the hills amicably flowed into one another while the bus with its placid passengers rolled contentedly toward Jerusalem. Then, in the distance, atop the crown of one of the hills, much like all the others, appeared a cluster of buildings, sitting like a happy ending: the Temple mount, the Holy City. Oskar felt at peace with himself, and at peace with this setting. In the days to come, when the Messiah delays no longer, Jerusalem will be like all of *Eretz Yisrael*, and *Eretz Yisrael* will be like all the world. The bus grunted and heaved around another bend, the community of buildings perched on the hilltop drew nearer. The sun passed into the open between two hills and spread some of its gold along the crowns that interlaced and joined together like a tasteful embroidery. The city drew them to it like the pilgrims they were, like travellers turning aside to lodge for the night. Dusk cloaked the streets as they entered Jerusalem and left the terraces behind them to the soft mercies of evening, which arrived like a courteous guest.

That same sweet night, he left the hostel, refreshed, settled in, his few travelling things carefully arranged as though he had arrived back in his true home after years of instability and wanderlust, and caught the rickety Egged bus to the centre of town. The centre of the centre. As he ran for the bus he tried to breathe in the fresh new smells of the night air and rocky surrounding hills. Why not wait for the next bus? Or when he returned, give himself time to appreciate these unique scents? The bus driver, explaining the fare, addressed him in Hebrew! More of the every-day miracles of this unreal place. He arduously translated in his mind – numbers are always the most difficult part of a new for-eign language, he reminded himself, all educators know this – and then carefully separated the coins into the required amount. The driver eyed him with tolerant boredom. A Hebrew-speaking Jewish bus driver who treats an inept passenger as though this is a normal occurrence: the marvel of it might never fade.

He descended at King George the Fifth Street and proceeded directly to Ben-Yehudah Street. He paused to luxuriate in this, a major artery recalling the father of the recreation of the Hebrew language. A block and a half up he found the Finjan, a restaurant the hosteliers recommended. He hesitated carefully over the choice between kofta and kebab. He knew one was minced lamb, like patties; the other was chunks of meat broiled over a flame. Middle Eastern to their heart. He was passing backward at great speed through the epochs of his people's history: the age of Napoleon, the era of the Enlightenment were already gone; then the Renaissance, the time of the Polish *shtetl*, the late Middle Ages, the Golden Age of Spain. Swifter now: the Dark Ages, the Jews of Provence, the Rabbinic periods – Amoraim, and before them the early rabbis, the Tannaim; the age of the Apocrypha, the Maccabees! And when he had scarcely realized it, here he was, again, where he began this meal: in the land of the Bible. He ordered a plate of felafel. This too they talked of in the movement back home, that is in Berlin, and he stopped to won-der, while his order was being prepared, at the astounding and complete overhaul of national life that even included the creation of a new menu for a new kind of restaurant. The rebirth of his people included everything, but what touched him deepest were the things he had not anticipated: the bus driver and felafel. It came with a dark green salad of parsley and cucumbers.

He walked home, that is, to the hostel. He was unsure of the way, but he did not fear. The path seemed to lead down one hill, then up another. He was away now, from the shops and restau-rants and cinemas of Ben-Yehudah Street and Zion Square, and from the low houses and duplexes that surrounded them. The stars above were bright, and the sky seemed lower than it ever had to him like, like . . . a firmament! Not the endless abyss of modern astronomy, relativizing all dimensions and directions; rather a finite dome, a vault, as the story in Genesis says, arching above the concrete world below, enclosing it protectively, into which the stars are stuck like pinpricks, and which holds back the waters of the heavenly realm and prevents them from washing over the fragile earth along with its carefully created and nominated species.

As he walked and marvelled, another urge seized him. He had to urinate. Surely not here, on the very ground over which *David ha-melech,* David the King, grazed his flocks as a shepherd boy, awaiting news of his brothers off in battle under mighty King Saul. David, not merely king but king of poets, who wrote, just as Oskar now felt, "The earth is the Lord's and the firmament declareth his handiwork." Yet what else, thought Oskar the traveller turned aside, would David the King have done on a night like this in this very spot? *David ha-melech* had a bladder too. Oskar was seized with a sense of divine mischief. He unbuttoned his fly with a flourish, he whipped out his dink and peed happily on the rocks, scrub, and dust of the Judean hills.

Those were days of awe in the life of Oskar. His experience seemed full of a quality it had always before, and would always afterward, lack. Full of fullness. He travelled the land from end to end, from Metuleh to the Negev, from the sea to the deserts of the Aravah. Never had he seemed so firmly set in the here and now, as Buber might have said. Yet he did not feel disconnected from the life that had preceded. On the contrary, his earlier life appeared now as preparation for this journey. The experiences he had here seemed to contain for the first time the real meaning of all he had done before. He went camping everywhere in the land, as if he was obsessed with sleeping on the same ground his biblical forebears had slept on. In the ruins of Hazor, in the north. On the shores of the Dead Sea, or those of Kinnereth, for that matter, the Sea of Galilee of Jesus and his disciples, who also seemed a part of his heritage now. At the oasis of Ein Gedi, and at the foot of Masada, the fortress from which the martyrs of Bar Kochba hurled themselves, rather than fall into the torturers' grasp of Roman legions. He took friends and comrades, old and new, or went alone, and each night he spent in his sleeping bag on the earth of *Eretz Yisrael* seemed more wondrous and more normal. Surely this was the inner meaning of all those hikes and campfires in the Grunewald and the Black Forest—but a meaning that could only be revealed here, never there.

One night they camped among Roman ruins at the ancient port of Caesarea on the Mediterranean. A British patrol stopped on the road above, evidently in search of illicit attempts to land Jewish refugees as darkness began to fall. They asked for Oskar's papers and those of his companions, and travelled on. With dusk came heavy seas, waves beating against the remnants of the docks and breakwater constructed so long ago by the engineers of an earlier empire, repaired and reinforced through the centuries by the passing powers: Saladin, the crusaders, Napoleon, the sultan. Those works now stood in disrepair. Out beyond the breakwater, he first thought it was simply the waves playing to create fantastic shapes. No, it was boats and figures, struggling to reach the piers behind the breakwater, looking up and noticing him alone on the beach, wandered down from the campfire his companions shivered around. He moved closer, the shapes waved for help, he pressed forward, to connect with this tattered remnant, returning with such stealth and tenacity from whatever captivity they had come, as he had, through the heart of seas.

Closer up, they were swarthy and dark, their voices harsh and guttural. Fellow Jews from the northern shores of Africa – Tunis or Tripoli? Or Yemenites, or Falashas even, from Abyssinia? Or farther: the Jews of India, or of China? None. Local Arab fishermen actually, beaching their boats as they did each night when the seas began to kick up like this. They grinned at his arrival and smiled more when he indicated by gestures he would be pleased to help. When the deed was done, their boats rolled over on the sand, they beckoned him to their quarters, a crumbling enclosure that must once have been a watchtower on the breakwater's edge. He sat with them for hours, drinking their strong coffee. They seemed to discuss many things, Oskar and these Arabs, for by the end he knew about their families, the number of their children (a few had photographs), and something, at least impressions, of their lives as fishermen and fathers. Yet he realized, as he stumbled dreamily back up the beach toward the fire around which his friends snored, that he and they had no language in common. They could not speak Hebrew, he knew no Arabic, German was not a possibility. How had they passed this time and shared so much? By what power? They even invited him for lunch next day at their home in Acco.

There were no street signs in Acco, not even Arabic. Like a camper in a wood on a dark and starless night, he allowed his feet to discover the path in the going, and put faith in his body to follow. They rejoiced in his coming, like a joy they had anticipated confidently, not an unlikely event they had joked about or bet on, and they indicated graciously he should remove his shoes before entering the room for dining. He was embarrassed, for the only time during this enchanted journey, and touched that they made no reference, even subtly, to the white of his skin showing through his threadbare socks, or the smell he feared rose from them. They laid a splendid meal at his feet, literally. The food was spread on a cloth around which they settled, by women who appeared and withdrew wordlessly. There was no cutlery. Each man deftly swooped down on the various dishes with a piece of pita bread employed as a scoop. It seemed so logical, so efficient, not at all unsanitary or undignified. Yet he knew there was another Oskar, perhaps awaiting his return across the seas, who would have felt disgust. Was he a different being in this land? Did he have a different soul? Was a different soul for each Jew laid up in storage in the Holy Land, awaiting distribution in the Days to Come? How could simple acts and words hold meanings for him so contrary to those they held when he was at home, that is, in Berlin?

He sat and gazed across their table, that is, the cloth laid on their immaculate packed earth floor—everything here so close to the land itself. He looked out the window, that is, the square opening in the whitewashed clay wall—all things here so simple

190

and transparent. Across the bay sat Haifa, the new Jewish port, while he squatted here in the Arab quarter, the crusader city of Acco. An encounter between the ancient cultures of this ancient place, and Oskar himself the transposable part. A human being full and whole, and a Jew without diminution. They asked him, though he could not afterward recall how, to give them something of his own in return for the meal when they had done and the dishes had been replaced by a *finjan*, as they explained their elaborate coffee pot was called. A song perhaps, he knew they were saying. He had no idea what to offer, but he did not panic. He paused and waited for the answer to come. *Artza alinu*, he raised his voice. *Artza alinu, artza alinu, artza alee-ee-nu.* We have gone up to the land, we have gone up to the land, we have gone up to the land. *Kfar harashnu*, we have already ploughed, *v'gam zarahnu*, and we have sown, *avahl ohd loh katzarnu*, but we have not yet reaped.

All things were new here. *When I cause you to return to the land I gave your fathers, I will give you a new heart.* An inverted heart. The impossible was possible, mysteries were revealed, even faith and prayer became the stuff of his daily life. On a Saturday morning in Jerusalem he walked slowly and feelingly through the narrow streets of Mea Shearim. He had been warned against entering here, above all on *shabbat*. The zealots of the Tradition were likely to stone him, or any outsider desecrating the day. But since, for him here, all things were inverted, he went. A semi-musical babble of voices poured from a window above. He looked up. He saw a narrow balcony with a railing. On it stood a boy, dark, with earlocks and a silk *yarmulke* on his head. His little hand, like the little paw of a bear cub, beckoned urgently to Oskar: Come up, come up. He went.

There were few of them in the room, a *minyan* plus one or two. The women must be behind the cardboard partition with the two small holes in it. Most of the men were gathered around the Torah, its scrolls already spread on a shaky reading-stand. No one showed awareness that Oskar had entered. He reached for a *siddur* and pretended to find the correct page. They muttered and shuffled their way through the *parsha* of the *shavua*, absorbed in routine and praise. A *Cohen*, a Levite, and then ordinary Israelites succeeded one another to the scrolls, blessing them before and after the reader chanted his way, section by section, through that week's biblical reading. Suddenly one of them was at his elbow. "*Attah Yehudi?*" said the scrawny man: You Jewish? Oskar nodded. The man swivelled his head toward the front and gave a Jewish wink to the little crowd gathered there: both eyes closing and opening together with a slight grin while his whole head slowly bobbed and rose. Their collective approval ushered Oskar forward. Someone draped him in a prayer shawl as he arrived at the table. With the hem of the *talit* gripped between his fingers he delicately touched the word in the scroll indicated by the reader – so far have we come in this week's reading, it is now my task to move us along. He inhaled tensely, trusted himself again, and plunged as he had so often since he arrived. Again it worked. The phrases of the blessing to be chanted during the Torah service sprang spontaneously from his throat to his mouth and from there out over the scrolls of the Law. The members of the congregation nodded as though the world was firmly set in the order established during the seven days of creation, and the reader read the designated portion of the portion. At its end, Oskar calmly and fluently produced the blessing to be chanted after reading a Torah section, and returned to his seat amid many warm handclasps and congratulatory grunts. These were Jews, he recalled from his earlier life, who would have appalled him: ritualistic, narrow, uncultivated, and, to be frank, dirty. Polacks or Litvaks or Galitzianers. Ghetto Jews. Someone else named Oskar had thought those thoughts. Here all Israel was one body, Israel was their name.

He returned once to Mea Shearim, shortly before his departure. It was *Simchat Torah*, the birthday of the Torah, celebrated by rolling the entire scripture back from one overfull scroll to the other, so that anyone hoisting the twin rollers is bound to teeter over to the left-hand side, until the balance is redressed and then reassigned to the right-hand side, all the way to In the beginning God created and so forth. Imbalance to balance to imbalance, like the course of a Jewish life in our times. Oskar suspected on his first chance visit that they might be *hassidim*. He discovered now that they were. He lurched into the second-floor room again, just the way the last rays of day slanted through the window from which the boy had summoned him. They were already running through the preliminary prayers of the service. Running, that's it, they truly were, in a hurry to get somewhere. They reached the *Sh'ma* – perhaps that was their goal – the *Sh'ma*, affirmation of divine unity, heart of the service in the austere, Protestantized synagogues of Berlin. No, they were already past it, they were well beyond, people pacing restlessly throughout the room, prayer books in hand, as though looking for wastebaskets to empty at the end of a workday. They were halfway through the *Amida*, the standing prayer, everyone tripping and traipsing through it at his own rate (or hers, with a glance at the partition with the two round openings) wandering hither and yon in this cramped chamber, miraculously avoiding each other like taxis in a Roman rush hour, treating Oskar rooted to his spot with familiarity, not exactly as one of their own, more like a fire hydrant, a liturgical fire hydrant, which they take for granted as they amble or scurry by.

Then they opened the *aron kodesh*, the ark of the convenant, the repository of the Torah scrolls, and the tempo changed. They removed the *sefer Torah*s, they began to parade them about, they would doubtless lay them delicately on the reader's table and begin to read. Perhaps Oskar would even get another *aliyah*, another call up to the reading-stand, though this time there were more than enough men even if they extended the number of *aliyah*s beyond the required seven, in honour of this once-a-year occasion. But no, they did not. Not lay the Torahs down and advance through the service, but merely laid them aside, and paused a long pause in the liturgical course of things. Instead of proceeding straight to the Torah readings – and rewindings – those *hassidim* hauled long wooden trestle tables from somewhere into the narrow low room and laid the tables end to end. Others fetched benches and stationed them down the length of each side. On top of the tables appeared mountainous platefuls of shmaltz herring and bottle after bottle of Slivovitz brandy.

Everybody was drinking. Everybody was bolting forkfuls of herring. But mostly, everybody was singing. They sang as if this was the Olympics of singing, and they had trained and rehearsed for it over many years. Oskar craned his neck toward the centre of the table, lowered his eye line, and sighted down its length. From this angle their motion looked like the beat of oars inside a Roman galley. Everyone with an elbow on the table, raising his hand, then slapping down his palm, all in unison, not just unison but frenzy, and singing with abandon. *Emis*, they sang. Not *Emet*, as the *sabras*, the native-born Israelis, would say, but *Emis*, as in the ghettoes of Eastern Europe. *True.* "True it is that You are first / And true it is that You are last / And beside You there is no other." *Emis, emis, emis, emis, emis, emis, emis, emis.*

There were only a few glasses on the table, little shot glasses, and they skittered across the tabletop like billiard balls. One slid to a stop before Oskar. Across from him a head in a furry *shtreimel* tipped forward, a bottle of Slivovitz enfolded in a huge hand, and poured a full glass right in front of Oskar. He knew the procedure instinctively, or via peripheral vision, which took in the same drill up and down the room, or just because he knew, being here in this place at this moment. He raised the glass, looked left, looked right, barked, *l'chaim, l'chaim* – they chorused back, *l'chaim, l'chaim* – he tossed it down his gullet in one motion and one swallow. It scorched a passage along his throat and across a strip of his stomach lining. No time to recuperate, he seized the bottle and poured a glass for someone else. This was the ethic, this was their code. None pours for himself, each pours for another. Eternal reciprocality, true community. The meaning of life according to the teaching of Hassidism. But experienced directly, here and now, not via Buber, for once. Top it up, shout it out, down the hatch, on to the next. Oskar reached for the herring. It was permitted to serve oneself herring. The salty taste mitigated the searing of his insides. The volume rose, so did the temperature. The Torah scrolls leaned patiently in a corner. He wanted a break, he strolled outside. No one noticed, nobody looked after him as he went. The sound subsided. He stood in the street and stretched toward the stars.

When he returned, minutes or hours later, they were sliding the tables back against the walls. Empty plates and bottles outnumbered people. The rhythm continued, the singing never ceased, though now they were not eating and drinking. They were dancing. Not alone, not with one another – with the Torahs! Spinning, whirling, dipping. Old men cradling a Torah in one arm and somersaulting on the bare wooden floor while with the other hand they reached for their *yarmulke* to see it didn't fall from their heads. On and on. For a while he lingered at the side like a wallflower, then he let himself go, followed his feelings, and joined. *Al tifrosh min ha-tzibbur.* Do not separate thyself from the community. Eventually they spread the Torahs on the reading desk, read them perfunctorily, and returned them to the *aron kodesh*. Mere words, even words revealed to Moses Our Teacher on Mount Sinai, were bound to be an anticlimax after one had seen a Torah dance. It petered out. He departed through the twisty streets of Mea Shearim, then began crossing the terraced hills of Judea on his way back to the hostel. He paused, and peed, and went on his way. He was feeling amiable.

When he left finally, after a visit that lasted, or should we say lingered, seven weeks (though such a thing cannot be measured in the kind of time that is applicable outside the land of Israel), he wondered whether he was "going down" as he had seven weeks earlier – by outside time – gone up. But he knew "going down" was the derogatory term applied to those who abandon the land after having earlier committed themselves to it. This was inappropriate, since he had come only on a visit, to see and learn (and become whole) and report back to those who were unable to see for themselves. Still, if he was not going down, that suggested he had not really gone up. Yet he had rarely felt anything so clearly as that he had not only gone to, but gone up to, the land of Israel, that is, Israel, his people.

He left on a Greek freighter, from the old Arab port of Jaffa. He felt such a sweet sadness. Even a departure from *Eretz Yisrael* is unique nourishment to the soul. Better to leave *Eretz Yisrael* than to come and stay in any other place. He had only one regret: he had not met up with Greta and the members of the movement who were, at almost exactly the same time, making *aliyah* and establishing a kibbutz. They were to have arrived in the midst of his own stay, and nothing would have better suited him than to leave a bit of himself, a memory of Oskar, to be planted with their first crops. Their boat however was delayed.

He stood on the deck of the freighter as the shore line gently released its grip and allowed the ship to steam slowly away. He would have liked to experience and re-experience this exquisite parting, and afterward relive it in his mind, in a way that would become common only much later in an age of television and replays. He gazed over the harbour, the docks and the little buildings behind it; to the north squatted the burly young frame of the new Jewish city of Tel Aviv. His eyes were like a hose, like a pump, drawing in the sights, sounds, smells; like a block and tackle determined to haul away events and impressions that filled this magical time. He knew eventually, some time before the shore line completely faded from view, that he would reluctantly turn his gaze to focus firmly and responsibly on Europe and the future. But while they were still withdrawing, while they were still just at the harbour's edge, he heard a medley of voices from over the water, joined together in one united cry: "Oskar!" He looked around, he swung his gaze like binoculars on a swivel mount: it was Greta and the others from the movement, on a little ship across the harbour, entering as he was leaving and though surely intent on drinking in their own first sights of the Aretz, by some grace that he knew was typical of this place, they had seen him on deck. "Oskar!" they cried again, and he managed to wave through his tears. He had felt close to them many times but he never had and never would feel so close as he did in this instant of connection. He smiled the forerunner of his crazy grin and waved jerkily at them till not even specks of each other were visible in the sunlight that played over land and sea as he descended and they went up.

The book he wrote when he returned to Berlin was dry and

comprehensive. It contained chapters on the geography of the land and the demographics of Jewish settlement. It discussed obstacles to agriculture and analysed the politics of immigration in the light of indigenous Arab opposition and the prerequisites of Mandatory, that is, British, policy. It was informative and, as he said in the copy he wrote for the jacket, indispensable for those seriously considering migration and resettlement in Palestine. Nothing in what he wrote conveyed even a slight fragrance of that enchantment he experienced incessantly from the instant of his arrival to the moment when the shore line of Jaffa dropped below the horizon. Just as, for that matter, the entire experience of his time in the land contained neither a hint nor an echo of all the terror and anxiety that weighed on every moment of his life in Berlin before he left and after he returned. The centre for education published the slim volume, and members of the movement responded appreciatively by buying the odd copy and passing it around among themselves till the pages fell out.

Each Jew has a soul that awaits him in the Holy Land and exists for him only there. When the Messiah, the son of David, comes and arranges the conveyance of all Israel back to the Temple mount, via the clouds of heaven or whatever form of transportation he has in mind, then and only then will each Jew make the acquaintance of the special soul that awaits him there. In the meantime, which has lasted a long while, a slight glimpse of this soul is occasionally vouchsafed to a Jew on the Sabbath, particularly during its waning final scene, the Havdalah service. Still it is possible that on rare occasions a visitor to the Holy Land will chance to encounter his special soul there. However, even if such a delectable meeting occurs, it is unreasonable to expect that its effect would be transferrable to any place outside the Holy Land, even by way of mere description or reference to what occurred there. At the very most, a dim memory might persist.

Shortly after publication of the modest *oeuvre* that Oskar based on his journey, a note arrived in a packet from the publishing arm of the centre for education. It was from Buber. Oskar immediately wondered wherein he had failed with this, his first and now very likely last, published work. The note however was a brief, scribbled, and heartfelt congratulation. "I find only one element lacking," wrote Buber in an afterthought: "the inclusion of your own feelings about all that you saw and described." The return address was Department of Comparative Religion, The Hebrew University, Mount Scopus, Jerusalem. It was the first he learned of Buber's emigration, that is to say, his *aliyah*.

The cabin tilts. The ground approaches. The problem remains: How does one set foot in the land of Israel, Israel the state that is, in the middle of the 1970s?

So many passengers have crowded over to the left side of the airplane that their weight seems to be causing the tilt. It is not. Captain Uri Levinger of El Al airlines is banking his 747 as part of the approach to Ben-Gurion airport, and to provide his passengers with their first view of the Promised Land. "Sit down, sit down please, ladies and gentlemen," says stewardess Aviva Bar-Ott, forgetting to use her microphone, then seizing it and holding it too close to her mouth. No one pays attention. Jack Katz, sitting next to Oskar, raises his voice huskily and melodically, "*Kol ohd ba-levav pneemah, nefesh Yehudi homeeyah*." People join in. Some straighten up, to stand at attention for "Hatikvah," Israel's national anthem. Those over whose seats they have been leaning try to stand too. Others are constrained by their seat belts, which the sign illuminated by stewardess Bar-Ott instructs them to fasten. The result is a kind of milling-about, comprised of moving, singing, rising, and sitting. As the strains of "Hatikvah" die, a bustle begins for the hand luggage in the overhead racks, most of it containing gifts for relations here in the *aretz*, family whom one may never have seen. By the time the jet liner touches down, few of its passengers remain seated. Oskar, though, waits for the aisle to clear. He is thinking about this moment of arrival. He waves goodbye to Jack Katz, with whom he has sat for the past fourteen hours. When he first met Jack, in the bungalow off the muddy stretch of Toronto called Lawrence Avenue, Jack struck him as a model of America: a new kind of Jew, vigorous and confident, a powerhouse of a person who built housing subdivisions with a combination of will, greed, financial acumen, and his bare hands. Now he is bald and bombastic, but the old energy remains. He looks like a Ray-O-Vac flashlight battery, with tufts of hair and slits for eyes. The new wing of the old addition to the school building back in Toronto is named after Jack. During this trip a dormitory of the nursing faculty at the Beersheba campus of the Hebrew University will be dedicated to him. Their partnering on this flight was accidental. Oskar has come ostensibly to attend a convention of liberal Jewish educators, the first time their association has convened outside either Canada or the United States.

The cabin is emptying. Oskar cannot wait much longer, he still has not solved his problem. When he steps jerkily down the ramp and onto the tarmac, will he rediscover the *kavanah* that once upon a time enabled him to step decisively yet imperceptibly from one reality to another?

The problem is solved for him. There is no ramp, there is no tarmac. An enclosed tubular passage is hydraulically accordioned up to the door of the airplane. Through it the *olim* of the late twentieth century enter the airport directly. Oskar eyes its entrance. Stewardess Bar-Ott has seen this response before. "It will soon be standard at airports throughout the world, sir," she says. "It increases security, and as you are aware the security of our passengers is our foremost concern." She speaks these words so fluidly, unlike her other English phrases, he would not be surprised to hear the needle catch on one of the grooves in her brain: "Our foremost concern – CLICK – our foremost concern – "

His first step onto sanctified terrain has ceased to be an issue. In a sense it has ceased to exist. For where does it occur? As one proceeds into the tubular passage? When one emerges from the tubular passage into the lengthy corridor of the airport proper leading to the baggage carousel? When one clears customs? When one steps through the electronic doors into the arrivals area? The crush here is enormous, it is hardly possible to exercise *kavanah*. When one steps outside then, before one picks up the rented car that ought to be waiting if all proceeds as arranged? Yes, surely now, as one steps into the open.

He is almost dismembered by a khaki-clad teenager cutting across his path like a cleaver. He is barely brushed, but the slipstream seems to hurl him against the outside wall of the airport. The youth stops, turns back, he is suddenly casual and solicitous. He extends a hand to Oskar's elbow, and says with a harsh and difficult accent, "Are you all right, Mister?" Oskar nods, "*Hakol b'seder*." The youngster smiles back with – is it ever so slight derision? The cousin of a look Parisians give anglophones who dare try and address them in *la belle langue de Molière*. "You are looking for the rental car pickup?" says the boy. Oskar nods again, this time no words. "By there," points the youth, marking the way with the barrel of the submachine gun hanging from his shoulder like a pair of skates. Oskar follows his lead. The moment of arrival has come and gone.

He pulls the Fiat to the side of the highway just past the crossroads, but the three hitchhiking soldiers are picked up by motorists immediately ahead of him before he has time to reach a full stop. This society looks after its young protectors. Instead a teenage couple with a knapsack run breathlessly to the door of his car and smile beseechingly. She climbs in front and her companion settles with their pack in the back seat. "How far are you going?" says the young man in Hebrew. "Haifa," says Oskar, "and then to kibbutz Hakatzir." His Hebrew holds up, but so far this has not been a severe test. "What part of the *aretz* do you live in?" the young man goes on. Oskar is still following effortlessly. "*Anee mee-Kanada*," he says: I'm from Canada. The boy laughs with glee. "*Anachnu gam ken*," he chortles: So are we! Oskar leers with delight over his shoulder, then glances sideways at the girl, who is blank. "She doesn't speak Hebrew," says the boy in Hebrew. "Let's not tell her." No wonder my Hebrew has sufficed with these two, thinks Oskar as he drives. The joke lasts a few kilometres, then they all switch to English. He feels they are a little delegation from the Canadian Diaspora. "Where do you come from?" he asks. "Toronto," they chime. He screeches with pleasure. "And what synagogue do you belong to?" There is an awkward pause. "We attend the Port Credit Tabernacle Church," says the boy. "We're Christians," adds the girl. "We were born-again."

He is appalled. She looks like Old Dutch, on the labels of Old Dutch Cleanser, stooped and gnarled, Old Dutch the old witch, from the time before they switched the name to *New* Old Dutch Cleanser and changed the aged crone with the broom for a fresh young blonde, a lick of golden hair falling from her kerchief across her forehead. *New* Old Dutch is the type of woman he can abide, the kind he often pictures when he jerks off in his tower office, though they rarely pass through the school and just as rarely continue on as student teachers where he could really get to know them.

For this bag of bones he stopped here at the Centre for Adult Education in Tel Aviv, instead of driving straight to Hakatzir? Ugh. Ancient, dry skin, crinkly flesh. When she first walked in and out of the classroom, he assumed she was the cleaning lady, looking for something to sweep. Next time through he decided she was a vacuous pensioner taking a Bible class to while her time as she dies. Now she stands at the front like the Ancient Mariner and starts to teach. This is *her* class. He was seduced by the name. Chaviva. His colleagues said, You must see Chaviva teach. You are going there for an educators' symposium, and she is an amazing pedagogue, a legend in the Jewish state. Can she teach Bible? Are frogs waterproof?

Chaviva is young and vibrant, he thought as he drove. Chaviva is ripe like a fruit. Chaviva is a *sabra*, an Israeli, a new Jew: spontaneous, urgent, rapacious. This withered presence is not a Chaviva, she is a Rivka or a Yetta, from the Old Country; she probably murdered a Chaviva somewhere, disposed of the body, and kept the name and other valuable effects. He is so disappointed.

Does her class compensate him for his fantasy? Is he inspired by her teaching despite the letdown? Does the experience reconfirm his commitment as a Jewish educator?

In all honesty, he hates it. He cannot stand her or her teaching. After two thousand years of Rabbinic obscurantism – two more hours. Here they sit in the light of an Israeli day. For the first time since Imperial Rome drove Oskar's people into exile, Jews can again study *their* Book at home. They are surrounded by the same hills, the very streams, the skies and constellations mentioned right in the text, along with artifacts and memorabilia of those times. Is a biblical word or name unclear? Check it against the Ugaritic or Akkadian equivalent on a tablet or inscription unearthed by some young scholar or archeologist, probably on leave from the paratroops. He has often inspired his staff in Toronto with the *newness* possible in Jewish education because of advances in modern Israel. He has followed their investigations keenly from his distance and passed on scraps and insights to his bedraggled Canadians. Someone discovers that Hebrews are the *hapiru* of an old Chaldean manuscript – gangs of marauders and mercenaries ubiquitous in the ancient Near East. Or the delightful interplay between ancient Hebrew and ancient Greek that a linguist hypothesizes occurred on the isle of Crete. (Crete? Of course! Why didn't Oskar think of it?) Or meteorological information that might or mightn't explain the sudden shift in fortune of the Israelite army under Gideon, when the sun stood still.

What does it mean? the staff sometimes ask. It makes it real, Oskar tells them, it'll make it real for the kids. That seems to satisfy his teachers, they don't question further, as he probably would: "So what, real? Lots of things are real. Why should we care about them just because they're real?" If they did challenge him, what would he say? Maybe just heap scorn on the question – that usually works. Sometimes he simply gets tired of the search for relevance. He has been at it so hard and long, wondering what it's all about. At least while he's here he can take a rest from it. So what if this archeological Israeli *stuff* doesn't mean much? You can't have everything. Why on earth, then, have they sent him to sit at the withered feet of this relic passing under the name Chaviva?

"*Ma kahshe lo?*" she is asking. What's his problem? He who?

202

Whose problem? Not Oskar's problem, not the problem of the technicians trying to radio-carbon date the latest Dead Sea scroll, but Rashi's problem, old Rabbi Shlomo Ben Isaac, a bottomless pit of biblical and Talmudic overinterpretation, dead a thousand years, a man who wrote so many commentaries he must never have paused for food, sleep, or sex.

They are studying the tale of Cain and Abel from Genesis. That's all Oskar needs after eighteen hours on a plane: brothers! God says to Cain, "Where is Abel thy brother?" And Rashi writes: "To soften him with gentle words so that he will repent." And this old bag wants to know, What was his problem, what was bugging Rashi, that he inserted this phrase ("to soften him with gentle words . . .") as if it explains something that needs explaining about the original murder between the original brothers. Who cares? Here they sit in a classroom at the gateway to the scriptural panorama, a piece of the puzzle itself, and perplex themselves about what bothered a medieval Jew, the longest journey of whose life took him from his birthplace in Provence to Worms, exactly the opposite direction from the biblical homeland! Who cares what's his problem? Why should it be our problem? Oskar is purple over it. She is eyeing him. Good, he must be making her tense with his shifting and sighs. She continues. Why does Rashi give a psychological interpretation to God's words instead of accepting them as a simple inquiry about Abel's whereabouts? All God asked in the text is, where's your brother? *Ma kahshe lo?*

"Because God knows exactly where Cain's brother Abel is. The poor sod is lying right there in the dirt, and God of all people knows that, so He can't seriously be looking for a straight answer, can he! The question is obviously rhetorical."

Oskar is astonished – *he* is the one who said that. He is flabbergasted that his Hebrew works, not just to express himself but to convey impatience and derision. "Right," says Old Dutch, *Nachon l'gamrei, adonee!* Absolutely correct. In an unplanned outburst meant to express total contempt, he has managed to become her star pupil. Next day he is shocked to find himself there again. The trip to Hakatzir for a rendezvous with his past and his mismanaged destiny has been delayed. What has hooked him? It can't be that bizarre method of hers. It is like an idiotic television quiz show that the kids and housewives in Toronto watch. The quizmaster gives the answers and the contestants have to guess the questions!

She argues with them, the biblical scholars of twenty-four centuries, as though they are all in the Tel Aviv classroom alongside her students; the way Hermann carries on seminars with the long-gone immortals of Jewish philosophy. What unites her with those dead scholars is neither time nor space but the holy text and its inexhaustible surrounding of commentary. She swims in it, along with them, as if they are all kids in the lake at camp. He sees her before class, or during coffee break, diving into the oversized pages of her multivolume *Mikraot Gdolot*. She opens it lovingly, as if she never knows what joy she'll find inside. He strolls casually by and glances down over her shoulder and the small hump on her back. In the upper right corner, in the heaviest possible typeface, stands a biblical verse. "Where is Abel thy brother?" Or, "In the beginning God created." Immediately below, in smaller type and less dignified script: the inevitable Rashi. Beneath him, still on the right-hand half of the double page: the obscure analysis of Ramban, Rabbi Moses Ben Nachman, a medieval mystic, and to his left, the commentary of Rabbi Abraham Ibn Ezra, so concise and cryptic it requires its own commentary, double its length, immediately beneath it. Below them, bottom right, is Rabbi Joseph Sforno, and lower left, the Rashbam, Rabbi Shlomo Ben Moshe. Oskar has no idea who they all are or by what right they are still present in a Jewish classroom. Meanwhile, above, flowing like a stream from the biblical text itself across both upper pages: Aramaic translations by Onkelos the Greek and someone called the Yerushalmi, presumably from Jerusalem. There are notes to each translation, and notes to the notes in the margins and between the commentaries, along with commentaries on commentaries everywhere.

All those voices on the same page, shouting, squealing, and pleading, a mockery of chronological order and priority, a jumble of history, a hard slap at that logic of cause and effect so ingrained in Oskar the would-be historian. So unorganized, so unkempt, so un-German! He eyes her behind the desk and the books, her gaze darting from one precocious interpretation to another, judging and mediating between them, twitching her nose and nodding in connivance: oh, the confusion and point-lessness. Oh, for life to possess such unity in its chaos. What else could provide a sense of connection like her unassailable belief that everyone—meaning every Jew, or at least every Jewish reader—exists in the same context: our Tradition, because of which we *know where we are*? We live our true lives there on those hectic pages. What comfort can Oskar's fragmented historical titilla-tions – the *hapiru*, the hypothesis about Crete – provide to a human life compared to her incomparable security that it all makes sense, it all comes together in the endless meditation upon itself of the Tradition, as we ourselves enter the chain by walking into her classroom and become one more serpentining link. Time and space, incongruity and doubt, are resolved in that overarch-ing vault, as the ceiling of a medieval cathedral supports and resolves conflicts and tensions beneath it. It's such nonsense; it is irresistible. She is having fun, she is happy, she is at home, and she transmits her delight and complacence to anyone with the curiosity or misdirection to wander in. This unblessed hump-backed creature, this mound of joy and spreader of her joy to others. He is falling in love again. After that class, the second, they talk. Come home, she says, you look like you don't eat properly.

An aged gnome opens the door to them. "Meet Nehemya," she says. Oskar's heart falls. "I have to look after him since we were kids," she says, knocking a can of tuna from an upper shelf with the stick end of a broom. "He's my brother." Oskar's heart takes another leap, sideways this time – he refuses to let it remount. "What do you think of our fascist country?" says the gnome. "He makes trouble," she says. "Always. Since we were shrimps." The gnome, to Oskar's surprise, has a complex anal-ysis of political, economic, social, and geographic forces in the Jewish state. The result, in his view, is pushing Israeli society in a fascistic direction. "Going to pee now," he says. "Anybody wanta come?" In his absence, Oskar tells her Nehemya seems reasonably competent. "Yes," she says, "that's why he got the job." Oskar looks quizzical. "Oh," she says, "the Institute for Advanced Nuclear Physics. He's the president there," as she stirs the tuna surprise.

Romance is out. The gnome is banging around in the next room. After supper, in lieu of a grope on the couch, she shows him her complete works: the *gilyonot*. It takes hours, there are thousands – smudgy legal-length sheets of crumbly paper, each bearing the signs of the Gestetner machine, like the mark of Cain. Oskar has lived through the Era of Death Camps, the Rebirth of Israel, Flight to the Moon, but he feels he really belongs to the Age of Gestetner. Her too, but in Hebrew. Each week of the year, she produces a *gilyon*, based on the Torah portion for that week. In each *gilyon* she treats a few verses, or just one, maybe only a word or a phrase. Fifty-two a year and she has been doing it, she's not sure, twenty-four or twenty-five years. That makes . . . many.

She plods through them with him. It's not just his Hebrew that's rusty, it's the damned machine they were cranked out of. Fragments of insight from her gang: Rashi, Rashbam, Ramban, Sforno, occasionally a modern like an Italian rabbi who wrote in the 1920s, or Buber even – followed by her badgering questions. She mails them to her students everywhere in the *aretz*. They reply by return post with answers, which she corrects and sends back. Through this bizarre correspondence course, he thinks, she has found a way to expand the ludicrous dialogue on those folio pages, a dialogue she could never have joined on its own terms in its own times, because she is a woman.

Ma kahshe lo? Ma kahshe lo? This is her method: What's his problem? What's bothering him? Perhaps it is just the repetition, but Oskar starts to think it has a certain . . . sophistication? Yes, yes, the adorable witch replies to his fumbling praise: It's much like the New Criticism in literature, or the French *explication du texte*. Has Oskar read *The Meaning of Meaning* by I. A. Richards from Harvard? What about *Seven Types of Ambiguity* by William Empson? "Northrop Frye," Oskar says, floating the name of a literary critic, at least he thinks the man's a critic. "Oh, no!" she coughs. "That one is no more than a classifier, that's not criticism." "He's from Toronto," says Oskar weakly, "and so am I." She is hurtling farther through the *gilyonot*; they are her children, he thinks.

When he leaves the cluttered bungalow and drives toward Hakatzir, a full set of *gilyonot* is piled on the back seat of his Fiat. Twenty-five decaying bundles of fifty-two sheets each. They sway and totter as he corners or brakes, but they do not fall. He *shleps* them along as faithfully as his camera on every stage of this trip, and then home, to a high shelf in a corner closet in his tower redoubt. He doesn't look at them again and he never shows them to anyone. (When he dies and we go through his effects–photos, letters, curriculum outlines–we find them, and wonder where they came from.)

From now on, there is an addition to the bric-a-brac of his mind. *Ma kahshe lo?* he asks as he lurches through the remainder of his life. He has always envied those he knows who experience life as a series of answers, who have faith in the answers though they may sometimes be uncertain what those answers are. They are full of answers, and he himself doesn't even know the questions. "What's his problem? What's bothering him?" he will remember to say to himself in the future when he encounters confident words and stances in others. *Ma kahshe lo?* he will respond, and it comforts him.

Hakatzir means "The Harvest." *We have already ploughed / And we have sown / But we have not yet reaped.* The kibbutzniks themselves sometimes alter it to Hakotzim, or "the thorns," referring to their increasingly oppositional role in Israel's expanding urban and capitalist society. Still, they play their role with zest. Rumour even has it that a pig farm nestles just past the hill, though the religious parties, with their strategic handful of seats in Israel's parliament, have seen to it that pigs and pork products are illegal and officially non-existant in this country. Supplying bacon and pork to a population frustrated by this situation could be a profitable sideline here at Hakatzir. Moshe (the former Max) saunters each day over the hill. When he is asked, Moshe says blithely that he runs the chicken coop, which everyone on the kibbutz confirms. But surely the coop is in the other direction. Oskar sometimes sniffs it, he is sure, from the bungalow shared by Moshe and his wife, Galyah, the former Greta, where Oskar is an honoured guest.

This place, Hakatzir, has the air of paradise. It is aromatic; it smells of fruits and lemons. The darkness of night is thick and warm. The bungalows that house kibbutz members are small and safe, like gingerbread houses. The boughs that overhang the walks and pathways are protective. The sounds of music from the dining hall and of cleanup in the kitchen are orderly yet vital. Oskar moves, he follows the others along the path, it is like a graceful dance. She goes ahead, and before her, the children; they are her grandchildren, Ilan and Batsheva.

Is it because he just left the company of Chaviva, the mistress of multiple meanings, that he finds this place so layered with significance, the way a faint smell can trigger a flood of feelings and memories? In Rabbinic lore the term for paradise, PARDES, represents four levels of understanding for any verse or symbol: literal (*Pshat*), metaphorical (*Raz*), analogical (*Drash*), and mystical (*Sod*). The reality in which Oskar moves now seems even more complex.

It *is* a garden. It is green, it blooms, yields its scent. A garden whose inhabitants blissfully pass their lives and raise families. It is the garden into which they were expelled from the inhuman Europe they left forty years ago. A man and a woman came here and bred. The woman was his (Oskar still thinks). He and she were the first man and woman for each other. Now he is with her again, in this garden. But she has a different Adam to her Eve, though right now Oskar strolls through the garden with her at the end of a day as though it is theirs. Either this is a foretaste of the life to come, such as the righteous are granted, or it is an aftertaste of a life that might have been.

The original couple, the biblical pair, contained all future souls, according to lore. They learned something, were driven from the garden for it, and forced ever after to work by the sweat of their brow: to plough, sow, and reap.

This garden into which Oskar's friends were expelled, they came happily to it, because in this garden they could work. They entered the garden on the promise they would be permitted to live by the sweat of their brow. It was a fate they yearned for. Over numberless generations, Jews were denied the kind of labour by which Adam and Eve were punished; here, at long last, they toil and sweat. It is not a fate Oskar can imagine choosing. He smells the oranges and lemons and steps awkwardly along the path.

The first Adam gave names to all the animals brought before him. Apparently he knew who they were as soon as he saw them. On Oskar's other trip here, in what seems like a previous life, he too seemed to know the names of all things. When a response was required, he simply opened his mouth and found a name on his tongue. That trip was full of answers. This one seems to hold only questions. He opens his mouth on this trip, and gapes. *Ma kahshe lo?*

She has renamed herself, since she was expelled into this workaday paradise. She was Greta, she has become Galyah, which doesn't mean anything, she says when he asks. Many people change their names, she adds. Perhaps, he thinks, it is just a matter of knowing who you are without being able to say why, with the kind of confidence he once possessed. Others he knows, when they moved to Canada or the United States, also changed. Wilhelms became Williams, Rolfs became Ralphs. Even Oskars became Oscars, and sometimes Ozzies. How did they know they had changed? Did Oskar really become an Ozzie, but mistakenly stay an Oskar? Some educator. *Ma kahshe lo?*

Galyah is tall and gawky. Her neck extends, it stretches as though it may not quite reach her head, which hovers among the leaves of the drooping boughs. The head is large and bony, covered with freckles and blotches like a giraffe. Her hands are massive, they dangle at the ends of her looping arms. He must have loved her with a zany narcissism. Being with her was like meeting himself in a hall of mirrors. In those days he looked fine, even dashing, but he sensed a freakish character would emerge, as though the ugly duckling would come after the swan. She awaited him like his fate, his analogue, the *sod* to his *pshat*. With her he could be himself, because she was like his name, the real one, that says what he really is. He is so relieved to be in her presence again. Letters were not enough.

The kids are not giraffes, they are prickly fruits, *sabras*. He can picture Batsheva's dark head poking from the turret of a tank like an inquisitive sprout. Ilan will doubtless become a soil scientist, absorbed in this earth from which he has been nourished. Galyah is following them at a leisurely pace. They have urged Oskar to come along and say goodnight. They adore him. Perhaps they see an analogue to their grandmother in him, his *sod* to her *pshat*. They don't live with their parents, as their parents never lived with her and Moshe. Not even when they were tiny. "What is the sleeping arrangement for the children?" Oskar asked clumsily. "Beds," said Moshe. "At what age do they move into the collective care?" – unable to stop sounding like a thick anthropologist. "From zero," said Galyah. He knows this, he has read it, it was standard discussion in the movement long ago. How can you know something and not know it at all? What does it mean to know anything? He has never known what collective care of children *means*.

Now, as the kids skip ahead on the path, he thinks of us, his Great Class, our separate fates consigned to the chance selection of parents on whose confidence, ability, or luck everything will hinge; at the mercy of two people we never chose, who might or might not succeed in protecting our welfare, and even our survival. These kids on the path a few yards away are so different from all the Freddies and Fredas he knows in Toronto. What do these kids feel? Of what are they certain? From their point of view, each member of this community – in other words, every human being in the world as they know it—accepts responsibility for their well-being. To them the world is a secure embrace.

He stands still on the path as Galyah, Ilan, and Batsheva pass out of sight, round the corner of the low nursery. I have no responsibility for "my" kids in Toronto, he thinks, because I guarantee them nothing. What does Jewish education have to do with their lives, their survival? Everything can be a way of not doing what it seems to be doing.

Inside, the kids clamber onto their bunks. Across the hall a baby cries. From zero, as she said. "Over here, Oskar," shouts Ilan. "Here I am, Oskar," yells Batsheva – *Hineni*, the word Abraham and Moses and all the biblical heroes used when God called them. Brother and sister in the same room, of course. From zero, everything together. Sometimes they seem to draw the same breath. They took him camping a few days ago, to the shores of Kinnereth. In the evening, as the sun faded and the lake turned misty, they grew pensive, almost moody. At the same moment, collectively. These kids even get depressed together. Is this community? When he sends his kids at home on study weekends and exchange trips to Erie or Cleveland, there is teenage conformity but no melding. His kids arrive for their shared experiences, each comes from the compartment called My Nuclear Family. They are a convention of intergalactic representatives; they exchange thoughts, but they never join. He is the perfect convenor of such events.

(*Ma kahshe lo?* He is wondering whether you can justify a childless life.)

"*Jeder Anfang ist schwer*," she says. All beginnings are hard. They are outside again. He smiles his crookedest. She's right, they have to start somewhere. "I would not be able to survive here," he says. "I would expire." "*Warum?*" she asks. "Do you know what central heating is?" he says. "Do you know what air conditioning is? I cannot live without them. I need my comfort. I have changed." She cocks her oversize head. "No," she says, "you were exactly like this."

He protests. "I was in the movement, I was a leader. I believed in community. The connections between Jews, between people. And Buber–" He breathes in and out. This is incoherent. "I and Thou," he says. "That always made sense to me. Relationships between people. Not just I and Thou. We and Thou. But I changed."

"Yes," she says. "*Aber–*" She is searching for something. She switches to Hebrew. "*Attah loh ratzeetah l'hitkashair*." She says this as she said *jeder Anfang ist schwer*, a shopworn phrase, a piece of ordinary wisdom. As though she has said it many times to herself. When, for instance, his name came up in a conversation, or a letter arrived from Canada, or a postcard announcing regards from their old friend Oskar conveyed by some acquaintance of his who was touring the *aretz*. He translates laboriously, word for word, in his mind. *You didn't want to connect.* "*Niemals*," she concludes in German. Never.

"Never," he says. "Never?"

She shrugs. "I don't think so," she says. "When?"

"I thought maybe there was a time," he says. "And then it stopped."

"Ah," she says. "Does it really matter now?"

"Only in the abstract," he says, thinking about Kierkegaard, of all people, who would have stayed with someone named Regina, if he had had faith.

"Well," she says, "you may be right. I don't remember."

He is relaxed now. These feel like the last words of the last conversation they had the last time they spoke. They are back together. "Here we are again," he says. It is natural to take up where you left off, where else are you going to start after so many years? She relaxes too. "So, Mr Religious Educator," she says, "what do you think of the way we raise our children here among the atheists?"

He tips his own odd head. "What do I know about raising children?" he says. "I have none."

"You have many," she says. "You always did." He shrugs.

"Doing anything can be a way of not doing that very thing," he says. She smiles and shakes her head with slow indulgence. He feels it wash over him as it used to. "What I mean," he says, "is that having many children can be a way of not having any." She keeps shaking that head. "If I have to be exceedingly precise," he says, as though they are arguing about who left the cap off the toothpaste, "I mean that I do not have any children who are my own offspring."

212

"Oh," she says breezily, "not all of us are meant to. Many people here" – she looks around at the darkness and listens – "have none of their own, but they have the children we all have."

"Then maybe you think I should have come here in the beginning," he says.

"No," she says confidently. "If you had come here in the beginning, then you wouldn't need the children we all have, because you would have children of your own." He melts. Forty years of his life fall into the wrong place. His own children, his and hers. He pictures himself a normal human being capable of uncertainty over the ordinary choices of marriage and family. His tongue hangs out of his mouth, he looks like a contented kibbutz cow. Is it pathetic that the mere thought of what he might have had makes him so happy? No. Probably more satisfaction than this would be too much for Oskar. Real children, real responsibility for others, a real woman across the breakfast table each morning – enough is enough. For him the delicious thought of what might have been will do.

(What is the answer to the question: "Can you justify a childless life?" The answer is: "It's better not to have to.")

"I love you," he says among the pomegranates and orange blossoms, perfectly secure in the thought and all it does not require. He's never said these words to her before and he's not certain what language he said them in now. Perhaps in none. Maybe she didn't hear him at all. "Me too, Oskar," she says. "Come inside and we'll all have a cup of hot milk."

There is a letter from Jerusalem. It is from Hermann. Hermann, his lovely wife Merle, and the kids are in Jerusalem, where they now live. They moved here a year ago; they have made *aliyah*. It started when Hermann took a sabbatical and lectured on Philosophy of Religion from Fichte to Schopenhauer. That was at Bar-Ilan University in Tel Aviv. His Hebrew was weak and they wouldn't let him go directly to Jerusalem. Next sabbatical year he was in Jerusalem itself. For a while Hermann seemed to spend alternate years in the *aretz*. Oskar is full of envy, again. Being a tenured professor is like a foretaste of the messianic days.

The letter is actually from Merle; she has assumed responsibility for relations with Oskar. We know you're here, she writes, we know you're coming to Jerusalem for the Jewish educators' convention, well, we insist on seeing you. This is the commanding tone her summonses to *shabbat* dinners always had. She sounds like Jack Katz in 1943 inviting a pathetic Polish *yid* for charity supper. He feels like he just stepped off the boat in Toronto.

The survivors of Bergen-Belsen are having a do, writes Merle, and we've been invited. If you get here in time, you can come too. Let us know. Hermann says hi . . .

Scholem is the anti-Buber. No beard, no flowing mane, no penetrating gaze followed by a soul-shattering aphorism. Scholem is bald like an eagle. He looks like the garment manufacturers on Spadina Avenue in Toronto who *schrei* over blintzes in United Bakers Dairy at lunch, then meet in the sauna of the Jewish "Y" after work to trade conquests of buyers and secretaries. Scholem is the number one international scholar in the field of Jewish mysticism and the history of Jewish religion. He doesn't need to act like God, thinks Oskar. He has it all.

Scholem is lecturing the members of the American Jewish Education Association, gathered here in Jerusalem to, among other things, make Oskar their next president. Scholem has granted them a brief audience. He is not exerting himself, yet he is awesome. Scholem has made it his business, hell his mission, to excavate the hidden darknesses of Judaism through all the reaches of its history. Anywhere there is ambiguity, heresy, superstition, irrationality, the antisocial, or antinomian, Scholem finds his way, pitches camp, and stays till he has lifted the rug and uncovered what was concealed. Oskar licks his lips. Talk about perverse. This man, this genius, has set his face against every effort of liberal Jews for two centuries, from Moses

Mendelssohn down to Oskar's Aunt Hilda with her subscriptions to progressive magazines like *The Journal for Political Psychology and Sex Economy*; and beyond them to the righteous members of the Pillar of Fire Parents' Council, so concerned about those high school fraternities and sororities their kids slink off to. Scholem does not discriminate; he torpedoes the mighty strivings of all those generations to make Judaism modern, rational, and acceptable. What motivates this sorcerer's apprentice? People wonder, but Oskar knows. It is the urge to scandalize. The way Buzz Friedkin scandalized the Jews of Toronto when he came from Long Island and said "Gawd" like he was calling them for dinner. To the well-spoken respectability of every Jewish community leader Oskar has ever known, from Leo Baeck to Jack Katz, Scholem turns and drops his pants. A curse on your respectability and good intentions.

Scholem reserves a special scorn for Buber, his long-time colleague here on the faculty of the Hebrew University, dead now many years. Maybe they were friends, as Oskar and Hermann are friends. Both Scholem and Buber came here from Germany, the way Oskar and Hermann went to Canada, though Scholem, much the younger man, came–came up, Oskar should say – before the Nazis, and Buber came up after. The kind of friends who are full of hate and resentment. Friends like brothers, who need not worry about pleasing or offending each other, since they'll always be connected. Oskar wants to call out, Where is Buber thy brother? as Scholem pours a mountain of contempt on Buber and his ideas, especially his ideas about Hassidism.

Ma kahshe lo? Why is Scholem so livid and unremitting over Buber's version of Hassidism, the marvellous tales Buber found, translated into limpid German, and explained in a deft, modern, even existential way, in answer to the need of his contemporaries for meaning and solace. Lovely and comforting ideas like: to sanctify the ordinary, and to hallow this place. *Crap,* says Scholem. *I can prove to you conclusively, by means of all the central texts, that Hassidism will bear no such interpretation. Buber's thoughts may be attractive, they may be comforting, they may even be true – but they are not Hassidism!* Behind Scholem's scholarly veneer is the will to destroy. He is like a U-boat under the Atlantic. Does Scholem know what a staple Buber's tales have become in North American religious schools and Friday night sermons? Does he know how Jews in the placid American Diaspora have learned to feel Jewish through the tales Buber (re)told? Is it because Scholem knows all this that he speaks with such menace to this group? Or does the man simply have a mission to destroy? Would he be a destroyer anywhere, among any people? When Scholem steps onto an Egged bus to go home after a day of lecturing at the Hebrew University, do his fellow passengers quake as he casts a deathly glance up and down the aisle before choosing his seat among them?

A denunciation is not what Oskar's AJEA colleagues have come to hear; on the other hand they are spared its most severe effects because few understand what he is saying. Oskar marvels at their insulation. They are such nice educators, well-protected from the feelings of people like Oskar and Scholem, both of whom happen to be resettled German Jews. His colleagues are shielded as no ghetto walls ever sheltered Jews. To them Scholem is not the satan, the Accuser; they look and see one more Israeli professor, another proof of the intellectual success and, yes, respectability of the Zionist enterprise.

Not Oskar. He knows the sound of mischief. He sees where it leads: facts piled on facts, documents mentioned and categorized in a terse phrase, then appended to the developing thesis. He is ready to play this game. He sits through the lecture, noting the vague, almost subliminal discomfiture of his fellow educators. They don't understand, but the shrewder among them intuit, at the far end of their sensing apparatus, something of menace. When he concludes, Scholem responds curtly to a few questions and storms from this auditorium in the Sciences of Judaism building on the campus. The educators file out, content to survive another session of heavy-duty scholarship. Perhaps they look forward to Oskar's session this afternoon, Audio-Visual Aids and the Sexual Restlessness of Adolescents, their final session, just prior to the election for their incoming executive. Oskar stays seated. He basks in Scholem's aftershock. He stretches his limbs and sighs with pleasure. If he smoked he would have a cigarette. But something is missing. He has not had his fill.

He steps into the large foyer of this stolid monument to the *Wissenschaftlich* approach to Jewish studies. Four floors of offices and classrooms ring this central space, they run around it off balconies, like the upper level of the sanctuary in the Pillar of Fire. Oskar scans the far reaches. High above, on the fourth floor where eagles dare, he spies his prey. Scholem the eagle, whooshing along the balcony and vanishing into an office, leaving some turbulence and a shuddering door. Oskar, no eagle himself, follows recklessly. He tears up floor after floor and arrives at the top, wheezing. Now he must compose himself. No, that's a mistake. If he delays he will lose his resolve. He steps to the vault – whoops, office – in which the wizard works, cocks his fist, bares his knuckles, hesitates almost too long, and raps.

"Enter!" booms the voice within. Oskar crosses the threshold. Scholem barely looks up. Perhaps he flicks his eyeballs briefly and peers through the top of his skull. He is writing, or studying, or boring a hole in the desktop with his gaze.

"I was in your lecture with the educators from America," says Oskar. Scholem is impassive. "You just talked to them," Oskar explains. No response. "I want to know one thing." Still no movement. "Why do you do it?" Like a stone. Like the man has ears of stone. "I want to know why you bother." Oskar feels like a whiny child demanding something. I want what I want when I want it. He charges forward. His is not to reason why. "What is the purpose?"

Scholem elevates his forehead as though the tomb of Tut is being opened. "I thought I smelled that – somewhere in there," he says slowly. Oskar feels like the rat in a trap he set for himself, but he must go ahead. "What is the" – Oskar searches – "the relevance of what you do, its meaning? Explain to me please, why you bother. All that material. All that learning. For what?" he finishes desperately. He feels like a Christian taunting a lion, like he has offered blood to a shark. Scholem opens his maw. "It . . .

217

has . . . no . . . relevance," Scholem says sonorously, like a Puritan preacher denouncing the frivolities flesh is heir to. "Relevance has nothing to do with it. Relevance." He repeats the term as though it has the taste of the forbidden. "Then why," retorts Oskar with abandon, "do you do it?" This is like a tennis match played with lead rackets, hard to get underway.

Scholem explodes. "Because it interests me!" he shrieks. Suddenly he is yapping like a magpie. "It interests me! *Ça m'interesse! Das interessiert mich! Zeh m'anyenet ohtee! Verstehst? Moovan? Comprenez?* That is all. Nothing more. No point, no meaning, nothing. It interests me. So I do it!"

Oskar is ecstatic in victory. He has got what he came for. Scholem's outburst rolls past him. He feels again that he is Moses sheltering in the cleft of the rock at Sinai and the Lord has granted him a further look as He passes by. Scholem thunders on. Oskar misses the precise words but he feels the power, like a pre-orgasmic tickle. Scholem is on his feet now and around the desk. He is herding Oskar to the door, he has bullied him out onto the balcony, bellowing still. In the hollow core of the building, Scholem's outrage echoes from floor to floor and bounces off the marble below where acolytes of the Sciences of Judaism shade their eyes as they look upward toward the source of this tirade. "Interest. Nothing more. That is all. That is why. Do you understand? Buber is dead. God is dead. Relevance is irrelevant. I smelled this. I told you I smelled it in that roomful of nincompoops. Educators they dare to call themselves. The most degraded word in the Jewish life of the twentieth century. Have I answered your question?"

Oskar retreats down the steps from floor to floor. At each landing the reverberations rise again. At ground floor he emerges, he arches his neck and cranes toward the top railing. All is sudden silence. Every office door on the fourth level is shut. Life goes on. Did it really happen? He steps outside the edifice for the Sciences of Judaism into the harsh sun of a Jerusalem afternoon. Along the hilltops of Beit ha-Kerem stretches the sturdy architecture of the Jewish intellectual renaissance, one faculty after another. Cradles of Jewish agronomists, engineers, lawyers, historians, librarians, educators. A real people, just like everybody else. What a difference from that which came before.

For two thousand years, Jews neglected this world while they spun wondrous visions of God and His heavens. Now all that no longer has meaning, if Scholem is right. Well, thinks Oskar, there had to be a price for the changes we've made. He strides along the walkway that passes before the many practical buildings, he feels like a gambler on the boardwalk at Atlantic City, he could try his luck anywhere. He has no idea if the result was worth the cost.

A rap on the door of Oskar's hotel room. It disrupts his schedule: now is packing time, followed by travel to the final AJEA meeting, scene of a well-planned triumph in his measly and unsought career as a religious educator – election to the association presidency. Then will come a leisurely drive to the airport for his flight home, with ample time for check-in and the exhaustive El Al security procedures. The rap repeats, urgent. Oskar opens, expecting, since this is Jerusalem, maybe *Eliyahu ha-nahvee*, Elijah the Prophet, appearing like room service. "The Messiah is downstairs, sir, in the lobby." "Let him wait," Oskar will answer, "the way we have."

It is Hermann, tenured professor. Oskar feels he should apologize. For what? Whatever. "I didn't call," he says. "I know," says Hermann. "Maybe it was because the phones didn't work," says Oskar. "Was it?" says Hermann. "Of course not," says Oskar.

"Don't worry about it," says Hermann, blinking first. "So," says Oskar, winding up for the pitch, "how was the social event of the survivors' season?" Hermann ponders, the way a food critic might halt his pen in midflight before composing a precise phrase: My companion's duck was a trifle dry.

"Sorry," says Oskar, blinking too. "Maybe we could take a walk," says Hermann brightly, "and have something to eat, like the old days." Oskar shakes his head. "I'm packing," he says. "I have a tight schedule. Sit down while I do it." Hermann starts to settle on a suitcase. "Not that one," says Oskar, "I haven't done it yet. Sit on that one." Hermann does. "You carry a lot of baggage," he says to Oskar. Oskar smiles a crooked smile, a little spittle drips from the edge of his mouth. "You've still got your dead pan," he says to Hermann. Hermann dips his head in appreciation. "Anyway, you can't get a hot hamburger here," he says. "I've tried everywhere."

They have a desultory conversation covering little as Oskar finishes packing. Then Hermann accompanies Oskar downstairs to the desk and fidgets while Oskar checks out, as people do during an unsatisfactory farewell. They linger at Oskar's car, two German Jews not quite knowing how they got from there to here; it is as though Canada has no reality, as if neither of them interrupted their lives with thirty or forty years in a huge country with almost no people. They are speaking English, leaning against an Italian automobile in the ancient land of Israel. "So, is it everything you thought it would be?" says Oskar.

"You have to live a thing through," says Hermann with indirectness, "to find out what it means in your life. You can't just think it out."

"You knew that," says Oskar brusquely. "That's basic existentialism. Even I know that."

"I knew it," says Hermann. "But I still had to live it." He hunches his narrow shoulders. He looks more like a tired body and less like an embodied mind than Oskar remembers.

"Do you think you denied Hitler another victory again when you moved here?" asks Oskar.

"I think so," says Hermann. "What do you think?" As though Oskar might have answers!

"I've been thinking," says Oskar, as though he really has and he really might. Then he stops. He is not used to being asked for answers. Perhaps he fears his lifelong identity, built laboriously on a rock-hard foundation of uncertainty, is about to crumble. But he carries on. "It depends," he says, "on what Hitler wanted. It depends on what Hitler had his heart set on." Hermann doesn't argue or question, he doesn't even wrinkle his forehead. He waits.

220

"I've been thinking about why I didn't come here," says Oskar. "I was sure it was because I didn't want to work hard picking crops and go to sleep on a hard bed every night. Everything hard."

"That *is* why you didn't come," says Hermann. "You said it often."

"I know," says Oskar. "But maybe I was also trying to give Hitler a bad time."

"You never said that before," says Hermann.

"They didn't want us to stop being Jews, at first," says Oskar. "They wanted us to stop being Germans. They wanted us to stop contaminating their Aryan society. Maybe that's why I left the Zionists even though I was with them for a while." He seems to be daydreaming out loud. "They just wanted to get rid of us. They didn't care where we went. They wanted us out. Maybe that's why Buber stayed so late, even though everyone wanted to know why he didn't go on *aliyah*. Maybe that's why I almost didn't leave. Because they wanted us to go."

"It was your way of giving Hitler a hard time," says Hermann.

"Maybe it was," says Oskar. "Maybe it did give them a hard time. For a little while."

"You're so stubborn," says Hermann. "It would be just like you."

"I thought I got so active in the movement to affirm my Jewishness," says Oskar. "I thought I was defying the Nazis. But I have a sneaking suspicion they didn't mind if we affirmed our Jewishness. It separated us from them."

"Maybe that's why you're always so crabby about Jewish education, even though you're a Jewish educator," says Hermann.

"Maybe I won't do anything that would make Nazis happy," says Oskar. "It's my way to not give Hitler another victory."

"You won't do anything that would make anyone happy," says Hermann.

"The point is," says Oskar, "that anything can be a way of not doing what it seems to be doing." He looks around at this slice of the modern Jewish state. "When the Messiah finally comes"—

he takes in the traffic and the many signs urging people to buy things – "he may have some surprises."

"But look here," says Hermann. "The Nazis said Zionism was like Bolshevism. They said they were the same thing."

"Sometimes they said that," Oskar agrees.

"And as for a Jewish state," says Hermann, "they would hate it. The State of Israel would not make Hitler happy."

Oskar shrugs. "Don't expect me to have all the answers all the time," he says.

Hermann looks around at the cars and signs and soldiers. "It upsets me very much," he says, "some of the things that happen here. It is a surprise to me."

"You didn't see it coming," says Oskar.

"I didn't see my reaction coming," says Hermann. "That's what surprises me. The rest –" he shrugs a shrug of his own, "it was here if you had eyes. While we were over there, you know," says Hermann vaguely, meaning Canada, "the view was different."

"I didn't see it coming either," says Oskar. "And I'm the historian. Anyway, I'm still over there."

Hermann squints. It may be a smile. "At least in this place a Jew is at home," he says, "after all the trouble we've seen."

"Yes," says Oskar. "He is."

"But what?" says Hermann.

"But what what?" says Oskar.

"You tell me," says Hermann. "With you there is always a question for every answer."

"Well," says Oskar, "what's the point of being Jewish, if it isn't any trouble?"

"There's plenty of trouble here," says Hermann, "in case you haven't noticed. But at least we're at home."

Oskar chews this briefly. "Maybe what I meant," he says, "is what's the point of being Jewish, if you're at home?"

"The last time I looked," says Hermann, "the Jews in Toronto seemed pretty comfortable where they were."

Oskar looks directly at this person next to him, a rare event in the life of Oskar. He gives Hermann a light visual embrace with his eyes. "They are," he says with a sly smile to his oldest friend, "but I'm not."

It is now time for Oskar to leave the *aretz* and return . . . home. He thinks he understands something. A visit to the *aretz* during the time of waiting is different from a visit there after the time of waiting. During the time of still waiting, a visit to the *aretz* contains a taste of the days to come. It is infinitely sweet and cannot be found anywhere else in this world. Even miracles happen – small ones. When the time of waiting is over, a visit to the *aretz* is a trip. One books a flight, arrives, maybe enjoys, and goes home. There are no miracles.

He is having trouble, though, with the Fiat. It is a ticklish situation. The door is caught on the curb outside the Knesset, Israel's parliament, where he parked before he ambled over to the final convention session at the Teaching Faculty of the university and was duly elected president for the coming year. This delay is no laughing matter. He must fly home and assume his duties. The plane leaves in five and a half hours and he has left a margin of only ninety-five minutes for emergencies such as this: he can open and close the door while standing on the curb, but when he occupies the driver's seat, his added weight lowers the door into contact with the curb whence it cannot, with the leverage available to him from a sitting position, be budged. He steps outside again where he can close the door but not drive the car. He ponders the matter. "Get in," says a voice.

He barely turns, the sense of command is so firm. From the seat once more, he looks up at her. "All right," she says, "ready when I say." She braces her sensible shoes against the curb and leans against the roof of the car. "Okay," she says, with minimal strain in her voice. He freezes, unsure what to do. "The door," she says, and he closes it. He rolls down the window to thank her. "Where ya from?" she asks. "Toronto," he says, "and Berlin. Where are you from?" "Milwaukee," she says. "Whaddya doing here?" He tells her and adds that he is on his way home now. "Hmh," she grunts, "take care," and passes a large leathery hand through the little window of the car to shake his. He gropes for the ignition with his right hand and adjusts the no-draft of the driver's window with his left as he watches the bulky figure of the prime minister trundle along till she reaches and enters her own little car.

He is in ample time. He is checked in, his seat preselected, the in-flight movie vetted. He sits on one of the seats that sprout like toadstools in the waiting lounge. He is watching the incoming gate. He senses, despite his new realism about this land in this time, that something may occur, as it did last time he left the *aretz*. Someone goes, someone comes. The law of arrivals and departures.

Instead, a disturbance at the entrance doors to the terminal. Less a disturbance than a gust. And standing there, blown in like a puff of desert air, straight from the Negev or the Aravah, a figure like Lawrence of Arabia. It is aged and ruddy; it has weathered well. More Laurentian than Lawrence. This is how Oskar pictures Moses Our Teacher as he took his last trudge up the mountain for a look over Jordan. The figure casts its gaze round the airport lounge, as Moses often surveyed his rambunctious flock. Its mobile scrutiny halts on Oskar. "Aie!" it barks. It is Munch of Union Seminary, Munch from Good Friday! He strides right to Oskar and bending forward offers a stiff embrace.

"How did you know I was here?" says Oskar. "Hadn't a clue," says Munch, setting down a small valise and himself. "Then why are you here?" Oskar asks. "Like any traveller," says Munch, "I must go home." Oskar looks down at Munch's lack of luggage and thinks: Travelling light. "That's not the only baggage I've ditched," says Munch, replying to the thought. "Wait while I check in."

They pass through security together. On an Israeli airline this is always a journey, arduous and detailed, and begs a companion. Oskar listens as the old man recounts his odyssey of recent years. Munch has been to the desert and returned with a stunning tale. Not the Negev or the Sinai, wherever he was on this current visit, for some particular scholarly purpose. The true desert, the metaphorical one, unbounded by time or space, while the actual desert only seems unbounded. Munch was tempted out there – and he succumbed! This Oskar gathers indirectly, for instead of biblical theology, Munch now talks only of Marxist analysis. Marxist analysis of the Bible!

They move slowly forward as the line advances, check by check, one potential terrorist, then the next. The security examiners are methodical, virtually Germanic. The passengers stand like cows waiting to be milked. They will leave the ground eventually, on time and with perfect faith that no danger lurks in cabin or cargo. Oskar toddles forward beside Munch, like Joshua supporting Moses, like Tonto riding with the Lone Ranger. Munch explains his conversion with patient passion. Oskar doesn't really understand. He feels lost and inept as so often in the past, with Hermann, with Buber, with former Father Gerald expounding from behind an armature of dinner dishes.

It is clear Munch has abandoned faith in God, or the trinity or His Saviour or whatever for most of his life he believed. He says he has done this for the sake of his beloved Old Testament. He feels he has now sunk himself deeper into its reality. "Without God?" says Oskar, as they shuffle forward a few paces. Not without God precisely, Munch explains, but the God of the Bible – Whom Munch in his atheism still refers to with an awe beyond Oskar's ability at the height of anything he's ever felt – that God of the Bible Munch now sees was an expression of the total social reality of ancient Israel. "They said God," Munch fiercely explains, "they even spoke with Him, but they really meant the concatenation of factors in their own social experience."

"Then He doesn't exist," says Oskar. It is a whine, a moan, and a question. "No," says Munch, "not like you or I or any human being exists."

Oskar misses the God he has never been able to believe in. He especially misses Him in the life and words of a man like Munch. He realizes how important the faith of others has always been to him. "Couldn't you let Him exist alongside all the social factors?" he asks. "Buber believed in sociology too." Munch shakes his mane sternly. His is a Barthian *Nein*, an Old Testament "NO!" in thunder and tremor. Like all true Protestants, he will not quibble; either God is, or is not. Either Marxism is explanatory, or it is not. This absolutism is moving, it is attractive, there is something almost sexual in its energy. Oskar starts feeling turned on.

"Do you think maybe you have just changed one religion for another?" Oskar asks, while a stern woman with her hair pinned back begins to examine his hand luggage as if she is on a dig. "No way, compadre," says Munch. "I know what you are suggesting, but once you've believed in the real God of the Hebrew Bible, the only true God I can still say, and then lost Him, you aren't going to accept some paltry substitute like social analysis or Karl Marx, no matter how useful they are in themselves. No God–and no idols either!" Oskar is irredeemably lost again. He hasn't a clue what Munch is saying, but he loves to hear him talk.

"What is this social reality of ancient Israel which was happening when they thought they were talking to God?" Oskar asks.

"It is," says Munch, handing his tiny bag over the counter and getting it back instantly, "the vision of a radical social egalitarianism utterly hostile to the prevailing imperial and feudal models of the ancient Near East."

"And what did it all have to do with Yahweh," asks Oskar, about the clumsy name Gentiles at Union often used for the God of our Fathers.

"He functioned," says Munch, "as a religious servomechanism providing societal feedback to reinforce the radical social model."

Oskar is calmed. Munch has spread salve on his wounds. Munch does still believe, and it is a wondrous vision he has. He believes in the truth of the Bible, and even in the God of the Bible. He has merely adjusted his terms. Here is a man of advanced age who leaped from a jet airplane without a parachute but with absolute confidence and drifted safely to ground. "Just one other thing," says Oskar as they approach the electronic arch. "Don't you feel it is a bit late in your career to change everything?" He is through, his pockets are being radiated by an electronic prod, he is explaining this or that beep. "You mean," says Munch, speaking still from, as it were, the near shore, "what will people say?" Oskar nods, he supposes that is exactly what he means. Munch steps majestically through the arch. "Just art Thou, O Lord," he says as he comes, speaking words Oskar knows must come from the Book of Jeremiah, "therefore will I contend with thee: surely shall I speak my judgements against Thee."

Here on the other side, they part, each moving to his own gate. They are men with different destinations. Oskar thinks, as he lurches away from Munch, about Albert Schweitzer, the great biblical scholar and organist of the early twentieth century. He wonders if Schweitzer too lost his faith as an old man, and if that's why he returned to university to study medicine and then went to Africa to die among black lepers. Perhaps Schweitzer just didn't have the guts to say so, even to himself; it doesn't sound so different from what Munch has told him. But Oskar doesn't feel that Munch has lost his faith exactly. There is something else going on. He tries to recall what Buber said the time they talked about faith and love. "I thought your problem," said Buber to a very green Oskar, "was whether you can have faith without God."

When Oskar leaves the *aretz* this time he does not linger on deck, urgently devouring his last view of the land; instead he buries his nose in the inflight magazine. Whether others, whose lives are intertwined with his, are setting down as he is lifting off is of no interest to him. In the *aretz* these days, there are no miracles.

He travels back irrationally, via California. He is not ready for home yet. They've assured him he can route this way on his ticket, though budget is no motive; he wants to see Tocchet, as he once went to Buber. It is the Bubering impulse in him. He needs help with the current phase. After stops in Lisbon, Miami, and Salt Lake City, he is at last on a freeway, driving north in a rental car to Santa Celeste and the Institute for the Enhancement of Liberal Values. Tocchet is dean of the institute: the most recent station on his pilgrimage.

It looks like the estate of the governor of California in a Zorro movie. The offices of the resident scholars are like cabanas on Miami Beach; inside each sits a notable with many books to his name, thinking. The graffiti on the washroom walls say Stamp Out Reification and Nietzsche Is Pietzsche. It is a think-tank in the sun. The door to Tocchet's compartment swings open at Oskar's knock and Tocchet steps forth, a shrunken, sunburnt Buddha. Tocchet's hair is grey and stringy to his shoulders; his smile cracks into lines baked like clay all over his face. His white shirt is open, it has frills and no collar. This is California Tocchet; he embraces Oskar like one hippy to his fellow.

They talk as sunny shadows cross the cubicle. Tocchet listens with his sweet smile; comments and chuckles, approves and forgives. They speak till Oskar feels a slight, nonspecific ache. This talk is unlike their earlier ones. Tocchet's words do not run straight to Oskar's heart and snuggle there. He does not speak memorable phrases that Oskar can carry with him for the rest of his life like a charm. It is a sad fact that Oskar cannot remember anything Tocchet says in their conversation.

He assumes it's his own fault, as usual. He didn't bring Tocchet a problem to solve. In the old days when he went Bubering, he usually had a particular question. It might be stupid, like, What can I do about the sunset? but at least it was something. Now he doesn't have a question. Instead he is one, twisty and broken.

Oskar looks at his old confessor, at the beads around his scrawny neck; he doesn't feel his former confidence. Tocchet, his knight of insight, has been bashed about over the years since they met; he has passed from joust to joust, foiled in his crusades often by the likes of Harry Hall. He seems at peace here. Oskar is unable to share Tocchet's sense of completion. Is it possible:

does Oskar now feel older than Tocchet? He hates the thought
that he might never again feel anyone is older than him.

No, he says at the end of the talk that wasn't, he won't stay
over, he can make a direct flight from the local airport and yes,
all right, he will accept a ride there from Nick, Tocchet's youngest, who lives in Oskar's memory as a Christmas present bounc-
ing up from under the tree in the house near Casa Loma.

"Are you still a virgin, Nick?" he asks as the subdivisions and
sea cliffs flash by. This is a typical opening when he tortures
confirmands, student teachers, and other defenceless beings.
Maybe he is angry at Nick's dad for wearing lovebeads and not
alleviating horrible pain as he used to. Nick shakes his head. He
is behind the wheel. He is not a virgin. "It was two years ago,
when I was fifteen," says Nick, in a brilliantly nonantagonistic
counterattack. "I went to Mom and Dad," he says, switching
seven or eight lanes, and then deciding to return to where he
was, "and told them my girlfriend Karma and I were going to
sleep together." Oskar says nothing, but his balls start to tingle;
life is lifting a corner of her skirt for him to snatch another peek.
He is going to gain one more ounce of the ordinary knowledge
others inherit naturally. He remembers Aunt Hilda's words
about his genital structure. He feels he is edging over to the big
dictionary again, now that aunt and mother have left the room,
to seek the meaning of the words they used.

"Dad said he and Mom were very happy. He just wanted to
know two things. Did I have contraceptives and would I like
him to get me some. I said that was okay, I had them." Oskar
moons, he nearly swoons as he turns toward the window; this
is life as it ought to be, generous and giving; living as learning,
the world as teacher. "The other thing is, they wanted our first
time to be at home. Upstairs in my room." Would Oskar like to
know more about it, he asks, but Oskar is content to absorb this
for the remainder of their ride. Tocchet has lent him comfort
after all, through the boy beside him. At the airport Nick walks
Oskar to the gate. No one sees Oskar to airports, no one meets
him when he arrives. This seems absurdly romantic. He wants

to say something appropriate to this beautiful youth. "*Naar hayyeetee*," he says, "*v'gam zakahntee*." "What does that mean, Oskar?" says Nick. "It means, I have been young," says Oskar, "and also old." He knits his brow, he hopes he doesn't sound dotty. Nick grasps him with a hug that would crush a linebacker, and nuzzles Oskar's neck like a rooting pig. Oskar can't remember a more intimate physical moment in his life.

He is still unready to end his wander. Not Canada, not yet. Oskar prefers to circle out here in the real world, like a satellite in space before falling to earth. In Canada these days they have Trudeau. They are excited about him: he is sophisticated, he is world-class, he is a Canadian JFK. Oskar is happy for the Canadians, they should have one of their own to be proud of, but he does not partake. It isn't just that Trudeau dates Barbra Streisand, though Barbra Streisand panics Oskar–she reminds him of dynamos on the Sisterhood and the Parents' Council, like Wilhelmina Barkhouse and Cecilia Lubetsky, the ones you know would be high-energy dealmakers and powerbrokers if they weren't women. Maybe it's simply that Trudeau dates. The leader of the country, an international statesman: he dates? In Fran's he and Herman always asked, "So who're you dating?" If Trudeau had been there they would have asked who he was dating. He thinks he might take Trudeau more seriously if he were the leader somewhere else.

He flies from California to New York. What has he in mind? He would tell no one, he probably does not admit it to himself, but . . . maybe he will meet Bella again. It could be the effect of Nick's narrative. Has Oskar received indirect permission for something he feared to do or be all his life? If Tocchet were Oskar's father it is possible that every guilt-racked overanalysed encounter with a woman he's ever had might have ended swiftly and serenely in bed. He takes the same bus, the same walk from Port Authority. He descends at 72nd and looks for the pizza place, which is right where it was long ago! He lurches by. And who does he see, actually standing at the counter, aiming a slice mouthward? Can it be her? Of course not. It's Gerald the former Jesuit and . . . Lorna the ex-sister of Saint Winnifred! Who Oskar introduced to each other the night of the blackout. The same day Oskar met Kroitermann, when she rescued him from the police. Bella is nowhere in sight. Kroitermann is dead, according to the newspapers. But Gerald and Lorna are, of course, married.

They wriggle with delight at the sight of him. They rush out, slices flapping, and embrace him with their immense interest, the quality they shared—he should have known they'd stick once they found each other. They dragoon him along 72nd, over to Central Park West, past a beribboned doorman and up the elevator to a marvellous grotto of an apartment, stocked with kids, Gerald and Lorna's, and friends of the kids of Gerald and Lorna. Yes, says Gerald, quite a pad. Al Pacino lives upstairs, Meryl Streep is below, last month Merv Griffin the talk-show host offered me seven million for it.

They tell him what they do now. Oskar's jaw drops, then he smacks his forehead with his palm. This gesture is the emblem of his life, its leitmotif. If Oskar had a family crest it would be a dropping jaw rampant on a smacked forehead. Of course he should have guessed – therapists! Gerald works with his customers there, in the study jammed with his old religion books, Max Weber, and all the sociologists; Laura treats hers here in the living room alongside the enormous piano. Oskar asks who comes. "They're people with some money to spend," says Gerald, "who wonder what happened to their lives." Lorna starts to nod off in the puffy armchair near the piano. She looks beatific. A young teen with flowing curls tears by the French doors in the hall. Gerald beams as he never did behind the breastwork of plates he built each night in the 24-hour restaurant, while explaining the unquenchable human need for meaning.

This encounter reactivates in Oskar the same thought that propelled him to New York years ago: I must act. To what act is he inspired – marriage and family? No, that is out of the question. He has substituted for that sort of closeness. Substituted what? People, in unpredictable multitudes, all kept at a distance.

Life as a potpourri. But Oskar no longer fears his return to Toronto. There will be no further delays. He knows what he was seeking, and where to find it. As soon as he arrives home, he places a call.

Paltz is mine, thinks Oskar. A shrink of my own. He inspects the office. It is dim. Good. Like a cave, a maze, a treasure trove he has taken years to penetrate. He is in, but it wasn't easy. The moment of decision came yesterday when Paltz returned his call. Paltz was reluctant, he said he was tired, he can't handle as many patients as he once could. "Maybe I lack the courage," said Paltz. Oskar took his words as code. They meant one thing: this man can't bear the thought of me when he recollects the great hours of analysis he shared with Hermann my nemesis. Oskar sighed himself. "Buber once said something like that," he mused into the mouthpiece. Paltz sounded more alert. "Buber?" he breathed, "Mordecai . . . Martin . . . Buber?" Oskar calmed down. This one was hooked, like Freud himself, who never lost his fascination with Judaism. Freud, with all his analysis and sophistication, his reductions of everything to complexes and resistance and toilet training, who felt nevertheless that maybe, just maybe, he'd missed something that didn't reduce all the way down. Perhaps even that his ancestors from the *shtiebelach* in their ignorance and superstition knew something he, the genius who created psychoanalysis, didn't. Jewish analysts – Jewish doubt. Maybe the same key unlocked this door for Hermann decades back. Hermann never even met Buber. Now, inside Paltz's office, through the door like an encyclopedia salesman, Oskar relaxes.

Many months later, nothing has happened. What are they doing? Where are they bound? Paltz waits, somewhere behind him, he supposes. But Paltz might have gone for a pee, or downstairs for coffee. Oskar doesn't know for sure, because Paltz is out of sight from here on the couch. One day he wants to go for a pee himself. He says so. Paltz actually speaks. "Why don't you stay there and see what happens?" he says. Oskar asks why. Paltz says nothing. "Is it because you suspect I am trying to avoid confronting a repression by pissing it out in my stream?" Oskar asks. He thinks he hears Paltz shift in the chair. He has become expert at interpreting the creaks and moans of furniture. But you never know. It might be the floorboards, it might be the pipes, it might be the effect of a passing plane or the wind. Or the elevator. Or a truck unloading far below. Oskar knows he is meant to express these thoughts, it is the primary rule, which Paltz revealed the first time they talked. The *only* time they talked.

He tried to comply. In that first hour they had together he really did. He opened his mouth and said, "I had an unhappy childhood." He was mortified at his triteness. He was certain he had lost Paltz's interest and would be turfed back onto the street. But he tried again anyway. "I suffer from sibling rivalry," he said. Then he gave up. The silence began, and the waiting. Paltz became the brooding presence at his shoulder.

Does Paltz take notes, does he snooze? Yes, he does from time to time. Oskar can tell from the breathing. How he yearns to crane around and look on this presence who forever looks on him. Like God, The Unseen, Who sees all. But does Oskar dare? What if he was wrong? Imagine the horror: slowly turning your head, leaning up on an elbow, swivelling to gaze on a dozy Paltz – and him looking right back at you, face to face as they say of God and man in the Bible. A huge craggy unforgiving visage. Oskar would not survive. No man shall see My face and live. I can't stand it, he says, the time he has to pee. He leaps up and bolts for the wc in the outer office. He doesn't look back. He knows what happened to Lot's wife.

He feels like Lot these days, he thinks he knows how Lot felt. Lot's brother Abraham had an excellent relationship with the Lord. The two of them went back a long way and did many things together. Just like Hermann and Paltz. Here is Oskar the interloper, little brother trying to make his mark and failing pathetically by comparison. No one thinks about Lot. He was a loser. Even his name is forgettable. Lot lived in Sodom, or Gomorrah, out of the way places notable only for the fact they were obliterated. The sole reason he's remembered at all is his big brother Abe, who had such a super relationship with the Lord. Oh, for a world without brothers!

Maybe Paltz is past it. Sometimes he seems to slip into another realm. He becomes garrulous, a Dutch uncle instead of a silent judge. "You're too good for this society," he announces after weeks of dead air. "There's nothing wrong with *you*, there's just no place in this stifling system for anyone sensitive and creative." During these effusions Oskar trusts Paltz far less than when Paltz is at his stoniest. Oskar is certain that the instant the door shuts behind him after one of these sessions, Paltz explodes in a string of epithets and denunciations: "Ass, degenerate, pervert, pariah!" As though Paltz has spent numerous lifetimes – his own and those of others – wading patiently through human inadequacy and anxiety, and now that his own end is near he has grave doubts whether any of it was well spent. They are garbage – the entire human mob as he's analysed, soothed, and salved them – and the best he can do at this point in his travail and theirs is extend a bromide and usher them back onto the grimy streets.

Mostly, though, Paltz waits. Even at these prices, Oskar finds it impressive. Sometimes he wants to scream, "Good heavens, man! LIFE IS PASSING as I lie here on your couch!" It is a godlike patience Paltz has. Why is it the attributes of God appear in people Oskar knows with the regularity of the man from the gas company who reads the meter?

He is dead certain this is not how Paltz treated Hermann. They engaged in a lively dialogue. Maybe not a Buberian dialogue – that would be difficult with one of you stretched like a mat before the other. But Oskar knows they talked. Paltz was always presenting Hermann with interpretations of his fascinating childhood. Oskar heard them in tedious detail. Is Oskar's own childhood so dull it evokes no comment? Or might Hermann . . . is it possible the little shyster actually *invented* all those experiences and conversations Oskar lusted for during dinner at Fran's?

One day dialogue strikes – in reverse! Oskar has been babbling about Buber and Hermann and God. Paltz speaks. There is uncertainty in his voice. As though he is . . . a person! "I think I'd like you to change chairs with me for the rest of this session," he says. There is weariness in his voice. Even sorrow? "You need not get up," he goes on, "but please listen."

Paltz, it turns out, has a grandson. This means Paltz also has a wife, children, a home, all the paraphernalia Oskar does not associate with the omniscient asexual divinity shifting weight behind him. Oskar is unhappy at this turn. He feels as he did when he thought Buber was trying to unburden himself. The trouble with these godlike figures is they want the glory but they try to avoid the perfection that goes with it. Once, since he entered treatment – or the effective lack of it – he ran into Paltz at a function for Jewish educators and social workers. "Oh, Oskar," cooed Bee Lilienthal, "you must meet Dr Paltz, he's *very* interested in Jewish symbolism." There he stood, Paltz incarnate, the non-word made flesh, holding out a hand with a grin that said, Let's play this game! Oskar swiped at the handshake and walked away. This was his confessor and judge. He didn't want to exchange chitchat. What an indignity, what a joke played on his long odyssey to arrive in the sanctum of Paltz's practice. Now, while Oskar lies on the sacral couch like an offering in the days of the Second Temple, Paltz turns to him again as a person. What is Paltz trying to do, dissolve the transference when it has barely got started? I want my transference, Oskar howls in his mind.

Paltz's grandchild, it appears, has been a rocker and a punker and a rebel in his time, none of which satisfied him. At the urging of his elders the young man visited Israel last summer. He went to a kibbutz. Oskar's interest overcomes his grumpiness. "In my experience," says the voice of Paltz, "the kibbutz over the years offered meaning to many jaded children of our society." In this case, though, the kibbutz failed. The young Canadian Jew caught a train for Tel Aviv, on his way home. There an unappetizing religious man approached and asked the boy as a charity to lay on a set of *t'fillin*, so the pious traveller could fulfil the commandment of causing another Jew to perform a religious act. They began to talk. The man was a *Lubavitscher Hassid*, a recruiter in effect, and now Paltz's grandson is a member of the Lubavitsch community, Kfar Habad, outside Tel Aviv. "Do you know the place?" asks Paltz. "Yes," says Oskar, "it is a perfect replica of a pigsty of an eighteenth-century Polish Jewish community." Does Paltz gasp? Is it just the cushion of his chair exhaling as he shifts? He continues.

The young man is no mindless enthusiast. He is thoughtful and concerned, just like those Oskar tells his staff "make it all worthwhile." On Kfar Habad he has discovered something he values. He has written his grandfather about it, and Granddad is impressed by the boy's earnestness. Then, just this past weekend, the *Lubavitscher rebbe* was here in Toronto on a rare excursion away from world *Lubavitsch* headquarters in Brooklyn, N.Y. At the request of the *rebbe*, Paltz and the missus went to meet him.

"He's a great man, you know," says Paltz. "He has a degree in engineering from the Sorbonne. He keeps track of his thousands of followers throughout the world and helps in their life decisions. You know how he does it?" Suddenly an oversize index card with categories to fill in, printed in Hebrew, is floating above the couch. The card hovers there, facing Oskar's upturned face, like a helicopter, then slowly descends. Oskar plucks it from the the Unseen Hand like a revelation, like the Tablets of the Law handed down from Sinai. "I'd like to know what you think of all this," says Paltz.

Oskar scans the card, then he shrieks "You are an idiot!" and wheels to a sitting position. "Do you know what is on here? Do you know what is the basis on which your great man guides the lives of his believers? Astrological data! Birth date, time, year, phase of the bloody moon! That is how he tells them who to marry, where to move, what job to take, when to go on vacation, everything to do with their pathetic existences. You with your respect for human autonomy, for the possibility of rational victory over the neurotic wellsprings of behaviour – how come you don't deplore this manipulation of dependent and childish and superstitious tendencies? It is not just infantile – it is primitive, degrading, disgusting. . ."

Oskar is rising now from the couch, profile to Paltz, like
Lazarus from his bed, Jesus from the tomb, Lucifer the rebel
angel climbing back from the depth to which he was hurled for
insubordination, up again to the exalted state in which he began.
Oskar turns to face Paltz, the face which faces his a surprise:
shrivelled and doubtful, its godliness has vanished, gone on a
trip, the face is uncertain, fearful, intimidated even. Ugh! He
has managed to terrorize even Paltz, what is the point of anything? "You. You—fake. I had faith in your wisdom, your insight,
your sophistication. I am so embarrassed! My shrink is a push-
over, a sucker. Engineering school in Paris? Since when are you
so impressed? What if he went to the DeVry Institute?" Paltz is
cringing. "He has your number, you little Viennese afterthought.
You reminder of something Freud would have shaken off the
end of his penis after a good pee – a *teepah s'roochah*, like the
Talmud says, that's what you are, a stinking little droplet! You
know what Freud wrote? *'Surely infancy was meant to be over-
come.'* Brilliant, compassionate, immortal words. Not, hand in
your file card and the *rebbe* will tell you what to do with your
life. He knows how to manipulate your Jewish past and your
Jewish guilt and your narcissism and he uses it on you! Sigmund
Freud – be glad you're dead!"

Paltz recovers. He sucks it up. He stands too and faces Oskar.
They look like two stunted gunfighters in the streets of Laredo.
But what can Paltz say in this moment of truth? "I may," he
pronounces coldly, "not know much about Judaism. But I am
one of the goddamn best psychoanalysts on Avenue Road!"

It is the last insight he leaves Oskar, who steps moments later
into the declining sunlight on Avenue Road. He knows how
Samson felt right after he brought the temple down around himself. He looks north toward the hill that marked the shore of
Lake Ontarionensis during the Ice Age. He feels feisty but not
fit. He pivots southward, along the gentle incline toward the
current lake. He tips gently forward, past the boutiques of Yorkville and the bar of the Four Seasons, across Bloor, looking for

someplace to park the sense of liberation he feels. Thirty years of yearning for this thing, this access, access to himself, through this man who held the key, the gatekeeper to ME, and he just tossed it. It's so satisfying. Why are you banging your head against that wall? *Because it feels so good when I stop!* It is the end of a lifelong search, he feels it in his thin bones. He will get off now. Is it the end because there is no one with the wisdom he sought, or because he is tired of looking? Is it the end because you find out there are no answers, or because you get bored with the questions? Who cares, it feels good. Across the broad street is the Royal Ontario Museum, where his fitful induction by Goldberg into what is Canadian began. Some American play? The museum is history. Fie on it. But next door, where nothing was in years past, rises the new planetarium. *Parfait!* Oskar is feeling cosmic.

He sits alone in the indoor amphitheatre. He stretches luxuriously across several seats. Above him the galaxies unfold. (Somewhere in the darkness the projection machine hisses.) *When I behold the heavens*, he thinks, *the signs of Thy handiwork* . . . He leans back farther, as if he'd like to transform himself into the biblical firmament that arches over creation and protects it. He's never felt so clearly that, as the psalm says, "*The heavens declare the glory of God.*" Whatever He is, and whether He is – not to mention His glory, whatever that is – the heavens declare it. Here in Toronto, one is almost never aware of the sky. It's that kind of town: day or night, your gaze is rarely drawn upward. But inside this planetarium on a dusky evening, alone, Oskar is overwhelmed by the grandeur, just as he once was. Where was that?

The camp! The Canadian one, where they were sent after the Plains of Abraham. It was north of the St. Lawrence River, on a late August night shortly after they landed. The Canadians were so unprepared – the searchlights weren't even in. They lay on concrete platforms the sergeant-major said were their beds; they'd been foundations for heavy machinery when the place was still a sawmill. That night, through a window high in the wall, the sky seemed to lighten. Then it stopped, and he wasn't sure it had happened. Then it flickered, and flickered again. Then it glowed, in shifting patterns. He thought: searchlights. But not in colours! It was the northern lights. The first time Canada had a content of its own. Not just the place that wasn't Europe, where he wasn't dead. Later, when they took kids to retreats or JYGGL camp, they'd hope for a run of the lights; they'd rouse the kids and hustle them into canoes and out onto the lake for a quick, meaningful experience. "Are we going to have a singsong?" the kids yawned.

Something else is in his mind. The sunset, the one he *shlepped* into Buber's study and presented to the Great Man. How Oskar yearned and pined to connect to the grandeur he knew was there; grandeur that here, in the McLaughlin Planetarium, his limbs flung erratically over plush seats, he feels at last. He is in touch with nature, the divine handiwork that eluded him in the days of Hitler's rise, and his own.

How did he know, that psalmist? How did he sense exactly what Oskar feels? The explosion of ego, when your heart swells like a bladder, you can't stand the joy, like you're being tickled to near death. Here is Oskar, sprawled almost flat beneath these heavens, the sign of His handiwork, as though someone has drenched him with an emotional fire hose, while the psalmist, he'd have been out in the soothing hills of Judea, with the odour of the sheepshit or the hint of rain coming and a sky so total he feared he'd tumble right off the earth down into it.

And then, "*What is Man, that Thou art mindful of him, and the son of Man, that Thou thinkest of him?*" Exactly! *What the hell are we, anyway?* they both think. The distance between them squirts out of the gap that separates them. Oskar knows what the fellow meant! I am a failure, I am a nobody, I am so insignificant that I sit here in the twilight of my years in a tourist attraction in a provincial backwater.

"*Yet Thou hast set him but little lower than the angels, and hast crowned him with glory and honour.*" They feel *so* unworthy, Oskar and the psalmist, but what can you do, here they are, poised before the menacing deep heaven, the vault of the planetarium, the aurora borealis above the internment camp, the trite

sunset of his poser to Buber. Foolishly, incomprehensibly, awe-
somely present.

Oskar sees Paltz once more, in the soft news section of "Street
Beat," an evening newscast over a local channel, a long time
later when Oskar not only owns a television but watches it often.
Paltz is the subject of a special segment. A young reporter says
Paltz has abandoned private practice and devoted his final years
to practical research. Practical, but crazy. Paltz has invented a
calibrated test tube, which he places over the erections of perverts to measure through displacement by volume their reactions
to various erotic stimuli: photographs, voices, passages in
books. In a kind of frenzy as death moves in, Paltz is gathering
data with a will. He seems to have no interest in collating it or
formulating explanatory hypotheses. He appears determined to
avoid explanations. In the final analysis what he leaves will be
a mountain of pornographic calibrations.

Is this the final act? The Oskar Memorial Banquet, with the
Incorrigible One himself as honoured guest. They are gathered
at the call of Jack Katz, those still alive, to mark Oskar's retirement. Even Buzz Friedkin has flown from New York to speak.
We come too, Jimmy, Joey, me, and Teddy the Temple Torcher
– the remnants of his Great Class. They seat us on the outer
reaches, in the foyer of the new Congregational Hall, not inside
it. We wonder if this was Oskar's last command.

Is he bitter at being retired? Did Moses lay down the Law?
His replacement is Gloria, from Scarsdale, Westchester, Great
Neck, White Plains, or Yonkers. She is divorced. At her first
meeting with Sisterhood, she told them, "Ladies, I'll be frank. If
it ever comes to a choice between a man and all those headaches,
or my career and alla those, and it's up to me – I'm gonna be
honest, it's my nature. You'll find me socked right in to the split-
level with the screeching kids, the pile rug, and the snow blower.
But while I'm here, you got me body and soul! Do you hear what

I'm saying?" This was enthusiastically received. How do we know? Oskar says so. How does he know? He has spies. Aging spies, but they still report.

As the tributes flow that evening, does he humbly glow, does he pout, or graciously banter? He records them on tape! This is a historic summation in the life of Oskar, who is a historian, in his failed dreams though nowhere else. Has his vision of a vocation come to this? He will ply the trade anyway. When a tape reaches its end, he leaps from the seat of honour, calls a halt in mid-praise, replaces the tape, and waves the ceremony on.

During the non-alcoholic socializing before dinner, he runs into Hermann. It has been a while. Hermann still lives in Israel; he now sabbaticals in Toronto as he once did in Jerusalem. He has become a *shaliach*, Oskar thinks; one of the emissaries the movement sends to hearten Jews in the Diaspora and urge them to migrate. Their meeting feels like an accident in a foreign place, as though they glanced up on the Rue de la Paix or the Friedrichstrasse and saw one another. They radiate a spontaneous warmth, like some former lovers. "So," says Hermann, "we'll get together and talk." Oskar bobs his head like a plastic perpetual motion duck in a store window. "Lunch," says Hermann. Oskar is going to propose the Famous Food of Israel restaurant, where Hermann can order a kosher chicken fricassee, but Hermann's lovely wife Merle sweeps in. "Come for *shabbas* dinner," she says, like the presidential appointments secretary. Oskar bobs his head sadly.

Afterward, Hilary Zacks drops by our distant table. Maybe she is on her way to the coat check. She is still *zaftig* as she was when I learned my bar mitzvah portion from her. Teddy the Torch sits among us beaming, out on a day pass, or maybe already stamped stable by the shrinks to whom he was entrusted by the courts, and returned to reality. He is amiable though ashen – no surprise after his recent experiences. Maybe that is why Hilary doesn't place him. "Did I teach you too?" she burbles. "I'm Teddy Stein," he says cheerily. Her composure dips miles. "Was it grade five or grade eight," she stammers, "or are you going to send me up in flames?"

On the road again. We are both visiting at the summer camp Sammy bought after years of running the Pillar of Fire youth program. We straddle a wooden bench facing each other, on the deck attached to the dining hall, which overhangs the waters of Lake Missigami. It's a bit like the balcony on which Oskar bearded Scholem. Or the one that runs around the upper level of the sanctuary in the P of F. Or even the little ledge from which the child in Mea Shearim beckoned Oskar aboard the good ship Hassidism. The sun lowers casually toward the far shore line. The campers buzz around us like black flies: the young ones on scavenger hunts or seeking green sticks for their marshmallows and hot dogs; the older kids in earnest pairings asking, Will I see you in September? Everyone knows Oskar won't stay long on this visit, he probably won't last the night. It is a comfortable ritual, developed over the years, hardly less revered than, say, the Consecration Service every autumn. He receives many invitations from those who adore him, he does not answer, then he declines with an insult about the discomfort of the drive and the inadequacy of the accommodation. Finally he phones from the highway, an hour away; he supposes he will drop in, as if he had some other purpose for the five-hour trip from Bathurst and Eglinton to nearly Sudbury. Everyone strives beyond endurance to please him, he fails to conceal his disgust with their miserable efforts, then late at night when all seems unalterable, he leaves, preferring the nocturnal return drive to Toronto and his comfortable bed to the Procrustean exigencies of a summer camp or cottage.

"Where are they now," he says as we look out on the lake, "my Great Class?" A set-piece is beginning, something he has worked on most of his life. It is apparently ready for his public. I wait like a first-nighter as the curtain rises. "This one's a Maoist," he says, meaning me. "This one's married to an Indian princess in Saskatchewan." That's Izzy, who wore the little blue suit and shared my contempt for the inefficiency of the Pillar of Fire Religious School when we were eight. "This one's a sexually obsessed sculptor with penis drawings on his walls." That's Jimmy the ark-maker, and penis wallpaper is a libel on his excellent taste. "The other one is a mad arsonist." Teddy would insist he was not mad, he was performing a symbolic act.

Oskar leans back. I don't quibble, his point is made. We let him down, his life is a failure. I gaze into the middle distance, like an old trapper from these parts who's seen just about every-thing. Before I can grunt a folksy reply, he announces he is leaving. It is his best exit speech ever.

CHAPTER

7

OSKAR HAS BECOME a celebrity. It is his least likely role.

He knows he is a celebrity because he watches television. It is a new feature of his life. In the past, though not bookish, he spent his free time indoors, reading. His apartment on Shallmar Road is furnished mainly with books. He doesn't really like books, but they are a settled part of his life, like eating, sleeping, and regretting his major decisions. Now there is a television set in the apartment. They gave it to him at the Oskar Memorial Banquet. He took it as a message: stay home, stay out of our hair, do not haunt this building, your time here is past.

So he sits on Shallmar, except when he is invited to dinner with one of his teachers: Maida, Rita, Myrna – the bidding for his company is fierce. It means nothing to him. He continues to snarl and revile his fate. He slouches in his armchair. He reads a book. He despises it. He reads another. He loathes it. He eyes the television. It squats in the corner like a big square book with a cord running out of it. He switches it on. "Sveetch on!" he says, like the commander of a tight ship he once was. What does he see?

Abba Eban. This is PBS, the American educational network. "Watch PBS, it's very serious," they said when he recoiled from their gift. They set the channel selector at PBS, for when he weakened. He tries, at this pass he'll try anything. The former Israeli diplomat has aged well. He looks less shiny than he once did. He is worn and comfortable like a sofa. The voice survives, the Oxonian tones to which a generation of Canadian Jews *kvelled* when it rose righteously in the forum of nations. He talked like a lord, that one, not like a greenie. He speaks now, voice-over as they say, for a multi-part documentary called "The Jews." Florid. Oskar has heard it before. He flips.

Peter O'Toole, the actor. He likes O'Toole from *Lawrence of Arabia*. In this one, O'Toole is a Roman general commanding legions in Judea. He has laid siege to Masada. Oskar climbed those heights, it was on his first trip to the *aretz*. The second time he took the elevator. O'Toole loves a Jewess. She is every film Jewess since Elizabeth Taylor was Rebecca in *Ivanhoe*. O'Toole is torn between love and his orders to decimate those rebellious Jews in their desert fortress. Oskar knows the grim end, and awaits it. At the moment of mass suicide the camera pans up: in the sky over the second-century Jewish martyrs a squadron of Israeli jets flies past, a *Magen David* flutters. Oskar flips.

Another American station. This one has Ingrid Bergman. No, it is Golda Meir. No, it is Ingrid Bergman as Golda Meir, looking much as she did the day she heaved his Fiat off the curb. Here she is running a cabinet meeting. Now she is cooking *kugel*. She is running a cabinet meeting *while* she cooks *kugel*. The American defence secretary is in her breakfast nook. She passes him a plate and persuades him to supply more heat-seeking missiles. Oskar frowns. Ingrid Bergman is dead. Golda Meir is dead. He flips again.

This one is Canadian. He just knows. Maybe it's the sound, which is hollow and echoes. Perhaps it's the background movement, that is, lack of background movement. It isn't about Jews. The hero is a real Canadian: strong, gentle, unaggressive. Mr WASP. He comes from a pleasant Canadian town during a pleasant time, maybe fifty years back. But wait. The Canadian Gentile goes to Europe. He is helping Jews escape from Nazis. He has been caught. They put him in a concentration camp. The inmates are pudgy and well-fed. Their striped pyjamas are clean and pressed. A Canadianized Auschwitz. *Flip*.

American: tough Charles Bronson as an Israeli paratrooper rescuing hijack hostages in Uganda. *Flip*. Canadian again: a comedy about growing up Jewish in a small town. Funny sound. *Flip*. PBS again. A Jewish family in Germany during the Nazi years. *Flip*. American: gruff but lovable newspaper editor sends pretty girl reporter to cover neo-Nazi march through Jewish community in Illinois. *Flip*. Rod Steiger as Jewish pawnbroker in Harlem. Oskar has seen this, it's a movie, it must be the late show. *Flip*. Gregory Peck learns about anti-Semitism by pretending to be Jewish. This one is old. *Flip*. Marshall Dillon helps a rabbi in the old west – a rerun. *Flip*. Israelis. *Flip*. Survivors. *Flip*. Nazis. *Flip*. Nothing. *Flip*. Nothing. *Flip again*. Nothing. *Sveetch off*.

He slumps in his chair. He sinks his fingers like talons into the cloth. He rubs his eyes with his palms, trying to adjust his inner set. When he first came to the Pillar of Fire, they gave bar mitzvah boys a book called *They All Were Jews*, or for the dullards, *Great Jews in Sports*. Those books were stuffed with proof that Jews could be heroic, or at least interesting. As the boys turned the pages (or their parents turned for them), the family squealed, "Him too? I never thought *he* was Jewish!" It changed, perhaps forever, when blue-eyed Paul Newman crawled dripping from the sea as Ari Ben Canaan, Israeli *Übermensch*, in a film of the novel, *Exodus*. Here was a new Jew for public consumption: steely, brave, and irresistible to the blonde Aryan, Eva Marie Saint. Oskar summoned his teachers and department heads, like the tribes and elders of Israel. Send your kids, he told them, like Joshua despatching spies across the Jordan. Arrange group rates, charter busses – but get them there! He had a sneaking suspicion he might never need another carton of *Great Jews in Sports*.

He rubs his palms in reverse direction. He is back in Berlin. Everyone around him knows who is Jewish. They are all trying to prove that Jews can be German! They quote the greatest figures of German literature in support of their claim. Oskar grew up thinking Lessing, Schiller, Goethe, Herder, and Fichte were Jewish names; he heard them so often in defence of Jewish rights. Education is pathetic, he thinks, rubbing away the memory, and coming back to the bewildering present.

Jews as stars. And stars as Jews. Elizabeth Taylor converted. First she was Rebecca in *Ivanhoe*; then she was the real thing. Marilyn Monroe converted too. Jack Katz told him a joke. Liz and Marilyn are powdering their nose in the Ladies'. In walks Kim Novak. "*Shach!*" says Marilyn to Liz in Yiddish: "Here comes the *shiksa*." Even a black tap dancer converted – Sammy Davis Jr., Oskar doesn't understand. These famous people want to be Jewish?

Canadian Jews used to react with a myclonic jerk when the word "*Jew*ellery" appeared in a headline. Now they take stories about Jews for granted. There is always something about Israel in the press and usually on television, as if there is news about Jews and news about everyone else. Jewish editor jailed in Argentina. Falashas smuggled out of Ethiopia. Jewish intermarriage rises in Britain. Lady rabbis in the U.S. Jews are newsworthy, as he and Goldberg would have said at *World Press Review*, when they talked constantly about the Jewish Problem but never put it in the stories they wrote. A banner outside the museum, the good old ROM, in whose basement he met Canadian culture, advertises a display of Jewish religious art from Hungary, redeemed, unlike the rest of Hungarian Jewry, from the Nazis. Down at the waterfront, the Hadassah Bazaar is on. Everyone is going, it is the place to be on a day in November. Last weekend was the bar mitzvah of the son of Loony Larry Electronics, *hundler* supreme. It was a gross affair. Oskar knows because he reads the daily papers. Loony Larry dressed his boy in an ermine cape and a crown. His own rabbi criticized him on the nightly news! There were *editorials*! Don't the Italians or the West Indians ever do anything?

Sometimes he drives downtown and parks in the lot beneath City Hall, then surfaces and sits on a bench in Hartley Harvey Park. Affable, avuncular Hart was one of Toronto's first Jewish mayors; he called himself the mayor of all the people. Politics wasn't so slick then. Every Yom Kippur, he came to Temple and was called to the pulpit. He always read the chapter from Jonah that mentions "all the people" again and again: God sent Jonah to tell all the people, all the people heard, and so forth. Jewish mayors are small potatoes now. There are Jewish cabinet ministers, federal and provincial party leaders, supreme court judges, heads of royal commissions, even bankers. Oskar looks over toward University Avenue and ogles the secretaries. They cross the street, they ride the escalators, they clamber up from the subway. He liked it better in the sixties, when they wore miniskirts.

Around the time Oskar started at the Pillar of Fire, Rabbi Rosen wrote an article for *Canadian Capers*, the magazine that came in the Saturday paper along with the comics and a pin-up of a hockey player. The piece was called "It's Fun to be a Jew!" Oskar found it transparent. If it's such fun, he thought, why get so solemn? Now, nobody protests too much; it *is* fun to be Jewish.

One day, the temple calls. Will he come Sunday and speak to the confirmation class? Yes, certainly. He washes and shaves with care, he arrives, that is, returns. The class, they explain, deals with the Holocaust. In fact, the whole course is about the Holocaust – he created it. Ah, he says, as though he finds it a clever idea. They take him before the students.

"This is our guest," says the teacher. "He isn't exactly a survivor." She sounds apologetic. "But he did live in Germany during the Nazi era." The class lean forward, they are attentive. "He's going to try and speak to us about his experience," she says.

Try? Why *try*? What does she mean? He considers where to start. A forest of hands rises and sways before him. He points to one, she has tight dark curls. "Were you in a concentration camp?"

"I was," he starts, and feels they are with him. "For a few

weeks," he says. "After *Kristallnacht*. It was before the war. Then I was released. Then I came to Canada."

What just happened? He lost them, they've gone away. "I was in a camp for a longer time," he says, and they lean in again, "when I came to Canada. It was in Quebec." There is a flicker of disappointment, maybe even anger. They want the Nazi hell, no substitutes. He'd like to give it to them, he wants them back. He describes the disintegration of the Weimar Republic, and the re-emergence of anti-Semitism, never far from the German surface. They seem neutral, they wait for more. It perplexes him. He recalls the anxiety of Jewish youth at the time – there is a spasm of interest. He mentions his own role, and the determination everyone felt to be proud of being Jewish. He has them now. He decries the cowardice of the League of Nations. They are gone again. The stark terror of *Kristallnacht*, and the moment he was picked up himself. The terrifying arrival at Oranienburg. The kids' eyes fill with tears. It's clear, they want a survivor, and they deserve one.

Why not? They face lives of withering dullness. A bourgeois existence in a bourgeois suburb, self-absorbed and smug. Their parents are models of success and their future is dreary and predictable. Yet their ancestors fell under a mighty hammer. This nightmare in their past singles them out, it adds grandeur to their identity, prestige even, and to acquire it, they need only plug in to those events. True, Oskar does not feel this need himself, but he has always been inadequate to life's opportunities. They have a right.

Yet he fails them. He is not really this, which they want, nor that either. Not a fully fledged survivor of the camps, nor a trenchant historian who can make the era live. Not a DP and not a true-blue Canadian. He is never quite enough of whatever others find desirable, and he always withholds what the moment requires. He is a Churkendoose, and his time will never come.

"You could have got a better survivor," he says to the teacher later. She shrugs it off. "I tried," he says, but it doesn't seem to bother her, something else is on her mind. "It's like they're in a

sealed container," she says, "and the only thing that ever pene-
trates it is this thing called Holocaust. When it's gone, they're
numb again."

"I know what it's like to bring a guest in," he says. "It ought
to be special. You're looking for a star. I'm sorry."

She looks perplexed. "Oh no," she says, "we didn't think of
you as a star."

"No?" he says. "Then what did you think you were getting?"

She smiles her timid smile and shrugs again, embarrassed. "A
hero," she says shyly.

He travels. Travel was the great seduction of retirement. You
can travel, they said. As though retiring him when he never asked
was a favour.

He starts each trip on the subway. This is prudent, economic,
and German. Everything in one suitcase, one long ride on the
subway to the airport bus, and you are here, Pearson International.

The flight to Zurich is delayed. Unfortunate but unavoida-
ble. Oskar did check before he left the apartment. He flipped to
the TV channel that gives arrivals and departures: Air Canada
only, but that's why he books Air Canada. Then, coat on and
hand on the doorknob, he phoned the airport direct. *Hakol
b'seder. Alles in Ordnung.* Now, at a late point, trouble. We
have an equipment problem, says the redhead with glossy lipstick at the check-in. What equipment? he asks. We don't have
a plane, she says. He looks around terrible terminal 2 and frets.
If he'd taken a cab, he'd have left later. He might have learned
about the equipment problem in time to adjust his schedule. Is
the subway a false economy?

"Anything else sir?" say the red lips. Yes, there is something
else, but he doesn't know what. It is Zurich. He has been to
Zurich on every holiday for years. At first he pretended it was a
stopover to ease the haul going to and from Israel. Gradually he
abandoned subterfuge. He loves Zurich. It is clean like his bathroom. It is sane and predictable. It is typically German with one
advantage: it is Swiss.

So what suddenly is wrong with Zurich? Nothing. There is no problem with Zurich. The problem is Oskar. Why is he going to Zurich again? To revisit Germany by proxy? To contact the past but not touch it? What is the point? He is old, he is retired. And he *still does not seem to connect*!

The lips are still smiling. She waits patiently, she'd like to help. He needs help. He wants to connect. But how? Connect with what? Anything. Start somewhere. The easiest place.

"Is there something wrong with Zurich, sir?"

"No. Nothing. I just – don't want to go there."

"Where do you want to go?"

Here. Wherever that is. He has never gone anywhere *here*. Not to Hamilton, Halifax, Ottawa, or Winnipeg. He has lived here more than twice as long as he lived in Germany, and he has never been anywhere here. He avoids it, he is never here. He has spent a lifetime not being here, wherever that is.

"Have you got a flight here?"

"Here, sir?"

How do you get here? He has been south, to New York and Florida. He has been east, to Zurich and Jerusalem. All right, clearly here must be in another direction: north perhaps. He starts to shiver. In that case – "Do you have a flight to the West?"

"Like . . . the Prairies?" she says. He tries to nod, his head jerks up and down and his eyes glisten. She seems to catch his fervour, she senses this is a historic moment in the life of Oskar, she doesn't ask reasonable questions. "What about Calgary?" she says, glancing over her shoulder to be sure her supervisor is busy. Calgary, he thinks. Calgary, Calgary . . . Alberta. Calgary – Stampede. Calgary – cowboys, Rocky Mountains, oil wells, Wayne Gretzky the hockey player!

"Yes," he says. "The first flight."

The Dodge Dart flits across the countryside. He took it at the rental desk because it is a Dodge and recalls its predecessors, but he's never been in a car this small and racy. It is a sub-compact at most. He's never seen a landscape like this either. At first it seemed flat, lacking character. But the more he drives through it the more complicated it gets. It unfolds subtly. Slight features demand attention. It's because I'm Here, he thinks. The driving looks after itself. Straight ahead at a constant rate. No turns, no curves, no rises or falls. He is normally a finicky driver, checking the meters for speed, heat, fuel, glancing in the rear-view, the side-view, watching for approaching and passing traffic – that would be superfluous out here.

There is an unfamiliar quality he can't finger or name. This discomfits him. Name it and you take control. Like God at the Creation: call it this, call it that – the names don't matter, but the power to name does! As a lifelong sadist, Oskar covets the ability to name the deepest fears of those he seeks to intimidate. Name what they are afraid to admit, and they are his. Out here, he has no names.

There is a *newness*–that's the quality. He didn't go on *aliyah*, because it would be strange to him; instead he came to Toronto, which felt strangely familiar. He doesn't even stay overnight when he visits friends, because he yearns for his own bed. He has spent more than forty years – a standard stretch in the wil- derness – in his new country, without getting to know it. Every- thing can be a way of avoiding what it seems to be doing.

But this landscape is different. It looks like a place that has never yet been, and still somehow isn't. Like the pre-Creation! That time before God named all things and fixed their character forever. The mystics of the Kabbalah were fascinated by the pre-Creation, as are children. What was there before anything was? In the beginning, the real beginning. Before that meddling God of the Bible got busy creating and precluded all possibilities except those He decided to make real. Before Him, say the Kabbalists, there was another divinity, called the Ayn-Sof, the Endless One, who just was, but who didn't *do* anything. Oskar looks around at this flat bare place containing little beyond hints and implications. Nothing is set. Out here all is still, it waits, it does not force Oskar's hand or exhaust him with its undeniable values. It releases him from preoccupation with himself and his

252

horrible duty. It lets his attention drift from his task to his context.

Perhaps this place represents the kind of religion he was made for. Perhaps his problem was that Judaism came to him pre-formed – it was preform, not reform, Judaism. He'd like to try getting behind that kind of religion, to the the Ayn-Sof, the Endless One. He suspects he would find the Ayn-Sof a nice impersonal deity. Oskar has never been good at personal rela-tions: *Attah loh ratzeetah l'hitkashair,* Greta said. You didn't want to connect. Well, the God of the Jews was nothing if not connected: He summoned His people, formed a relationship with them, made demands, complained furiously if they failed, and dispensed humiliation, not to mention death and exile, in the bargain. He was always looking on at your dull life, like a psychoanalyst paid to examine every slip and indiscretion. But look at this prairie – flat and endless; like the Ayn-Sof. Its rare features, abutments, dips don't oppress you with their dialecti-cally necessary implications as you whiz past in your Dodge Dart. They don't foretell every detail of their end in their begin-ning. A divinity like this Oskar could relate to, maybe. You wouldn't pray to it, that would be like praying to a sand dune, a sagebrush, or a tumbling tumbleweed like the one that just rolled across the blacktop in front of him. This is the sort of godhood that would lay back and let a fellow come to it. Oskar could be a devout man out here – a *Hassid* of the Prairies. Maybe he should have been a Gnostic.

The Gnostics were a sect who flourished, he once read, in the ancient world. They attracted Oskar because they claimed the God of the Bible was an impostor: He was really the devil in disguise. The true divinity, according to Gnostics, was like the Ayn-Sof, a vague being who let existence flow slowly along on its own till that biblical Devil-God took over and tried to force things according to his own wilful personality. The snake tried to tell the first humans, Adam and Eve, what was going on, to give them knowledge – in Greek, *gnosis*; the snake's been vilified for his good intentions ever since. And Oskar the educator, the inquirer, the one with the questions who is dissatisfied with the answers, hasn't he always wondered whether he became a teacher because he *wanted to know*, even if he's been in a fog about what was missing? Maybe it's the snake with whom he identifies, wily and slippery with a secret agenda on his twisted mind. Oskar can relate to the snake better than he could to priests and prophets, not to mention rabbis. Perhaps Oskar *is* the snake, his mouth wriggling across his face, tantalizing ideas issuing from it, winding their way toward the ears of his innocent students at the Pillar of Fire, urging them to question received wisdom and challenge authority. Has he finally found a biblical hero after his faint heart? In the primary grades they never sing about the snake. He hums tunelessly as he . . . snakes across this landscape, this flat memento of pre-Creation, a country he never knew was here. Something has begun for him. Canada. Because out here nothing changes, history takes a holiday. It is so implacably stable.

Till now. In his bland career across uniform space he suddenly realizes his motion is uniformly accelerating! So smooth he barely notices, then doesn't believe it. But the needle on the speedometer is climbing. It makes no sense. They are on level ground. There *is* nothing but level ground. He lifts his foot lightly, the needle keeps climbing. He lifts some more. His foot is off the accelerator. The needle keeps mounting. He reaches down, the accelerator peddle is right up, it's not stuck on the floor – yet the car still speeds. He hesitantly tries the brake, the car starts to swerve, no help there. Some traffic approaches: a car and a truck. More than he's seen in hours. What if the car tries to pass the truck. WHOOSH. They are by him. In a creative burst he reaches for the steering column and turns off the ignition. The engine cuts. The car glides silently, like a divine spark from the shattered holy vessels of the pre-Creation, drifting down through world after world, to finally settle in the murky and crass husks of the lowest of all worlds, our own. But settle it does, because Oskar found the key. Proudly, he eases onto the brake, which works properly now, and slows the Dodge to a stop on the shoulder of the road. In the dim flat distance squats

a very small town. BLANTON, says a sign right where he stopped,
A GOOD PLACE TO BE. 2 KILOMETRES.

Vanderveen has returned with him. Vanderveen opened the door
of the trailer, the first place Oskar came to as he lurched toward
Blanton. Oskar never knocked on a trailer door before. It was
surrounded by a picket fence, with a neat garden and a sign,
The Vanderveens Live Here. Lanky Les Vanderveen stood in the
aluminum door and gazed down. Not just from the natural
height he towers over Oskar, but add in the distance from the
trailer to the ground. A look like the opening shot in a western
movie spread slowly across his expansive face. He looked Oskar
up and down and stretched his neck as if he'd like to see this
creature from behind and beside as well.

Vanderveen didn't know what this apparition meant, but he
was sure it meant something. Les's mind was dedicated to the
belief that everything meant something, though never what
everyone else thought. Thus, if others agreed an event meant
one thing, Les took it as a sure sign the opposite was true. Since
everyone said this attitude showed he had a conspiratorial frame
of mind, Les figured he was on the right track for certain. Why
else would they all try and put him off it? In addition Les was a
westerner: hospitable in his bones and incurably generous. The
real pastime of the Canadian prairies has always been helping
other folks out. "Right with you," he said immediately.

Back at the Dodge, Les slips behind the driver's seat and
releases the hood catch. Oskar marvels. He searched in vain
beneath the hood itself for that release. Just as well, only a
revelation would have told him what to do had he penetrated
the car's innards. Les scrutinizes him for a moment, as if there
should also be a hidden release to raise the lid on the meaning
of this man's appearance at his door. He ducks under the hood.

He fiddles and twitches. He adjusts and resets his shoulders,
as though putting on the right body for this job. He knows what
he is doing, thinks Oskar. I came to the right man. Or is everyone
in this enchanted barrens a natural auto mechanic? Something

they're born with or acquire as they grow, like their manner of squinting toward the sky and sniffing for rain. Les shifts his weight from one foot to the other and reverses the elbow on which he leans. He slides the screwdriver, which seems to grow out of his palm, to his other hand in a fluid motion. He jabs, feints, jabs again, and twists. "All right," he says, with satisfaction. It's almost a prayer, this All right. Oskar looks back uneasily. Big Les enfolds him with a paw on the shoulder. "You drive my car," he says genially, "and I'll test yours, to be sure." Oskar looks down sheepishly. He likes this large alien creature. "I don't know much about automobile mechanics," says Oskar. "I'm a Jewish educator."

An inner light floods Les's face. As though he knew all would be well, as though he has received an epiphany, a hasty message of great importance from a superior source. He puts out his hand. "I'm a teacher myself," he says. "History and shop. See you back at the trailer."

The Indian girl at the desk of the Moccasin Motel on the outskirts of Blanton says to Oskar, "Your room is ready." Vanderveen phoned for his reservation from the trailer, after Oskar resisted an offer to stay with Les and the missus. It is now 8:30 in the evening.

The room is a horror. The bedspread, carpet, and drapes are all stained. He does not look at the sheets. The toilet is broken and noisy. Noise comes from every room up and down the hall. There is a single unshaded bulb, and the smell of disinfectant, as one finds in a hospital or whorehouse. "Can I see another room?" he asks.

Five rooms later he says, "Aren't there any decent rooms in this motel?" No, says the housekeeper. He goes downstairs and steps onto Blanton's main street. Dusk has fallen. He lurches up one side and down the other. There is a Radio Shack. It makes him lonely. An Agnew Surpass shoe store and a Kentucky Fried Chicken. At the movies is *Conan the Barbarian*. He's seen it. Oskar arrives back at the motel. This is the end of the earth. He yearns for home, his bed, his television set. His exhilaration of the drive is a lost memory. Still, eighteen dollars a night isn't much to pay for such misery. He could do worse. And he already has a friend. Aha! Twenty minutes later he is back at the trailer. No, he hasn't decided to stay with them, the motel will do, but he is happy to pass more time in Les's company, now that Lily is in bed.

Les unpacks his library for Oskar. It is in an attaché case he fetches from the bedroom of the trailer, where Lily soundly sleeps. It is not his whole library. Other books are spread around in cases purchased at Consumers Distributing and assembled at home, or shelves that come from the K Mart and hang on the wall. But the small selection of booklets and pamphlets that emerge from the attaché case is clearly the essential Vanderveen. This little holder is the Holy of Holies, you might say, the ark of the covenant in the sanctuary of his trailer. Les removes them with the delicacy and affection of old men in Mea Shearim as they take out the Torah scrolls. The booklets and pamphlets are well thumbed. Often in the mornings, confides Les, he rises early, gets them from their place, and comes in here to the living room to study. Others watch TV in the morning, but he doesn't have it in him to waste time. He's too interested, he says, in the meaning of life and related matters. Oskar doesn't need to be told, he knows it's an honour to see these documents. He fingers them. He isn't sure what to say.

"No such thing as a dumb question," says Les robustly. Oskar is moved. The man seems to have the heart of a teacher. "Tell me about them," says Oskar.

Les starts with a pamphlet called *Is Humanism Molesting Your Child?* "Have you read it?" he asks, hoping the answer is no. "No," says Oskar, thinking, Who else worries about humanism? Of course – Hermann! What a connection: big, dumb Les and wiry, brain-huge Hermann. "What do you mean by humanism?" he asks. "Humanism, eh?" says Les, and Oskar has a quick vision of life in history class at Blanton High.

"Humanism is a godless way of life," says Les. "Humanism is the stupid arrogant idea that people are smart enough to run their own lives and the world without guidance from a divine source." *Look around you* – Oskar can hear him saying to his students – *Look in a mirror. See that silly grinning puss? You think you've got the smarts to figure it all out? You so dumb you think you're that smart? You in back – you couldn't even pass geography. You there – you jammed the plugs just trying to do a minor tune-up on your dad's pickup last week. I had to sort it out for you.*

Oskar is drawn in by Vanderveen's colloquy more than he often was by Hermann's literate theses over waffles. Humanism is "a man-made selfish system," explains the teach. Communism is an offshoot of it, but the main thing about humanism is that it doesn't work! "How," asks Oskar, "do you know?"

Vanderveen grows still. There is a charisma to the man. "I have studied history," he says, "and if you go back five hundred years, or a thousand, in every case you will find that systems based on a supreme being have done better than systems which are not." Oskar stares at the capacity of a human being to say such a moronic thing. An impulse stops him from asking for an example. Maybe it's human solidarity. Les moves steadily forward, like Oskar's rented car; like it, he even accelerates. He reaches into his attaché case and plucks out *Life's Daily Disasters: Mockery or Messengers?* "My favourite," he says, and Oskar pictures him on frosty mornings bent over the small tome.

"I grew up on this dusty prairie," says Les. "Can you picture it in the Depression? We went years without rain. Locusts we had. Heat we had. Debt collectors and bailiffs and greedy bankers. No rain, though, not a drop. Once, after a storm we held my baby brother by his heels and pounded his back till he vomited a stomach full. Maybe it was my sister. I don't remember hardly anything but dust." Oskar tries to picture it. He cannot. For him this place is outside history. He sees Nuremberg. *Kristallnacht*. Oranienburg and the afternoon they came for him. At the same time on this same planet, Vanderveen remembers only dust. Dust is not history.

"I laid awake nights while the dust came in under the screen door and through the walls," says Oskar's new friend, "and I wondered, what am I doing here? You can't farm dust, and when you don't farm around here, you've run out of things to do. You just lie there and think – why, WHY?"

"And when it ended?" says Oskar, with a curiosity he rarely mustered for Hermann.

"That's the funny thing," says Les. "It didn't seem to. It ended for others but not me. Even when the Depression was over and the war came. Even when the war was over!" Oskar's eyes are bright with questions. Encouraged, Les continues. "I remember the end of the war," he says. "The celebrating. People sort of saying: Okay, we can relax now. I just couldn't get into it. I tried, but I couldn't. I felt they were relaxing too much. It made me nervous. It was like the tension had gone out of the society. But the danger was still there. When the worst part is over, *that's* when you have to really worry! I felt so lonely, worrying by myself. I felt lonelier than ever!"

As Vanderveen talks, Oskar slips deftly out of their conversation and onto his other track. He thinks he smells an opportunity. He stepped through the looking-glass into this wonderland, Alberta. He has been skittering across its surface like the ball in a pinball machine, pinging and ringing, lighting up and being lit. Now he feels if he is to maintain momentum, if he is to stay in the game and not slip down the hole – Game Over, Next Player – he must do something different. He came here with purpose. Not *a* purpose, but purpose nonetheless. Perhaps this is the chance to unleash a person he never (yet) was: Oskar the historian. Where better than this Canadian Here, where there is only pre-history, where history itself has still to begin; it is perfect for the novice historian. Like a young doctor going to his first post in some northern mining town where they've never had medical service, he can't help but be appreciated. He turns to the odd case before him, this ahistorical prairie being, and starts to work. Where it seemed there was only dust, he is going to try to make – history!

All right! says a voice in Oskar's head, *You have now located a pivotal event that shaped this creature, this brooding Samari-*

tan fixer of cars who has crossed your path. A historic trauma – the Depression – engendered him.

Oskar likes the sound of it so far: an objective interpretation of the phenomenon, based on Vanderveen's own testimony. He is enjoying himself.

In the same manner, the voice continues, *another network of catastrophe – Nazism,* Kristallnacht, *the events in the barracks at Oranienburg – accounts for you, Oskar, historian* manqué *and dybbuk of Bathurst. It made you possible as the Depression made him possible.*

He scowls. The voice has turned round and started talking about Oskar! This displeases him, it's unprofessional, he's sure. No true historian winds up analysing himself. The voice continues thoughtfully.

Yet no mere Depression could account for a being this strange. There must be more, in his genes and molecules, in his tortuous relations from birth onward. Doubtless the Depression – a veritable Holocaust of the Dirty Thirties in this place which is still, even today, a wasteland – did not lighten the load that was twisting his soul, but he would not have been a straight shooter, an ordinary Rotarian or an average citizen, had economic catastrophe never happened.

This satisfies Oskar. It is explanatory, it expands the discussion, it is part of the historian's role. And then it happens, the cursed turn again.

Nor would you, Oskar, the voice goes on, *have been a normal soul had Hitler never been. Hitler was bad for you and everyone you knew, but you were in trouble anyway and your life was not going to be a movie matinee even without National Socialism and World War II. Do not overstate the role of a few catastrophes.*

Oskar is squirming now.

Oh, what the hell, the voice says, sounding frustrated. *Does history have to explain things? Perhaps, as Scholem said while kicking your ass downstairs, it's interesting – that's all!*

And thus it happens again in the life of Oskar. History dissolves in autobiography; analysis, in confession. Must it always go this way? He begins with a step back, a little distance from which to observe. He wants to provide some insight, to make his small contribution to the march of knowledge. Then suddenly confusion enters, anxiety mounts, he is obsessing about himself, his life, his identity, his many failures, his doubt. He has not shed light, he has only spread more gloom in his own heart. Is this why he never succeeded as a historian? Is he really unconcerned with everything out there in the world? Does he examine the past only to locate it on a loop leading back to himself? Even here?

Oskar has no idea why he hears voices in his head at this moment, when other people would be merely thinking. Of course he is not the only member of his tradition to hear voices. Perhaps it is the Jewish way of thinking. Sometimes those who heard the voices ran from them, like Jonah. Or tried to pass, like Moses. Or whined, like Jeremiah, a man who knew from snivelling. Oskar wonders if Les Vanderveen hears voices. Maybe. There's not much prestige in it these days. If you hear voices in your head, you get it shrunk, you cut down the area for the voices to operate. Anyway, in Oskar's case it's probably just loneliness; when you've been on your own this long you welcome company, inside your head or not. At least in Bible days, when you heard voices, you might come out of it with dignity. People saw you twitching and frowning. *Oh, that? I just heard the voice of the Lord.* Even back then you could be tagged a false prophet, like Jeremiah. All the other prophets were taken seriously; he was laughed to scorn. But at least Jeremiah lived when hearing voices *could* have cachet. Is timing everything?

Meanwhile, he still does not know the purpose of his journey. Why has he come here, to Alberta? Did he really expect to solve something by fleeing to this place, as Jonah fled to Nineveh? Did Oskar – or Jonah – think they might find answers that would actually change them? Or does being here just interest him? What is the point? If it isn't to fulfil his lifelong fantasy vocation, what is the point? "Can I come to your history class tomorrow?" he says to Les.

Oskar sits in history class at Blanton High, and his ears burn.

His knobby knees knock against the top of the desk. The PA system belches unpredictably and throws the voice of the vice-principal into the lesson's most forceful moments. The kids fidget. Oskar had forgotten the inelegance of teaching. He feels a sudden admiration for those like Les who subject themselves to it daily. As for his own presence, the class seem oblivious. They cast casual looks at him as they entered, and occasionally during the lesson, but these are adolescent throwaways, signs of teen sophistication. One look, that's all you get: as in New York. He feels like an invisible guest, a spectre Les Vanderveen has conjured. Meanwhile his ears burn.

His new friend is teaching a history Oskar has never heard, but it has a familiar ring. Vanderveen's version begins in 1776, not the year in which American revolutionaries fired a shot heard round the world, but when a sinister Jewish figure named Adam Weishaupt founded a secret sect in Germany. They were called Illuminati. Vanderveen's pupils seem as familiar with them as with their bicycle combination locks.

Illuminati? thinks Oskar. Who? He pictures a boxed advertisement they often carried in *World Press Review*. Or was it the crime and vice magazines he devoured in those days to practise his English? (Sure, sure. The way he went to strip shows at the Victory to study sociology.) Anyway, those weren't Illuminati—they were Rosicrucians.

The students attend their mentor closely and take wads of notes. Either they sense a usable secret lies in this tangle—a clue to clarify their combustible teenage sensibilities—or they are just responsible for the stuff on the exam. Vanderveen is leisurely and circuitous. He starts with a review of last lesson, but it goes on so long Oskar suspects the recap is for his own benefit, though his presence remains unnoted. What about those Illuminati? Yes?

A sect of Jews (answer the pupils) determined to conquer the world. Les nods as if this is routine, like going over the causes of a land reform or the functions of bureaucracy. Nobody looks at Oskar. How did the Illuminati work? This is more technical and the response is slower, or does Oskar's presence lumber them? Slowly answers come, like the dawn.

"They destroyed monarchies and legitimate governments . . ."

"They attacked religions, especially Christianity . . ."

"They abolished marriage, they handed children over to the State . . ."

"They eliminated private property–"

"Right!" says their teacher, tipping off the answer he was looking for. "Anything else?"

It is effective teaching, no question, none of the kids look bored. They listen to each other, they puzzle, some even have the wonderful expression that says: Caution, teenager in thought. Oskar adores this pose, which marks arrival in an unknown country. The wonderful realm of mind, imagination, the ability to think your way through, to open up the world by your own mental processes. You never knew such a possibility existed: previously all had been given by authoritative parental figures; now suddenly the world is there to interrogate, reject, even alter. This is the inner meaning of education: leading young minds from the cave of tutelage to the light of their own power. It thrills Oskar whenever he sees it.

But what of the drivel they are testing their ripening intellects on? Does the adolescent mind awaken in a vacuum? Is content irrelevant? Then why has Oskar squandered eyesight and insight on curricula? Is he an educator or is he a Jew? He is a Jewish educator! He makes bold. "May I say something?" he asks. His voice scratches and cracks. The students look at their teacher. It is up to Vanderveen to confirm or ignore this request, along with the existence of the alien among them. Les beams, a smile wide as his leather belt with the big cowboy buckle. He doesn't mind, absolutely one hundred percent not. He is a teacher, isn't he? This is a classroom.

"How do you know?" says Oskar weakly. He was not quite ready. He regathers his forces. "How can you say so," he starts again, "when none of this is contained in any standard texts, encyclopedias, or histories?"

Les nods serenely. "It's not," he says. "That's exactly what proves the success of the Illuminati. If their conspiracy wasn't successful, then we would all know about it." The students turn

to Oskar now, boring in; he feels like a gladiator in the Colos-
seum. "Does that mean," says Oskar carefully, "that the less
evidence there is, the more *proof*?" He knows this is a dialectical
thought; Hermann would be proud. Vanderveen's big head, his
broad face, nod slowly in approval. "Exactly," he says, in a
further twist of the dialectic that Oskar didn't anticipate, while
every student copies down their exchange.

Did Oskar just miss his moment? An opportunity has been
granted. This is his chance to connect. To what? His destiny, his
fate, his own corner of history. What if he had met Hitler in,
say, 1923? Or ten years later? We make our own history, but
not in circumstances of our choosing. If we are to make it at all,
we must accept the less than ideal contexts we are given in which
to act. True, this is Alberta, in the 1980s. Vanderveen is merely
the Führer of Blanton, but he is the only Führer Blanton has and
the only one Oskar is likely to meet. Oskar has spent a lifetime
avoiding. He sought avoidance the way others pursued wealth,
power, or sexual ecstasy. Will he now redeem a life of inaction,
along with the fact that he survived while others did not?

"I am a Jew," he blurts, and just like that is committed:
teacher against teacher; anti-Semite against Jew; worldviews in
conflict. That's all it took, it's easier than losing your virginity –
a lot easier – and now there is no escape: one role is reserved for
each player, there will be a winner and a loser. This is Oskar's
punishment, or his reward, for those years of letting others do
it, playing the skeptic and loving the role. Past is past. Now
comes confrontation. Oskar will finally take them on: the storm
troopers, the Hitler Youth, the ss and the Gestapo, the Führer
too. This is the time and the place. What a relief, at last, to take
a stand. But – as Oskar looks around at their puffy, friendly faces
– what a time! And what a place!

Their heads turn toward him. They regard him as really
present, he is not going to go away. Vanderveen keeps his distance, assessing the foe with respect. "We knew that," says a
kid, "we knew you were a Jew." They all nod.

Oskar looks back defiantly. His expression says: Call me to
my face, then, the slurs you just flung at my people. They con-

sider this challenge. "Not all Jews are money thugs and gutter rats," says a pretty girl with short hair. Oskar noticed her when they came in. She speaks thoughtfully, trying not to offend. These are, he thinks in a pet phrase, basically decent kids. "Only the Jews that come from the Khazars are bad, not the old-time Jews," says an undersize boy. "The Khazars got converted to Talmud Judaism and then they took over from the real Jews." They are all nodding and smiling, as if they will gladly let Oskar off the hook because maybe he isn't really one of "them"; and anyway, this isn't anti-Semitism, it's history class.

The Khazars? Oskar ransacks his memory. They were converts to Judaism in the Middle Ages. Turks or Bulgars or something. Judah ha-Levi wrote a treatise about their conversion called *The Kuzari*. Hermann overanalysed it in Fran's one night when they were trying to choose a topic for his thesis.

"Those Talmud Jews call Christians *goys*," says the girl. "That means dog, and they have sex with the dead." Oskar stays calm. "That's not true," he says. But where should he start in refuting this nonsense? He chooses terminology. "*Goy* doesn't mean dog," he says. "It means nation." They look doubtful. Dog made sense, but nation? Why would Jews call Christians nations when they think of them as dogs? Oskar decides to deal with this later. He turns to her other proposition: sex with the dead. He's not sure what to say: We don't have sex with the dead? The board on which they're playing this game is hard to see. He returns to language. "We call other people nations," Oskar says shakily, "because in the Bible, Jews are the people of God, and all the others are the nations of the world." There is a vague if silent reaction, and Oskar breathes easier; he got them thinking about it; he moved them off dead centre.

Oskar now makes a small error: he pauses for self-congratulation. Their problem was not that dog made sense and nation didn't; they just don't think in collective terms; they are complete North Americans, like his own kids at the Pillar of Fire; introduce them gently to the notion of people in groups, and they can join you. As Oskar reflects on his success, Vanderveen acts.

Les cleverly withdraws from the primal combat for which

Oskar is braced and depersonalizes the blooming encounter between his students and the Jew; in his own way he intellectualizes the subject and removes a dangerous emotional charge. "This is a special day," he says, "and I think we should take advantage of our guest's presence. Instead of going ahead with the provincial department curriculum, we'll review everything we've learned about Jews, so we can find out what he can add to our understanding." He has interceded with such benevolence, such concern for truth and his students' education. The face of hate is rarely hateful.

The lesson unfolds around Oskar, for his benefit. What can he do? If he is to confront them, he must enter their world. He tries to focus, but it isn't easy. Reality is a social construction, as they said in sociology seminars at Columbia. A roomful of lunatics creates a consensus.

"The Talmud teaches Jews to hate Christians."

"They use Israel to fool Christians into believing Jews are the chosen race."

Oskar doesn't follow their logic. He is floundering already.

Les comes to his aid. "See, that's why I left the Baptists," he explains. "Those Baptists thought the state of Israel proved the millennium was here. Well, the minute you accept Israel as a sign of the Second Coming, you've bought the Jews as the Chosen People!" What should Oskar do now? Deny the importance of Israel? Deny the chosenness of Jews? Interpret it as a universal mission to proclaim brotherhood, the way he often did for his uneasy staff? Vanderveen has already waved his flock onward.

"The Jews are behind all the Socialist and Communist governments."

"They use the United Nations and NATO and the Warsaw Pact because they're easy to infiltrate."

"Whoa," says Les with a smile that's a plea for indulgence. "Let's get some historical order into this." There is a rustle of loose-leaf pages as students lean into notebooks, then heads rise again like morning glories, ready to nourish the record.

"Their first revolution was the French Revolution. In 1789 they held food back and got riots going. Then they sent in groups of anarchists with Adam Weishaupt." Oskar feels an inane relief at hearing a name he has heard before, even if was just minutes ago.

"The Jews guillotined everyone who disagreed with them. The Napoleonic Code was based on the metric system and the Talmud."

Someone is pumping her arm like she's going to launch it from her shoulder. She has the desperate sound of a student with only one answer to give. "The Talmud says it's okay," she reads, "to have pederasty."

"Then came the Civil War. When Lincoln tried to get the South back on its feet, a Jewish actor named John Wilkes Booth assassinated him."

"Germany had a leader named Otto von Bismarck," says a boy across the aisle, reading from a binder. "He had a Jewish alter ego named Lassalle." Oskar peers over at the page. "Auto von Bismarck," it says.

"In Russia, Czar Nicholas would get a reform ready to go and then the Jews would assassinate somebody. They knew if people were going to revolt, they had to have something to revolt against. Nicholas got fed up and became a reactionary."

What prevents Oskar from breaking in, challenging this tide of misinformation, and reversing it like a Jewish Canute? He could punch a thousand holes in their "facts"; he could turn his fabled sarcasm on their bumpkin mentor. He was about to, he was pulsing with it, then something changed. Now he is enjoying this lesson! It happened when he leaned across the aisle.

There is a limit, even to atrocity, and with Auto von Bismarck, Oskar reached his. He's been so earnest about history. It wasn't just vocation for him; it was salvation. Now the whole redemptive package veers in another direction, toward hilarity. Take the Third Reich. Please. The book Oskar learned English from, while interned in Dorset, was called *1066 and All That*. He read that book, with a dictionary in his other hand, until the words started to repeat. Then he knew he knew English. The Norman army was equipped with crossbows and snu. What's snu? Nothing, what's new with you? When Oskar crossed the ocean, he discovered Canadians like this kind of history. *Just when Columbus despaired of sighting land, a lookout cried "Indians!", so Columbus ordered his ships to form a circle with the women and children in the middle, and while the women and children were splashing around and drowning . . .* Oskar read that in a Canadian book someone gave him when he had his appendix out. He would have bust a gut if he hadn't already.

The Canadians treat their own history as a joke. In 1837 – the same year the Prussian police arrested the archbishop of Cologne and nearly started a war – there was a comic-opera rebellion here in Canada against the British Empire. That's what the Canadians call it – comic-opera. In Canada they don't wait for others to ridicule their history; they probably think no one else would bother. What a place to choose to become a historian. Could he have known what he was doing? Perhaps.

Think about the German way of doing history. Think about the Jewish-German method, *die Wissenschaft der Judentum*, the science of Judaism, with its exorbitant detail and finicky analysis. Perhaps Oskar always harboured a sneaking suspicion about the seriousness of the craft. What can you actually say in the most exhaustive scholarly examination of a single life, or even a single event in a life, much less an epoch? It will be skimpy compared to the thickness of one moment in that life itself, even if it's as ordinary and chaotic as Oskar's own. Chutzpah! Better maybe to smile wryly and enjoy the sight of those who try. He listens on.

"In 1851 Engels and Marx got the Crimean War started. They used Jewish control of the news."

"In 1903 twenty-three Jews decided to bring Russia to her knees. They figured they could finish her off if they got a world war started, so they sent in a Bolshevik Jew to assassinate Prince Ferdinand."

"They wanted a homeland. England fell for their story."

"Jews are responsible for debts and revolutions and everything else in the world today."

Vanderveen nods to this last comment like a conductor at the final bar of a symphony who is amazed his players have reached the end together. Not everything he heard pleased him, at points they struck wrong notes, at others they were painfully off. It is a children's symphony Les is conducting, a learning experience, and not a finished performance. Still, as an educator he seems proud. He turns to Oskar. *À ton tour, mon cher.*

This is one of those rare moments in the life of Oskar in which he finds The Move. It is rare in any life. At one instant we feel locked into a situation that defines us. How do we break free and pass to another position? It seemed impossible. Then it has happened.

So it is with Oskar now. For he has moved to the front of the class! He is no longer their guest. He has transformed, and they know it. He didn't think this move up – it came to him. It is the closest experience he will ever have to receiving an instruction from on high. He is no longer the object of their examination, the demonstration Jew, poised on a slide under their microscope. He knew that he should become, for a little while, the teacher of this class, and he did it. It just . . . came. He does not feel the battle is won because he made The Move, but he feels suffused with the power to win it.

(It recalls another moment in his life, a half-century ago, when he shifted his body's weight from the gangplank onto the firm earth of *Eretz Yisrael*. Both are moments of *kavanah*, acts performed with utter certainty.)

"All right, my friends," he says, and his posture announces that a potent force has entered him. He takes a pointer. He will do nothing with it, but it proclaims his new mastery. He proceeds to cover the material under discussion. Merely the history of Jews and Judaism through all time. He employs every technique he has ever known and communicated to others. He draws in the students and extracts knowledge and wisdom they had no idea was theirs. They hear themselves saying the opposite of what they thought they thought and thought they knew was true, and sense themselves understanding as they speak the unexpected words.

It may be the most dazzling lesson ever taught. Near its end Les intervenes, attempting to recapture his hijacked students. "I ask myself," says Oskar, turning to face the Führer of Blanton, so that the students now see these contending authorities in profile, nose to nose as it were, "I ask myself: what if Adolf Hitler had been my teacher in a country school in Bavaria when I was young? He might have sounded exactly like you! Should I therefore find you sinister and menacing, or should I have found him ludicrous and inconsequential? I don't know. Is a Hitler in Alberta still a Hitler? To tell you the truth, I don't even know if he was really the monster we think of in Bavaria. What might he have been—or not been—without the war, the revolution afterward, fear of the Soviet Union, the Depression? Maybe he would have been a you! An overcompensating provincial with a likable side. You too, my young friends – what if I had met you many years ago on the hiking paths around Berlin. And as a matter of fact I did. Our experience would have been very different. That is why I am grateful to you, for my meeting with you here has been extraordinary. It has been like walking into a mirror of my past and rearranging the reflection. I know that sounds a little impossible, but all it required was the willing suspension of disbelief. How many people ever have such an opportunity? I hope the experience has been as useful to you as it has to me. Thank you for letting us learn together." Ending properly – this too is a kind of blessing, which arrives unbidden.

Oskar has passed from one stereotype to another during his magnificent lesson. He was the ghetto Jew, pinned and denigrated under the glare of their small-mindedness. He has become the suave continental, a man of the great world beyond adolescence and Alberta. They know they are in the presence of worldliness, and they are charmed. His final smile and nod—even as his mouth leaks spit – conquers all. He takes his leave. He walks outside and enters his rental car as though it is a charger that has always been responsive to him. He turns the ignition. "Sveetch on," he mutters, and Blanton is, in the life of Oskar, history.

Let us take a moment, while Oskar's Dodge Dart scoots away over the blacktop, to reflect on a final role in the life of our hero. In many ways it looks like his natural, lifelong role, the one he seems suited to yet always declines: the survivor. If sufferance is the badge of my people, as Shylock said, then Oskar is their name. He even looks like the past of his people; he is a walking sandwich board of Jewish travail.

Yet all his life Oskar has said a hearty *Nein* to this role. He has refused to be the character he obviously is. Every actor feels in his heart there is a part made for him. Oskar knows his part, but he won't play it. His identity lies less in who he is than in who he refuses to be.

It is this stubborn refusal that makes me think Oskar is heroic. Of course heroes are not what they were in the days of Jacob or Odysseus. They don't consort with gods; they stumble around among us. But it seems to me noble that Oskar refuses to blame the bizarre behaviour by which we all know him on the unique and catastrophic circumstances of his youth. He has always had a sneaking suspicion there is less to his problems than meets the eye, and he has never used Hitler as his excuse. However trivial – and also embarrassing – are the sorrows of his present, he prefers to live his life in their terms rather than those of a mythic past.

Looking back, it would be possible for Oskar to realize there was a moment that made it possible for him to refuse that role in Vanderveen's class. It came when he scanned the classroom, just before finding The Move. Much as a Beliveau or a Gretzky – foggy names to Oskar, but heroes too – scan the ice in a wink, surveying every variable, before deciding where and how to pass or shoot. What did Oskar see when he looked around? A small human society in which the Jew and Jewishness were not necessarily mythic. Among whom he was not absolutely required to represent a prototypical human experience. In the eyes of whom there was no pressure to play the part, and being a survivor was only an option. *Hinter allem steht der Jude*, said Goebbels. Behind everything stands the Jew. Vanderveen agreed, many people agree, but in his glance at those kids Oskar could see it need not be so for them. They didn't need it, and he didn't need to play it. They freed him, and he freed them.

That's why it seems to me that we have just imagined a heroic

271

moment in the life of Oskar, even though it only involves being what he is. What is he? A Jew. And a teacher. In Canada. That's all. He is like Rabbi Zusya, who shuddered on his death bed, according to one of Buber's tales, and whose disciples asked why. Because, said Zusya, when I get to the Throne of God, I won't be asked, Why weren't you Abraham? I won't be asked, Why weren't you Moses? I'll be asked, Why weren't you Zusya?

Has Oskar this choice? Has anyone? He aims to live free of his mythic past, but can he? Maybe his obsession with his missed calling is a yearning to exist outside the power of history and myth, to escape history instead of being its outcome. To move from passive to active, as he did in Vanderveen's classroom. As, for that matter, Oskar's people have tried for two hundred years to climb off the mat of history, cease to be history's mythic plaything, with consequences difficult to reckon.

From an objective viewpoint this may be unachievable, but from Oskar's own viewpoint, or anyone's, what we can or cannot is close to what we will or will not. From our own point of view, it *is* a matter of what we decide. Oskar, the walking myth, wishes to be free from his mythic past, in a modest personal way, and he is.

Life changes for Oskar. He is in the Montreal Forum, at a hockey game. This place is unlike Maple Leaf Gardens, where Oskar went with Goldberg to see the Sadler's Wells ballet and be initiated into the culture of his strange new country. This arena is low and intimate; the ceiling hangs just above the crowd, forcing attention onto the ice. It has the aesthetics of a theatre, rather than a urinal. From the roof hang giant pennants. They mark some accomplishment: many victories in the Stanley Cup. Stanley was an Englishman, appointed to govern Canada. The sight reminds Oskar of waving rows at Nuremberg, Nazi legions, a pennant billowing before each.

He thinks about Nuremberg – not the rallies but the laws, which legally eliminated everything that was German about Germany's Jews. In its way that was nothing new. In the old days

Jews were in exile too, officially homeless. But the old exile was ordained by God, it had a purpose, we could even take pride in it. The homelessness after Nuremberg was ordained by Nazis, not God. It was the sign of Jewish failure to accomplish what Jews had set their hearts on: to become full German citizens. He thinks about the patriotic works of his parents and their parents: heartfelt efforts that stood out from their other achievements, which were mostly accumulations. The crowd roars. It occurs to Oskar he has avoided Canadian crowds because he connects them with Nazi rallies.

On the ice below, patterns form and dissolve, falling toward this end of the rink and away from that, then tipping back. He is standing about halfway up, there were no seats available. At the aisle an usher's pocked face scans the crowd. A peasant face, thinks Oskar, as the eyes hold on his and jerk toward several unoccupied seats in the section just below.

On the ice a form detaches itself. Unlike the others, he wears no helmet, and his blondish hair flares behind him like a cape, like the plume on a centurion's helmet. The excitement of the crowd follows him like his slip stream. He is Gallic, this one, he is not Toronto or Alberta; he is surely the spirit of Quebec. He crosses into the other team's zone – Hartford? the Whalers? – he whirls and corners, his opponents rush him, they miss him as he sweeps by, swish at him with their sticks and grab with their grotesque gloves; he leans but does not fall, his whole body seems to drop till it is nearly parallel to the ice, his thin nose could carve figures in the surface, then he is back up, still moving; it is unnatural, he defies nature. The eruption as he scores, as the puck enters the net, is an anticlimax. No, it is exactly a climax, like coming with a gush and shouting as you do – seventeen thousand at one moment!

The usher is at Oskar's elbow. Did he do something wrong? Is he being singled out for ejection, should he have continued to avoid this Canadian reality? The usher is pointing to one of the empty seats. Maybe they recognize his newness and want to help him relax. The usher halts before the seat, expectant. Oskar understands. He reaches into his pocket and hands over a two-

273

dollar bill with the Queen of England on it. They have let him in. He belongs.

He listens for the hiss of French in the chatter around. These sounds of Europe comfort him, they make him feel at home where he didn't feel he could. The two over his left shoulder must be arguing about the game; perhaps they have a bet. But the sound is too blocked, too guttural, for French. Could be *joual*, Quebec French. No, it's not French at all. Greek! There are many Greeks here in Montreal. The crowd hums its low hum like the start of a siren, the centurion is streaking again. *Yofi, chabee-bee, Yofi*, says the voice just behind. They are speaking Hebrew.

He walks the Terrasse Dufferin. He thinks of Sunday in Berlin. But this terrace is named for an English general and overlooks the St. Lawrence River. Now, near midnight, Oskar is alone. He feels like the ghost in Hamlet. He looks up at the ramparts on the wall that surrounds the Old City of Quebec and into the shadowy bulk of the Chateau Frontenac. Old is quite young here in Canada. In Europe, old is maybe a thousand years. In Jerusalem the Old City is three thousand. But in Quebec, a mere four hundred, and in Toronto or Blanton even less. Oskar is getting old himself, and these distinctions don't fascinate him as they once did. For Oskar at sixty and some, historical is not a matter of age but of meaning. He wonders if he'll ever feel wise.

He came here after the hockey game in Montreal. He is finding his way in Canada – better late than never – in unsystematic fashion. No guide book, no plans, no bookings. He plays it as it lays, as they say. He drove toward Quebec, reached it, rolled under the wall of the Old City, and lurched about till he found a street with an irresistible name: Rue Ste-Ursule. He pictures Ste-Ursule like the young wife on an orthodox kibbutz with strands of silky brown hair slipping from the kerchief on her head. Was that someone he saw in the thirties, or just last year?

He rapped on the door of Maison Acadienne and Madame

Bergeron showed him a room on the third floor. This could be the Swiss Alps – *Suisse-française*, not *Deutsch* – or overlooking the rooftops of Paris. When he needs a new bulb for reading, she brings it herself. Is she saying something with her eyes, her body evident beneath her close-fitting dress?

One night he stops in a restaurant for hot chocolate. He glowers into his cup, the old morbidity is moving in like the tide. But all around he hears a heavenly choir. They are singing something by Bach in childlike harmonies. They *are* children, they've come from rehearsal at the cathedral next door. They order hot chocolate too, and sing. He has been given a gift.

One day her son is at his door with a note. Would Monsieur like to join Madame for a carriage ride to the Plains of Abraham? No thank you, but he would be pleased to take a stroll together on the Terrasse and a cup of tea in the Chateau. They parade together. With her at, if not on, his arm, he feels like a true son of the bourgeoisie. Later they go, by carriage after all, to the *champs du bataille*, where the battle that settled the future of this huge little country was fought.

He looks at her. Her future was decided on this plain. She might have been on the battlefield, searching afterward among the carcasses for a husband or a son. One empire battling another up and down the body of a distant colony, a coveted outpost. Egypt and Assyria perhaps, over the body of little Judea. Was that any more significant? Has he lost the urge to denigrate? He doubts she would make great claims for this place. It is a tragic site in the history of her people, but theirs is just one of many stories. They have their pretensions, but not the *hubris* of the Chosen People, *am s'gulah*, God's special treasure, who spawned two other great faiths, and survived in Exile, and thrived, and have even been reborn as a State in his and her own lifetime: a national rebirth, which the descendants of the losers on the Plains of Abraham perhaps envy here by the waters of the St. Lawrence.

Abraham was a river pilot, she says, he owned a plot west of the town. Namesake of that other Abraham, thinks Oskar, Abraham Our Father. What a paltry difference. Egypt and Assur,

England and France, Palestine and Canada, promised lands of here and there, then and now. Abraham this or Abraham that. All moments in an indifferent history, all just life slipping away. Oskar and Mme Bergeron–it is his first date with a *shiksa*. These distinctions too once meant much to him. Think of it, think of what came of that tiny Semitic people, all it begat, the influence, the literature, the pain! He thinks of it. He considers telling her he has been here before, greeted by the Canadian army in a shipment of Nazis, bivouacked in tents right . . . about . . . here. But he does not. Perhaps it was not this spot after all. It hardly feels the same.

The experience feels complete. Next day he leaves.

As he drives home toward Toronto, he hears on his car radio that a high school teacher in Alberta has been charged with spreading hate in his classroom. He will go to court, perhaps to jail. Oskar changes the station.

What is it that rankles, as he drives? Is it that Les Vanderveen befriended him and fixed his car? Does one cancel the other? Of course not. Is it something else, that in another society in which Oskar lived, there were also court cases against anti-Semites, who were convicted, fined, and jailed for slandering and assaulting his people–the legal division of the *Centralverein* of German Jews was assiduous; while the Jewish Defence Service, the veterans and athletes, patrolled the streets against anti-Semites, just like the NeverAgainers of recent years – and it all ended as it ended anyway? So? Was it wrong to fight them? Was it wrong to fight any way you could?

Or is it just that all his adult life Oskar has told students and teachers, "Go ahead, question. Don't be afraid. It's not a crime to be wrong!"

The night sky is lit with fire. It rises from the west. He noticed it when he awoke in his armchair and stumbled forward to extinguish the television. It flickered stupidly, then expired.

276

Behind, though, through the window, all is aflame. Something out there, perhaps as far as Dufferin Street, the Dufferin of Toronto, past the streets Jews live on – a lumberyard, maybe – is crackling and incinerating. Did the sirens rouse him as he lolled, mouth open, before the blank screen? He could retire to his bedroom and his bed, but why? Instead he will go in search, he will go west again, it served him once.

He strides along Elm Ridge Drive. He accelerates the lurch to a purposeful gait, as though he is driven toward a goal. The sky grows brighter, he hears sirens to the south along Eglinton, and north, on Glencairn. He walks into the fiery night.

There are figures on porches, stick figures, shadows wakened as he was and drawn outside. Puffballs of people appear in their picture windows, gaze toward the flame, then withdraw. Only Oskar moves confidently on. Toward him, out of the flaming sky, strides another person. They do not notice each other, they are absorbed in their separate advance and withdrawal. They pass as though travelling in different dimensions. Oskar realizes. He whirls, he must act quickly. "Wetherford!" he screeches at the receding back, which halts and waits as Oskar reverses course to make up the distance between them.

"It's Oskar," he says. Their faces are illuminated. It is like meeting in a furnace.

"No, it's not," says Wetherford decisively. They study each other. "I knew an Oskar once," says Wetherford, "but he was no . . . wild-eyed man from the mountains, or whatever you are."

They sit in the garden. The backyard really. Wetherford has let the garden go to hell, he says. It is the next day. After Wetherford denied Oskar was Oskar, he clasped him firmly and said, "Come tomorrow. We'll have tea in the garden." They wait as the tea steeps. He offered Oskar sherry or whisky, but Oskar said he'd take whatever Wetherford was having. Wetherford was pleased, he despises alcohol, drugs, all artificial stimulants, because they substitute for reality, and veil it. It is hard enough to touch reality without chemical barriers, he says. Anyway, his doctor forbids it. Booze, not reality. This bungalow on Hilltop is two and a half blocks from Oskar's apartment on Shallmar. He finds it strange.

"You encamped in their midst," he says to Wetherford. Wetherford says, "So did you."

"An apartment is different," says Oskar. "It is nowhere." Wetherford nods. "I taught their children for decades," he says. Oskar smiles and says, "We both did." Wetherford says, "I chose to teach them because they did not interest me at all. They were so mundane and meaningless, I could pursue the Truth without distractions."

"I heard you agreed to head the mathematics department," says Oskar. "It didn't sound like you. It would distract you from . . . you know . . ."

"I did it," says Wetherford, "on the strict understanding I had no interest in improving the teaching of anything at the school. Especially mathematics." Oskar cackles. "I got it in writing," says Wetherford.

"But they too are reality," he continues. "How stupid I was. The Truth does not wait somewhere for you. You have to visit it wherever it is. Wherever you are."

"To hallow this life," says Oskar, knowing this is not what Wetherford means.

"What?" says Wetherford.

"So you moved in here where they all live," says Oskar. "And have you found . . .?" He smiles sheepishly. He still cannot say these words without embarrassment: ". . . it?"

Wetherford rises from the plastic folding chair. He steps to the unruly bushes that ring his yard. He peers through the thicket toward the next yard. It is hard to see anything. "I have had a love affair this year for the first time in my life," says Wetherford. Oskar straightens in his chair. He understands why Buber preferred a visitor with a hard choice between two women over one with a philosophical dilemma. "Have you ever had an affair, Oskar?" Perhaps only Wetherford could ask this question with no suggestion Oskar might have done so, and none that he might

278

never. "I have no idea how they stand it," says Wetherford, glaring through the bushes, as if he would like to burn a channel with his eyes through to his neighbours. "All these people entangled all their lives with each other, from their teen years on. The anger, the need, the hate, the terror, the doubt, the boredom, the humiliation, the exposure, the jealousy. I couldn't bear it for a few months. How do they put up with it through lifetimes?"

I have never been interested in the Truth, thinks Oskar. I couldn't care less. Why am I as lonely as this man? Why do we sit here like two spinster sisters? What have we in common? Oskar always envied Wetherford. He envied his quest. It made sense of a life, as love or faith do. Why does he feel so familiar and compatible with this *goyishe kop*?

"I don't understand anything," says Wetherford. "Not one thing." He is stretched out now, on a plastic recliner. You get them at the Bi-Way. Oskar did. His is on the balcony of his apartment. Wetherford coughs, he is clearly ill. He sounds consumptive, thinks Oskar; what a fine old disease that was, consumption. "I don't understand the bushes, I don't understand the birds – not the least small thing. I suppose that's why I let it all go. I used to garden, cultivate, expecting it would reveal itself . . ."

"What did you expect to find?" says Oskar. "I never knew what you were looking for."

"Ah," says Wetherford, with a note of his ancient vigour, "you never knew. You never would know till you arrived. That was what kept you going. The trip."

My Death

I LIKE MY BROWN HYACINTH the best. She is like a package of candy wrapped in cellophane. All her good parts bulge exuberantly in her packing. When she touches me, I feel manly. When she turns me, I roll against her breasts and I can tell she is smiling. She is generous, she has room in her. Nothing really matters to me now but being touched.

They have hired her for me so I will have around-the-clock private care and not suffer unnecessarily. They don't understand at all. They have never understood how important it is to me to suffer. Misery is the basis of any relief I ever feel. They are full of good intentions. They are determined to show me how much they care. They take my ill-humour as a sign I cannot express how touched I am by their trouble over me. The truth is, their affection and attention make me feel how far from them I am. When my brown Hyacinth from Jamaica lets her heavy breast slip lower and brush my shoulder as she leans over me to reach the edge of the blanket, then I feel no doubt, no guilt, no missed communication. Her breast and her; my warm feeling and me.

They have made an around-the-clock schedule to assure I will never be left without someone who knows and cares. The only time they leave me with her is when they go and stand in the hall

280

while she changes or bathes me. They think of her as someone they have hired to help me with some technical matters, while they remain close, near my heart. She is far closer; she is my only real companion here.

They sit beside me; the ones who love me most sit all night. Sometimes I talk, but it is exhausting. It is exhausting to talk with people who don't know you well, though they have known you so long. It is exhausting to respond to their need for me to need them. It is wearisome to matter so much. I don't want to be cruel, which I sometimes am, but it does no real harm because then they think of me as Bitter Old Oskar, unable to show how grateful he is for how good we are to him. I avoid causing real pain by never saying how far they are from me and that their around-the-clock presence only makes me feel farther. They might know it was true. Instead I fade. I swoon. I sink onto my pillow and lean away from them. Hyacinth enters. They say, "Is he all right? He just slipped back. He seems to be asleep." She nods and smiles as though she understands nothing; she lays a cool brown palm with the lines and creases of her hard life on my forehead, and I sigh quietly. They sit content in the armchair near the bed, or lean against the counter by the window. They thumb through *Newsweek* or *Toronto Life*, satisfied she has verified my survival. For the moment I am not dead.

Some, a few, know what I feel. With them I don't have to pretend.

Ida came last week – I think it was last week. I told her she could draw me, finally. She asked if she could on our first date, when the war was on and I was new to the staff. I said no. I was haughty. She knew why: I didn't respect her skill. Anyway, why should I admit her to the intimacy of a portrait? I didn't care for her and I didn't want her, though I liked her. When I said she could do it, forty years after I refused, she said she would think about it. She came again and said no. It surprised me, to tell the truth. She said she was afraid I wouldn't like what she did, and she couldn't stand the disapproval. Well, not exactly. She said she didn't want to have to put up with it. What do I need it for?

she said. She doesn't worry about hurting me, even though I am dying and so forth. I feel we are at the real beginning of our relationship. She has accepted my rejection.

I don't perform for Willi Schropp either. Willi comes often; of course he has other visits to make here in the new New Mount Sinai. He sits by my bed, we don't say much. He comes in. "How are you, Oskar?" I look out the window, he lowers himself into the chair, looks out the window too, or at the ceiling, through the lattice of his fingertips he makes as though he thinks it is a sign of profound thought. We sit quiet awhile, as though we are passing slowly backward through time to where we used to be, and when we have arrived, we are on different terms, as we once were, and we begin to talk as people no one knows today.

Sometimes with Willi I realize I have broken my silence. I have been speaking, though not to him. "Don't hit me any more. Please don't hurt me. I will clean the floor. I will clean your boots. I will do anything if you don't cause me more pain. I beg you." I say this in German. It is as though, on my way back to our fine times together – Willi's and mine – I had to pass through the afternoon in the barracks at Oranienburg; and I don't mind doing it with him present. Then I realize I have stopped. I turn toward him. He looks back and says nothing.

How comforting I find Willi's presence now, near my death. It is proportionate to how odious I found him these last decades of my life. Willi knows me, though I don't think he understands the way he knows me. Not with his mind, which is mediocre, despite his own high opinion. Anyone else, Hermann, Tocchet, Wetherford – to mention Buber would be an obscenity – in their light Willi is nugatory. But his life touches mine the way Hyacinth's breast brushes my shoulder. I feel it when he looks at me after I have been screaming in German to the men in the barracks. His face is full of wonder but no questions. He is with me there.

The others fall into groups. Individuals are less unique than groups, though in the school we always taught the uniqueness of each human soul. "For man mints many coins with the same stamp and they are all the same; but the King of King of Kings, the Holy One, blessed be He, marks each man with the stamp of Adam the First, yet not one of them is the same as his fellow."

My women. My staff. They are full of sentiment. Sometimes it approaches feeling. They sit by me all night; I don't wonder why, I know they need to, it provides something in their lives. They are all married, they are devoted to their husbands, with whom they have good relationships, and their children, with whom they are open and honest. They have constructed their supportive roles with care. Why do they seem like such children themselves, these wives and mothers? I sense as they sit near me, prayerful, as I sleep, that they lack respect for themselves. These are women I have yearned for, with a deep spiritual need and raging lust. I wanted them; their parade through my day and my life kept me going; I anticipated their comings, brooded when they left. I daydreamed and wet-dreamed and masturbated to thoughts of their bodily parts. They sit before me now like prim, undeveloped children. Like the little ones we marched onto the steps of the sanctuary each autumn to be consecrated by our rabbis – so unformed. They would not have been enough if I'd ever had them as I pined; I'd have discarded them like spent rags, which they knew. What they want and need from me is greater than the fantasies I required them for. I am to them like the sign of a hard but valid life, a life of pain and challenge, which they lacked the courage for themselves. I wouldn't have guessed, or did I?

The uncomfortable men, husbands of my women, so tentative in their manliness. They are successful. Marv's firm has just merged; now they do criminal *and* civil; he teaches at the law school. Srul used to be a fat music teacher who dabbled in real estate; he has become a gourmet and sophisticate. He doesn't drive a station wagon any more; he has a Mercedes. He discusses vintages and travels between the fine collections of Europe. He's not even fat, except his face. Neil is president of the Pillar of Fire; imagine, someone who ran clubs for me. He is respected, although he's not rich. They have worked for me, the uncomfortable men, like their wives; but unlike their wives, they did it for the money, and only until their real careers blossomed. They wanted me to know it wasn't for the sake of meaning in their lives – or only a little – but we don't speak of that between men. Their wives can do things that are merely humane, because they are women. I have a sneaking suspicion my men doubt their virility. They stride into my sick room with fatuous male authority, come to lend competence to the deathwatch. Yet I sense self-doubt. Is it because they have been associated with me and the school, with the feminine and spiritual? Does this leave a limp in their egos? Did they lack male confidence all along? Or is it only in my presence they are unsure, while they are firm and fine at the office? Maybe this is why they bluster so much at me, they expand their chests and blow windy assurance my way. They say I am lucky to have this chance – they mean my painful lingering cancer – to "settle accounts." Then they feel courageous; they have looked (my) death in the face; but I see them shift their feet. They are unanchored. I'd like to pat their hands and whisper, You need not fear. But I cannot raise my hand to do so, and they would experience my touch as deathly, and men do not touch. They are good people and my friends, and I suppose I love them.

The ones I barely know. They were students. Some I recognize but most I recall only after they say their names. They have heard I am dying, so they come. I mean something to them. This surprises me, and seems to surprise them. They stand awkwardly. Are they embarrassed or perplexed? They look on my crinkly translucent skin, puzzled. Like Miss Rosenzweig. She is one of five children; they went through the school, they didn't join clubs or youth group or student teaching – just the minimum for bar mitzvah and confirmation. I call her Miss Rosenzweig because I cannot remember which she is. They passed before me like the flock of a nonchalant shepherd, then moved on. She saw me briefly, we did not interact, I made an impression.

She stands straight, as always. Ah, then I do remember. She is bony, she juts. She does not retire, she exists out into the world. I think of her with crossed arms, though they are not now, and an inquisitive nose and jaw. Perhaps she has tried law but failed at it, she says something like this. She is married but seems uninterested. She looks at me as though she is in the museum for a special exhibit, which she had to wait in line for; she is here to acquire something. She thinks of me, I'd say, as an odd being but with integrity, full of pain, bizarre, and a failure. None of this matters to her. All that matters is her impression I was in touch, connected to a reality that evades her. So vague. It took very little to stamp her with this impression. My contortions as I whizzed by in the hall; she was six, or twelve. My foolish announcements over the PA. My talk about sex in the Bible when I taught confirmation. A being trying to be human – it impressed her and stuck. Not my tireless curriculum, nor my well-trained staff, nor her years of instruction, reinforced by examinations and grades. None of that mattered.

My Great Class. They stayed awhile after confirmation; they took courses with Hermann, became student teachers and teachers, but it is ages since I saw them. I hear about them occasionally, and sometimes read of them. None belong to Temple. None have children in the school. My Great Class.

They come, but not together. They are no longer a community. Nothing binds them now, except the will to see me as I die.

James, once Jimmy, maker of the ark. A sculptor. I have followed his career. Not a Jewish motif. There is something sexually ambiguous about him, he is not comfortable with it. I tell him about Hans, my friend of long ago in Berlin. I do not exactly say Hans was a bisexual; I speak of his creativity and his sensitive spirit. Jimmy bends forward as I speak as if to peer behind my words. He wasn't expecting this, and I can tell he draws a message of encouragement from what I say. I had no friend named Hans in Berlin.

Teddy the arsonist. Of all the students who went through my school, only he looks like another person. In the others I see the child in the man, in most cases I see the child as the man. Teddy, though, has been through the valley of the shadow of death. Either because of what he did, or because of where they sent him for it.

Joey Banks has hardly changed. He is a television writer. I have watched his shows. They rarely mention Jews. When they do, it is an embarrassment. I preferred his series about the secret sex lives of professional hockey players. He has written a stage play, he says, a serious work. It will redeem him from the frivolity of television. He hopes I will attend when it opens. I say I can hardly attend the toilet ten feet from me, but I will read the newspaper reviews; however, I die before they are printed.

It is strange: all the members of my Great Class were male. I hadn't known.

I feel I am teaching my last class. What are they learning? They are people equipped with a sense of historic insignificance, like most of the people who have ever lived. Theirs is a comfortable, bourgeois, untroubled moment well off the main track. They don't challenge this place out of the sun they occupy, but they are troubled. Is this all? That is the question they bring with them. I am the Jewish educator, the conveyor of a thin layer of their identity which is not trivial. The people of the Book, the eternal people, the epic of suffering and survival. As they amble about the tree-lined streets of their suburbs and the underground malls downtown, they carry in their back pocket a touch of meaning – and I put it there.

This is not quite correct. Excuse me, I am weary, and it is hard to finish a complex thought. This idea is only the start of an insight. It is true for those who passed through my school but did not know me. For them significance is Jewishness, transmitted in my classrooms. But for these others, who remember me and visit me, significance is personalized, because they know *me*. *I* am their contact with meaning. I not only teach them Jewish history; I am it. Look at me, as they do. I am the smashed face and persecuted body. I come like Daniel from the furnace, barely alive, and I exhibit the life of sufferance that is the badge. They do not neglect me as a person, but they are drawn to me by what I mean. I give their lives a point of contact. With what Hermann calls transcendence. For them I am history. It is no fault of mine; nor is it to my credit. It has nothing at all to do with what I want. Some must try to find the meaning of their own lives through the lives of others. It could as easily have been reversed, so that I sought meaning through them, but it was not. This chanciness is the nature of history, I comprehend.

I lie here and they pass before me, as though I am God on Rosh Hashanah, the Day of Judgement; the one which occurs each year, not the Final one. They stand at the foot of my bed, like the accused before their judge; they sit only at my invitation, as in court. They come intending to ease my pain and my end, yet it is clear I am dying this way for their sake, in order to ease their way. I *am* an educator! I am astounded by my lucid sense of what is happening and what it means. I make no effort, yet I know I am getting things right. Perhaps all that wisdom requires is cessation of striving. I have reached Koheleth's conclusion by my own route. I have no stake, I fear nothing my thoughts may reflect, prove, or establish. My life is done, the results are in. All I see is seen for its own sake, it is *lishmah*, as the Talmud says; what a wonderful freedom. I never understood: for its own sake as opposed to what? As opposed to tedious, pointless self-justification. I feel for the first time capable of wisdom. I simply open my mouth. As it were. I do not actually speak these thoughts. My wisdom is the direct result of lack of effort.

When I die, I am alone with Hyacinth. She gently loosens the grip of my hand and goes into the hall to tell her superintendent, who will inform the others, who will set in train the arrangements for my funeral.

Many people are here for the funeral. It doesn't surprise me; I've touched their lives – though I've only begun to understand the ways. Most who enter through the rear doors of the sanctuary look around with surprise and pleasure. As though it is their own funeral and they are glad at the turnout. Though really, they are pleased because they think it would please me, and that it would irritate and anger me if there were fewer. They can't stand it when I am upset because I always take it out on them. Anyway, I am glad to see them, and I hope my funeral is as satisfying as they want it to be. I lament a few absences: Rabbi

Rosen sends regrets from Texas or somewhere; I suppose he means it, but he probably also thinks: "Oskar is dead, it won't make any difference if I *shlep* my aged bones through the sky and expose them to high-altitude radiation in order to be there; when nobody's around I'll sing him a *kaddish* by the side of the pool." And Buzz hasn't come from New York. I miss him. I wish he were here.

Young Rabbi Shatz gives my first eulogy. It's a pity, he misses the point. The point of me, that is. He says I was an honest seeker and had a deep faith of my own, though it was not apparent. I would sigh had I breath. He says I was very emotional and moved by all those who loved me, and my gruffness and legendary temper were a façade. Hundreds of heads nod without conviction. They would like to believe it. I think as he speaks that in my feelings toward these people was much genuine hate, not a great deal of love, considerable sympathy, and a deep attachment based on something none of them understand. He tells how I helped when he came here from the States, a junior rabbi, and that I understood his experience of being a Jewish foreigner. He says I conspired to introduce him to Helga the kindergarten teacher whom he married. This part is true. He tells some little incident showing I was a lovable codger. He weeps, he sits.

Willi Schropp gives my other eulogy. I am happy now, that he came twenty-five years ago on the worst day of my life, because no one else would have been correct, right on as they used to say, the way Willi is, without trying. He does not weep for me, I have no wife and no children and no one will live with emptiness next to them for a while because I am gone. But Willi's words are true to me as the odd person I was. He says little about the meaning of my life; unlike young Barry Shatz, he does not get it wrong and does not try to get it right. Instead he recounts our times together, early and late. As he speaks, his tone grows more reflective and interior – unlike all his sermons and his public statements–as though his attention is being drawn toward his own heart. I think this change in his tone occurs when he describes my outburst *auf Deutsch* in my hospital room that day. Instead of drawing a conclusion and pointing a moral, as he always does, he says, "There are things that happen, and leave a mark, and we never know they are there." Because he knows me better than the others, he wonders most about me; it is a sign of our closeness, and our importance to each other, though I don't think he understands how much I mean to him. Like other egocentric people, he notices his own centrality to others and misses their importance to him. But he is not much different from all those who are here. They come to reconcile themselves to my death and their own lives; it has little to do with me.

They rise now for my *kaddish*. There are many covered heads in the congregation. When I came there were none. They were proud to stand bare-headed in worship as a declaration of their modernity. Their parents wore *yarmulkes*, even *shatls*. Now as a sign of their lately renewed pride in being Jews, they wear not only *kippot*, mostly the bright-knitted Israeli type, but even *tallitim*, prayer shawls. I underestimated the tenacity of tradition and the difficulty of change. Or was I right, but only at a certain time? I am glad I am done. I did not yearn to die, but it has been a comfort over the years to know that miscalculations and frustrations would not continue forever. That knowledge made it easier to persevere, as one must. In the school we always told the children not to feel queasy when they rise for the *kaddish*, even though it is part of the funeral service: it is not a prayer for the dead, we told them, it nowhere mentions death; it is a declaration of praise, an affirmation of life raised in the face of death. I insisted on this, it suited me. It required no faith in anything beyond life; I found faith in life tortuous enough. Now, though, as they rise and intone—*yitgadal v'yitkadash shmeh rabbah*—and then file sombrely up the centre aisle and out to the parking lot from which some will drive to my burial—I mildly resent the fact that nowhere in my final moment in the sanctuary at the Pillar of Fire is there mention of my death.

They are gathered around my gravesite, the hole into which I will be dropped. There aren't very many. Far fewer than were at the funeral service, which is the main event and doesn't require a long journey by car. But I thought there'd be more. They are standing in a large clump, like a bush. It is raining, though this is winter, I believe. The weather is indeterminate, it might be almost any time of year; it is cold and it is damp. Lack of comfort.

Apart from the clump, on the other side of the mound of earth that will cover me, stand Willi and one from my Great Class. He went and stood there alone when the cortège arrived, he declined to join the others. Not an act of defiance, just separateness. Willi moved to his side. They had high hopes for him once. He would be a rabbi, perhaps return to the Pillar of Fire —one of their own in the pulpit. Or reincarnate Buber, to whose books I introduced him, and to whom I promptly lost him. As I lost him to Hermann and others of larger faith than my own. Somewhere they all lost him; no faith, no loyalty to the community, an anti-Zionist, I think.

The wind is cutting through to their necks, they shift and stamp their feet in the grip of the cold; they are older now, these who knew me, they revere my final moment among them, but they are drawn to the warmth of their cars and their homes. The final words are spoken, I am lowered, not dropped, the first shovelful of earth is showered down on me. I cannot tell who does it, then come others, each takes a symbolic turn. Then it stops. They move off to the long line of cars filling both sides of the cemetery road. Feet trudge away, along planks laid over mud, car doors slam, engines start. A more serious filling-in of the hole has begun. One, and two, and . . . The professional grave-diggers have come out of their shelter against the rain; they mutter as they work, joking and grumbling like characters in Brecht. I can tell from their voices the chill is reaching inside their skin.

Someone else has remained. I don't know who. He – I think it is he – stands there, shoulders hunched against the chill, hands thrust in pockets. He stands. Perhaps he considers offering to help the workers, but he does not. Still, he is tucking me in. The earth continues to fall, and he stays. Eventually it has spread all above me. The grave hole is not filled to the top yet, but now it doesn't matter. I am covered, I am inside. Thank you. You can go now.

LET US CONCLUDE with the best moment in the life of Oskar. The sweetest moment. He is in Paris.

Well, we will say Paris. It might be Zurich, or Lausanne. It might be Berlin or Jerusalem or New York. It might even be Toronto, though that is unlikely. But it could be Paris, so it is. Let us say he is returning from his trip to the *aretz*, the one which caused him considerable *angst*, the time he saw Greta again. He has stopped here in Paris for . . . whatever. To contemplate the meaning of life. To commune with great art. To have a meal. To postpone Toronto. He is crossing one of the bridges over the Seine, heading toward Châtelet; maybe he is to meet a colleague or an old friend there. Suddenly he is aware of someone tracking his steps, stride for awkward stride. He glances to the side. She is small and pert and perhaps nineteen. She wears jeans and a woolly sweater beneath which she has attractive round breasts. Her hair is sandy and short, a knapsack is slung over one shoulder. In it no doubt are her university books. Nothing about her mirrors him.

And they are talking! He doesn't know how he managed this. Because he didn't think about it? Because he takes her for a student, or student teacher, and falls into a familiar role in relation to her? Did he start or did she? No matter how much he frets on his other track, he continues to talk easily with her. They are over the bridge, she stops. She plants her feet in their sneakers and faces him squarely, face to face as it always said. They are still talking. An ordinary miracle in the life of Oskar. "I must now meet an old friend," he says. She nods, she continues to stand there on the spot, looking up at him; she is quite short. She seems to know him, she appears happy to remain there smiling, taking pleasure in his company, until he says it is necessary to break off. "Could we meet again?" he says fearfully to this adolescent—no, wait, surely *he* is playing the adolescent. He tries again. "Shall we meet again? Would you want to?" She smiles and nods all at once, as if this is an obvious solution. He looks around, an awful weight of decision bearing down. "That café," he says, of the first one to enter his field of vision. It is right by the river. "Tomorrow evening, at seven?"

Wonder of wonders, she comes. They smile, they talk, they sip wine. He tells her about Toronto—it seems to interest her—about the Pillar of Fire, his work, Israel, his childhood and family. He tells her not because she is special, but because she is here. She talks about her courses. It's not hard at the Sorbonne, she says, though most students miss many classes because they have to work to pay their fees. He asks how they keep up. We tape the lectures on cassette recorders, she says. You only have to be there at the start of a lecture, set your tape running, and then retrieve it at the end. In between you go to your job. Someday, she thinks, there will be no students in the seats of the lecture hall—only cassette recorders. Then one day the professor will bring in *his* cassette recorder, start it running with his taped lecture on it, and depart too—and then the educational process will be complete. He asks about her marks. Very good, she says, because I've learned the secret of high grades at the Sorbonne. Just end every exam question with the same phrase. Oskar asks if she'll reveal it. She says, "And what is the solution? It is necessary to nationalize the means of production!" Oskar laughs. It may work here, he says, but he doesn't think it would be effective in confirmation class. She laughs. He looks around. They have been here for hours. He is tense, he has come this far

293

before but rarely farther. He screws up his courage, falters, speaks.

"Would you like to walk a little?" he says. Not what he intended, but not bad, he realizes. She smiles and nods in her economic way. He pays. They walk beside the river. They pause under a tree and chat some more. They walk again. This pattern continues. On and on. And on. He is stymied. Then the words make it from his thoughts to his lips. "Would you like to come back to my hotel room for the night?" She answers, after a silence that indicates ease, not doubt. "If you want."

Si tu veux. He thinks it is the sweetest phrase ever spoken. Ever spoken to him. It is a line from the Book of Psalms. It outdoes the Song of Solomon. If you want. She accepts what he wants. She wants it too. He aches for this response, always has, and she – she says she is happy to be a part of what he wants, if he wants.

In the middle of the night she wakens him. Not intentionally, but she is whimpering, like a small animal. He realizes what she wants. Him. More Oskar. To his wonder, he responds. He slides into her. After, she sighs, he relaxes, they tumble against each other in sleep.

He dreams of Abraham. Abraham Our Father, as he is known. Normally Oskar is inclined to dream of Moses Our Teacher, rather than Abraham Our Father. This is reasonable, as reason goes in the irrational realm of dreamlife. Oskar identifies with teacher, not father. Abraham has always seemed distant to him. Stern too. Moses on the other hand is accessible. He stutters, he'd rather not do what he is required to do, he loses patience with the children of Israel, he argues with God. Altogether Moses is an approachable and sympathetic fellow human. Abraham is so severe, so obedient, so iron-willed. God says go and Abraham is gone. Leave it all: your country, your homeland, your father's house – just be off into the great unknown and by the way, don't worry, eventually I'll show you where you're bound. And oh yes, take your son, your only son, whom you love – oh, how the Lord can stretch it out to make sure no ounce of horror in his commands passes you by – and slaughter him to My greater glory on some distant mountaintop. Father indeed. All the paternal, patriarchal attributes a soul could be terrorized by.

Now, in the early morning of a Parisian, let us say spring, day, Oskar finds himself feeling not as Abraham's children would have felt; nor Abraham's brother Lot; nor his wife Sarah; nor his faithful foreman; nor his beleaguered concubine Hagar and her little bastard Ishmael. Amazing – Oskar feels like Abraham himself, not at any of Abraham's most glorious moments, not when he is, as Kierkegaard says, the knight of faith, but Abraham at his most *fatherly*. At the moment when old withered Sarah finally bears him a son, the last yearning of his fading internal vision, little Isaac, whose name means laughter: "he will laugh," or "one will laugh," maybe "there will be laughter," or best of all, "people will laugh." Funny old Abraham, a father at last in his dotage, and hardly in accord with the dignity and severity that mark his destiny throughout the biblical narrative. Here at the end, just a kind of joke. Did you hear about Abraham? A *father* – at his age! Did Abraham mind? Perhaps, but just for a moment. Then he must have joined in. He *was* old, his time was past, his glory over and about to become the mere stuff of myth and legend. What could he have cared, really cared, about what people might think? He'd be dead soon enough and then they could laugh their little hearts out. And in the meantime he had his son. His son to carry on. Dignity was just a whistle in the wind. But Isaac the joke on his dad was bawling his tiny lungs out. Oskar feels akin to Abraham Our Father, in their mutual absurdity.

She whimpers once more in her half-sleep. He thinks the thought of fatherhood. Oskar a father! What a joke. At his age, in this place. He grins the smile of the demented, it remains plastered over his shattered features as he turns toward her and gently enters. All through, this time, he thinks the thought of fatherhood, because he wants to connect – with her, with others, with the future. Not as a teacher, not at a distance. He is committed to this thought. When he ejaculates, with a quiet, happy groan, the thought of fatherhood is in his mind. They inhale deeply. He falls asleep inside her.

This time he dreams a myth. At the beginning, there was just a big human mass. There were no separate human beings. Only one great personal mass. Then something unfortunate happened. The original mass fragmented into many pieces. Gradually some of the pieces lost sight of the fact that they were only accidental results of a chance fragmentation. They became deluded. They thought their randomly misshapen individual existences were a natural state. The longer this state lasted, the more natural it seemed. A few pieces still thought they belonged together somewhere with all the other pieces, but this was a minority view, and seemed unrealistic, even to themselves. The dream has a calming quality because Oskar the dreamer knows what the separate fragments do not: that they *do* belong together, because they did come from the same place, and their separateness is a temporary mistake. It is one of those dreams whose most important part is the dreamer's knowledge that he is dreaming.

We could call this myth that Oskar dreams the ultimate demythologized, humanized version of pantheism. We could, but why bother?

As Oskar drifts from his dream into a deeper sleep with no dreams, he hears a voice, soft and insistent, repeat a single word. The voice is saying, *Connect* – though Oskar cannot recall this afterward. All he remembers is a calm assurance that he knew what the word was. When they awake together, it is day.